THE SHEARING

STEEL CITY SERIES: BOOK 1

N.J. COLESAR

Copyright © 2017 Entanglement Interactive LLC
All rights reserved.

ISBN-13: 978-0-9989280-0-5
Hardcover: 978-0-9989280-6-7
eBook: 978-0-9989280-1-2

This book is a work of fiction. Names, characters, businesses, organizations, places, events and incidents either are the product of the author's imagination or are used fictitiously. Any resemblance to actual persons, living or dead, events, or locales is entirely coincidental. Some locations described within the story are real places. Certain details may have been altered to better support the story.

Author: N. J. Colesar
Cover Art: Vanette Kosman

Publisher: Entanglement Interactive LLC

For information visit:
www.ENTANGLEMENT-INTERACTIVE.com

10 9 8 7 6 5 4 3 2 1

STEEL CITY SERIES

THE SHEARING
ORIGINS OF MYTH
BIRTH OF LEGENDS

*To everyone that helped make this book possible.
Thank You*

CONTENTS

PROLOGUE.............................I
CHAPTER 1 1
CHAPTER 2 16
CHAPTER 3 25
CHAPTER 4 31
CHAPTER 5 41
CHAPTER 6 51
CHAPTER 7 61
CHAPTER 8 76
CHAPTER 9 82
CHAPTER 10........................ 92
CHAPTER 11...................... 101
CHAPTER 12...................... 113
CHAPTER 13...................... 123
CHAPTER 14...................... 131
CHAPTER 15...................... 137
CHAPTER 16...................... 145
CHAPTER 17...................... 153
CHAPTER 18...................... 160
CHAPTER 19...................... 169
CHAPTER 20...................... 184
CHAPTER 21...................... 194
CHAPTER 22...................... 205
CHAPTER 23...................... 220
CHAPTER 24...................... 230
CHAPTER 25...................... 241
CHAPTER 26...................... 252
CHAPTER 27...................... 261
CHAPTER 28...................... 272
EPILOGUE 276

PROLOGUE

Today, we make history.

At least that was what Francis told himself as he checked all his calculations for what must have been the hundredth time that morning. Everything had to be perfect. One misstep and something catastrophic could happen. But he wasn't about to let anything go wrong. He was a brilliant physicist and had been working on the Large Hadron Collider upgrades for years. Nobody knew more about it than he did and his mind raced with visions of what they would discover.

Sweat ran down his neck and matted what little white hair he had left on his head. Even though the facility was kept rather chilly so all the enormous machines didn't overheat, Francis was still sweating. He was getting more anxious by the second. He wasn't nervous, he told himself. It was excitement. *Yes, that is what it was.*

Looking up from his desk in the control room, Francis watched all the other white-coated scientists scurry about various tasks as everyone prepared for activation. The white walls were covered in monitors and other sensor equipment. The large, curved desk he sat at was also made entirely of switches, monitors, and LED screens. Lights flashed and announcements rang out over the loud speaker as the different systems came online.

Francis watched as an attractive young woman in a lab coat walked up to one of the LED control panels and typed something into the screen. She watched the screen for a moment before making a small adjustment to whatever information she was given. As she turned away, Francis said, "Alicia, how are the energy levels looking?"

Alicia kept her head down as she read off the tablet in her hands. "Energy levels are holding steady at one hundred thirty teraelectronvolts, Dr. Burkhalter."

Good, he thought. *Everything is running perfectly.* "Wonderful! Thank you, Alicia. That will be all." He dismissed her with a smile. She nodded and hurried away.

A brilliant young woman that Alicia Worland, Francis thought, *and pretty to boot! If only I was forty years younger*, he thought with a sigh. *Hey now, stop that!* He scolded himself. *There is work to be done.* He was on the brink of one of the greatest scientific discoveries of the modern age and here he was daydreaming about girls!

Getting back to his monitors, Francis ran a diagnostic on the coolant systems one last time. Everything was looking good there as well. The superfluid helium four was maintaining the superconducting quadrupole electromagnets at a constant -271.25 °C.

There was enough liquid helium running through the 27-kilometer collider that the LHC was technically the largest cryogenic facility in the world. And at between 50-175 meters below the surface on the border of France and Switzerland, it was also one of the safest.

Francis continued to watch the monitors as streams of data flashed by. He remained engrossed in the screens for several minutes until at last he pulled himself away. All factors had been accounted for and everything was in the desired parameters. He had to control himself from checking the data one last time. He had done it a hundred times already. Everything was perfect. His heart beat faster. They were ready!

He reached down and pressed a button on his console then spoke into a microphone sticking out of the desk. "Attention! This is Chief Physicist Dr. Francis Burkhalter. Everyone to their monitoring stations and standby for collider activation. All systems are fully operational and particle acceleration will commence in T-minus five minutes."

He switched off the microphone and watched as the announcement set all the scientists into a flurry of activity as they ran about their assigned tasks. They all knew their business and within minutes the room was nearly silent as everyone took their positions around the various monitoring stations.

A low, rhythmic humming slowly built up as the massive electromagnets charged. The scientists watched their monitors as the final countdown began.

Ten....Nine.... Eight...

The rhythmic hum grew louder until everyone could hear it over the countdown.

...Six....Five...Four...

The air vibrated in time with the rhythm of the pulsating magnets and a static charge filled the air causing the dust to dance in the air.

...Three...Two...

Francis held his breath as his precious particle accelerator prepared to fire. Years of hard work and countless, sleepless nights were all finally going to pay off. He was about to oversee the greatest feat of modern science that would launch the human race to new levels of understanding.

...One... FIRE!

The upgraded Large Hadron Collider fired the protons through the 27 kilometers of pipe faster than the speed of light. The distinctive digital sounding *pings* of the passing protons rang out through the control room as the detectors monitored their passing. Within moments, data were streaming across all the monitoring stations.

Letting out his breath, Francis watched the information filter across his screens when the *pings* of the passing protons rang out again. That wasn't right! There should have been a much longer pause before the protons passed by again. He didn't need the data on the monitors to tell him something was wrong.

The hum grew in intensity and the vibrations began to shake the control room. The *pings* escalated and before the last one ended they started over again. Within moments, the sound of passing particles was constant. The machines couldn't keep up with the data they were receiving and started to smoke. With a crash, one of the monitors abruptly fell off the wall and shattered, as the vibrations got worse.

Francis tried to access his controls and power down the magnets, but a sudden jolt knocked him off his feet and sent him crashing to the floor. Before he could right himself, the central control panel exploded, spraying him and those nearest him with razor sharp pieces of glass and plastic.

"Shut it down!" he screamed from the floor. "Now!"

He knew they were in trouble, but the system was so complicated that there wasn't a single off switch. Other monitors crashed to the floor as the vibrations grew ever more intense. The humming was getting so loud that it was hurting Francis's ears. On top of that, the particles kept accelerating, filling the room with a steady stream of *pings*. The computers tried to gather all that information, but were overwhelmed and started exploding all across the room. The confined space was quickly filled with smoke as the burning machines belched toxic fumes.

Some of the scientists ran for cover while others remained at their stations and tried to stop the acceleration. The electronic vibrations increased and everyone had to cover their ears as the rhythmic hum grew even louder. A sudden jolt then knocked everyone off their feet and sent more equipment crashing to the ground.

Francis tried to raise his voice over the chaos. "Everyone out! Evacuate the facility!" He climbed to his feet and tried to get to the exit, but the room was shaking so badly that he couldn't stay upright.

He decided to try crawling, but as he made his way across the rubble strewn floor a sudden tremor rocked the facility and a massive crack split the floor between him and the exit. Two scientists fell into the sudden opening and were lost to the blackness.

The old physicist stared dumbly into the pit, shocked at what he had just seen.

The vibrations grew and the *pings* came so quickly now it was almost one steady note. The hum was hurting Francis's ears and giving him a serious headache. But as he shook off his horror and began to franticly look for an escape, he realized somebody needed to stop the collider. If it kept going who knows what kind of damage it would do. It might create a black hole and suck the entire planet in.

Francis suddenly realized that he must stay and try to stop such a catastrophe. He looked around the room and saw the motionless form of several scientists that lay either unconscious or dead. He didn't know which. All the others had either escaped or fallen into the expanding cracks in the floor.

He pulled himself up to one of the few remaining workstations. The billowing smoke was making it hard to see and the ear-splitting hum made it hard to think. Another quake nearly knocked him down again, but he held onto the station with all his might and just barely remained upright.

Looking at the monitor, Francis's worst fears were realized. The power levels were off the charts and the particles were moving so fast the detectors couldn't even track them accurately. The whole collider was going critical and there was nothing he could do.

A sudden flash of light blinded Francis and he backed away from his controls. Temporarily blinded, the old physicist stumbled backward as he blinked away the glare.

When he regained his sight, there was a glowing anomaly twisting in the air before him.

The anomaly slowly rotated and began to spin. It spun faster and faster until there was a horrible tearing sound and a sudden burst of energy. Where the crack had been a second ago, a swirling vortex had formed. Francis watched, awestruck. A tear in the very fabric of space!

Colors and shapes formed inside the vortex as it spun and grew. Small bolts of multicolored energy arched from the expanding maelstrom and where the bolts touched, tiny new vortexes formed. Francis backed away as he stared at the growing rifts in disbelief.

What had he done?...

CHAPTER 1

IT WAS A BEAUTIFUL DAY IN PENNSYLVANIA. A cool spring breeze blew through the rolling hills as the trees were just beginning to get their leaves back after a long, cold winter. Nestled into the point between three connecting rivers sat the sparkling city of Pittsburgh; its skyscrapers gleaming in the morning sun.

Perched on one of the hills outside the city were several neat rows of small, identical houses, a relic from the old steel industry. Vehicles lined the streets as people scurried back and forth like a swarm of ants to load things into their waiting cars.

The door to one of the row houses opened and a beautiful young woman stepped out.

Elizabeth McAllister stood on her small porch and watched the people run around. She was tall with an athletic build and her wavy, brown hair fluttered in the breeze as the morning sun kissed her olive skin.

Watching all the activity, she was glad that she had loaded her car up the night before. Thinking of last night reminded her of the last several months; lots of long lectures, boring classes full of tests, and studying. *So much studying...*

Taking a deep breath, she pushed all that out of her mind. No more thinking about classes. It was spring break and she was going home to Clearfield.

"Hey Liz! What are you waiting for? Let's gooo!" a voice shouted.

Snapping out of her daydream, Liz looked to where the voice had come from.

Parked in front of the small house was Liz's little white car, packed with boxes. Sitting in the passenger seat was another young woman who was the source of the shout. She was pretty, with pale skin and wore a small black fedora from under which her long, black hair fell in tight ringlets down her back. Her arm hung out the open car window with her ring-covered fingers tapping impatiently on the door.

"Yeah, yeah, I'm comin'." Liz shouted back as she headed for the car. As she walked down the short sidewalk, she smiled and waved at some of the people next door. Going around the car, Liz opened the door and slid in.

"Thanks for coming down and helping me pack, Emily." Liz said as they drove away. "And having some company on the ride is nice."

"My pleasure. Besides, you have been trying forever to get me to one of your 'events'." Emily replied. "So, what is it we are going to again?"

Liz smiled. "It's an SCA event. They do historical recreations."

"So, it's like a Renaissance Fair then?" Emily asked.

"No, not quite. Renaissance fairs just focus on the Renaissance. The SCA covers most of history up to the Renaissance. So, you could dress up as an ancient Egyptian if you really wanted."

"Wait, so I have to dress up?"

"Well, you don't *have* to. But everyone else will be dressed in period garb, so you would stand out like a sore thumb. But don't worry, I brought a dress you can wear and it's even in black."

Emily breathed a sigh of relief. "Cool, thanks. Black is my favorite color." Emily grinned wickedly. "Spikes are fun too."

Liz groaned.

"So, what are we going to do there anyways? Walk around and watch people joust or something?" Emily asked.

"Well, some people do the heavy weapons fighting. They wear armor and use rattan weapons."

"Rattan?"

"It's a type of flexible wood. Keeps anyone from getting too injured. Anyways, there is that and lots of other stuff." Liz started ticking items off on her fingers, "There is fencing, archery, thrown weapons, heraldry, calligraphy, cooking, singing, sewing, brewing, I'm sure there are others that I can't think of right now. Basically, if it was done pre-seventeenth century then there is probably a group doing it."

Emily's eyes lit up. "I am pretty good at archery. I'll have to check that out. Anything with horses?"

Liz rolled her eyes. "How could I forget that, with you being a horse trainer and all? Yes, there are some equestrian things."

"Awesome. I like the sound of this so far. How many people will be there?"

Liz shrugged, "No idea. A few hundred, maybe more."

"Really? That many? I thought there would be like twenty or so."

"Ha, no," Liz laughed. "Some events are small like that, but the biggest ones have thousands of people attending. The SCA is a worldwide organization."

"Interesting. I didn't think it was that big since I've never heard of it before. How do they keep it all organized?"

"It's broken into kingdoms. There are kingdoms all over the world and each is ruled over by kings and queens. Then, they are broken down into smaller duchies and such."

"Wait, you have kings and queens? How do I not know about this? How do you get to be the king?" Emily asked.

"Win a crown tournament or something." Liz waved a hand dismissively. "I don't really understand how all that works. I just go for the archery and fencing."

"Sweet. I can't wait to check this out! I want to be a duchess." Emily bounced happily in her seat. "Duchess Emilia has a nice ring to it," she smiled. "So, how long until we get there?"

****

The ground trembled as the two armies charged each other and with a thunder-like crack, the two forces collided. A sea of spears boiled and rolled as the two sides fought for position. Weapons rose and fell, and bodies hit the ground as the tide of battle swirled, with Mike caught right in the middle of it.

The press of bodies was overwhelming, and the stink of sweat and metal filled his nose. Men shouted from all sides as the two forces ground together. Sweat ran into his eyes and his arms burned with fatigue as he fought desperately. Blows rained down in all directions and more men fell.

Quickly raising his shield, Mike blocked a spear thrust. But before he could counter, another spear stabbed towards his face. He deflected it with a swipe of his sword then started to step forward to engage the swordsman in front of him. But before he completed the move, he remembered his job was to defend, not attack. Pulling back, Mike rejoined the phalanx.

His company was holding the center and he, along with the row of other swordsmen, were to keep the spearmen behind them safe. So far, they were doing a good job, but Mike didn't think the left flank would hold out much longer because they were losing people too fast.

Mike peered out of his helm at the opponents in front of him. Each enemy that fell was replaced by what seemed like three more. The opponents were outmaneuvering them, and Mike's line kept thinning. He looked out to see if there was a weak spot where they could surge and take the offensive. Suddenly between the enemy spearmen in front of him and surrounded by his guards, was the king!

****

Numerically, the armies were about even with several hundred on each side. However, the nearest army was a combination of several smaller companies, all fighting together.

The Scadian fighters had a wide variety of armor on. A few had full sets of steel, but most had scrapped together sets. Pieces of football and hockey pads were common along with other homemade plastic pieces. Rusty steel helmets and gauntlets were also common, and duct tape was everywhere.

A few small banners could be seen flying above some of the companies.

But as a whole, the army was a very ragtag bunch. While they may have looked rough, they fought well and were holding their own.

But as the nearest army was a crusty-looking group, their opponents were quite impressive. Their bright plate armor and clean surcoats shone in the sunlight, and many colorful banners rippled in the breeze. Nearly all of them wore long white belts and had large, open-linked chains around their necks. Some had white baldrics slung across their chests and a few even had crowns attached to their helms.

All of their spears were in nice even rows and everyone was neatly organized. The banners flying depicted many different symbols, but there was one that stood out. It was a massive banner that dominated the center of the white-belted army. On it was a white, eight-pointed cross within a gold laurel wreath topped with a gold crown, all on a field of red.

Liz and Emily stood on the edge of the field and watched the battle unfold. Liz wore a simple, but elegant, red and white dress, with a gold belt around her waist. Her wavy, brown hair hung loose about her shoulders. Emily, on the other hand, wore a long, black dress with silver scrollwork around the borders and a silver chain belt. Her black, curly hair was tied back with a piece of silvery chain.

Emily pointed to large red banner. "What does that big, red flag mean?"

"That is the kingdom's royal heraldry. It means the king himself is on the field," Liz answered. "The army with him is called the Chivalry. They are the knights and masters at arms of the kingdom. Along with other Royalty."

"Cool, and it looks like the king is about to enter the fight," Emily noted.

"Oh, no," Liz groaned.

"What is it?"

"Meduseld is right in the center of the line," Liz answered.

"Who?" Emily stared down at the battlefield. "And what does that matter?"

"That is the mercenary company Mike fights for," Liz groaned. "And it looks like the king is headed directly for them."

It seemed Liz's observation would prove true. As they watched, the banner moved from the very center of the army to the front and when the banner reached the combat line, the fighting grew in intensity. It seemed as though the presence of the king spurred everyone to even more furious combat.

Liz and Emily couldn't make out what was going on as combat swirled around the King's standard as both sides pushed forward.

After a few more moments of intense fighting, the king's standard fell, followed by a loud cheer from the ragtag army, and with a sudden push they drove into the king's army. Their victory was short lived though, as a few seconds later their left flank collapsed.

Trying to recover, men shifted to try and bolster the left. However, this weakened the line and soon the right flank collapsed as well. The army shifted again and drew itself into a tight circle, and within moments the ragtag army was completely surrounded.

They fought desperately and held out for several more minutes, but the press was too great and eventually they were all cut down. The kings' army let out a roaring cheer as the last enemy was defeated.

"And another victory for the Chivalry," Liz sighed, as the defeated fighters picked themselves up and made their way off the battlefield.

As Liz and Emily watched the fighters leave the field, a group of men headed in their direction. They all wore white tabards with three interlocking red horns emblazoned on the chest. As they got closer, two of the men broke away from the group and walked up to Liz and Emily.

One was a very large man. He stood slightly over six feet tall and was very broad across the shoulders. He wore heavy steel armor and his helm was a modified Norman style. On his left arm hung a well-worn heater shield and his rattan sword was clutched in his right gauntlet. He moved with a grace that spoke of years of training.

As he approached, Emily couldn't help but think how impressive he looked and she was glad she didn't have to face him across a battlefield.

The other man was even taller, although not near as broad, with a rather goofy looking walk. He had mismatched armor, some steel and some plastic visible on his arms and under his tabard. His helm was a beat-up, modified bassinet and he carried a long, rattan spear propped against his shoulder. While he didn't move with the same predator-like grace, intelligent eyes glittered from under his dented helm.

Emily had the impression that while he didn't look that much like a warrior, she was sure there was definitely a keen mind at work under that helm. Looks could be deceiving. Perhaps this one was more dangerous than he first appeared.

As the two men stopped in front of them, they tossed their weapons onto the grass and removed their helmets.

The taller one was an average looking guy, probably in his early thirties, with dirty blond hair and a strangely braided beard.

Emily thought the tall one looked familiar, but she couldn't quite place from where.

The broad fighter turned out to be a handsome young man with very short-cropped brown hair and a reddish goatee.

Emily's eyes grew wide as she realized she knew him. "Mike?"

"Hello there, Emily." The broad man smiled. "Liz, I didn't know you were going to be here."

Liz smiled back and threw her arms around his neck and gave him a big hug. After a moment, she pulled back and said, "Hey, Mike. I just thought that since you guys were here and that we were headed this way anyways, that I would stop and show Emily an event."

Liz went over and gave the taller man a hug as well.

Mike looked at Emily and suddenly caught her in a tight embrace. "It's about time you made it to an event," he said as he let her go. "I think you will like the archery stuff."

"So, I've heard," Emily smiled back.

Mike turned to his tall companion as Liz backed away, "Ted, this is Emily. You two have spoken, but never actually met."

Now, Emily knew why he looked familiar. He was one of the guys they played online with.

"Yes, I remember. It's nice to finally meet you, Emily," Ted said with a bow.

"Nice to meet you, too," Emily laughed.

Mike bent down and retrieved his sword and shield. "Ted and I need to get out of this armor. What do you ladies say to joining us at our campsite?"

"And I need a beer," Ted added.

Liz grinned, "Sure." Then she turned to Emily. "What do you think?"

"So long as we stop at the archery area first," Emily replied.

"Awesomesauce," Mike smiled, and slung his shield over his shoulder, "We can do that." He turned and started walking off the field. "Follow me."

The campsite was rather small, with less than a dozen tents in total. They were positioned in a ring around a large fire pit and the whole area was roped off from the other campsites nearby. Liz and Emily sat together on a wooden bench next to the campfire as they waited for Mike and Ted to emerge from their tent.

"So, what do you think so far?" Liz asked.

"I like it. Using a recurve bow and wooden arrows will take some getting used to," Emily replied. "But it was a nice change from my old compound bow."

"Good. I'm glad to hear it."

"Next time, I want to try out one of those longbows. They look neat."

Liz raised an eyebrow at that. "Oh, so there is going to be a next time, huh?

Emily shrugged. "I don't see why not."

Just then, the tent flap was pulled aside and Ted emerged, followed closely by Mike. They had removed their armor and were now in their period clothing.

Ted wore a long, reddish-brown coat with fur trim that concealed most of him, while a tall, furry cap was perched on his head, making him look even taller. A white tunic and tan pants tucked into worn, black boots could just be seen under the coat. His left hand rested on an elaborate saber that hung from his hip, while a large unmarked bottle was held in the other.

Mike appeared a lot plainer in comparison. He wore a simple blue tunic with black pants tucked into calf-high brown boots. He had a large dagger and leather pouch hanging from his black leather belt.

"Would either of you lovely ladies care for some homemade mead?" Ted asked, as he held up the large bottle for them to see. "My best batch so far."

Liz wrinkled her nose. "No, thanks. The last time I tried that stuff it tasted like gasoline."

"But that was years ago!" Ted pouted. "I have made several adjustments since then."

"Let me think about that... um, no." Liz looked at Emily, "You want to try the rat poison?"

"Hey now!" Ted laughed. "It's not rat poison." Then he thought a moment. "But, I bet it could be," he added with an evil grin.

Liz rolled her eyes. "You're ridiculous."

Mike just shook his head and walked over to the large cooler at the end of the bench. "While you two are arguing over the quality of mead, I will be having a beer," he said as he reached into the cooler and pulled out a bottle.

"I'll take one," Liz said quickly.

"Me, too," Emily added.

"You guys are no fun," Ted complained. "You don't know what's good." He uncorked the bottle. "Where is your sense of adventure?"

Mike handed both girls a drink and sat down on the bench across from them. "I know what's good, and it's not that stuff," Mike laughed as he took a swig.

Ted took a long swallow from his jug. "You just don't have a refined palate like I do."

"No," Mike smiled. "We still have all our taste buds from not drinking that battery acid."

"Oh, that was cold," Ted groaned. "Last time I offer you any of my special brew!"

Mike shrugged. "Ah, well. It's not the end of the world."

"Unless you watch the news," Emily said. "Ever since the accident at that particle place in Europe a few days ago, the news has been all about the world ending or whatever."

"Just like Y2K was going to shut down the computers and kill us all." Ted chuckled.

"Or when we were all going to get Raptured," Emily laughed.

"And then the Mayans were going to come down out of their spaceships in 2012 when their calendar ended," Liz added with a grin.

"Yeah, what a bunch of baloney," Mike snorted and took another drink.

"That's why I don't watch the news. It's either over dramatizing things and beating them to death, or it's high school drama."

"Agreed," Liz said. "But you have to admit there have been some strange things going on since then." She took a sip of her beer and continued. "Like the day that I felt all tingly. It was like there was static electricity all over or something."

Everyone nodded at that. There had been a strange feeling in the air the day after the accident was reported. And what was even weirder was that everyone across the world seemed to have felt the same thing. Then all of a sudden, it disappeared. Most people blamed a solar flare or some other natural event. But a few, including the media, said it was a result of the particle collider accident and that it heralded the end of the world.

"Then, there are all the earthquakes," Liz continued. "We even had a few here and that never happens."

"Actually," Ted interrupted, "Earthquakes do happen in PA, just very infrequently." He knelt down and began rummaging around in the cooler. "But, there have been more in the past week than the last fifty years combined." He dug a little deeper into the cooler, "Ah, ha! Who wants some hotdogs?" Water ran down his arm as he held the dripping, plastic pack of hotdogs for everyone to see.

Everyone shook their heads "no."

"Nobody? Really?" Ted shrugged. "Fine, more for me." He sat down next to Mike and ripped open the bag. "Now, it is possible that the things happening are a result of the particle collider malfunction, mostly because nobody actually knows what could happen. It's the reason they are smashing the particles together in the first place; to make discoveries."

"Sounds dangerous to me," Emily shuddered. "I've heard that it could create a black hole and suck everything into it. Or crack the earth in half."

"Those are all extremely unlikely." Ted said has he jammed a hotdog onto a sharpened stick. "But, theoretically, it is possible. Like I said, nobody knows what could happen for sure."

Emily moaned. "Great. That makes me feel so much better."

"Anytime!" Ted replied happily as he held his soggy hotdog over the small fire.

Not giving up the fight, Emily continued, "But that doesn't explain the strange creatures people have been reporting."

Mike rolled his eyes, "Psh, all those so-called "sightings" are unconfirmed. Just like Bigfoot and the Loch Ness Monster. There isn't one shred of proof that anything was there."

"But there were footprints. And even some videos," Emily insisted.

Mike scoffed. "Yeah, prints are easily faked and all the videos were shaky and out of focus. How convenient."

"Oh, believe what you want. But there *is* something strange going on," Emily maintained.

"*Anyways*," Mike emphasized as he set his empty bottle down, "who wants another beer?" He asked as he got up and reached into the cooler.

"No, thanks. I need to drive home," Liz replied with a sigh.

Emily shook her head. "One was good for me, thanks."

With a shrug, Mike grabbed another beer and sat back down. Ted's hotdog hissed and spit over the fire as the juices dripped onto the hot coals.

Liz tipped her head back and finished her drink. "Speaking of home, we should get going. We have a two-hour drive yet."

"Yeah, and I need to check on my horses," Emily said. "I left them with my father," she grumbled. "Hopefully, he didn't kill them yet."

Liz laughed. "I'm sure they are fine." Then she stood and stretched. "Shall we?"

"I guess," Emily groaned as she stood as well.

"You guys don't have to run off," Mike said and stood up, "The party won't start until tonight. That's when the fun happens," he added with a wink.

"Ugh, even more reason for us to go," Liz laughed.

"Fine, be that way. But…" Mike stopped talking, held up a hand and looked like he was trying to concentrate on something. "You guys feel that?"

Everybody was silent for a few seconds as they all tried to feel what Mike was talking about.

Emily nodded, "Yes, the ground is shaking."

"Great," Ted sighed, as he continued to rotate his steaming hotdog.

"Another earthquake."

A few moments later everyone could feel the tremor and it quickly grew in intensity. The ground shook uncontrollably and tents started to vibrate and sway like they were caught in a strong breeze. Suddenly, the ground heaved and seemed to drop away.

Ted fell over backwards; his steaming hotdog flew off his stick and sailed through the air. Emily started to fall and Mike reached out and caught her, but another sudden lurch sent them both crashing to the ground. Liz stumbled and fell. She continued to lay there, eyes squeezed shut, clinging to the grass with her fingers dug in and praying that the earthquake would end. It didn't appear her prayers would be answered as the earth heaved and bucked like a raging bull, knocking down tents and trees all over the place.

The rumbling and shaking lasted for a few more moments before it suddenly stopped. An eerie crackling sound filled the air as the quake ended. It reminded Liz of the faint static sound that you would hear from an old TV. Refusing to look, she was keeping her eyes closed and waiting to be sure the shaking was actually over when she heard Emily breathe, "Oh... wow."

Liz slowly opened her eyes and couldn't believe what she saw.

All around them, as far as they could see, curtains of colored light floated through the air. Streamers of bright red, blue, green, and yellow light danced all around. It was as if they were standing in the aurora borealis. Motes of pulsing golden light danced through the featureless glow while areas of multicolored mist floated through the air. The whole scene was both bizarre and beautiful.

Liz took a deep breath and realized that there was a strange scent in the air as well.

And it was amazing.

It was like every good smell she could think of was all smashed together. She couldn't describe how wonderful it was.

She took another deep breath.

She felt more alive than ever! Looking around she wanted to see if the others were having similar reactions.

Emily had her arms spread wide, as if she were trying to touch as much light as possible. Her mouth hung open and her eyes were closed as she let the warmth fill her. Emily spun in slow circles with arms spread wide, allowing the colorful lights to glisten all around her and they pulsed with her movements as if choreographed in a strange dance. She appeared so childlike, as she spun with a soft smile on her lips.

Mike stood in wide-eyed amazement at the brilliant display all around him, but his left hand gripped his large dagger. With a dreamy smile, Liz watched Mike scan the lights. Using his dagger, Mike tried to stab one of the golden balls of light. When his dagger touched it, the light winked out. *Fascinating! Did Ted have an explanation for this?* She thought, as she turned to face him.

Ted waved his hand through the mist suspiciously while inspecting how the particles moved. Ever the scientist, Liz thought.

Moving her own hand through the light and mist, she did notice something strange. Some of the mist reacted to her movement, like she expected, by being dragged along with the motion of her hand, like smoke. But strangely, other areas didn't react at all. It seemed as though her hand passed right through them. The golden particles were the same way. No matter how hard she tried, she couldn't actually touch them.

That didn't make sense at all. *Why don't they move,* she wondered? And when Mike stabbed one, it disappeared. How was that different than her hand touching it? *Oh, well,* she sighed. What matters was that she felt fantastic. The lights and the smells combined in the perfect symphony with the cracking buzz to make everything seem great. She was in Heaven.

But then, the lights started to fade. Very slowly at first, but with increasing speed. Some just disappeared like they had never been there, while other rays appeared to get sucked into the ground. Looking at her arms, she noticed that some of the colored mist was clinging to her arms. Was it just her imagination or was it soaking into her skin?

Just her imagination, she decided as the mist slowly vanished. Turning around, Liz saw that all the lights were going out along with the crackling noise and the fantastic smells.

All too soon, all the beautiful lights were gone like they had never been there. It was like waking up from a dream. Everyone blinked in the afternoon sun, confused.

Mike spoke first, "That was fun."

"Yeah…" Emily breathed dreamily. "But what was it?"

Ted shook his head. "That, my friend, is an excellent question."

Liz came out of one of the tents. "Alright, I'm ready. Let's get out of here."

Emily and Liz were still at the campsite, but now they were back into their normal clothing. Liz in her blue jeans and t-shirt and Emily had her usual black fedora, dark gray tank top, and black mini-skirt.

The camp had been put back together, and people were running around everywhere trying to learn what had happened. So far nobody had any answers.

It seemed the quake followed by the light show had scared everyone into leaving. A flurry of activity followed, as tents were being torn down and packed into waiting vehicles.

"I agree," Emily nodded. "Before anything else happens."

"That is a good idea," Ted said. "Hopefully, the roads are safe after all that shaking." He was dumping water onto the fire and then kicked the ashes around. Once he was satisfied that the fire wouldn't start back up, he turned and went back into his tent.

Right after Ted went in, Mike pushed the tent flap aside and came out carrying a large wooden crate full of armor. "We will be leaving, too, as soon as we get the tent and gear packed away," he said, as he walked through the camp and over to his car that had been backed up to the edge of the camp. He set the heavy crate in the trunk.

Mike went back into the tent and after a few moments came back out with his sword and shield. He threw them into the trunk as well. As he was going back for more, Ted came out carrying a large plastic container filled with his armor that he put it in the back of his little red truck, which was parked next to Mike's car. "Okay," he said. "That's the last of my gear." Then, Mike came back out of the tent with one small bag that he added to the pile in his trunk. "Mine too."

Ted turned to Liz and Emily. "You ladies have a safe trip back."

"We will. Don't worry," Liz replied. She walked over and gave Ted a big hug goodbye, followed by one to Mike.

"You drive safe, too," Emily said, as she gave Ted a hug next. "It was nice to finally meet you."

"Agreed," Ted smiled, as he pulled away.

With their goodbyes said, Liz and Emily prepared to leave. "Oh, hey!" Ted yelled, as they started walking away. "Gaming tonight?"

Emily laughed, "You don't give up do you? I may be online. Depends."

"On?"

"On if I feel like it or not. Duh."

Ted turned to Liz. "What about you, Liz? Since we are leaving early I figure we can group up and kill some virtual baddies tonight," he said hopefully.

Liz shook her head sadly. "Things are going crazy and you are worried about gaming. Why am I not surprised?" Then she smiled. "I will if we ever get out of here. I can't be up too late. Have church in the morning."

Mike had been unwinding the ropes holding the tent down, but he looked up when he heard that. "You can't be serious?"

Liz looked at him, "Of course I'm serious. Tomorrow is Sunday, so I am going to church."

Mike stood up. "But St. Francis is over twenty minutes away from your house, through windy back roads. I don't think traveling that far would be such a good idea. Not with all the earthquakes and things going on."

"I *am* going," Liz replied stubbornly.

"Fine, then. I am going with you."

Liz breathed a silent sigh of relief. "Deal." Although she wouldn't admit it, she was nervous about traveling alone, so she was glad that Mike had offered to come along.

"I will be at your place by nine, so be ready." Liz said.

"Yes, dear," Mike replied.

Liz shook her head as she turned back towards her car. Emily waved to Ted and Mike, then turned and followed Liz out of the camp.

CHAPTER 2

"Ugh, do we have to?" Complained Mike.

"Yes, I'm going and since you won't let me go by myself, you are coming too," Liz replied.

"Ugh," Mike groaned again. "But with all this weird stuff going on, it would be better to stay here and wait it out. I'm sure things will calm down soon," he pleaded.

Liz turned around. "All this 'weird stuff' is the perfect reason to go to church."

Mike shook his head sadly. "Look, the world is going to pot already. This new stuff is just more proof we are alone. Or better yet, if there is some kind of God up there, it just proves that He either doesn't care, or is punishing us. So, either way you look at it, we are screwed!"

"Now, you know I would like nothing more than to have all that God stuff be true. Going to an eternal paradise for being good sounds wonderful. Even better are all the a-holes out there being sent to Hell forever. But right now, I have some serious doubts."

"You always have doubts," Liz said with an exasperated sigh. This was not the first time they had had this conversation. "But that is why they call it Faith. You have to believe it, even when it doesn't make sense to you."

Mike let out a big sigh of his own. "Why on earth would I believe something that doesn't make sense? That doesn't make sense!" He argued. "I will believe it when I see it. I won't just follow along blindly. Just give me proof."

Now, it was Liz's turn to shake her head. "Faith doesn't need proof."

"Maybe," Mike replied, "but I do. I have seen way too many bad things happen to good people that a 'loving' God wouldn't let happen."

"No." Liz shook her head again. "We may not understand it, but everything happens for a reason."

Mike laughed. "Of course it does."

Liz bent down and pulled her shoes on. "So, are you coming or not?"

Mike groaned again, "Yes, yes, just give me a sec."

Mike pulled open the large wooden door to the church. "I still say this is a waste of time," he said, as Liz strode through the open door.

"Oh, it won't hurt you," Liz replied as Mike made a face.

"It's not church hurting me that I don't like," Mike replied sourly. "Didn't you hear all those gunshots as we walked in? And I'm positive that one was something blowing up."

Liz laughed. "This is central PA. There are always gunshots."

True enough, Mike agreed, as Liz found them a place to sit.

St. Francis was rather sizeable, being able to hold several hundred people. The rectangular room had one long, red-carpeted aisle down the center with a smaller aisle along each side. It resembled a Cathedral with its rows of wooden pews and large, stone columns supporting the ceiling, only on a smaller, less grand scale. The altar was on a raised area at the far end of the main entrance. When Mike and Liz entered, the church was less than half-full, with people scattered across the wooden pews.

Liz led the way and chose a seat near the back, because she knew Mike would complain if they sat too close to the front. She entered the row first, knowing Mike liked to sit near the aisle.

Mike leaned over and whispered into Liz's ear. "We are sneaking out at the last song."

Liz smiled and with a look of fake annoyance whispered back, "Fine." Just then, the music started and everyone stood up as the Mass began.

Liz joined in the singing while Mike stood there silently, like he always did. First, the servers entered, followed by the deacon, and finally the priest himself. Mike groaned when he saw who the deacon was. Liz stopped singing and whispered, "You are doing an awful lot of groaning today."

Mike leaned closer. "That's because we have Deacon 'Fire and Brimstone' today. If I have to hear one more time how we are all going to Hell, I'm gonna go crazy."

Liz grinned. "You and me both. At least we have Monsignor today. With any luck, he will give the sermon."

Mike shrugged helplessly. "We can only hope."

At this point, the procession had made it to the front of the church and they were all taking their places around the altar. The monsignor and deacon stood off to the side in front of their respective chairs, while the two servers took up places back behind the altar. The singing continued for several minutes until the song ended and the monsignor raised his arms in a gesture to encompass the whole congregation. He opened his mouth to speak, but before he could say anything an ear-splitting scream erupted from somewhere in the group of people near the center of the church. With another shriek, the source of the noise was revealed as a man stood up clutching his head between his hands. The man kept his head between his hands as he attempted to get out of the row. People moved aside to let him out and as he stumbled his way out of the pew, he let out another cry of pure pain.

Everyone turned and watched the man as he fell into the center aisle where he tried to get back up, but fell back to his knees, pleading and moaning. "Somebody help me!" He tried to stand again, but before he could he doubled over still clutching his head, and let out a long, low moan. One of the men nearby approached the sick man and reached a hand out and asked, "What's wrong?" But before the good Samaritan could reach him, the sick man jumped up and pushed his would-be helper away with such force the other man flew backwards and crashed into a nearby pillar. There was a sickening crack, and the man collapsed and lay very still.

The sick man was now on his feet and yelling incomprehensible babble. He started to stumble towards the front of the church, but as he got closer his yelling grew louder and changed pitch with each step to become deeper and more pained.

Liz grabbed Mike's arm. "What is wrong with him? Do you think that other guy will be ok?"

Mike scowled, "No idea, but it sure doesn't look good for either of them." The sick man was halfway to the altar now and struggling to stay upright. He stumbled a few more steps, still clutching his head, before stopping. His pained yelling transformed into mad laughter. As he laughed, his voice continued to get deeper and he began sweating profusely. Now, the rest of the people were starting to panic, with everyone near the sick man trying to get as far away from him as possible.

The deacon chose this moment to step forward. "Son, what is wrong?" he asked, with concern evident in his voice. But the man seemed to ignore the deacon and continued his insane laughter. The sweat was pouring off him and a mad light had entered his eyes.

"Ah, I will show you, holy man," his deepening voice giggled.

Then, his laughter turned back into a horrible scream. His fingers dug into the flesh of his face, drawing bright ribbons of blood to mix with the sweat and run down his arms. Suddenly, his skin started to stretch as his body began to swell. He continued his screaming as his body expanded at an alarming rate.

Then, as if a dam had burst, his skin shredded as his body erupted outwards. As the skin fell away, it started to burn, then disintegrated into dust, revealing a huge, red-skinned monster.

It was roughly man-shaped and stood nearly eight feet tall. Its skin was a deep red that barely contained its bulging muscles and was covered with strange, branded tattoos. Two goat-like horns sprouted from its forehead right above its coal black eyes. It stretched to its full height and unleashed a hideous booming laugh as it flexed its huge claws.

People screamed and were running towards the exit, but before they could reach them, the doors swung closed and could not be opened. They were trapped.

Liz and Mike stood rooted in place, not quite believing what they were seeing. Liz gave Mike a panicked look. "What the Hell is that!?"

"Hell if I know," Mike mumbled distractedly.

Liz looked even more panicked and Mike added. "Don't worry, the priests will take care of it."

The demon let out a short bark of laughter and said "Now, now. You aren't going anywhere. It has been ages since I feasted on the flesh of mortals."

At this, the deacon mustered his courage and shouted at the huge monster. "Be gone demon! This is a house of God!" The demon's laughter boomed throughout the building.

With lightning quickness, the demon struck out with a huge clawed hand and tore the deacon's head from his body. Blood fountained as the deacon's head flew across the room to splat against the far wall. The headless corpse remained upright for a few heartbeats before slowly toppling over to land in a heap at the demons clawed feet.

"It killed him! It killed the deacon!" Liz gasped in astonishment. "We need to get out of here now!" The rest of the congregation had the same idea as they clawed in terror at the unmoving doors.

Mike grabbed her by the shoulders "Liz, calm down." He stared her straight in the eyes. "We will get out of here. Don't worry. Have some faith."

The demon turned to face the nearest group of people trying to escape, and strode toward them. Right before it reached them, a loud voice called out, "Stop!"

The demon froze in place, unable to go any further.

"Be gone foul demon!"

It was the monsignor. He stood behind the altar pointing at the demon with a large cross in his hand. He was sweating and appeared to be struggling with some unseen force. The demon roared and slowly turned to face the monsignor.

Mike looked down at Liz. "Somebody needs to stop that thing. After what it did to the deacon, Monsignor won't last long if that thing reaches him." That was when a strange sense of peace came over Mike and he knew what he must do. "Liz, I am going to do something really stupid."

"No," Liz said. "You can't. It will kill you!"

He smiled and shrugged his shoulders. "It's going to kill us all anyways. Might as well put up a fight."

Before Liz could react, Mike quickly turned around and raced towards the demon. He noticed that it had nearly reached the monsignor. Mike realized he wouldn't make it there in time, so he did the only thing he could think of. Stopping and reaching down, he grabbed a discarded songbook. "Hey, Ugly!" he shouted, and threw the book. His aim was true and the book struck the demon in the back of its huge head. The massive red monster let out a low growl and turned to find out who dared interrupt its next meal.

It saw Mike defiantly standing there and its eyes blazed with anger. "You will regret that, morsel," the demon growled.

Mike spread his arms wide. "Come at me, bro!"

The demon roared in fury at being mocked and suddenly launched itself at Mike. Not expecting such a quick response, Mike only had time to close his eyes and throw up his arm to ward off the demon's claws. The impact sent him to his knees and numbed his arm, but surprisingly there was no pain like he had expected.

Mike opened his eyes and was shocked to see a thin layer of some kind of blue-tinted energy in front of his outstretched forearm separating himself from the demon.

The demon appeared just as surprised, but it recovered quickly and with a horrible bellow it launched a thunderous blow at the shield. The force of the strike shattered the shield and blew apart the energy. Mike tumbled backwards, stunned. He rolled over and crawled to his knees as he tried to clear the stars from his vision.

"That was a neat trick, morsel. But it availed you not. I will enjoy devouring your soul," sneered the demon.

"Oh, I'm full of tricks, Ugly," replied Mike.

Before the demon could respond, Mike launched himself at the demon, his arm outstretched and something glittered in his hand. Caught off guard, the demon was taken by surprise when a blade made of the same blue-tinted energy punctured its thick, red chest. Black blood exploded from its back as the blade passed completely through its chest. A howl of pain and rage burst from the demon as it reeled backwards. The monster retreated, pressing its huge hand to the wound in a vain effort to staunch the flow of gushing, black blood.

The monsignor used the distraction to pull out a ceremonial staff from an alcove near the altar. Staff in hand, he raced down the wide stone steps to join Mike in facing the wounded demon.

The flow of black blood was slowing down and the demon stopped its slow retreat to face the two humans. Monsignor and Mike spread apart to surround the demon.

"Do you really believe you can defeat me?" it roared, as it tried to keep both of them in its line of sight. "Why, I will-" before it could finish, Mike struck at the demon, which it easily avoided, but before it could turn back around Monsignor swung the staff and connected with the side of the demon's head. There was a crack like thunder and a brilliant flash of light accompanied by the smell of ozone as the demon was sent crashing into a pillar. As it tried to pick itself up Mike struck again, stabbing the demon's exposed back with his ethereal sword.

Howling in agony, the demon pulled itself up and turned back to defend itself. Recognizing the staff as more dangerous, it focused on avoiding the next attacks by the monsignor. Mike stayed back, waiting to see if Monsignor was going to land another blow, but it became obvious that the demon was putting its full attention on the monsignor and his staff. Monsignor was starting to tire and Mike realized they had to end this quickly before he was overpowered.

"Prepare to die, priest!" roared the demon as it launched a series of devastating blows at the monsignor.

Mike stood ready and when the opening appeared, he leaped forward and with a mighty two-handed swing he severed the demon's head from its thick shoulders. Black blood fountained from the stump and the body continued to swing wildly as if trying to avenge its killer.

"You talk too much," Mike spat at the demon's severed head.

After a few more seconds of flailing, the demon's body finally collapsed in a bloody heap. The body was still twitching when it suddenly started to disintegrate and then abruptly burst into a pile of dust. The moment it turned to dust, all the doors opened and everyone poured out into the sunlight.

As the victors stood over their defeated enemy, the soft glow surrounding the staff slowly faded and the ghostly weapon gently dissipated, as if it never was.

Mike and Monsignor looked at each other, not quite believing what had just happened.

"Monsignor, that was a demon, right?" Mike asked.

"Yes. I believe so…" replied Monsignor, clearly shaken.

"But how did it get in here? I thought demons couldn't enter a church," asked Mike.

"That is a good question." Monsignor thought a moment. "Perhaps it used that poor man as a kind of doorway to enter this holy ground. Did you notice its body was steaming the whole time it was here? I think being in the church was weakening it and that is how we were able to kill it."

Mike had noticed the steam but hadn't given it much thought, believing it was just another aspect of the demon itself. But thinking about it now, Monsignor's theory made sense.

"I must report this to the Bishop and see what is going on. It is no coincidence that all these odd things are happening at the same time," Monsignor speculated.

The monsignor nodded to Mike and then turned and left, heading to contact his superiors and tell them what had happened.

As he left, Liz pushed her way through the last of the fleeing parishioners. "Mike! I can't believe you killed it!" She threw herself at him and gave him a warm embrace.

Mike laughed, "Me either!"

Her happy expression quickly fell from her face as she pulled away. "But I have bad news. It's not over yet."

After a breath, she continued. "I called 911 when the doors opened, but the dispatcher said they couldn't do anything because everyone was busy. Police, ambulance, fire departments, everyone. Apparently, everything is going crazy outside" She grew more upset as she talked "Maybe all those crazy apocalypse people were right after all and this *is* the End."

"Whoa, calm down sunshine. This is not *The End*. And even if it is, I'm not about to take it lying down," Mike answered. "Let's get back to my place and try and learn what's happening out there. That," he winked, "and my guns are there."

Mike and Liz turned from the ash pile that was slowly blowing away from the breeze of the open doors. They walked up to the doorway and together stepped out into the light to face the unknown.

CHAPTER 3

The arrow whizzed through the air and slammed into the bull's-eye, a hairs width away from the other arrow already protruding from the target. Emily reached over her shoulder and pulled forth another arrow. She set the arrow and looked down the sight of her old compound bow. She took a deep breath and released. The arrow sped through the air and struck the space between the two embedded arrows.

"I wish I shot this well all the time." Emily mused.

The large German shepherd lying near her feet looked up when she spoke. It gave a happy woof and continued gnawing at its large bone.

It was a beautiful spring day, perfect for some archery practice. Emily stood in an empty cornfield bordered by some thick woods. On the other side of the field, across from the woods, sat a cozy little house partially surrounded by trees. The trees were just getting their leaves back after a very cold winter.

The wind picked up and blew a chilly blast of cold air, whipping Emily's black hair wildly around. She reached up and gently pulled some of the stray ringlets out of her face. Another blast of cold wind nearly ripped the small, black fedora off her head and she barely got a hand on her head to keep the hat from blowing away.

Maybe she should change her clothes, she thought. She was getting a bit chilled in her mini-skirt and sandals. She thought about it a moment, but decided not to. She wouldn't be out much longer anyways.

When the wind finally died down, Emily set her bow down and walked over to the target. She tugged the arrows out and put them back in her quiver.

"Well, fifty yards was easy. How 'bout we try one hundred?" Emily asked.

The shepherd barked his agreement, picked up his half-chewed bone and followed her back another fifty yards. He rooted around until he found a comfortable patch of grass and then sat down to enjoy his meal.

"Here goes nothing."

Drawing and knocking another arrow, she released and it sailed through the air to hit the target nearly dead center again. A look of disbelief crossed her face, followed by a sly grin.

"Now, that's what I'm talking about," Emily beamed.

Without any warning, Emily quickly drew and fired another arrow. This one hit true also and landed quivering right next to the first. Before the second arrow could stop vibrating, she fired again and this one split her first arrow down the middle!

"What is wrong with me today?" Emily wondered aloud. She never shot this well. She must have gotten more sleep than she thought.

What was even stranger was that her dog was listening to her more. He had a reputation for running off and getting into all kinds of mischief, but in the past week he was listening to nearly everything she said.

"Must be all this strange weather we're having."

The words no sooner left her mouth than the earth began to shake. The trees shook and Emily had to reach out and grab onto a nearby branch to steady herself. Her dog merely tilted his head and looked at her as if asking, "What is that?"

"Getting real tired of these earthquakes," Emily complained as she clung to the branch. The quakes were getting more frequent and had been happening for the past week. The timing was suspiciously aligned with her improved archery skills.

After a few seconds, the quake subsided and her dog continued devouring his bone like nothing had happened. Emily released the tree she was holding and headed back to the target to recover her arrows. Before she reached the target, her dog started barking furiously at the nearby wood line.

"See a squirrel, Klaige?" Emily laughed.

Klaige stopped barking and looked at Emily. He let out a sad little whimper as he looked at her, then turned back to the woods and continued his barking.

"Ok, ok, I'm coming," Emily chuckled. "Let's have a look at this big, bad squirrel."

She had just reached Klaige when he suddenly stopped barking and froze. Out of instinct, Emily also froze and looked into the woods.

There was something moving out there.

She couldn't quite make out what it was, but it definitely wasn't a squirrel. As they watched, the sound of rustling leaves and snapping twigs reached Emily's ears. As she continued watching, she could make out several different shapes moving through the woods. But before she could see what they were, they disappeared behind the curve of a hill. Curious now, Emily started creeping towards the sounds with Klaige at her side.

Making their way through the thick undergrowth, they eventually reached the location where Emily had last seen the figures. Searching around the area, Emily found several strange tracks that resembled a small, oddly shaped four-toed foot. She knew the tracks of all the animals that lived in these woods and this one she didn't recognize.

Now more curious than ever, Emily and Klaige began following the strange tracks. After several minutes of following the creatures, it became obvious to Emily that she wasn't getting any closer to her query. Frustrated, Emily picked up her pace, hoping to catch sight of these elusive creatures.

Rounding the next hill, she caught a glimpse of movement between the trees far below them. Excited now, Emily increased her pace as she picked her way down the hill. Before she was half way down, there was a bone-chilling shriek from the direction they were heading. Klaige stopped and shook his head, whimpering. Emily agreed. That sounded like a large animal being eaten. She shuddered. Whatever made that noise sounded big, so whatever was eating it had to be worse. After finding the strange footprints and being unable to catch up, coupled with the recent earthquakes, Emily's imagination was running wild with ideas of huge creatures being kicked out of their underground homes and now lurking in the woods.

"This is nonsense," she tried to tell herself. "There is no such thing as monsters. "

Just then, another shriek erupted from the nearby hill, only this time it seemed to have moved further away. So whatever it was, it wasn't dead yet and it was still moving… slowly. Her curiosity got the better of her and she started off after the sounds. She made it about ten steps before she realized she was alone. Turning back, she saw Klaige still standing there.

"Well, are you coming or not?" she asked. In response, Klaige slowly laid down and let out a soft whimper. "Be that way then, you big baby," Emily said, as she turned back around and hurried towards the place she last heard the noise.

At the base of the hill, she found several more tracks meeting up with the ones she had been following. "Great," she muttered. "More of them…"

Picking up speed, Emily quickly moved through the trees trying to catch up to whatever it was she was chasing. Not for the first time, she considered what she was doing. Maybe this wasn't such a good idea, but she was committed now. She had gone this far, so she might as well see it through. Besides, she knew if she turned around now she would forever wonder what she missed.

Emily no sooner finished that thought as another shriek lit up the woods. Instead of slowing, this time the sound only drove her faster. Racing through the woods, she became aware of sounds coming from ahead of her. She was gaining on them! Seeing that she was coming up to a small valley surrounded by large rocks, Emily slowly crept up to a nearby boulder and peered over the edge.

Down below was the strangest thing Emily had ever seen.

Marching in a ragged line were a dozen of the ugliest creatures she could have imagined. They were roughly human shaped, but short. She figured they were only about four feet tall, but it was hard to tell from her perch. Their skin was various shades of green, from very dark to almost a sickly yellow. They had very long arms and huge clawed hands that nearly dragged on the ground. Their heads were rather small with large, pointed ears. Some had gaudy jewelry hanging from stretched earlobes and beady, red eyes peered out above broad, flat noses. Possibly the strangest part of the creatures was their extra wide mouths that had rows of small needle like fangs.

The creatures shambled along at a deceptively quick pace and were making a horrible racket. Apparently, they were not concerned with being heard. They were dressed in assorted clothing scraps; some wore leather and cloth, while others had what appeared to be metal armor. All held crude weapons like cleavers and rusty daggers in their large hands. The strangest of all was the creature they were dragging along behind them.

Four of the ugly green creatures were struggling to carry one large, hairy monster. This new creature was a head taller than the green monsters and looked twice as heavy, but it was hard to tell just how big it was because of its shaggy coat of long hair. It thrashed about in the green monsters' grip, desperately trying to break free.

Emily's first thought was that it looked like what all the stories said the mythical Sasquatch looked like, but this poor creature was far too small to be a bigfoot. But it was obvious that this hairy creature was terrified and it was taking all the green monsters' skill to keep it subdued. As she watched, the captured hairy creature shrieked and struggled even harder.

So, that was what that noise was, Emily thought. It was this poor creature's cry that sounded like someone dying.

Emily decided right then that she was going to help the hairy creature if she could. She couldn't say why, but as she watched she had the distinct feeling that the hairy creature was peaceful.

Her mind made up, Emily crept forward and silently followed the ugly, green monsters.

Following the curve of a small hill, the monsters marched their captive around until they came upon a small cave. When they reached the cave mouth, dozens more of the green monsters emerged, jabbering wildly as the new arrivals presented the hairy creature to one of the monsters.

This monster was slightly shorter than the rest, but it had an almost reddish tint to its warty skin. It was even uglier than the rest, and wore a mangy looking feathered cape. It carried a knotty staff topped with a skull of some creature

Emily couldn't identify. After saying something in its squeaking voice, the other monsters cheered and carried their hairy captive over to a pile of stones that could only be described as an altar.

They stretched out the hairy one on the large, flat stone in the center of the small clearing. One of the green monsters held each of the hairy one's arms and legs down as the feathered leader took up a place behind the altar. Emily watched, horrified as one of creatures brought forth a wicked looking dagger and handed it to the feathered leader. The leader took the dagger and leaned its skull-topped staff against the tree behind it. The gathered monsters cheered and called out in their strange gibbering language. Taking the serrated dagger in both hands, the leader lifted the blade high above its head right over the chest of the thrashing hairy creature.

Emily drew an arrow and took aim at the feathered leader. Without hesitating, she fired.

The arrow whizzed through the air and struck the dagger-wielding monster directly in the forehead. The arrow blasted into the monster with such force it knocked the small body backwards, where it became pinned to the tree behind it.

The dagger fell from its nerveless fingers to lay forgotten at its feet. The assembled creatures howled in shock and anger, looking for the attacker.

Emily took the distraction to fire four more arrows, each striking one of the monsters holding down the hairy captive. As soon as it realized it could move, the hairy creature leapt off of the altar and bolted towards safety.

Taking the extra time to free the creature gave the assembled mob of monsters time to find where Emily was hiding, and when they discovered her, they screeched in rage and raced towards her.

Emily jumped up and turned to run, but as she turned she slammed into something and fell backwards hard. Dazed, she looked up at what she had crashed into.

The shadows moved as a gigantic creature loomed above her.

CHAPTER 4

The garage was a complete mess.

Tools and parts were scattered about everywhere. Old engines and tires were stacked in the corners and assorted tools where mounted on the walls, along with taxidermy animals. In the center of the room sat a large, black pickup truck. The truck was lifted and had huge, studded tires that were covered in mud. Its driver's side was propped up on two large jacks and its front tire was off.

A golden "Don't Tread On Me" flag hung on the back wall above a long workbench that stretched the whole length of the building.

A man sat hunched over the workbench putting something together. There were worn tools and greasy parts lying all around him.

The man stood up with the part he had been working on and walked towards his truck. He was of average height with short-cropped, black hair and several days' worth of stubble on his chin. He wore a white beater with his army-issued camouflage pants and combat boots.

Jack Treno was not the kind of man to pay someone for a job he could do himself.

Wiping his greasy hands on his camo pants, Jack strode over to the truck and repositioned a large piece of cardboard under the exposed wheel well. He then sat down on the cardboard with his back to the truck. After he set the part next to him, Jack reached into a nearby toolbox and pulled out a small wrench. He leaned back and with a small grunt, slid under the truck.

Jack reached up and was in the process of attaching the offending part of the truck when the ground started to shake. The tremor increased in intensity, knocking piles of junk over and rattling tools on the walls. The part slipped from Jack's hand and fell, landing painfully on his nose.

"Ouch!" Jack cried, as he rubbed his injured nose.

A few moments later the quake ended and Jack got back to work. After several minutes with lots of grunting and cursing, Jack pulled himself out from under the truck and put his tools back in the toolbox.

Gathering up the cardboard and placing it on a pile of parts, Jack walked over to where a huge tire rested against an old refrigerator. He shoved the tire off the refrigerator and rolled it over to the open wheel well. Because of its large size, it took Jack several moments to position the huge tire correctly in front of the opening. Once in position, he squatted down and prepared to lift the monstrous tire.

Jack straddled the tire, with his feet and knees touching its muddy sides. He wrapped his arms just under the enormous center of the tire. Lifting up with all his might, muscles bulging, Jack only got the tire an inch off the ground. The axle was still several inches higher than that.

Slowly easing the tire back to the floor, Jack stood up and walked over to the second car jack that was positioned in the center of the truck's frame. Taking hold of the long handle, he slowly turned the small lever counter clockwise. The pressure in the jack released and the arm holding the truck up slowly dropped. When the arm came to a rest on the jack stand, he gave the lever a few quick clockwise twists, locking the arm in place. He then rolled the jack out from under the truck and headed to the other car jack.

Taking hold of this one as he did before, Jack slowly released the pressure of the last jack. With only the one jack holding the truck up, the truck began to slowly descend as the pressure was released. Carefully watching the descent of the truck, Jack let it drop a few inches before quickly locking the arm and stopping the drop.

Repositioning himself back against the tire, Jack squatted down again. Straining, Jack slowly lifted the huge tire off the ground. Ever so slowly, the tire ascended the necessary few inches and lined up with the axle bolts. Jack carefully leaned forward and edged the tire into position.

Using one hand to hold the tire steady, Jack reached down and grabbed one of the lug nuts and quickly screwed it on. He was fitting the third nut when he heard a noise outside. Glancing over his shoulder, Jack peered out into the surrounding woods.

Jack's house sat at the end of a long dirt road, surrounded by forest. He was no stranger to hearing animals rustling through the brush. So, when he didn't see anything he shrugged and went back to putting the lug nuts on.

He just finished tightening the last one when he heard another rustling noise.

What was making that sound? Jack wondered. He reviewed the possible animals in his head. Deer would usually stop and listen every few steps unless they were running away from something, so it wasn't a deer. Squirrels bounce around and run in short bursts, so it wasn't a squirrel either. Coons, opossums, rabbits, and any other small critter he could think of were also too random in their movements to make such a steady, stealthy sound. Only predators move like that. But it still made too much noise to be a predator. Even a bear would be quieter if it wanted to.

Straining to hear, Jack listened as the noise got closer. Someone was trying to sneak up on him and failing miserably. Perhaps it was just his imagination or some remnants of PTSD, but to his combat-trained ears the rustling seemed too slow and steady to be a wild animal. Now more curious than ever, Jack slowly crept over to the garage door.

With the lug wrench still in hand, Jack reached the door and peered out into the woods. Unfortunately, the brush was very thick around his garage and he couldn't see anything. Staring hard into the trees, Jack searched for the source of the noise.

The rustling grew louder as it got closer, but then all of a sudden it stopped. Jack stood there in the doorway listening for several more moments, before he finally shrugged and turned back into the garage. Must have been a squirrel after all, he thought.

With the four-way wrench in his left hand, he walked over to the last car jack. Taking the lever in his right hand, he lowered the truck to the floor. Locking the jack up and rolling it out of the way, Jack started to tighten the lug nuts one final time. He was bent over, muscles straining to finish securing the tire when he heard the tapping of small claws scurrying across his garage floor.

"Great," he muttered. "Now there are coons in here."

Straightening up from where he was bent over the tire, Jack turned to where the scratching was coming from. As he approached the junk pile where he could hear the sound coming from, there was suddenly another scratching of clawed feet scampering in a different corner of the room. Jack spun around to find this new noisemaker.

But when he turned, there was nothing there. So, he went back to the nearby junk pile where he had heard the first sound come from. Just as he started to peer around it, something crashed in yet another corner of the garage.

Jack quickly turned around again, but still there was nothing there. That made three separate critters in there with him. "This is just great," Jack grumbled. "Now I have a full coon family in here."

Then, he heard the scurrying sound again, and it was right behind him!

Thinking a rabid raccoon or opossum was behind him, Jack spun back around and raised his lug wrench, ready to bash the animal before it could pounce on him. Jack's military training was the only thing that saved him as a rusty dagger slashed at his stomach.

Jumping backwards and bringing the wrench down in a quick swipe, Jack knocked the blade away. Holding the wrench up in a guard position, Jack got a good look at his attacker and it was unlike anything he had ever seen.

The creature was short and scrawny, standing approximately three feet tall. Its skin was a reddish green color with a covering of fine scales. The creature had a dog-like head, but with very reptilian features and beady red eyes. Small horns sprouted from its forehead, while other even smaller horns lined its jaw, progressing down its back where they merged into a long rat-like tail. It had large, clawed hands and feet, and wore a dirty red leather vest with a leather kilt. There were several gold hoops hanging from its small pointed ears.

The creature barked something in what appeared to be some kind of language. Suddenly, creatures started jumped out from everywhere!

Jack's head swiveled back and forth trying to keep them all in sight, but they were scrambling everywhere. *There must be a dozen of them*, Jack thought, as he quickly backed away from the sudden horde of monsters.

Backing into the wall of the garage, Jack found himself surrounded by the short, scaly, dog-like things that stalked him with a variety of weapons. Some had small rusty knives while others had assorted clubs and chains. All wore the same patchy reddish leather clothing, and none wore any kind of footwear. When Jack bumped into the wall behind him, the nearest dog thing pounced.

Jack kicked out, catching it in the chest and sending it crashing backwards into some of its fellows. Three of the creatures went down in a heap. Jack saw a short crowbar lying nearby, but he couldn't reach it with the monsters all around him. The dog-like creature directly in front of Jack lunged with its dagger pointed at his chest.

Jack brought up his wrench just in time to deflect the dagger. Knocking it aside, he brought the wrench down on the creature's head with a terrible crack.

When the monster fell, the others all let out a haunting howl like a pack of rabid dogs. Seeing his opportunity, Jack dove for the crowbar. Grabbing it in his right hand and with the wrench in his left, Jack turned to face the pack.

"Come on, you filthy little demon jackals," Jack taunted. "I haven't got all day."

The dog things didn't need any more encouragement. As one, they all howled and charged.

Jack grinned and sprung forward to meet them. Swinging the wrench and crowbar with ease, Jack laid into the creatures. Swinging the crowbar in a swift arc, he crushed the skull of one with the crowbar, and then blocked the stab from another.

Jack kicked out and knocked two of them backwards to crash into a pile of old parts. A large, broken engine had been propped up with the old parts and when the creatures crashed into it the engine fell. With a sickening crunch, the engine pulverized one of the creatures, while the other had gotten tangled in a pile of junk with an old metal can stuck over its head.

Another of the monsters swung a spiked club at Jack's back, but seeing the creature from the corner of his eye, Jack dodged the swing and returned with a backhand with the wrench. The heavy tool smashed into the strange beast's chest and sent it sailing across the room. Jack had no sooner finished the motion than three more of the monsters lunged at him from different sides.

Parrying furiously, it was all Jack could do to keep the slashing blades away. Giving ground, he had to slowly retreat back to the wall or be gutted by one of the dog things.

Two more of the creatures threw themselves into the fray and Jack dodged the clumsy swing from the first one and then spun around in a tight pirouette, arms outstretched, knocking the creatures away from him. Now with a little breathing room, Jack stabbed out with the crowbar at the creature to his right. The beast dodged, but Jack pulled back and caught the creature in the back of the neck with the hook end of the crowbar. Dragging it towards him, he used his momentum to fling it past himself and sent it flying into another dog thing that was charging from his left. The two collided with a crack and Jack turned just in time as another monster swung a brutal looking mace at his knees. Jumping up, the mace passed harmlessly under him and the monster was caught off balance. Bringing the crowbar down in a swift arc, Jack flattened the mace-wielding creature before it could recover.

The monster that had its head stuck in a can finally managed to extract itself and ran at Jack just as he finished off the mace-wielding brute. Not seeing the threat in time, the weaponless creature crashed into Jack's back, sending them both crashing to the floor. The monster clawed and bit furiously as Jack tried to get the creature off of himself.

Out of the corner of his eye, Jack could see the other two that he had knocked together were also getting up and he knew he didn't have much time before they reached him. The dog thing bit at his face, but Jack got the wrench up in time and the creature bit down on the steel bar instead of his exposed throat. Pushing with all his might, Jack threw the creature off and jumped to his feet.

Just in time, too, as the other two dog things swung at him in unison. Jack started to turn and swiftly brought the wrench across, deflecting the nearest one's attack and pushing its arm into its fellows, blocking them both. Finishing his turn, Jack drove the crowbar down, smashing both creatures to the ground where they crumpled in a bloody heap.

Hearing the skittering of claws behind him, Jack spun and punched out with the straight end of the crowbar. It caught this dog thing square in the chest and blood exploded from the wound as the creature's forward momentum pushed it further onto the spike. With a soft gurgle, the beast slowly slid off the crowbar to collapse in a pool of gore.

Suddenly, there was silence.

Straightening up, Jack surveyed the room. Small corpses littered the floor. A few of the creatures were still twitching, but Jack was confident that none of them was going to get back up.

Looking around his garage, Jack admired his handiwork and was surprised to notice that he wasn't even breathing hard. After such an encounter, he thought for sure he would have been winded at least.

He had been feeling rather strange lately, but he just assumed it was the strange weather. With the appearance of these monsters, now he wasn't so sure.

Jack was contemplating this when he heard another rustling sound coming from the nearby woods. Turning to face the open garage door, Jack prepared himself for another attack.

The rustling grew louder and now Jack could see the brush quivering as something moved towards him. As it got closer, it seemed as though the whole forest was coming to life. The undergrowth boiled with movement.

Suddenly, the woods erupted. More of the scaly dog things poured out of the undergrowth in the dozens. Brandishing crude weapons, the creatures barked and howled wildly as they charged. It was a sea of scaly flesh, and it was headed straight for Jack.

Completely unprepared for such a massive wave of monsters, Jack stood frozen in shock. His first instinct was to run, but his combat training kicked in and he quickly came to his senses. Jack dropped the wrench, spun around, and pulled open a nearby drawer. He reached inside and withdrew a worn pistol.

The sea of creatures was just reaching the open garage door when Jack turned back to face them, pistol in hand.

Raising his new weapon, Jack pointed the gun at the nearest creature.

It was an impressively ugly specimen. Even though it was smaller than most, it had larger feet than the biggest of the dog things. Large, sagging jowls hung from its pockmarked face, and extra small, bloodshot, red eyes stared out from under its shaggy uni-brow. It charged forward, the swarm at its back.

Taking quick aim, Jack pulled the trigger.

The deafening explosion echoed inside the garage. The lead creature fell, a hole between its eyes. The swarm briefly slowed at the sound of the gunshot and sudden death of one of their companions, but the horde trampled the body as they continued their charge into the room.

Firing in rapid succession, Jack unloaded the magazine into the oncoming swarm. The bullets exploded from the barrel to blast a bloody path through the dog things.

Jack stood his ground, arm outstretched, waiting for the mass of creatures to reach him. As he fired the last bullet the horde came to an abrupt halt.

The monsters howled in dismay as they suddenly began to turn and flee back into the woods.

Shocked, Jack just stood there and watched as the creatures fled.

"And don't come back!" he shouted at their retreating backs.

When the last one disappeared into the undergrowth, Jack turned back to the workbench. Opening a drawer, he dug around until he found another full clip. Replacing his empty one, Jack went back to the scene of carnage. The trampled bodies of these strange attackers were piled up, nearly blocking the doorway.

Newly loaded gun in one hand and crowbar in the other, Jack slowly advanced towards the door. Not hearing anything out in the woods, he walked up to the pile of bodies. Jack noticed as he got closer that the last monster he had killed was far larger than most of the others. It was also dressed differently.

This one had a more golden tint to its red scales and where the scales of the others were oval in shape, these were diamonds. The creature wore rough, red woolen robes with what Jack assumed to be writing around the edges. It clutched a funny looking stick in its dead hand and it had a large, golden talisman around its scrawny neck.

Jack bent down and pulled the talisman off the corpse. Turning it over in his hands, Jack inspected the item. It depicted a snarling wolf with a crown on its head. There were diamonds set in the crown and two red gems for the wolf's eyes.

Suddenly, there was a loud ringing sound. Jack jumped and almost dropped the talisman.

It was just his phone ringing. Taking a deep breath to calm himself, Jack reached into his pocket and pulled out his cell phone.

"Hello?" Jack said, as he continued his inspection of the talisman.

"Hey Jack. It's Mike. Look, I don't know if you heard, but there is some crazy stuff going on over here and I thought it would be a good idea if we got some people together to ride this thing out. I've even heard that there are monsters or some nonsense attacking people all over."

"Funny you should say that," replied Jack, "because I just killed a bunch of grubby little monsters here in my garage not five minutes ago."

"Really? Are you alright?"

"Of course. The little buggers didn't stand a chance," Jack answered. "But I know there are more of 'em out there. I guess I killed their leader and when I did, the rest retreated."

"Interesting," Mike muttered over the phone. *"Look, we need to group up. Can you get to my place? Liz is here with me, but I haven't been able to reach Emily and-"*

Jack cut in. "I can retrieve Emily."

"No," said Mike. *"If something did happen to her we should go out there together. Besides, she might not even be home. Give her some time to call us back."*

Jack stuffed the talisman into his pocket and walked over to his truck. "Rodger. I'll be over asap."

Ending the call, Jack looked at his dirty truck. That was when he had an idea. Walking over to the large wooden box laying in the corner, he unlatched the heavy steel clips and pulled the lid open.

Grinning to himself, Jack opened his cell back up. Punching in a quick number, he put the phone to his ear and after a moment someone answered.

"Hey it's Jack."

...

"Yea, I'm good. Look, you know that toy you have been wanting to help me put together?"

...

"Yeah, that's the one. Well, how soon can you get here?"

...

"Great, I will have it all ready. See ya soon."

Snapping the phone closed, Jack looked into the box and smiled.

CHAPTER 5

"They aren't answering either," Liz complained, as she threw herself onto the overstuffed loveseat. "First Emily, then my brothers, and now my parents!" she moaned, as she set her cellphone on the coffee table.

Liz lounged in the living room of Mike's second floor apartment. It had hardwood floors with a large grey and red carpet in the center of the room. Situated on the carpet was a small coffee table. On the carpet facing the table sat a large overstuffed couch and matching loveseat. A small lamp rested on the end table between the two couches. In the corner of the room was a small entertainment center with a flat screen TV and gaming console. The one whole wall was a large bookshelf, overflowing with books, while the other wall had three large windows and a door that led to a small porch.

The living room was separated from the dining room by a small hallway that led to a bathroom and two small bedrooms. Mike entered the room from the hallway and looked over at Liz who was sprawled dejectedly on the couch.

"Don't worry. I'm sure they are all fine. You know we get terrible cell service around here," Mike said, as he walked through the room and over to the windows.

"I know that! I tried their home phones, too, but still no answer. Did you get a hold of yours?" Liz asked.

"Yes. They are at home and just fine. They haven't seen anything strange. And both of my sisters made it back from college. They are all together right now," Mike replied. He reached out and using two fingers opened up a slit between the blinds and peered out.

Liz sighed. "Well, that's good at least. Are you going to go join up with them?"

Mike shook his head. "No, not yet at least. Once we get everyone else together we can decide what to do. Besides, my family lives so far out in the boonies I doubt anything will find them. And even if they did, Dad has enough guns and ammo to equip a small army."

Liz smiled. "Yes, I bet he could. But Jack could too and he still got attacked."

Still peering through the blinds, Mike replied, "The difference is Jack is out there by himself. There are four at my parents' house. It doesn't matter how many guns you have, you can only shoot one at a time."

Liz made a face. "This is Jack we're talking about."

Closing the blinds, Mike thought a moment and smiled. "Yeah, you are right. That crazy fool would try and shoot all his guns at once... and probably succeed."

Liz laughed. "Yes. He is the kind of guy you want on your team."

"Why do you think I called him?" Mike grinned back.

Liz sat up and reached for the remote control. Picking it up, she turned on the TV. "Let's find out what's going on out there."

Mike groaned. "Not the news! You know it's all trash."

"I know the news is a joke, but you know how they like to latch on to a story and beat it to death," Liz replied. "With all this crazy stuff happening, I bet they are eating it up." She flipped through the channels until she found a local news station.

Mike nodded. "This is true. Maybe they will actually tell us something helpful," he said without much conviction.

Sure enough, the news was speculating about the current unexplained events.

Reporter: *Breaking News: Strange, lizard-like creatures have been seen running rampant through the streets. In the Iron Heights development, these creatures are reportedly slashing tires, rampaging through homes, setting the homes on fire and attacking anyone in sight. Residents are encouraged to bar all windows and doors, and to stay inside. It is unknown as to whether there is a safe haven to escape to, as there have been multiple sightings of a variety of strange animal-like creatures. Do not attempt to engage these monsters, stay away from windows and doors, and try to keep your families safe. We will continue with up-to-date live reporting to help you stay informed on the matter. There has not yet been any information released as to where these strange creatures are coming from. Local government officials speculate that these creatures are just wild animals that have been mutated due to the waste expelled by the local power plant into the local river and streams.*

"See!" Mike grumbled. "Will you turn that crap off? Who cares what government officials think? It's probably some big cover-up anyways because of some government experimentation gone wrong! Stupid press is paid by the officials to report what they want them to..." Mike ranted as he paced about the room.

"Wait, isn't that where Ted lives?" Liz asked.

"Shoot! I knew Iron Heights sounded familiar!" Mike replied as he jumped up and grabbed his cell phone. Punching in the number, Mike made the call. Impatiently tapping his foot, Mike waited for Ted to answer. After several moments, Mike closed his phone and turned to Liz. "He isn't answering either and I know he should be home today."

"Then go over and see if he's there," Liz told him. "He could be in trouble and need help."

"I'm not leaving you here alone," Mike replied. "I already told Jack to come over here. When he gets here we can all go look for Ted together." Mike smiled. "Besides, knowing Ted, he will either show up here right after we leave or he isn't even home because he's at some game-con or science conference or something."

Mike and Liz turned back to the news just as the reporter announced a breaking story.

Reporter: *"This just in! More strange creatures have been spotted moving along Front and Pine Streets. These creatures are going into buildings by breaking into windows and doors, and attacking everyone they find. The monsters are reportedly carrying various types of weapons including knives and axes... "*

Mike looked over at Liz the same time she looked at him as the news report continued on. "That is right down the street!" Liz cried. "Maybe we should get out of here!"

"And go where?" Mike asked. "Anybody nearby isn't answering our calls and Jack is on his way here. We are probably just as safe here as anywhere else."

Just then a large explosion shook the building, making the windows rattle.

Liz jumped out of her seat. "Safe here, eh?" she said, as she ran to the window and peered out. In the distance, a fire burned and the sounds of sporadic gunshots could still be heard. "There is another building on fire," she muttered to herself. Was it just her imagination or were the gunshots getting closer?

Was that a scream? Listening closely, Liz strained to make out any sounds. *Yes, there was definitely screaming.*

Liz turned away from the window. "Can you hear that?" she asked.

"Hear what?" Mike asked. "The gunshots?"

"No, there are people yelling. And I'm pretty sure they are getting closer," Liz replied. Looking worried she turned back to the window.

Mike walked over to the remote and turned the TV off. "I've seen enough of that."

Just then, Liz screamed and jumped away from the window.

"What is it?" Mike asked as he ran to her side.

Shaking her head, "Th-there are th-things out there," Liz stammered and pointed out the window.

Peering through the blinds, Mike looked down at the street. At first, he didn't see anything amiss, but then he saw one of the manhole covers in the center of the street begin to shake. It quivered for a few moments before slowly sliding away, revealing small, pink, clawed hands that were followed by a furry black shape.

At first Mike thought it was a giant rat, but as the figure grew, he realized it was far more than that. It did have the appearance of a rat, but it was shaped like a man. Standing on two legs and with a long rat-like tail, it crawled out of the sewer. It was quickly followed by another, and then another. Soon, the rodents were pouring out of the open sewer. At first Mike thought they all looked alike, but as more emerged he started noticing differences between them.

The ratmen's fur were varying shades of black; the lightest resembled a light charcoal grey, while the darkest were a deep jet black. All stood on two small, clawed feet and had matching hands. There was no fur on their hands or feet, revealing skin that varied between a light pink to a dull grey in color. They had long, furry snouts and beady, black eyes. Large, sharp fangs protruded from between their lips and two small, pointed ears sat atop their heads.

Each wore a hodgepodge of scrap armor and strips of leather. Most of it appeared extremely worn, while some were just scraps held together with filthy pieces of cloth. Some had small, serrated daggers clutched in their paws, but most carried rusty, short swords.

The ratmen boiled out of the sewer and as they poured out into the street, they broke into packs and scattered in all directions.

"There must be a hundred of them," Mike muttered in amazement, as he watched the ratmen swarm down the street. As he watched, several packs peeled off from the main swarm and headed down the street towards them. "Oh, no. Here they come."

As the ratmen scurried down the street, they split into smaller and smaller groups to search every building they came to. Not only were they breaking into all the buildings, but they were also slashing the tires of all the vehicles they came across.

Mike wondered where they had learned that. Surely sword-wielding ratmen wouldn't know anything about cars, would they? Unless it was some secret government project and they were testing it out on civilians. He discarded the thought almost immediately; if this was truly happening everywhere, then surely there was something else at work here.

Mike turned away from the window. "Looks like we have some time before they get here. Stay here and watch them. If they get here before I get back, yell."

Liz gave him a hard look. "And what are you going to do?"

"First," he replied, "I am going to get my boom-stick. And then I am going to get my SCA armor out of the closet."

"Well, hurry it up before they get there!" Liz said, as she went back to peering out the window.

Mike quickly turned and ran down the hall. He went into his bedroom and pulled open the closet door. Inside was a small, black gun safe. Digging into his pocket, Mike pulled out his keys. He quickly found the one he wanted and inserted it into the safe's lock. A quick twist and the heavy steel door swung open.

Mike reached in and pulled out a well-used hunting rifle and laid the rifle on the bed. Going back into the closet, he then pulled out a large black shotgun. Setting this on the bed as well, he turned back to the gun safe.

Mike quickly picked out a small plastic box that sat on the top shelf of the safe. Setting this on the bed, he rushed back into the safe and took out several boxes of ammunition.

"Mike, hurry it up! They are getting closer!" Liz yelled from the other room.

"I'm going as fast as I can!" he shouted back.

Mike dove back into the closet and hauled out a large cardboard box. Tearing it open, he dug through its contents until he found what he was looking for. It was a steel breastplate.

Mike quickly placed the two pieces around his chest and laced it together. That finished, he reached back into the box, but just then Liz's panicked shout stopped him. "They are almost to our door!"

Abandoning the rest of the gear, Mike grabbed the rifle and two of the ammunition boxes. He dashed out of the room, armor clinking.

He entered the living room and ran up to Liz. "Here," Mike said, as he shoved the rifle into her hands. "And these are the only two boxes of ammo I have for the rifle," he said as he set them on the table. Liz bent over and started to open one of the boxes as Mike ran back to his bedroom.

She quickly opened the box and began loading the rifle. She had three rounds in the chamber when there was a crash downstairs at the main entrance.

Time was up.

Liz jammed the last two rounds into the chamber and then slammed the bolt closed. "Mike! What are you doing?" she yelled, as she positioned herself behind one of the couches as far away from the door as possible. Another crash rattled the walls as the door downstairs gave way.

Liz heard high-pitched squeaking and the sound of scratching in the hallway as the ratmen scurried up the steps. When they reached the door, the scratching stopped. There was a moment of silence as Liz held her breath. The doorknob rattled. When the creatures found the door locked, there was a pause, followed by brief squeaking voices.

"They can talk?' Liz wondered aloud. "Maybe they'll just pass by." She whispered to herself. "What if the monsters are waiting for more to come to bust in and overwhelm them? Could they really be strategic in their thinking? They are just overgrown rats!"

As the squeaking continued, Liz began to hope that they would give up and leave. Perhaps they thought the place was empty. If she just stayed quiet they might go away.

Her hopes were dashed when something heavy crashed into the door. Several heavy thuds and scratching followed as the ratmen threw themselves at the locked door.

The door started to splinter as the barrage continued and Liz knew it wouldn't hold out much longer. Kneeling behind the couch, she brought the rifle to her shoulder and prepared to fire. She was far too close to use the scope, but at such a close range it didn't matter.

With a tremendous crash, the door finally gave way and the ratmen poured in. Liz was just about to pull the trigger when she heard a roar from behind her. Glancing back, she saw Mike barreling down the hall.

He had the shotgun pointed forwards as he charged toward the creatures. A sword bounced around at his hip and a wooden Scadian shield was slung across his back. Seeing the large man running straight at them, the ratmen in front turned and tried to retreat while the ones behind crashed into them. Tangling themselves up in their haste, the creatures were massed around the door when Mike ran up to them. He pulled the trigger of his shotgun as he ran.

The blast ripped through the creatures, tearing many of them apart and knocking them all backwards. Mike fired again and gore splattered the walls as the trapped ratmen squealed and died. He fired three more shots in quick succession right before he reached the doorway. Standing in the entrance above the torn bodies of the ratmen, Mike aimed at the remaining creatures still scampering up the stairwell.

Seeing their companions obliterated so quickly, the ratmen ascending the stairs turned tail and fled. Mike pulled the trigger as they ran back down the stairs, but instead of an explosion there was just a loud click. Mike cursed. He was out of shells.

The last of the ratmen scampered down the hallway and disappeared around the corner. Mike took a deep breath and inspected his handiwork. Counting the bodies was difficult since many of them were in bloody pieces but he guessed there were around eight bodies in and around the door. He figured only five got away, bringing the total to thirteen ratmen. Mike wasn't sure why, but he felt that should have some kind of significance.

With a shrug, Mike stepped over the remains and went back into the room. He fully expected Liz to yell at him for charging in like that, but to his surprise she didn't say anything about it. Instead, she asked, "Did you get them all?"

"No," he replied. "A few of them got away."

Liz looked grim, "Crap. They will probably go get help. We need to get out of here."

"Agreed," Mike nodded. "I need to grab the rest of the supplies, then we can leave. Stay here and keep watch." Liz nodded and turned to the window. Mike strode down the hall and back into the bedroom.

Taking the free moment, Liz took out her cell and tried making some calls. but still nobody answered. Frustrated, she put the phone away and looked out the window.

What she saw horrified her. There was now smoke rising from many burning buildings all over the town. Small bands of the ratmen could be seen scrambling through the streets, destroying and killing wherever they went. Some people were trying to get away, while others tried to fight. As she watched, far down the street two men tried to hold back a pack of ratmen only to be swarmed and torn apart.

Liz was appalled at the viciousness of the small creatures.

Then, just a few houses away, a woman and three small children burst out of their home. A few moments later several ratmen sprang out after them. The lead monster was a huge creature, easily twice the size of its companions.

Liz could see the family was running to an old van parked across the street and she knew that the family wasn't going to make it in time.

Not able to stand idly by, Liz threw open the window and using the windowsill as a prop for the rifle, she quickly found the racing monsters in her sights. Liz was finding it difficult to keep the creatures in the scope as her hands shook from the adrenaline pulsing through her veins. Her heart was pounding, and the children were screaming and crying while their mother desperately pulled them along. All of their cheeks were streaked with tears and expressions of terror were plastered across their small faces.

Liz berated herself for shaking and letting the terror get the best of her. *I have to help them, or they won't make it,* she thought to herself. Liz pressed the butt of the rifle into her shoulder and once again found the leading monster in the scope.

Taking a deep breath, Liz squeezed the trigger.

The huge ratman crumpled like a doll with its strings cut as a hole blossomed between its eyes. When it fell, the monsters following got tangled up in its huge corpse.

Liz quickly worked the bolt and loaded a new round as the family was just reaching their van. The woman Liz took to be the mother was struggling to keep the children calm as she searched desperately in her purse for her keys.

"Hurry up lady," Liz muttered under her breath as she squeezed the trigger again.

The top of the second ratman's head disappeared in a cloud of pink mist and its small body was pushed aside by its fellows. Snarling, the remaining ratmen charged towards the fleeing family. The mother had finally found her keys, and now had the van doors open and was quickly loading her children in.

The remaining ratmen were nearly on them.

Liz reloaded and fired again, dropping the monster closest to the family. Finally, with her children in the van, the mother jumped into the driver's seat.

The ratmen were only a few steps away.

As the mother started to close her door, one of the monsters lunged forward, sword outstretched.

Liz took quick aim and fired.

The bullet sped through the air and caught the leaping ratman in the chest, hurling it backwards into its fellows.

The woman slammed her door shut and started the van. One of the ratmen slashed at the vehicle with its dagger, gouging the door as the mother hit the gas and peeled out. She sped down the street, narrowly avoiding burning debris and roaming packs of ratmen as she careened recklessly down the road until Liz lost sight of her.

Liz breathed a sigh of relief. She then picked up a box of ammunition and began reloading the rifle just as Mike ran back into the room.

He still wore the sheathed sword at his hip and the shield on his back. But there was now a bulging backpack under the shield. He carried the shotgun in one hand and held a small black box in the other.

"Everything alright out there?" he asked, as he inspected the room.

"Yeah, fine," Liz replied. "Just sighting it in," she said with a smile. Mike gave her a look that said he didn't believe a word of it, but he didn't argue.

"Here, take this," he said, as he tossed the black box on the couch next to her.

"What is that?" Liz asked, as she set the rifle down and picked up the box. She unclasped the lid and opened it. Inside sat a black pistol, two spare magazines, and a holster.

"The holster straps to your leg," Mike said. "One strap attaches to your belt and the others wraps around your thigh."

"Thanks, Mike," Liz said, as she pulled the holster out. "Where did you get this?" she asked.

"A friend of mine. I helped him out once and he paid me with that," Mike replied.

Liz inspected the pistol and noticed there was a strange symbol on the handle. But before she could ask about it, Mike took out his cell phone. "Put it on," he said. "I am going to try calling Ted again."

He made the call.

CHAPTER 6

The golden liquid was slowly coming to a boil in the Erlenmeyer flask. As the boiling intensified, beads of condensation began to form on the top of the vial. Once heavy, these beads slowly slid down the filtration tube that had been affixed to the top of the flask. As the beads slid down the tube, they were transported to another, smaller beaker. The beads of golden amber were mixing in the glass with two other liquids that were being filtered in a similar way.

Situated over a Bunsen burner, the flask containing these three liquids was being heated, causing the new combination to boil. The boiling liquid rose into a series of twisting glass tubes, where it wound its way to rest in a small, clear beaker at the end of the counter.

Ted stood nearby in a white lab coat and large plastic goggles, watching the process while taking detailed notes in a small, beat-up looking notepad. His dirty blond beard was parted down the middle with each half tied back to his ears so when he bent over and peered into one of the liquids, his beard didn't contaminate it.

Picking up a delicate glass mixing rod and placing it in the small beaker, he slowly mixed the final solution. He then used a dropper pipet to extract some of the solution. Moving around the counter, he put exactly three drops into yet another solution-filled beaker he had cooking on another table. When the drops were added, the solution started to smoke and changed colors from brown, to deep purple, to bright blue, and continued to change before becoming clear as water.

Smiling, Ted picked up the beaker and slowly began to swirl the liquid, examining its clarity. He lifted the beaker up to his nose to test the potency of the mixture. A slight frown crossed his face. Something was missing.

Frantically, Ted ran to the refrigerator and began rummaging through its contents. He had to have put the final ingredient in there! A grin began to spread across his face as he removed the last ingredient from the depths of the refrigerator. Opening the lid, he took one of the round, green objects from the jar and tossed it into the clear liquid. Without hesitation, Ted picked up the beaker and took a drink.

"Ahhh," Ted sighed happily. "That's good stuff."

Setting the beaker down, Ted took out his battered notebook and jotted down a few more notes before taking another drink. With the beaker still at his lips, the kitchen started to shake. Ted quickly put the beaker back down and reached over to steady his equipment. The quake grew in intensity and caused several unsecured vials to crash to the floor, spilling their contents all over.

Just as quickly as the quake started, it ended, leaving a mess of glass and colored liquids all over Ted's kitchen.

"Wonderful. Another mess," Ted complained.

He very slowly and carefully released the equipment he was holding and started to back away from the table. A sudden ringing filled his head. Startled, Ted almost knocked his equipment over.

Annoyed, he reached up to his ear bud and silenced the Bluetooth call. Ted backed up two steps and started to turn around when he slipped on some wet glass.

His feet flew out from under him and he fell over backwards. But before he could hit the ground, he stopped, floating several inches above the glass-covered floor.

Ted looked around, astonished. "Well, this is new."

Trying to right himself, he rotated his body hoping to roll over, but he only succeeded in spinning himself around. Hovering face down above his kitchen floor, Ted attempted to touch the ground. He put both hands out and tried to push them down. Instead of touching the floor, his hands remained floating above it. It was like trying to press the same end of two magnets together. No matter how hard he pushed, they wouldn't get any closer. He was stuck.

There had been several reports of strange phenomena these last few days, but Ted had never experienced any for himself. He had dismissed many of the outrageous claims as merely hoaxes and people looking for attention. But now that *he* was experiencing one himself, he was forced to reevaluate his previous assumptions.

Of course, there was a perfectly logical explanation for this strange event. Perhaps the Earth's gravity changed from the earthquakes. Ted looked around and saw that nothing else was floating, so he discarded that theory.

Ted came up with several more theories, but each was more outrageous than the last and he dismissed each of them in turn.

The minutes ticked by and as fun as it was to float, Ted was getting frustrated and needed to get back to his feet. He tried to push himself up one more time, but he still couldn't break free and his hands slid around like they were on a soapy floor.

"AAARRRHHHAAA!" Ted yelled, as he thrashed about helplessly.

After several moments of furious movement Ted calmed himself. Still laying facing down, he sprawled out, exhausted, above the floor.

"Okay, Ted, think," he told himself. "Concentrate. You are not floating anymore. You are back on the ground."

Pressing his fingers to his temples and squeezing his eyes shut, Ted concentrated.

After several moments, nothing happened. Ted opened his eyes. "Come on, you can do this!"

Closing his eyes again, he concentrated harder. The veins in his forehead stood out and holding his breath, he started to turn purple. Still, nothing happened.

Finally giving up, he relaxed. "Good job, Ted. You are going to die floating in your kitchen," he grumbled disgustedly. "What a way for a brilliant mind like yours to go."

Just then he fell the last several inches, smashing his face into the floor.

"Ouch!" Ted moaned, as he slowly crawled to his feet. "Let's not do that again."

Rubbing his sore nose, Ted walked over to his old notebook and jotted something down before reaching again for his drink. He drained the beaker.

Ted turned back around to his chemistry setup. Adjusting some valves and taking some more liquid into the dropper, he made another beaker full of the clear solution. He then topped off his concoction with an olive. Setting the now full beaker aside, Ted set about turning off all the burners and emptying the remaining fluids into separate larger containers as if nothing strange had occurred.

Once all the liquids were put away, Ted turned around looking for his drink. "Now, where did I put it?" he wondered. Glancing around, he saw it on the far counter. "Ah, there you are. Come to Papa." As he said this, the beaker rose up and floated right into his open hand.

Stunned, Ted could only stare at the beaker in his hand. "Maybe I've had enough to drink for today," he mused.

Setting the drink back down on the counter he had an idea.

Taking a few steps away, he held out his hand and said, "Come here."

Nothing happened.

"Come here," he said again. This time, he pictured the beaker in his hand. Still nothing.

Frustrated now, Ted stretched out his hand and concentrated. Picturing the drink in his hand he said again, "Come to Papa."

This time, the beaker floated up and flew into his outstretched hand. A huge smile split Ted's face.

"Now, go back," he ordered. Sure enough, the beaker flew back and landed where it had been sitting on the counter.

Taking a deep breath, Ted concentrated and several items around the room levitated. They floated around for a few seconds before settling back down.

Ted was ecstatic. He could control things with his mind!

He had always wanted telekinesis.

Now, his mind raced with possibilities and questions, like was there

THE SHEARING

something in his drink? Did he mix up the components wrong and now he was hallucinating? Maybe when he slipped he really did hit the ground and this was all just a dream. He sure hoped not. This was turning into a great dream.

To make sure he really wasn't dreaming, Ted walked over to his freezer and grabbed a handful of ice. Opening the front of his shirt, he dumped the ice down it.

Jumping a little at the cold, Ted quickly got the ice cubes out of his shirt and threw them into the sink. "That was… refreshing," he shivered.

Now, just to make sure he still wasn't dreaming, Ted opened up a drawer and rifled through it until he found what he was looking for. Pulling out a small pin, he quickly jabbed it into his finger. "Ouch!" Ted cried, throwing the pin onto the counter and stuffing his bleeding finger into his mouth.

After a few moments of sucking on his injured finger, Ted took it out of his mouth. "If that didn't wake me up I don't know what will."

Digging once again into the open drawer, he pulled out an old, pink cartoon-themed bandage. After wrapping his injured finger in the bandage, Ted inspected the room. What a mess. Picking up all that glass was going to be a pain, unless…

Ted pointed at the broken glass and spilled liquids and shouted. "Up!"

To his surprise and delight, the glass pieces and multi-colored puddles slowly rose into the air to hover at the level of Ted's outstretched finger. Holding out his other hand, Ted made the shape of a large ball. He then brought his hands closer together to form a very small ball. As he did this, the glass and liquid compressed together to form a large blob of floating debris. Giggling happily, Ted slowly positioned the blob above his garbage can and released it. The whole mess fell into the garbage with a soggy crash.

After releasing his mental hold, Ted noticed he was getting a headache. That was unusual for him. He never got headaches. Maybe it had to do with his mental powers. Or just the strange weather they had been having. Either way, he was having fun and didn't want to stop. He also didn't want to admit it to himself that he was half afraid that if he stopped using his new-found powers that they wouldn't come back.

Ted was immensely pleased with himself as he picked up his drink, walked into his living room over to his recliner, and sat down. He wondered what else he could do. Then he had an idea. There was one thing he had always dreamed of being able to do.

Sitting in the recliner, Ted held out his right hand and then made a fist. He then quickly opened his hand.

Nothing happened.

Closing his hand into a fist again, he concentrated, and quickly opened it again.

Still nothing.

Taking a deep breath and closing his hand, Ted leaned forward and stared hard at his closed fist. He opened his hand again and this time there was a brilliant explosion that threw Ted out of his chair and singed his beard.

Quickly righting his chair, he sat back down and tried again. This time he slowly opened his fist, and a small flame blossomed in his outstretched palm.

Ted laughed wildly and stood up with the flame still dancing above his open hand. "This. Is. Awesome!"

Closing his left fist, Ted opened it and a flame burst into life above that one as well. He stood in his small living room, arms raised, with a small flame burning merrily above each open palm. Ecstatic, Ted danced a happy little jig.

That was when he heard the first scream.

Ted froze in mid dance and the two flames winked out. Arms still raised, Ted strained to hear. A few moments went by before another scream could be heard coming from outside. He dropped his arms and ran to the nearest window. Peering out between the blinds, Ted didn't see anything amiss at first. But then he noticed the smoke rising from a blue house down the street, followed by another scream, this one coming from a different direction than the last two. As he watched, a neighbor two houses down from him suddenly ran from their home and jumped into their car before peeling out of their driveway and racing away down the street.

"Can't say I've ever seen Old Man Karver move that fast before," Ted muttered to himself.

The smoke was now billowing from the blue house and as he stared, Ted could start to see flames rise from one of the lower windows. Screams suddenly erupted from all over, and now people on both sides of the street were fleeing to their cars and driving away as fast as they could.

Ted was very confused. He acknowledged that one house on fire was bad, but to have everyone on the street run screaming from their homes?

Then he saw the first one.

It came shambling out of a house far down the street. Ted couldn't see it very well, but it looked like a scrawny kid wearing a lizard costume. Soon, several more of the creatures appeared from around the houses. As he watched, the number of creatures kept increasing until there must have been dozens of them. They split into small groups of three or four and then disappeared into every house they came upon. Ted watched in growing horror as more of the creatures appeared and another house was set alight. Neighbors were now flooding from their homes and into their cars to get away.

One poor old woman wasn't fast enough and as she hobbled down her sidewalk towards her car, a pack of the things caught her and dragged her back into her house. Further down the street, a man jumped out of a window to land on the roof of his car. The man scrambled down and tried to open his car door, but before he could a creature burst from the hedge behind him and stabbed him in the back. He collapsed in a pile of blood as the creature hissed in excitement and continued to break into the dead man's home.

Seeing the man stabbed finally broke Ted from his shock. Jumping away from the window he threw back the remainder of his drink, spun around and dashed from his living room. Running down the hall and turning into a small bedroom, Ted opened a closet door and dragged out a large plastic container. Tearing off the lid, he rummaged through it until he pulled out some hard-plastic shoulder pads. Throwing his lab coat aside, he slid them on over his head and quickly laced them up. Ted then reached back into the closet and grabbed a black bulletproof vest.

"Glad I've been saving this bad boy," Ted muttered, as he pulled on the vest. Luckily for him the vest was large and fit easily over the shoulder pads. Turning from the closet, Ted reached into a tall dresser drawer and brought forth a large pistol. Checking to make sure it was loaded, Ted clipped the holster to his belt and then rammed the pistol in it. He then grabbed the two extra magazines of ammunition and stuffed them into his pocket before throwing his lab coat back on.

Ted bent back over the plastic container and took out two steel gauntlets. As he pulled them on, there was a heavy thud against his door, followed by a crash as one of his windows shattered. Ted knew he was out of time and rushed over to where a large poleaxe leaned against the corner. Taking it in both hands, he turned around and left the room. As he made his way down the hall, he pulled the large goggles down from atop of his head. "Can't be too careful," he muttered, as he positioned the goggles securely to his face.

Ted ran down the hall, headed for his front door. As he rounded a corner, he came face to face with a creature from a nightmare.

It stood nearly five feet tall and was shaped like a skinny human. Its skin was covered in greyish green scales with patches of fur running from its forearms down to the backs of its hands and clawed fingers. In its right hand it held a small hand ax. The creature had large, webbed feet and stood slightly bow legged. A slender tail dragged on the ground behind it.

It wasn't wearing any type of clothing, but it did have an assortment of leather straps crisscrossing its body from which a variety of weapons hung. The top of its head had a spiny crest that continued down to the tip of its tail. The creatures face resembled a cross between a Neanderthal and an alligator. A large, hairy brow sat above very reptilian eyes. Its nose was only two holes at the end of a short snout where large, sharp teeth poked out from between its closed jaws.

Before it could react, Ted lunged forward and buried the tip of the poleaxe in the creature's chest. Ripping the blade back out, the creature collapsed with a gurgling hiss.

Leaping over the corpse, Ted charged into the living room where two more of the creatures were busy tearing things apart. Swinging the poleaxe in a large arc, Ted caught the first creature in the side of the head with the ax-bladed side of his weapon, and blood and brain matter splattered across the room as its head was split in half. The second creature, now aware of his presence, sprung at Ted as it swung a large, spiked mace.

Reversing his swing, Ted just barely managed to deflect the blow. He was shocked at how strong the scrawny creature's attack was.

With an angry hiss, the creature swung its mace again. This time, Ted didn't try to block it. Instead, he threw himself backwards, just avoiding having his ribs crushed. Thanks to years of fighting in the SCA, Ted recovered quickly. He stabbed forward hoping to spear the creature, but it saw the attack coming and dodged around the blow. Ted then kicked out and caught the creature square in the chest. Knocking it backwards, the creature crashed through the center of a small glass table where it got stuck. Seizing the opportunity, but not having enough ceiling room for a full swing, he had to shorten his grip. Ted swung the poleaxe in a short chop and brought the hammer end of the weapon down squarely on the creature's head. With a sickening crunch, its skull crumpled under the force of the strike.

Tearing the poleaxe out of the creature's ruined head, Ted scanned the room for any more threats. Seeing none, he ran to the smashed window and looked out onto a scene of utter chaos.

The street was being filled with a thick cloud of smoke that was pouring from the burning houses, making it difficult to see. Several more houses were on fire and trash now littered the street. He could still hear screaming and just make out people running through the smoke. No more creatures were in sight, but from the crashing and hissing he could guess that they weren't far away.

Just then, a ringing filled Ted's ear. "What the-?" Ted jumped and looked around for the source of the noise. It took him a moment to realize he still had his Bluetooth in his ear and it was ringing! Quickly pressing the button, Ted answered the call. "Hello?"

"Ted! Hey, it's Mike. Look I just saw the news and there are monsters in your neighborhood!"

"Tell me something I don't know." Ted replied as he wiped the gore off his poleaxe.

"Are you alright? What are they? What happened? Did..."

"Whoa, slow down. I have a bit of a situation over here." Ted interrupted. "Some crocodile-like monsters are attacking the whole street."

"You need to get out of there!" Mike said. *"Meet me at my place. If this is happening everywhere, we need to get everyone together."*

"Good idea." Ted answered as he turned and headed back down the hall and opened a door to his garage. "I will be right over-"

His car wasn't there.

Ted started to panic, but then remembered he had left his car parked in the driveway.

But when he opened the garage door, his heart sank. His car was smashed and the tires had all been slashed. It seemed these creatures learned fast and didn't want him to escape.

"Doesn't look like I'm going anywhere fast." Ted said. "These creatures smashed up my car."

Mike cursed. "Okay. I will come get you. We have our own problems with these large ratmen running around town, but I should be able to get to my car," Mike replied. "Gather up any food or other supplies you can think of just in case."

"Of course. I will grab all the goodies I can," Ted complained, as he closed his garage door and rushed back inside. "I'm not a noob. Jeez."

"Alrighty then, just hang on and I will be there as soon as I can," Mike replied.

"Oh, take your time. I'm not going anywhere." Ted muttered before ending the call.

Hurrying back into his bedroom, Ted grabbed an old backpack that was leaning against the wall. Returning to the kitchen, he opened cupboards at random and grabbed any foodstuff he could find. Turning to the refrigerator, Ted opened it up and stuffed as many water bottles into the backpack as he could. Seeing he still had a bit of space, Ted opened up a small cabinet and pulled out a few small bottles of booze and added them to the bag. Just as he zipped the backpack closed, he heard the unmistakable hissing of the creatures speaking to each other.

Out of the smoke, two of the monsters emerged.

Ted slid his backpack on just as they saw him. The creatures hissed a challenge and rushed toward him. Ted hefted his poleaxe and charged to meet them.

CHAPTER 7

"You can't be serious," Liz said, as she slid the pistol into her hip holster.

"He's in trouble and I said I would go get him," Mike replied.

"*We* are in trouble," Liz growled, as she swung her arm to encompass the whole area. "Or haven't you noticed the evil rat-things out there?"

"Actually, I have noticed, believe it or not," Mike replied testily. "But he is in trouble and I can't leave him there. His whole neighborhood is on fire and swarming with lizardmen."

"Dog things, ratmen, and now lizardmen. What is going on?" Liz moaned. "The world has gone crazy." She went back to the window and continued her surveillance. "We will go together. Call Jack and tell him to meet us at Ted's."

Mike pulled out his cell phone and dialed the number. There were several moments of silence before there was an answer.

"Hey Jack, change of plan."

…

"What?"

…

"No, you're breaking up."

…

Mike looked over at Liz. "Lost the call."

"Great. Now what?" Liz groaned and turned her attention back to the TV, watching as images scrolled across the scene of downtown Pittsburgh. Clouds of smoke were billowing into the area, the bridges were packed with cars, and people seemed to be in disbelief.

"...*reports continue to trickle in of strange creatures roaming the streets. You are advised to stay in your homes until-*" The screen crackled with static. "*-we will keep you up-to-date on what is happening, while it's happening. In other news, Tom Cruise is in a new movie featuring himself as three other characters. The movie had a budget of 250.6 million dollars and is expected....*"

The television set began to shake and then the picture blinked out.

It started out as a slight tremor, increasing in magnitude until Liz thought the TV was going to end up on the floor. Before long, the tremor passed and the ground quieted as if nothing had happened.

"How ironic, even the earth itself didn't want to hear the mind-numbingly stupid news!" Mike laughed. "All of this is going on, and they are still going to drone on about what the celebrities are doing?! It's disgusting. They really need to learn what real news is!"

Liz rolled her eyes. "Okay, Mike. Rant over. What's the plan? What do we do now?"

"Now we get to my car and go help Ted," Mike replied.

Liz turned from the window, slung the rifle on her shoulder, and strode across the room and then down the hall. Mike watched her go. "What are you doing?" he asked, as she disappeared into a room. No answer came, but several moments later she reemerged with a piece of paper and a marker in hand.

"If we are leaving then I am going to leave Jack a note so he knows where we went." Liz said.

Mike stared at her in disbelief. "Seriously? We need to go. Like now."

"It will only take a second," she replied.

Liz set the paper down on the table and began to write. As she was writing, Mike went around and gathered up all the supplies he could carry. He then went to the window and scanned the street. Liz quickly finished, picked up the paper and grabbed a piece of tape from the table. "Okay, let's go," she said.

With a backpack and an old shield strapped to his back, sword swinging from his hip, and shotgun in hand, Mike headed for the ruined doorway. "Stay behind me," he said. With the pistol strapped to her right thigh and the rifle slung over her shoulder, Liz followed him towards the door.

As Mike reached the ruined door, a low rumble shook the house. Mike braced himself in the doorway and Liz leaned against the wall. The tremor passed after a few moments. Carefully picking their way around the dead ratmen, Mike and Liz made their way into the hall. Mike turned towards the stairs and slowly worked his way through the corpses. He reached the top of the stairs and then began his descent, shotgun at the ready.

Liz turned back once she was in the hall and taped her note to the wall next to the doorway. Task completed, she unslung her rifle and followed Mike down the stairs.

Mike reached the landing and he pressed his back against the wall. They could still hear the sound of gunshots and screaming coming from all around. He edged along until he came to the front door and took a quick look out the door's window before ducking back behind the wall.

"I don't see anything," he whispered.

Risking a longer glance, he looked both ways down the street. He could only see a block or two in either direction because of all the smoke from the burning buildings. Far down the street, he caught a glimpse of some figures running through the smoke, but he couldn't make out if they were people or ratmen.

He could just make out his car down the street and thankfully it didn't appear to be damaged like many of the other vehicles. Now, all they had to do was reach it. Mike wished he hadn't parked so far away.

He slid back behind the wall again. "There was somebody moving way down the street, but they were moving away from us and disappeared into the smoke."

"How does your car look?" Liz asked nervously.

"Looks fine to me," Mike replied, as he risked another quick peek out the window. "Let's make a run for it."

Mike shoved the door open and rushed out with Liz close behind. They were sprinting across the small front lawn when a group of ratmen appeared between two of the houses across the street. Mike and Liz quickly ducked behind the nearest smashed-up car parked along the street. With their backs to the car, they held their breath and waited. The seconds stretched on as they expected to hear the squeals of approaching ratmen at any moment.

A sudden flash of light in the sky caught Liz's attention.

Looking up, Liz saw a little fireball streak across the sky high above them and as she watched, more fireballs lit the heavens with a shower of small burning objects.

"Well, that can't be good," Liz muttered, as she stared at the debris burning up in the atmosphere.

Mike glanced over and finally noticed what Liz was seeing.

"As long as nothing lands on us…" Mike grumbled softly, as he tore his eyes away from the spectacle. "We have more pressing things to worry about."

Taking the chance, Mike poked his head above the car and looked around.

The ratmen were gone.

But they were still trapped out in the open where creatures could appear from any direction. They needed to move.

"They're gone. Let's go." Mike said.

Staying crouched, Mike and Liz ran a few yards down the sidewalk until they reached a large tree along the sidewalk. Hiding behind the tree they both looked out for any signs of ratmen. Not seeing anything, they sprinted to the next tree. This one was an old, gnarly oak with large roots that were peeling up the sidewalk.

Only one more tree left, Mike noted, as they hid against the old oak tree. Once they reached the next tree, his car was parked between it and the tree after that in the line.

Mike glanced at Liz. "Ready?"

"Yep," Liz breathed.

Together, they quickly stood and ran for the last tree. They were half way across when a pack of ratmen suddenly appeared across the street. Both groups saw each other at the same time. A chorus of excited squeaks came from the ratmen as they spotted Mike and Liz out in the open. The pack scurried forward with weapons raised.

All the noise the ratmen were making was drawing the attention of the other roaming packs. Further down the street another group appeared, followed by yet another pack that came charging out of the house right next to where Mike and Liz were running.

Mike fired his shotgun as he ran, blasting several of the creatures and sending them crashing into the others. Mike and Liz reached the tree just before the nearest group of ratmen reached them. With their backs to the large tree, Mike and Liz turned to face the monsters.

Mike swung his shotgun around and pointed it at the pack of ratmen charging across the street. The creatures were almost on them when he pulled the trigger. The first two rows were shredded as the shot tore into the pack, and a second blast ripped even more of the monsters apart.

Liz ignored the nearest group to her left, seeing that they wouldn't last long against Mike's shotgun. Instead, she sighted her rifle on the group pouring out of the house to her right. Taking aim at the most tightly packed area, she squeezed the trigger. The bullet shot forward with pinpoint accuracy and took the lead ratman in the forehead and continued on straight through the pack, tearing a bloody path through the center of the horde. Every ratman in line with the bullet died. Liz was surprised that the bullet penetrated through that many creatures, but seeing an advantage, she took aim again.

As Liz fired her second shot, Mike took his last as the final ratman trying to cross the street died in a hail of lead shot. A river of small, furry corpses spread across the road and ended just a few steps from Mike's feet. Seeing Liz decimating the pack coming out of the house, Mike took the opportunity to reload. He quickly refilled the shotgun and was feeling confident they could overcome the monsters when he heard a noise coming from behind them. He turned to look around the tree.

Filling the street was an army of ratmen. They poured from the sewers like a furry tidal wave.

"Liz, we have company!" Mike yelled.

Liz took a final shot before she turned and glanced around the other side of the tree. Her eyes bulged when she saw the horde flowing towards them. She turned back and lined up another shot. Pulling the trigger, she killed the last of the pack that had come out of the house. She then spun around and began to furiously reload her rifle.

Mike aimed at the center of the mass of ratmen and pulled the trigger again and again. The shots scythed through the creatures, but the chittering mass came on in an unstoppable wave with the ones behind trampling the fallen. There seemed to be no end to their numbers and their frenzy seemed to grow with each shot.

The ratmen were almost on them when Mike pulled the trigger and heard the heart-stopping click of an empty chamber.

Just then, one of the ratmen sprang over the others and straight at him. Mike frantically brought his shotgun between himself and the leaping monster just in time. The ratman slammed into the shotgun, but the beast's momentum almost knocked Mike over. The ratman snapped and clawed at him, just inches from his face.

With a mighty heave, Mike launched the monster back into the coming horde. The ratman crashed into the mass, tangling the nearest clump of beasts and giving Mike a few precious seconds.

With no time to reload, Mike did the only thing he could think of, he threw the shotgun at the monsters, knocking one over and sending two others diving away. Reaching behind his back, Mike unslung the shield and drew his sword. He took a quick step forward and placed himself just in front of the tree, between the horde and Liz.

The shotgun had reaped terrible carnage among the creatures, but there were still far too many to even hope to overcome. Liz had the rifle reloaded and began firing into the mass of monsters just as the first one reached Mike.

The lead ratman was a tiny creature, smaller than any Mike had yet seen. It didn't carry any weapons, but it did have some very sharp looking claws and it lunged at Mike with those claws extended. Mike thrust his sword out and speared the creature in the chest. He retracted the blade just as another ratman jumped at him. Mike brought his shield up and the creature slammed into it. The ratman fell to the ground. Stunned and wasting no time, Mike stabbed the stricken creature before it could recover.

Another ratman launched itself at him as he withdrew his blade. This one wielded a nasty spiked club and had a patch over its right eye. It swung at Mike's exposed right side, but before it could connect, Mike dodged aside and the club whistled harmlessly by.

Mike countered with a backhanded swing, taking the surprised creature in the throat. As the ratman fell gurgling blood, two more creatures jumped in.

Liz emptied the rifle's magazine into the horde, successfully thinning their numbers around Mike and giving him time to fight the closest without being overwhelmed. But she was out of ammo and now the ratmen were too close around Mike for her to use the rifle anyways, so she slung it over her shoulder and drew the pistol from her hip.

Several ratmen broke away from the wave that was surrounding Mike and charged at Liz, but she shot all of them before they even got close. Seeing their fellows cut down so swiftly, the rest of the ratmen seemed to lose their desire to attack her.

The ratmen changed course and instead headed for Mike. It appeared that most of the monsters were ignoring her, so she took the opportunity to use her pistol to pick off more ratmen as they tried to surround Mike.

Mike blocked another ratman's swing with his shield, but before he could strike back, another creature charged at him from the other side. Swinging his sword in a wild sweep, Mike kept the creatures at bay, but soon he was surrounded by slashing, clawing ratmen. It was all he could do to keep them from hitting him, but he was slowly being forced backwards.

Mike clubbed one of the creatures in the throat with his shield and it collapsed at his feet. Continuing his wild defense, Mike didn't notice when the stunned ratman started to move.

As Mike furiously kept the ratmen at bay, the previously stunned beast behind him lifted itself up and pulled out a small dagger. When Mike swung at a large ratman, the crouched beast saw its opening and struck.

Mike howled in pain as the ratman buried its dagger into his thigh. Turning, Mike brought the hilt of his sword down on the creature's head with a wet crunch.

The dagger was small, but the distraction was all the swarm needed. They surged forward clawing and slashing with renewed frenzy. Mike defended furiously with both sword and shield, but he still took several more cuts across his arms and back.

Liz saw that Mike was in trouble and she quickly unloaded her pistol into the charging ratmen. She reloaded and to her dismay she realized that this was her last magazine of ammo. She scanned the area and saw that more ratmen were coming from all directions. The sounds of battle had attracted every pack around and Liz realized what she needed to do. She ran to the nearby body of a dead ratman and pried a slender short sword from its cold paws. Now with sword in one hand and pistol in the other, Liz charged into the chittering horde.

She hacked and slashed her way to Mike's side. There, they fought together with the large tree at their back and surrounded by a seething mass of bloodthirsty ratmen.

Up close, Liz saw that Mike was bleeding from several deep cuts and the small knife was still embedded in his thigh. Somehow, he was ignoring the pain, but the wounds were beginning to slow him down. Having Liz on his left helped, but he knew he couldn't keep this up for much longer. Every swing was getting heavier and his feet wouldn't move fast enough.

The ratmen must have sensed his weakening because they pressed the attack with renewed vigor. The fury of the ratmen's assault drove Mike and Liz back nearly pressing them into the tree. Mike blocked claws and blades with his shield and swung his sword at any creature that came too close, hitting some, but mostly he just kept them at bay.

Liz slashed away at the swarm of ratmen, but her arm was getting tired. The fencing lessons were paying off, but the constant rain of blows was numbing her hand and making it difficult to hold the short sword.

She blocked a wild swing from a ratman and then was forced to dodge aside as another creature stabbed a rusty spear at her. The ratman with the spear lunged again, almost impaling her on its corroded tip. She pushed the spear aside with her short sword and then shot the offending creature point blank in the face.

Before she could fully recover and get close to Mike, two more ratmen charged at her from both sides. She spun away from the one and brought her pistol around to the other, being careful to keep her back to the tree. Pulling the trigger, Liz took the creature in the chest and sent it sprawling. The other ratman lost heart when it saw her shoot its companion, and it turned and fled back through the throng.

Liz couldn't enjoy her short reprieve because just then the pavement beneath her feet seemed to drop. She staggered backwards and tried to keep her balance as the ground heaved underneath her.

As the earth shook beneath them, Mike struggled to stay upright. Each jarring tremor sent pain lancing though his injured leg. Luckily for him the ratmen were having difficulty staying upright as well as and they tumbled drunkenly into each other. They backed away from the pair of humans as the ground trembled.

The shaking slowly subsided, and Mike and Liz regained their balance. The ratmen squealed and swarmed back in with renewed energy. Mike set his feet and prepared to meet the charge.

Suddenly, the earth lurched again and Mike's injured leg finally gave out. He fell to one knee as a pack of ratmen sprang at him. Mike tried to stand as he brought his shield up and desperately blocked two of the creature's clumsy swings, but the third beast avoided the shield and it rammed its short sword under Mike's breastplate and into his side. Mike groaned in pain as the ratman twisted the blade further into his body.

"NO!" she cried, as the ratman withdrew its bloody weapon and raised its sword to stab again.

Before it could land the blow, its head exploded.

Liz lowered the pistol and jumped to Mike's side as the headless body fell away. The rest of the ratmen had regained their footing and resumed the onslaught. Mike tried to stand, but his injured leg wouldn't respond and the pain in his side made breathing difficult. He slashed at the monsters that came close, but his swings were slow and lacked the strength to do any real damage.

Liz fired her last two bullets into the nearest ratmen and she knew that they couldn't hold out against such numbers. It looked like this was the end.

The ratmen were almost on them when she heard a rumble in the distance.

The distant roar grew into a thundering growl as the source of the noise drew closer. Within moments, the air vibrated with the deafening roar, and the charging horde froze in confusion looking around for the source of the sound.

That source appeared a moment later when from out of the smoke a huge, black pickup truck came barreling around the corner.

Engine roaring, gravel flew as the truck tore down the street. It had oversized, studded tires and was covered in mud. It looked familiar to Liz, but she couldn't quite place it. She could just make out the sound of music that could barely be heard over the deafening engine.

A man was standing in the back of the truck with something large held in his hands. As the monstrous truck got closer, Liz saw who was in the back and where she had seen the truck before.

It was Jack!

Jack stood in the bed of his truck holding a huge machine gun that was mounted to the floor.

As the truck raced towards them, Jack swung the barrel around and pulled the trigger. The machine gun thundered to life and fire burst from the barrel as it spat a stream of lead into the furry horde. Ratmen disintegrated as the machine gun tore through their tightly packed ranks. Pavement burst as the rounds blew through the creatures and impacted the road.

Already startled by the roaring engine, the ratmen panicked and began to scatter in all directions as the bullets sliced a bloody path through them.

The truck barreled towards Liz and Mike, plowing through any creature not fast enough to get out of its way.

Those ratmen nearest the sewer dove for the open manhole as the rest ran as fast as their short, furry legs would carry them. Most didn't make it too far before Jack cut them down.

Within moments, all of the ratmen were either dead or on the run.

Liz couldn't believe it. One moment they were dead and now they were safe!

The truck slowed and came to a stop next to where Liz stood protectively over Mike's kneeling form. Jack jumped out and ran over to them.

"Jack! We need to get Mike to the hospital, now!" Liz cried, as she bent over Mike's stooped form. Reaching down, Jack slowly eased Mike to a sitting position and leaned him against the tree.

"Oh, this is not good." Jack muttered as he inspected Mike's wounds. He looked back at the truck and yelled. "Darrell! Get out here and help me move him!"

Darrell climbed out of the driver's seat and ran with a rolling gait around the truck to where Jack knelt. He was a scrawny little man dressed in woodland camouflage. His short, sandy blond hair was receding, but he made up for it with a large, scruffy beard.

He crouched down next to Jack and inspected the wound for himself. "Aw, that ain't so bad. I got a little black powder in the back seat. Pour that into the cut and light it up. Poof! Seal it up all perdy like."

"You are not lighting black powder in his side!" Liz cried. "That is one of the dumbest ideas you have ever had Darrell, and that's saying something."

"Hey, don't I get a say?" Mike groaned.

"No, you don't," Liz growled, and looked at Jack. "Let's go."

"Right." Jack nodded. "Darrell, help me lift him."

Jack grabbed Mike's right arm and swung it over his shoulders, while Darrell did the same with the left. Together they stood up and when they did, Mike's wounded side ran with blood. Liz quickly clamped her hands over the jagged hole. With Mike propped up between the two and Liz trying to slow the bleeding, they slowly made their way to the back of the truck. But poor Darrell was having a hard time keeping up because Mike was so much larger than he was.

"Jeezus Mike, you weigh a ton!" Darrell groaned. "Must be all that mac 'n cheese you been eatin'."

"Better than that bean slop you call food," Mike gasped.

"Now just wait one sec..." Darrell started to reply before Liz interrupted.

"Shut up both of you!" Liz chided. "Mike, you need to save your strength. And Darrell, you just shut up."

Together Jack and Darrell managed to haul Mike to the truck. Both were breathing heavily as they leaned him against the tailgate.

"Now, we have a problem." Jack wheezed. "Truck is too high. We can't lift him in."

"Well, who is the genius that had to put a lift-kit on their truck?" Liz asked.

This got a small grin from Mike as he tried to catch his breath.

Ignoring the comment, Jack grabbed the truck bed and pulled himself up. "Okay, Darrell. I am going to grab under his arms and you lift from his feet."

Jack squatted down from the tailgate and hooked his arms under Mike's shoulders. Darrell bent down and wrapped his arms around Mike's legs.

"On three." Jack said.

"One..."

"Two..."

"THREE"

Jack and Darrell strained and together they heaved Mike into the bed of the truck. Mike gasped as the wound tore even more as he was pulled up.

Darrell released Mike's feet as Jack backpedaled further into the truck. Jack slowly lowered him to the floor. "Hold on there, buddy," Jack said as he released Mike and pressed his hands to the wound.

Mike groaned as he tried to sit up. "Need my sword... and boomstick."

Jack pushed him back down. "Stay there boss and we will get them." He looked over at Liz who was starting to climb up the truck. "Before you get in, could you go get Mike's sword and shotgun?"

Liz looked like she was going to argue, but after a moment she jumped back down and ran over to Mike's discarded weapons.

As she retrieved the weaponry, Darrell ran back around the truck and hopped into the driver's seat. Liz returned with the sword and shotgun, and she set both of them in the bed beside Mike's prone form before pulling herself up. Once in, she pulled the tailgate up and joined Jack at Mike's side.

"Okay, let's go!" Jack yelled to Darrell.

Giving a thumbs-up through the window, Darrell stomped the gas and the truck shot forward. Jack and Liz tumbled backwards and crashed into the tailgate.

"Careful you moron!" Liz yelled, as they tried to right themselves.

The truck bounced and swerved crazily as Darrell barreled down the street. As they rumbled through the town, the scale of destruction became apparent.

Everywhere, houses and cars were smashed and burning. Bodies littered the streets, both human and ratmen. There were also a few corpses of creatures

Liz didn't recognize. Debris clogged many streets, forcing Darrell to get creative in his driving. He drove over sidewalks and through yards to avoid the rubble. The sound of scattered gunfire could be heard from all over as screams and explosions echoed through the valley.

"Y'all better buckle up back there. Looks like we got company." Darrell yelled, as he pointed ahead of them.

Mike had been propped up against the wheel well with Jack and Liz on either side of him. At Darrell's warning, Jack stood up and took hold of the mounted machine gun. Liz kept her hands pressed to Mike's injured side as he went in and out of consciousness. Mike's head rolled around as blood trickled from the corner of his mouth.

As the truck slowed down, Liz looked up to see what the issue was.

Up ahead, the road was blocked by a multi-car pileup. And to make matters worse, there were ratmen swarming all over.

"Can't we go around?" Liz shouted over the roar of the engine.

"We already tried every other road," Jack replied grimly. "They are all either blocked or swarming with creatures."

"Then just run them over!" Liz yelled. "Mike can't hold on much longer!"

"Don't have to tell me twice," Darrell yelled back. "Hold on to yer hats."

"YEEHAWWW!!" He cried, and floored it.

Tires squealed and smoke flew as the truck shot forwards. Jack saw the opening between a burning car and a tree that Darrell was heading for, so he swiveled his gun into position and fired. The machine gun thundered to life, spitting death at the milling ratmen.

Liz turned away from the carnage and concentrated on Mike. He was very pale and his breathing was coming in shallow gasps. She pressed her hands even harder against his side, hoping it would slow the bleeding more, but she doubted it would do much good as more blood oozed between her fingers.

As she knelt there in the back of the bouncing truck with Jack firing overhead, Liz blocked out the noise and concentrated on Mike. She imagined that he was getting better, that strength flowed from her and into him. She knew it was a foolish thing to imagine, but she couldn't think of anything else to do.

What was even more foolish was that as she closed her eyes, Liz actually thought she really could feel something. The palms of her hands started to feel warm and then a strange sensation passed through her. As quickly as it came the feeling left, but her hands got even warmer. Slowly opening her eyes, Liz gasped as she noticed the faint golden light glowing from between her fingers.

Shocked, Liz quickly pulled her hands away from Mike, afraid that she was going to hurt him. The glow disappeared as soon as she broke contact. She stared at her hands, trying to figure out what had just happened. Turning them over, Liz couldn't find any trace of the glow she thought she had seen. Confused, she pushed the thoughts from her mind and looked back down at Mike.

It took her a moment to realize what she was seeing.

His wounds were gone!

And not just the large wound in his side, but every one of them, including the slices on his arms. It was like they had never been. His color was back to normal and he was breathing easily.

Liz was stunned. What had just happened? Had she really just healed him? It didn't seem possible, but then again, nothing about what was happening today seemed possible.

Mike groaned and opened his eyes. "What happened?"

"I... I think I just healed you," Liz replied in amazement.

"Really?" Mike stared in disbelief. "That's amazing." Mike inspected where he had been stabbed. Then his face fell. "Oh, no," He moaned.

"What is it?" Liz cried in a panic as she leaned in to see what was wrong.

"There isn't even a scar," Mike frowned. "Couldn't you have at least left me a nice scar to show off?"

Liz slapped him on the arm. "You're impossible!"

"Hey, boss!" Jack roared, as he continued firing at unseen enemies. "Welcome back to the land of the living!"

"Thanks, honey. Did I miss anything?" Mike yelled back as he tried to stand in the bouncing truck.

Jack released the trigger, but continued to scan for possible threats. "Not really. A few of those rat creatures, but that's about it. Town is a war zone though," he added.

"So, you should be right at home." Mike said.

"Meh," Jack shrugged. "Don't get me wrong. I love me a nice fight, but I like them away from home," Jack replied grimly.

"I agree," Mike nodded. "So where are we headed?"

Jack scratched his shaved head. "Well, we were taking you to the hospital, but seeing as you're all better I guess we can go someplace else." He thought a moment. "I vote Grice Gun Shop since I am about out of ammo for Ol' Bertha here and it is the only place in town that carries it," he said as he patted the big machine gun affectionately.

"No, we need to get to Ted. Last I talked to him, there were lizard men attacking his development and I told him to sit tight until I got there," Mike answered.

A concerned look crossed Jack's face. "Well, if we don't get to Grice's and get more ammo, we aren't going to do much rescuing."

"I understand, but he might not last that long. We've taken too long already," Mike pressed.

Looking around, Jack realized he couldn't leave somebody out in all this chaos. Taking a deep breath, he leaned down and yelled into the truck's open back window. "Darrell, change of plan. You know where Ted Koldun lives?"

"Yesser," Darrell drawled. "But what do you want that know-it-all for?"

"Just take us there."

Darrell wrinkled his nose at that. "Aw, do I have ta? That smarty-pants agitates me."

"I don't care if he agitates you and, yes, you have to. We are not leaving him behind."

"Fine." Darrell rolled his eyes. "Yer wish is mah command!"

As the truck barreled down the street, Mike and Jack took up positions on either side to watch for any threats while Liz remained seated against the tailgate, knees pulled to her chest, silently staring at her hands.

CHAPTER 8

Smoke billowed down the street as cars and houses burned. A few of the homes had already been reduced to little more than smoldering piles of charred timbers. Ash floated through the smoky air and mixed with other debris as it settled on the ground. Dark shapes appeared through the haze, only to disappear a moment later. The echoes of gunshots and terrified screams could be heard in the distance, but muffled as though the smoke was holding them back.

Glass and gravel crunched as a shadow loomed out of the smoke. One shadow became many, and out of the haze four lizard-like creatures emerged.

All four of them had small, spiny crests rising from their naked backs and dark green scales covering their wiry bodies. They had swords and axes held in their long-clawed hands as they strode across the street. One of them pointed at a house that had several burned corpses lying in front of the open doorway and said something in a barking hiss to its companions. The others nodded in agreement and together they charged into the house. There were several moments of silence until a sudden clang of steel meeting steel rang out.

Hisses of surprise and pain echoed down the hazy street and the dull thud of something heavy striking a body ended one of the hisses in a wet gurgle. The ring of steel continued and the sound of a mighty struggle could be heard.

Thuds and crashes continued, when suddenly a ball of fire exploded from the open door, carrying with it the body of one of the lizardmen. It flew through the opening and landed in a smoldering heap in the yard next to several other corpses. Smoke rose from the charred doorway as Ted stepped out of the house.

Blood and gore matted his beard and covered nearly every inch of his tall, armored frame. He clutched his bloody poleaxe in a gauntleted fist. The edges of the gauntlet on his other hand glowed red-hot as if it had just come out of a forge. His eyes sparkled with an inner fire as he scanned the street for other foes. Seeing none, Ted began to turn back into the house when a chorus of barking hisses erupted from down the street.

Over a dozen of the lizardmen abruptly appeared from out of the swirling smoke. They were moving cautiously and they clutched a variety of weapons. Their heads swiveled back and forth like they were searching for something.

In the center of the group was a strange looking lizardman. Stranger than its fellows anyhow - it was taller and had a more delicate appearance. A long, black robe covered most of its thin body, and where the others looked crocodile-like, this one had features that reminded Ted of a chameleon. It had a striped scale pattern with small horns lining the crown of its head and one large, horned crest disappeared down its back.

"Ah, now you look like a leader," Ted muttered, as he watched the horned lizardman. What was his role? Some kind of priest maybe? Sorcerer? Either way, this creature was obviously more important than the others and the group of lizardmen were looking for something, but whatever it was, Ted was sure he didn't want them to find it.

The robed creature abruptly turned its head and their eyes met. With an excited hiss, it pointed directly at Ted.

"Come and get me you filthy reptiles!" Ted shouted.

They obliged.

The robed one stayed back and let its companions run ahead. Ted tried to hide a grin. This was going to be fun.

He held up his hand, palm out, and aimed at the charging group of monsters. A small spark flickered in front of his outstretched hand. The spark began to spin, quickly growing to the size of a baseball. The orb continued to spin and glow, looking like a globe of liquid fire. Suddenly, Ted released the fireball and it shot forward to strike the lead lizardman full in the chest. As it connected, the sphere exploded, annihilating the lizardman in a brilliant explosion.

The blast flattened several of the monsters and left them lying in smoking heaps. Unfazed, the rest of the creatures continued their charge.

Ted was surprised that none of the others turned and fled at the sight of him throwing a fireball. All the beasts that he had encountered had tried to run when they realized he had powers. The robed one must be giving them courage.

Or perhaps fear.

An interesting thought, but Ted had other things to consider just then. Another ball of liquid fire formed and shot forwards, exploding among the monsters.

Ted was surprised to notice that he was getting tired. He shouldn't be this tired yet, it wasn't even noon and all he was doing was holding his arm up.

To add to his discomfort, the gauntleted hand was getting to be unbearably hot and he suspected he knew why the wizards in his books usually didn't wear armor.

The surviving lizardmen were almost to him with less than a third of their original number remaining when Ted shot a third fireball.

It incinerated two more creatures and wounded the last three.

Why are they not trying to avoid his fireballs? They were sitting ducks just running straight at him like this. It was then that he noticed the dead eyed stare they all had. Coupled with the lack of their usual shouts, Ted began to suspect they were under some kind of spell.

His arm quivered as he summoned another spark.

The glowing orb shot forward and erupted amidst the last of the lizardmen. Body parts flew everywhere as the explosion ripped them apart as blood and charred bits splattered all over Ted. With a big sigh, he wiped some gore off his face and flung it on the ground.

Now, for the leader.

The robed lizardman stood several yards away. "Your turn." Ted muttered, as he summoned another spark.

Sweat ran down Ted's face, soaking his shirt, as he felt the mental strain. His armor seemed to get heavier with each passing moment and he was barely able to hold his quivering arm up.

Ted fired the orb. The fireball streaked towards the monster, but with a casual flick of its delicate wrist, the fireball was deflected and exploded harmlessly down the empty street.

A wizard then, Ted decided. How wonderful…

Arm shaking violently now, Ted tried to call up another fireball, but the spark kept going out.

Ted suddenly realized what was happening.

The robed sorcerer must have put a spell on the foot soldiers so that Ted would waste his energy on destroying them and thus making Ted an easy target.

Clever.

There was obviously some kind of rules for this magic use. And magic is what he decided it was. But what were the rules? His mind raced over the various books he had read that all had their own rules for magic, but which one was true? Or were any of them? Could this be something completely new?

The robed sorcerer saw Ted's failure to create a new spark and an evil grin split its wide mouth, revealing rows of small, sharp teeth. The lizardman began to wave its arms around as a strange symbol began to appear in the air before it.

Uh, oh, Ted groaned to himself, *looks like this creature knows what the rules are.* That put him at a severe disadvantage. This was a duel he didn't think he could win.

The sorcerer said something in its hissing language and suddenly punched the center of the floating symbol. There was a bright flash and a bolt of writhing black energy shot straight at Ted.

He dodged to the side and the black bolt just missed him to go flying through the open doorway behind him. It exploded inside the house, blasting debris everywhere and knocking Ted flat on his face. Somehow, he managed to hold onto his poleaxe and with his ears ringing, he used the tall weapon to slowly pull himself up to a kneeling position.

Just as he reached his knees, he heard another crack. Instinctively, he dropped and rolled to the side. The lightning strike just barely grazed him as he had rolled away. He had managed to miss much of the attack, but he felt a bit woozy from the energy that had grazed him.

"That was a bit too close," Ted mumbled, as the residual energy danced along the left side of his armor.

Ted shook his head to try and clear it. *Think!* he told himself. Glancing up, he saw the sorcerer had begun to chant and wave his arms again. Ted knew he couldn't beat the sorcerer with magic, it was just far too experienced. But perhaps if he could get close enough he wouldn't need magic, he thought as an idea took shape in his mind.

Ted concentrated and a small flame flickered to life in the palm of his hand. It wasn't like the liquid fire orbs he had created earlier. Instead, it was just a small dancing flame. Keeping it concealed in his hand best he could, Ted sprang up and ran at the sorcerer.

Caught by surprise, the sorcerer faltered in its casting and the almost-formed symbol disappeared. Ted was closing the gap quickly, but he was still a few yards away when he threw the concealed flame at the sorcerer.

The lizardman held up a hand and the flame hit an invisible wall.

The flames engulfed the shield and danced all across it, blocking the sorcerer's view of Ted. That was all the distraction Ted needed.

With a mighty yell, Ted swung his poleaxe with all his strength at the still-burning shield. The poleaxe broke through the shield in a shower of sparks and continued down to cleave the surprised sorcerer's head in two.

Breathing hard, Ted pulled his poleaxe out of the corpse and looked around to make sure there were no other creatures around. He didn't see any and relaxed a bit. Exhausted, he walked over to a burnt-out car and slumped down on its charred hood.

Taking the backpack off, Ted reached in and took out a small flask. Pulling the stopper off, he took a long drink. He sighed and sat there for a minute before he heard the sound of an approaching engine.

That was how Mike and the others found him: On a smoky, deserted street, covered from head to toe in gore, surrounded by bodies of charred lizardmen, sitting with his poleaxe across his knees on a burned-out car with a flask in his hand and one body split nearly in half at his feet.

CHAPTER 9

The truck rumbled down the curvy, wooded road.

Liz and Darrell were in the cab while Mike and Ted sat in the bed as Jack stood with his mounted machine gun. They were on a small country road that wound between some low hills. Trees covered everything as far as they could see. Liz sat nervously in the passenger seat while Darrell looked out the side window and whistled a happy little tune as he drove.

"Would you please keep your eyes on the road?" Liz begged.

"Aw, now I ain't gonna wreck Jack's truck," Darrell replied with a grin.

"I'm not worried about the truck." Liz rolled her eyes. "You will just take a 'little detour' through the woods."

"I won't," Darrell said with a sigh. "So, how long till we get to this Emily's house? We been driving for near half an hour now an ain't seen a soul."

"Almost there actually." Liz pointed up the road. "You see that road up there? Turn onto that."

Darrell nodded. "Bout time we got there. Hopefully, there be some critters about. I ain't got to kill nothin' yet an my trigger finger's gettin' itchy."

They took a left onto the road Liz had indicated and after a hundred yards or so it became apparent that the road was actually a driveway. It cut through the woods and led to a small house nestled between the trees. Opposite the house on the other side of the long driveway was a large cornfield surrounded by woods. As they drove up the driveway, Liz noticed that Emily's little black car was parked by a blue pickup truck next to the house. *Strange,* Liz thought. *If she has been home why hasn't she answered any of my calls?*

Cell service out here was spotty at best, but that didn't keep Liz from having the sinking feeling that perhaps something had happened to Emily. Maybe they were already too late!

Liz hadn't been very worried about Emily since she lived so far out of town, but now that concern hit tenfold as Darrell pulled up behind Emily's car.

"Keep it running," Liz told Darrell as she opened the door and got out. "And stay here."

"Aw, yer no fun," Darrell complained, as he crossed his arms and slumped back into the seat.

Liz ignored him as she closed the door. Mike and Ted had stood up and were stretching when Liz walked back to them. "You guys stay here, too. It should only take a minute."

"Fine with me," Mike answered and the other two nodded their agreement.

"She just better be here or we just drove a long way for nothin'," Jack added.

"Her car is here. So she must be as well," Liz replied. "I'll be right back."

Liz turned and headed for the house. Before she got halfway up the sidewalk, the front door opened and an older man stepped out. He was short with a good-sized gut, and what little hair remained on his head was grey and hung in wispy strands. His pale blue eyes looked tired and a few days' worth of stubble grew on his face. He was dressed head to toe in woodland patterned camo and carried a large cardboard box.

He stopped suddenly when he saw someone in front of him.

"Why, hello there Elizabeth. What are you doing here?" He asked in a gravelly voice, as he continued down the sidewalk and set the box into his little blue truck.

"Hello, Mr. Strega." Liz smiled. "I came to see if Emily was here."

"I haven't seen her all day." A worried look crossed his face. "I thought she was with you."

"I haven't seen her either and she isn't answering her -" Liz got cut off as sudden barking erupted from across the field. A moment later a dog burst out of the tree line and bolted directly for them.

"Klaige!" Liz and Emily's father said in unison.

Klaige ran across the field and right up to Liz and began barking wildly. He spun in circles and let out several excited yelps as he danced around.

"What is it Klaige? You know where Emily is?" Liz asked the dog.

He barked excitedly again and took a few running steps towards the trees where he had just come from.

"She's in the woods?"

Liz wouldn't be surprised if Emily had been in the woods this whole time, but she usually took her phone with her, or at least told somebody where she was going. It was very unlike her to just disappear like that.

Mr. Strega looked relieved. "Well, that answers that question." He seemed satisfied with that and went back inside the house. Klaige continued to bark wildly and dance around.

"Settle down Klaige. I'm sure Emily will be right out." Liz said to the distressed animal.

As if her words were a summoning, there was a rustle in the brush from near where Klaige had run out of the woods a few moments ago. A small figure dove out of the woods and rolled into the open field.

It was Emily!

She sprang up and made a mad dash for the house. There were sticks in her hair and she was covered in dirt. It looked as if she had spent days in the woods instead of only a few hours. Liz also noted that she wasn't in her usual outdoor clothing. Instead she wore a tight V-neck shirt, mini-skirt and sandals, of all things.

As Emily ran, she noticed everyone in the truck. "RUN!" she shouted at them without breaking stride. No sooner had the words left her mouth than a great roar erupted from the forest.

She was almost across the field when two huge, green monsters burst out of the forest in an explosion of sticks and leaves.

THE SHEARING

They were massive. Well over six feet tall with large corded muscles bulging from under their green skin. They looked like a horrible combination of gorilla and boar put into a human shape and then turned green. Both were bulky with huge shoulders and long, powerful looking arms that ended in massive hands.

One had long, pointed ears and an almost pig-like snout set between its beady, black eyes. Two large tusks jutted up from its lower jaw, one of which was broken off. Fur pelts covered most of its hulking form and a large, spiked club was clutched in one meaty hand. An arrow stuck out of its chest, but the beast didn't seem to notice as bright, green blood slowly oozed from the wound.

The other monster was even bigger.

It had a large hairy brow set over its small, black eyes and a large, flat nose dominated most of its face. One large tusk hung down from its upper jaw, causing a constant scowl and a steady stream of drool. A small fur loincloth was its only covering. Coarse, black hair covered the majority of its muscled hide and it held a crude stone ax in each hand.

"Orcs…" Ted breathed in disbelief.

The beasts quickly scanned the field and when they saw Emily they both let out a terrible roar that shook the leaves around them. They charged after her, wildly swinging their weapons as they bounded across the field. Their lumbering gait was surprisingly fast and within seconds they had nearly halved the distance between them and Emily.

Everyone reacted at once.

Mike and Ted leapt from the back of the truck and charged the monsters. Darrell and Liz reached for their rifles. But Jack beat them all.

He swung the machine gun around and pulled the trigger. Fire erupted from its barrel and the ground shook with its angry retort. The monsters were knocked to a halt as the bullets tore into them. Large chunks of flesh were ripped away as the shots shredded their green bodies. The smaller one's legs were cut out from under it and it fell with a dull thud while the larger one's arm was blown off a second later.

While Jack was firing, Emily used that time to sprint cross the field and dash into the house. Mike and Ted slowed their charge as they watched the carnage unfold.

The larger one was still standing when there was a loud click and then silence.

"I'm out," Jack said.

The big monster had half its face missing as it turned to look at Mike and Ted racing towards it. The green beast tried to take a step, but before it could its eyes rolled up in its head and it toppled over dead.

Mike and Ted ran up to the bodies and checked to make sure they were, in fact, dead. Satisfied with what they saw, they headed back to the waiting truck. But before they had gone two steps from the corpses, a chorus of ear splitting roars erupted from the surrounding forest. A worried look passed between Mike and Ted as they turned to look back at the tree line.

As the echoes faded, Emily and her father hurried out of the house together. He carried a large hunting rifle and a big sack slung over his shoulder. Emily had refilled her quiver and carried a large gym bag. She saw Mike and Ted in the field, "Run!" she shouted. "There are more of those things coming!"

They didn't need to be told twice. Mike and Ted turned and ran as fast as they could back to the waiting truck and not a moment too soon.

The tree line shook as more massive green shapes burst out. The primitive beasts howled and raced towards them with murder in their eyes.

Without a word, Mr. Strega ran by them and jumped into his little truck with Klaige close behind. He started the engine and peeled out, kicking up dust and gravel as he sped away.

"Whelp, I think it's about time to go." Darrell said as he put the truck in reverse. Liz ducked back into the cab and slammed the door shut. "Agreed."

Emily reached the truck and threw her bag in the bed and then hauled herself up. She no sooner sat down than Darrell threw it in reverse. Mike and Ted were almost to them with the monsters close behind. Darrell cut the wheel and the truck spun around so that the bed was directly in front of Mike and Ted.

Jack was propped against the center of the tailgate with his rifle resting on it and as Mike and Ted made the last few steps to the truck, Jack opened fire into the oncoming mass of green muscle. Mike and Ted pulled themselves up on either side of Jack as he shot at the beasts.

THE SHEARING

Darrell saw everyone was onboard and hit the gas. The truck shot forward as Jack continued to fire at the pursuing beasts, but they quickly pulled away from the racing monsters and sped down the driveway. The green skinned beasts were still running after them as they were lost from sight, but Darrell didn't slow down until they were miles down the road.

Emily sat in the corner of the truck bed and picked sticks and leaves out of her curly, black hair as they rumbled back towards town. Mike watched her for a moment before asking, "What were you doing out there?"

She took a deep breath and told them how she had been practicing with her bow when Klaige had heard the sounds in the woods and she went to investigate.

"What I found was a group of little, green monsters dragging along a bigger, hairy monster." She slowly shook her head in disbelief as she told her tale. "The green monsters weren't like the ones you saw; these others were short and scrawny with big pointed ears and beady red eyes. They wore what looked like scraps of armor and leather mostly."

Mike and Ted shared a look at that news before Ted interrupted her story. "And did they have big noses and wide mouths with lots of pointed teeth?"

Emily looked shocked that Mike had known what they looked like. She nodded, "Actually, yes. That is exactly what they looked like. How did you know?"

Ted looked thoughtful. "I've heard that description before in some books," was all he answered before continuing to brood in the corner.

Mike then told Emily what had happened to them and how Jack had shown up and saved them. "I had been stabbed, but Liz healed me somehow. I'm not sure what is going on, but it seems like some of us are getting magic powers or something."

"Magic?" Emily scoffed.

Ted nodded at this. "It's true. I can move things with my mind and throw fireballs. It's the coolest thing ever!" Then he sighed, "But you were telling us what happened to you, so please continue."

Emily tried to compose herself after all the new information she had just received and it took her a minute before she continued. "Well, the monsters were dragging along this bigger, hairy monster that looked like a small Bigfoot." With an embarrassed grin, she added, "It was kinda cute so I decided to save it."

All the guys groaned at that.

"Hey, now!" Emily argued. "You guys would have done the same thing."

That was greeted with a chorus of low mutterings of denial.

Emily shrugged. "Anyways, I followed them for a while until they came to this evil-looking altar, and then this green monster in a feathered outfit showed up and was going to sacrifice the baby Bigfoot. So, I shot it. Then I shot the monsters holding it down and then it ran off into the woods. That didn't make those green beasties very happy, so they chased me, but then-"

Jack looked confused. "Wait... So where did the big green ones come from?"

With an exasperated sigh, Emily answered. "If you would let me finish I will tell you."

She took a moment and collected herself. "You won't believe this but when I turned to run away I ran right into Bigfoot! And I mean a real Bigfoot," she said excitedly. "This thing was huge! I think the small, hairy creature was its baby. Anyways, the real Bigfoot looked at me for a minute then turned and ran away. The little, green monsters followed it and Bigfoot led them away from me."

"No, way," Jack said. "I call BS on that!"

Emily scowled. "You can believe what you want. but I'm telling you it happened. And that's not even the best part. Once Bigfoot and the little, green monsters ran away I thought it was safe to come out of hiding. Now, I have been through those woods a lot and I would remember there being a stone altar there, so I decided to snoop around a bit. I expected the altar to be rather new looking since it couldn't have been there that long, but when I got close to it I found it looked old. Like really old. There were layers and dirt and blood caked to it, and cracks everywhere with small roots growing out of it. That altar looked ancient. I don't understand where it came from or how it could look so old."

She shivered at the memory, but plowed on. "I was so caught up in the altar that I forgot about the cave. It wasn't until I heard a growl behind me that I turned around and saw those two giant green ape-men."

"Orcs," Ted interrupted. "Those green ape-men must be orcs. With their green skin, massive muscles, and tusks… what else could they be? And that makes the smaller ones goblins." He looked more and more excited as he talked. "Think about it; creatures popping up everywhere, people getting magical powers. It's like a fantasy novel come to life! How awesome is that?" Ted was practically bouncing with excitement.

Jack looked at Ted and asked, "What about the creatures I fought? Or the lizard guys you had? What are those things?"

"I'm not sure." Ted scratched his beard. "Could be any number of creatures. Kobolds or Gremlins maybe…. perhaps a type of Draconian… Different sources describe monsters differently, so it is hard to say what they are. I will have to inspect each one closer and if I can't place it, then we give it a name so we can distinguish between them." Ted's eyes glittered eagerly. "They all can't just be called 'monsters'. But those big ones we just saw were most definitely orcs, no doubt about it."

Emily sighed impatiently. "Yes, yes, whatever, orcs then. But as I was saying, they noticed me a second after I saw them. They roared and charged. I shot them a few times, but they didn't seem to notice my arrows. So, I ran. That's when one of them seemed like it yelled something back into the cave. I turned back around once to see what was happening and saw more of them coming out of the cave. They chased me through the woods and I tried to lose them several times, but they always found me again. I was getting too tired to run anymore and I was out of arrows from shooting at them. Finally, I gave up and decided to try and get home. That's when you found me."

Mike let out a long whistle. "Wow. That is quite the story. But why did you run into the house instead of jumping in with us? And where did your dad go?"

"I needed my extra quiver of arrows, and I grabbed some extra clothes." Emily said as she patted the gym bag next to her. "And my dad told me in the house that he was going to Big Jim's camp with the rest of his hunting buddies. He asked me to come along, but I told him I was going with you guys."

"Ah, that explains why he just took off," Jack said.

Mike shook his head. "But that doesn't explain what's going on around here or what we are going to do about it."

No one had an immediate answer for that. There were several minutes of silence as everyone was left to his or her own thoughts.

Finally, Ted spoke up, "I have a theory... actually there are several theories."

Liz chuckled and rolled her eyes. "Oh, here we go."

Ignoring her, Ted continued. "As we all know, these events started suspiciously close to when the Large Hadron Collider was turned back on."

"Wait, what?" Jack looked confused. "The Large Hadron Collider?"

Ted took a deep breath and opened his mouth to answer but Mike spoke first. "Look, it's a particle collider, meaning it shoots atoms really fast and smashes them together to see what happens. It's all very theoretical and science-y."

"Yes," Ted shot Mike an annoyed look. "It is all very 'science-y'. Now as I was saying, scientists turned on the newly upgraded LHC for the first-time last week, but something went wrong. There has been no word from the facility since they turned it on." Ted eyed his audience meaningfully. "There are reports of strange storms and other phenomena surrounding the facility and nobody can get near it. I think that everything that has happened so far; the earthquakes, vibrations, swirling lights, monsters, magical powers, and everything else are all a direct result of the collider malfunction."

"That is a wide range of things for just one machine to screw up." Jack muttered.

"Theoretically, all those things *are* possible," Ted replied. "Nobody knows what will happen and that is exactly why they are doing it. It is fringe science; the cutting edge of theoretical physics. Very exciting stuff."

Ted sighed heavily. "Anyways, the LHC could have torn a hole in space time, causing rifts to form. These rifts could be pulling alternate realities, or even other worlds, into our own. Or perhaps the energy given off by the particle collision altered dark matter somehow, causing a chain reaction that morphed all the other matter around it, giving us all the strange events we are experiencing. Or the collision could have warped our senses, letting us see things what were previously invisible. All these creatures could have been here the whole time, we just couldn't interact with any of it… or them with us for that matter."

Jack smiled. "So, what you're are saying is that you have no idea why this is happening."

"I have plenty of theories…" Ted frowned. "Just no answers."

Mike leaned forward. "What we need are answers. Hopefully, the gun shop is still standing and we can get some answers there."

"And if it's not?" Ted asked.

Jack answered, "Then we raid it for whatever we can find and then look for a safe place to hold out until all this craziness passes." He thought a moment then added, "The Armory would be a good place to go. I know they mobilized the National Guard. I bet it's safe there."

Everyone agreed. It was as good a plan as any. Now, they just had to get there in one piece.

CHAPTER 10

The drive passed uneventfully. They drove through the countryside seeing no one. No monsters and no people. They saw several abandoned homes and a few of them had been burned to the ground, but there was no sign of a single, living thing. It was eerie to drive for so long and not see another soul. The towering column of smoke, visible for miles, rising above the town wasn't helping either.

They crested the last hill outside the small town of Clearfield that was nestled in a valley alongside a winding river. The friends were going around a bend when they came upon two vehicles pulled off the road.

One was a small car and the other a large van. Four people stood in front of them, next to the railing, looking out over the smoky valley.

They spun around when they heard the approaching engine. It was two men and two women. The men carried rifles and the women each held a pistol. They pointed the weapons at the sound, but lowered them when they saw Liz and the others, and realized that it was other people. The strangers looked relieved as Darrell drove up and pulled in alongside the van.

Mike, Emily, and Ted started to stand when Jack held up a hand. "You guys stay here. I will go see what's going on." Mike shrugged, and sat back down with Ted and Emily following more slowly. Darrell and Liz had started to open their doors, but closed them again when they heard Jack's announcement. Jack jumped out, still carrying his AR-15 and walked over to the strangers along the railing.

"Boy, are we glad to see you," one of the strangers said as Jack approached.

The speaker was a short, stocky man with messy brown hair. He had a cut above one eye and favored his left leg as he took a step and held out his hand towards Jack. Jack shook the man's hand and asked. "Why are you standing up here?"

The other man answered. He was taller and thinner than his companion, with long, blonde hair tied back in a ponytail. He had his arm around a short, young woman with long, black hair.

"We were at home, a few miles back the road there, when we were attacked by these scaly monsters. I'm sure that sounds crazy, but it's true. Our neighbors here," he motioned to the short man and the pretty woman next to him, "came to our rescue. But we saw more of the monsters coming, so we all packed up what we could and headed for town until we got here and saw all the smoke. So, now we don't know what to do." The man's face fell. "We have to get the children somewhere safe."

At the mention of children, Jack noticed that the van had five kids sitting inside it. It looked to him that they ranged in age from early teens to the youngest that was still in a car seat. He was about to ask what the man hoped to find, but then Jack looked over their shoulders at the valley and what he saw horrified him.

The town was shrouded in smoke as fires burned everywhere. Jack heard gunshots and the chilling roar of some unknown creature echo from the town.

He tore his eyes away from the sight and addressed the two couples. "We believe you about the monsters. We have fought several different kinds already. I'm not sure that anywhere is safe right now. Your best bet is to find other people and stay together."

The short man nodded. "Safety in numbers."

"Exactly," Jack agreed.

"But why are they here?" the short man asked. "And why are they attacking us?"

"Does it matter?" Jack replied. "We know they are trying to kill us, so that makes them our enemy. We can ask questions once we are safe. Right now, it is our job to kill them and survive this nightmare."

"And how do you plan on doing that?" the blonde man asked.

"My friends and I are going down there." Jack motioned to the burning town. "We are low on ammo and are going to see if the gun shop still stands. After that, we hope to find other survivors and join with them."

The tall man looked surprised. "You are going down *there*?"

Jack nodded. "We don't really have much choice. All of our homes have been attacked as well. You can join us if you want."

The short man looked at his companions. "Should we go too? We can't go home with those monsters there and the kids will be getting hungry."

The woman next to him that Jack assumed was his wife, said. "Well, we can't stay here." She shrugged. "I say we go with them."

The tall, blonde man stepped forward. "Looks like we are going to be joining you." He held out his hand. "Name's Berry. And this is my wife Ellen," he said, as he motioned to the black-haired woman next to him. Jack shook Berry's hand and then Ellen's. "Nice to meet you. I'm Jack."

The short man's name was Terry and his wife was Judy. After introducing themselves, it was decided that Jack and his friends would lead the way into town with Berry, Ellen, and their children in the van behind them. Terry and Judy would bring up the rear in their car.

Having that decided, Jack went back to his truck and informed everyone what was going on. Nobody argued, so Jack jumped back in the truck bed and took his usual position standing with the big machine gun. Even though it was out of ammo, he could get a better view standing up. The two couples got into their vehicles and followed Darrell as he started down the hill.

The small caravan wove its way down the curvy road into the valley. As they descended, the air became hazy with smoke. By the time they reached the valley floor and the entrance to the town, the smoke was so thick they couldn't see more than twenty yards in front of them. It was like walking into another world. Everything was shrouded in smoke and it was eerily silent. Like being in a tomb, except for the distant crackle of burning buildings.

Jack held onto the machine gun with one hand and had his AR-15 in the other as the others all sat against the inside of the truck bed with their weapons pointed out into the smoke.

That smoke was also making it hard to breath. Everyone tried not to cough so the sound didn't echo through the deserted streets. The occasional breeze would pick up creating a clearing in the smoke, but all too quickly it passed and they were surrounded again.

Adding to the eeriness as they crept through the streets, they passed by sections of town that were completely burned down while other areas looked completely untouched. Cars and homes were equally smashed or burned. It didn't take long before they came across the first bodies.

Two of them were lying on the sidewalk along the right side of the road. Mike couldn't make out the gender because the bodies were so mutilated. They had been hacked apart and they looked partially eaten, as well. Mike suppressed a shudder. He hoped they had been dead before being eaten.

They had just passed the first two bodies when they came upon another. This one was in the center of the road and had also been torn apart. It was surrounded in small, bloody footprints. They kept driving through the smoke and soon there were too many bodies to count. Some hung out of burning cars, others butchered in their yards. It was the most horrible thing Mike had ever seen. The stink of charred meat and rotten flesh filled the air. They went another fifty yards before they came across the first dead creatures.

There were several small, green bodies lying across the road. It appeared the goblins had all been shot. *Good*, thought Mike. *Somebody was fighting back*. He hoped whoever it was had escaped.

As the small caravan made its way through the smoky streets towards the center of town, more and more goblins lay scattered across the streets. It looked to Mike that as people became aware of the threat, they began to fight back.

They turned onto a side street and came across a huge mass of bodies. At first Mike thought they were all goblins. But as they got closer, he realized that there was another type of creature in there. Sprawled alongside the dead goblins were small, scaly dog-men. When Jack saw the dog-men, he hit the roof of the cab. "Darrell, stop here."

Darrell stuck his head out the window. "Why?"

"Because those are the dog things that attacked me," Jack said as he pointed to one of the scaly bodies.

This announcement got Ted's attention and he jumped up before Darrell had completely stopped the truck. He leapt out of the bed and dashed across the road and knelt down over one of the dog-men bodies. Ted rolled it over and began poking and prodding at the corpse. "Hmm..." he muttered to himself. "Dog-like head with crocodile jaws... interesting..." He continued his examination, still muttering to himself. After a minute, he snapped his fingers and stood up. Ted walked back to the truck and said, "I believe those creatures to be kobolds."

Emily snorted. "What makes you say that?"

"Well," Ted began, "first, you have their short stature. I estimate that none of them are much over four feet tall. Second, is the very canine-like cranium. The older texts I have read refer to kobolds as short, scaly, dog-like creatures. Third, is the reptilian snout, more accurately a crocodile snout. And this is identical with more recent texts that describe the kobold. The small horns and tail are also accurate with many kobold descriptions."

"And that helps us how?" Emily asked.

Ted answered in what Mike liked to call his "lecturing voice." "Assuming the texts with the descriptions are correct, which they appear to be, then we can assume that the other descriptions about kobolds are correct as well. Like the one that says kobolds and goblins are archenemies. That would explain why they were fighting each other." Ted pointed back at the pile of corpses. "Do you see how most of the bodies inside are goblin and how they are surrounded by the kobold bodies? Kobolds are known for their tactics and that leads me to believe the goblins were ambushed and slaughtered."

"They tried to ambush me, too," Jack chuckled. "But I wasn't the one who got slaughtered."

"You were lucky," Ted said grimly. "If there had been a sorcerer or the like with them then it could have been a different story."

"I know," Jack retorted hotly. "But they didn't." Then he remembered the robed one he had killed. Reaching into his pocket Jack grasped the golden talisman. "There was a red robed kobold I killed that had this gold necklace around its-"

Before he could finish bringing it out, there was a yelping sound beyond the corpse pile.

Everyone readied themselves as they sought the source of the sound. It seemed like an eternity to Emily as they waited. But soon there was movement in the smoke. A small group of kobolds emerged, and when they saw Emily and the others they barked a challenge and immediately charged.

The kobolds brandished crude weapons and swung them wildly as they ran. They numbered around a dozen by Ted's quick estimate.

Everyone pointed their various weapons at the running monsters; Jack with his AR-15, Mike with his shotgun, and Emily drew her bow. Ted was still standing next to the truck when he threw up his arms. "Wait!" he shouted. "Let me handle this."

Nobody lowered their weapons, but they didn't fire. The kobolds were running hard and were almost to the corpse pile as Ted grinned and turned to face the charging pack. The kobolds yipped and barked like a pack of wild dogs when they saw that Ted and the others weren't going to try and run.

The kobolds were just running over the corpses when Ted made a fist with his right hand and held it up to his face. He opened his hand and a tiny glowing orb or liquid fire rotated above his palm. Everyone watched in amazement as the orb grew to the size of a baseball. Suddenly, Ted punched that arm out and the orb shot forwards directly at the barking kobolds.

Before any of the small monsters could react, the glowing orb struck the lead kobold and erupted in a massive explosion. The nearest creatures simply disintegrated as all the others were blown apart and sent flying. Adding to the bodily debris was the corpse pile that the living kobolds were running over. Burning body parts of both goblin and kobold rocketed across the area, and the stink of charred flesh filled the air.

"Wow!" Emily breathed, as she watched the destruction in amazement. She glanced back and saw the mouths hanging open on the faces of the two couples that were following them.

There was a scorched clearing in the corpse pile making a crescent moon shape out of the remaining bodies.

Ted dusted off his hands as he turned back to the truck. "Pretty cool eh?" he asked with a sly grin. Mike noticed that Ted's nose was bleeding and made a wiping motion to his own nose. Ted got the message and wiped the blood away, seemingly unconcerned.

Jack looked stunned. "Why can I not do that?" he asked aloud.

Mike shook his head in disbelief. "I should have known. So, does that make you some kind of wizard or something?"

Ted looked thoughtful at that. "I suppose it does." He scratched his beard thoughtfully. "Or maybe a sorcerer... hmm... I'm not sure if there are different types of magic and casting... it is an interesting prospect that will require further study."

Mike let out a big sigh and held out his hand to Ted. "You can ponder the Mysteries of the Universe as we drive. Come on."

Ted took Mike's hand and jumped back in.

Darrell slowly drove around the charred corpse pile and the other vehicles followed more slowly. At the next intersection, they took a left and through the smoky haze appeared an old steel bridge. When Mike saw it, he let out a breath that he didn't know he had been holding. "Finally."

Clearfield was split by the Susquehanna River with most of downtown located on the other side of this bridge. More importantly, that was where Grice's was located. Once they crossed the bridge, it would only be another two blocks before they reached their destination. That sounded easy enough, so long as there wasn't an army of creatures between here and there.

They just started across when a vehicle appeared out of the smoke in front of them. As they got closer they discovered that it was an Army Humvee. Alongside the Humvee were several soldiers behind a crude barricade that spanned the width of the bridge.

Seeing all the soldiers' gun barrels come up and point at them, Jack put his hands in the air. "Friendlies!" he shouted, as Darrell put on the brakes.

"Let me handle this," Jack said under his breath so the soldiers wouldn't hear.

The small caravan came to a halt on the bridge as two soldiers came out from behind the barricade to meet them. The soldiers were in full combat gear and looked nervous as they approached. They reached the truck and the younger looking of the two opened his mouth, but before he could say anything Jack said, "Status report?"

The young soldier's teeth snapped shut and a look of annoyance crossed his face. He looked at Jack closely for a moment before he said, "You military?"

Jack stared hard at the soldier and replied, "Marine," as if daring the soldier to challenge him. The young soldier must have thought better of arguing. "The town is in bad shape sir, but this side of the river is mostly secure."

"Mostly secure?" Jack said.

The young soldier nodded. "We have barricades on both bridges and there are command points located at the gun shop, courthouse, and police barracks, with central command at the Armory. Most of downtown has been cleared of creatures, but some keep popping out of the sewers. We have teams trying to clear them out now."

"What about the rest of town?" Jack pressed.

"Unknown, sir," the young soldier replied. "We have had very little contact with anyone. Last we heard, about half the town was on fire and it was estimated that one third of the citizens are either dead or M.I.A."

"One third!" Emily gasped.

"Yes, ma'am. That's the estimate anyways," the young soldier replied grimly. He seemed to realize he was talking too much and frowned. "Now, what are *you* doing here?"

Jack thought the question was stupid, but he answered it anyways. "We have been fighting creatures all morning and are running low on ammo, so we are headed to Grice's to resupply."

The young soldier looked almost relieved at the news. Jack thought that was strange as well. Why would he be relieved? "Oh, do you like it that our town is being overrun by monsters?" Jack snapped angrily.

"N-no sir," the young soldier stammered and then paused like he was going to say something else, but he must have thought better of it. "It's just that you guys look like you know what you're doing and we could use all the help we can get."

Jack saw his hesitation and then noticed the young soldiers name and rank. "Was there something else, Corporal?"

"No, sir," the corporal replied.

"So, can we go in?" Jack asked.

Corporal Allen looked embarrassed and turned to his companion. "Move the Humvee so they can get through."

"Yes, sir," the other soldier said, then went back to the barricade and got in the Humvee.

"Sorry about that," Corporal Allen said. "This is all just… unbelievable."

Jack smiled sadly. "I know what you mean, soldier. But these creatures die just like anybody else. We will clean them out and get our town back."

"Yes, sir," the corporal said eagerly.

The Humvee moved and now there was an opening in the barricade. Corporal Allen saw the opening and said to Jack. "Okay, sir. There you go. Good luck."

"Thank you, Corporal." Jack nodded back.

Darrell started forward again and moved slowly towards the opening as Corporal Allen watched them go by. Jack looked back and yelled. "Oh, and Corporal. If you see any beasts wearing a robe, kill it first!"

"Yes, sir!" Corporal Allen shouted back.

The small caravan drove through the barricade and crossed the bridge into downtown Clearfield. As they drove into the town proper, the soldiers and bridge dissolved into the smoke behind them.

CHAPTER 11

After crossing the bridge, the differences became immediately apparent. The smoke was less thick here and Liz could now see several streets ahead. Where most of the buildings had been destroyed on the other side of the river, here a majority still stood. Gone were the abandoned corpses and bodies of creatures, but signs of recent fighting were everywhere. Bullet holes and blood marred many of the streets and buildings.

Scared faces peered out from upper windows as armed groups of civilians patrolled the streets. Many were battered and weary looking, but they all carried themselves with a grim determination.

Some of the armed groups were being led by soldiers, but many of them were just average people armed with hunting rifles, pistols, and shotguns. Liz was surprised when she spotted a few people carrying axes and other improvised weapons. These were men and women who had seen their homes burned and loved ones killed by monsters pulled directly out of nightmares.

Darrell waved at a passing patrol and said, "Looks like we came to the right place."

"Looks like," Liz mumbled distractedly. Even though this section of town was in better shape than everywhere else they had seen, all the things that had recently happened suddenly hit Liz like a hammer blow. The demon in the church and Mike's powers, the attacks by the ratmen, goblins, kobolds, and other monsters, Ted's magic, and not to mention her own healing ability. A flood of emotions suddenly rose up and tried to overwhelm her, but Liz swiftly pushed them back. *This was not the time,* she told herself. They weren't out of danger yet.

Liz was snapped out of her thoughts when Darrell pointed ahead of them. "There she is," he said with a smile. "Grice Gun Shop."

In front of them loomed a large building with several smaller buildings attached to it. Its tall, steel sided walls made it look more like a warehouse than a store. Indeed, Grice's was so large it might as well have been called a warehouse; a warehouse full of weapons.

Surrounding the buildings were several military troop carriers and Humvees. Soldiers ran back and forth carrying boxes from the store to their waiting trucks. Other non-military vehicles were scattered around them with citizens standing around watching the activity.

Liz let out a sigh of relief. "Finally!" She had been worried that they were going to find that the Grice's had been burned down. Seeing it there before her made Liz feel a little better.

As the small convoy drove up to the gun shop, a soldier standing guard stepped forward and raised his hand, signaling for them to stop. Darrell pulled off the road and before he could come to a complete stop, Mike and Jack jumped out and headed over to the soldier.

Liz smiled and shook her head, "I guess we'll just sit here."

Mike couldn't hear what she said, but just then he turned back and said. "We'll take care of this, you guys go find some food." It was then that she realized how hungry she was. When was the last time she had eaten? Breakfast? It seemed so long ago, although in reality it was just now around noon.

****

Mike and Jack approached the soldier and saw that he was an older man with some grey in his hair. Jack still wore his military issue camo while Mike had his breastplate on and a sword hanging from his hip. Both of them were covered in blood and grime from their encounters with the otherworldly creatures.

Walking up to the soldier, Mike noticed he was part of the local 2nd Infantry 28th Division of the National Guard. The old guardsman didn't even blink at their appearance. *And why should he?* Mike thought. After what had happened this morning he doubted the soldier would be surprised by anything.

"Where are you coming from?" the guardsman asked.

"Rockton Mountain," Mike answered. "Then we crossed the Nichols Street Bridge to get here."

At this the guardsman did look surprised. "You came from across the river?"

"That's right," Mike replied.

The guardsman's jaw nearly dropped at the news. "We've sent several teams out there to look for survivors, but none of them has returned. What's it like over there?" the guardsman asked.

Mike took a deep breath. "Well, most parts are completely burned down, while a few other areas seem untouched. There are bodies scattered all over, but not as many as I would have expected. Either a lot of people escaped or the creatures may be taking prisoners."

"And it looks like the beasts have been eating people," Jack added darkly.

Mike nodded in agreement. "Yeah, that too. We didn't see any living people, but a group of kobolds did attack us."

The guardsman looked confused. "Kobolds?"

"The little, scaly dog thing," Jack answered.

"Ahh, okay," the guardsman nodded. "We have seen a few of those things running around, but there are a lot more of the little green monsters."

"Goblin," Mike said.

"Goblins, eh?" The guardsman looked thoughtful. "How do you know what these things are called?" he asked.

"Well..." Mike replied slowly, not sure how to explain. He looked over his shoulder at everyone getting out of the truck and figured the best answer was the truth. "You see the big guy climbing out of the truck?" The guardsman looked behind Mike and nodded. "Well, he is big into reading mythology and fantasy, and all that. Based on what he has read, the creatures we are seeing match the descriptions of some of the creatures he has read about," Mike explained. "So, he has been naming each creature we come across."

The guardsman looked satisfied with that. "Sounds good to me. We need a way to distinguish them. Do you mind telling the lieutenant what you just told me?"

Mike and Jack looked at each other and shrugged. "Sure," they replied in unison.

"Follow me," the guardsman said, as he turned around and headed toward Grice's.

Mike and Jack followed him over to in front of the gun shop where a pair of guardsmen were standing over the hood of a Humvee that had several maps laid out across it. Mike could hear them arguing as they approached.

"We are not going to blow the bridge!" A short, muscled guardsman with dark skin and short-cropped, black hair growled. Mike thought he looked Hawaiian and wondered why somebody from Hawaii would want to live in central Pennsylvania. Surely the weather would be nicer down there.

"But Lieutenant, we don't have enough troops to sufficiently guard everything," the other guardsman grumbled. He was taller than the lieutenant and much thinner. "If we blow the bridges we can move those troops to help clear out the rest of downtown and reinforce the other barricades."

The stocky lieutenant shook his head. "I told you no, Sergeant," he rumbled menacingly. "The Captain told me to hold this side of the river and that is exactly what I am going to do."

The thin sergeant looked like he wanted to argue more when Mike, Jack, and their escort reached the Humvee. The lieutenant and sergeant turned from their maps to look at the newcomers, but before the guardsman could introduce them the ground suddenly started to shake, causing everyone to grab ahold of the Humvee for support.

The quake only lasted a few violent moments, then ended just as suddenly as it began. Everyone slowly let go of the Humvee, waiting for another quake to happen. When none did, the old guardsman spoke. "Lieutenant, these civilians just came from across the river. They have information I thought you would want to hear."

The lieutenant raised an eyebrow at this, but he gave no other sign of surprise. "Finally," he said. "That whole half of town has gone dark." The lieutenant held out his hand. "I am Lieutenant Bowman and this," he gestured to the other guardsman, "is Sergeant Leah."

Mike shook his hand. "Mike Strazney."

Jack took his hand next. "Jack Treno."

The lieutenant eyed Jack up and down. "You have the look of a Marine."

Jack nodded. "Two tours."

Lieutenant Bowman didn't look surprised. "I could tell by the haircut." Then he smiled. "I will try not to hold that against you. Now, what intel do you have for me?"

Together Mike and Jack explained how they came back into town and found the burned-out sections and cannibalized bodies. Jack told of finding the mass of creature corpses that appeared as though the two groups fought each other.

"Good," Lieutenant Bowman muttered at that news.

Mike went on to tell of how they named the creatures and how they were discovering some of them had powers.

"Magic, eh?" Lieutenant Bowman breathed. "That's actually not the first report of such things. I've heard one guy threw some lightning at a group of these "goblins" and one little girl is said to have frozen some ratmen solid. Now, you are telling me a friend of yours can throw fireballs and another can heal?" The lieutenant shook his head. "If that last one is true, we could really use a healer around here. There are lots of injured and dying that need help, but with the hospital out of reach on the other side of the river, we can't take the risk of trying to get anyone over there. We don't even know if it's still standing."

Jack looked around at the patrols. "Status? How many casualties?"

"We have around one hundred guardsmen protecting this side of the town," Lieutenant Bowman replied. "There are also maybe fifty state and local police officers, as well." The lieutenant looked down at his map of Clearfield and the surrounding area and pointed. "We have barricades on these three bridges and on these roads." He indicated several of the roads leading into this side of the town. "But we are shorthanded. The creatures seem to pop up everywhere." The lieutenant growled angrily, "It is almost like they appear out of thin air sometimes. As you have probably seen, most of the civilians are doing the internal patrolling while the Guard and police are protecting the borders."

He pointed at three red circles drawn on the map. "These are our command centers, one here at Grice's, another at the police barracks, and the last one," he pointed to a red circle out across the river, "is the Armory. But we lost contact with them over an hour ago. All communications are down; no phone, television, or Internet. Luckily, the electricity is still on and we have running water. I have teams going from door to door looking for survivors and gathering any food or weapons they can find."

The lieutenant ran his hand over his head and sighed. "As for casualties, it's hard to say. Right now, it's looking like over half the population is M.I.A. We don't know if they are alive or dead. What I do know is that at last count there were around two thousand people in this area," he said, as he drew his finger around a portion of the map on the east side of the river. "Outside of that, I have no idea. The last I heard, the Governor declared a State of Emergency and activated all Guard units. Soon after that, the comms went dark and we have been on our own ever since."

Lieutenant Bowman took a deep breath. "First, those "goblins" as you call them, started popping up everywhere, killing and burning everything before we knew what was happening. Then the ratmen poured out of the sewers in the hundreds. Luckily, they don't seem to be the bravest of creatures and once we killed a few of them the others fled. But not before they did some serious damage. After that, we parked all available cars on top of the manhole covers to keep them from coming out again. That was Sergeant Leah's idea." Sergeant Leah nodded at this.

"Only good idea he has had all day," the lieutenant grumbled. Sergeant Leah made a face and opened his mouth to protest, but Lieutenant Bowman plowed right on. "It appears that the debris burning up in the sky are all of our satellites. Nobody has been able to tell me why they would be falling out of orbit, and as far as I know they all burn up in the atmosphere before reaching the ground. But it has left us blind."

Lieutenant Bowman's shoulders slumped and he hung his head. "What it boils down to is that we are alone, surrounded by an unknown number of hostiles, with no help in sight." The lieutenant looked up, and gave a sad half-smile. "At least this is central PA where everybody has at least one gun. If it weren't for the people fighting back, things would have been much, much worse."

"I don't know if things could get any worse," Sergeant Leah said.

Mike and Jack both groaned. "Oh, you just *had* to say it," Mike complained.

"What? Nothing else could be worse than where we are right now," Sergeant Leah argued.

"Things can always get worse," Mike shot back. "Do we even know why they are attacking us?"

Lieutenant Bowman shrugged helplessly. "Hell, if I know. As far as we can tell, they just like killing and destroying things."

Just then a guardsman appeared down the street, running hard and looking panicked. Mike, Jack, and Lieutenant Bowman all scowled at Sergeant Leah.

"Lieutenant!" The guardsman gasped for air as he stopped in front of them. "Lieutenant Bowman, one of our reconnaissance units made it back." He paused to catch his breath.

"Only one?" Sergeant Leah asked.

"Yes, sir," the guardsman gasped, "and he is in bad shape sir. I'm not sure how he made it back."

The lieutenant stepped forward. "What did he say?"

"Sir." The guardsman stood a little straighter. "He said there is an army of the green monsters gathering near the Shawville Power Plant. He thinks they are preparing to attack it soon."

"Damn!" Lieutenant Bowman slammed his fist into the Humvee's hood. "I don't have the men to defend it. But we can't let the power plant be destroyed."

"If we blow the bridges we could send those troops," Sergeant Leah started to say.

"No! I will not destroy our only way across the river. There must be another way," Lieutenant Bowman exclaimed.

Mike looked over at Jack and they shared a look. Both had the same idea. With a shrug, Mike turned back to the lieutenant. "Sir, we'll go."

"What?" all the guardsmen said in unison.

Mike looked at each in turn. "Jack and I will go help defend the power plant."

"You can't be serious," Lieutenant Bowman said. "There is no way the two of you can make a difference."

"Maybe not," Mike replied, "but we have to try. If nothing else, there are people working out there that need to know what is coming." Sergeant Leah looked dubious.

"Look," Mike continued, "my father used to work there and I know my way around. There are only a few entrances to get inside the plant and by blocking a few of them, we won't need many people to defend it."

"I appreciate your bravery," the lieutenant said, "but going out there is suicide. You were lucky to make it here in one piece."

Mike knew the lieutenant had a good point, but he would never be able to forgive himself if he left the men at the power plant to die. Even if he and Jack couldn't save the plant, at least they could get the workers out. That would be a victory. However, if they left, the goblins would no doubt destroy the plant and that would knock out all the electricity.

That couldn't be allowed to happen.

Mind made up, Mike looked at the lieutenant. "I know you can't spare anyone, but all Jack and I need is to resupply our ammunition and we can get back out there. The sooner we leave the better our chances are of getting there before the goblins."

Lieutenant Bowman looked at Sergeant Leah. The sergeant shrugged and shook his head. The lieutenant threw up his hands. "Fine. I don't see how I have any other choice. I can't spare any guardsmen and the plant needs to be warned. Save it if you can, but if not, get the workers out of there. You can use our supply dump to restock whatever you need."

"Thank you, Lieutenant," Mike said. He turned to Jack. "Can you load up your truck with everything we will need? I will go find the others and tell them what is going on."

"I'm on it," Jack said, then walked around the Humvee and entered the gun shop.

"Good luck," Lieutenant Bowman said to Mike. "You will need it."

"Thanks, Lieutenant." Mike replied. "Make sure the town is still here when I get back."

"Gladly," Lieutenant Bowman said.

With that Mike turned from the guardsmen and headed down the street, looking for where his friends had gone. Knowing that they were hungry, Mike took a guess and headed to Denny's Pub to see if it was open.

A few blocks down the street, Mike was proven right as he came up to the pub and found Liz, Emily, Ted, and Darrell sitting outside eating hamburgers.

Denny's Pub was a rather large bar and restaurant that was famous for its humungous hamburgers. Built onto a slight hill, it was laid out in two levels. One door led down a set of stairs to the lower level, another led straight into the pub. The lower level had no windows and was mostly underground with a long bar and several small tables, while the second level had larger tables and was well lit from several large windows. Dark, polished wood made up the floor and furniture, giving it a homey feel.

At the sound of his footsteps, Liz looked up. When she saw Mike, a huge smile lit up her face. "About time you got here," she said. "Darrell is going to eat all the burgers."

Darrell shrugged with a half-eaten burger in his hands. "If they are gonna keep handing out free burgers, then I'm gonna keep eatin' em," he said, and took another bite.

The smell of food made Mike's mouth water. He was ravenous. Nearly forgetting what he came down here to do, Mike walked into Denny's Pub and saw several large hamburgers all wrapped and lined up on the bar counter. There were a few people seated near the back, but no bartenders in sight. Assuming these were the free burgers, Mike went up to the bar and grabbed two in each of his large hands and then walked back out to his friends.

"Hungry much?" Emily asked, when she saw the four burgers in Mike's fists.

"Two for me and two for Jack," Mike answered. "We will eat them on the way."

Everyone looked up from their meals and Liz asked. "On the way to what?"

Mike took a deep breath then explained what had happened while they were meeting with the lieutenant, and how he and Jack had volunteered to go to the power plant.

"That's insane!" Liz complained when Mike finished his story.

"Yeah," Emily agreed. "You don't have a chance."

Mike knew that, but he wasn't changing his mind. "Look, I know it isn't a great idea. But like I told the lieutenant, even if we can't save the plant, at least we can warn the guys working there and maybe get them out."

"That *is* crazy," Ted laughed. "And I am going too." He shoved the last of his burger in his mouth and stood up.

"Me, too," Liz added, and she stood as well.

Emily groaned. "Well, I am certainly not staying here by myself," she said as she pulled herself up from the step that she had been sitting on.

Darrell stood up and stretched. "Suppose I'll tag along. You guys would get lost without me."

"No, no, no," Mike said. "Just Jack and I are going. You stay here and help protect the town."

Liz shook her head sadly. "Mike, we are going with you, so just suck it up and let's go before there isn't a power plant left to save."

Mike opened his mouth to argue, but then closed it again as he realized she was right. To tell the truth, he was glad to have them along, and their chances of making it out alive would be better together. "Fine," Mike said with a sigh. "Let's go. I'm sure Jack is loaded up, and if I know him there are several extra guns there as well."

Sure enough, when they got back to the gun shop, Jack was waiting for them in the back of his truck with several new guns and boxes of ammo. "What took you guys so long?" Jack asked, as the others walked up to the truck. Mike tossed the hamburgers up to him.

"Mike tried to talk us out of coming," Emily replied with a grin. "Silly boy."

"Of course, he did," Jack laughed. "He is too much of a paladin to recruit anybody else for a dangerous mission. Even though he is always the first one to volunteer himself."

"Exactly," Liz laughed. "Mike, this isn't one of your video games. No running off by yourself. We don't get to come back if we die now."

"Ugh," Mike complained with mock distress. "Yes, Mom. I'm pretty sure I know that we don't get a redo."

Ted jumped in the back of the truck and looked down at the others. "Fight nice kids."

"Oh, shut it, Ted," Mike smiled, as he hauled himself into the truck after Ted.

The others followed suit with Darrell hopping in the driver's seat and Liz joining him in the cab. Mike, Ted, and Emily nestled in between the boxes that Jack had put back there while Jack stood in the center with his mounted machine gun.

Darrell slowly pulled out and wound his way through the cars parked on the manhole covers. They worked their way out and soon passed through the last barricade north of downtown.

Darrell picked up speed and Emily shivered as the cool breeze blew over them.

Jack noticed her shiver and snapped his fingers. "I almost forgot." He grabbed a nearby box and pushed it over to Emily. "Here are some clothes. They are all different sizes and I also grabbed some other supplies, just in case," he said, as he patted the box next to him.

Emily gave Jack a warm smile. "Thanks," she said, then opened the box. The inside was stuffed with various articles of clothing from hats and shirts to coats and pants. Most of it was in woodland camo, but a few were dark, earth tones. Perfect for sneaking through the woods, but not much use in a power plant.

Emily dug through the box for a while until she found something she liked. She pulled out a small pair of matching camo pants and a long-sleeved shirt. She held up the pants and then looked around at the guys in the truck bed with her.

Jack laughed. "We are not stopping so you can change."

Emily stuck her tongue out at him. "I didn't ask you too." Staying seated, she kicked off her shoes and carefully slid the pants on under her skirt. She buttoned the pants and left her black skirt on over top of the pants. Emily then put the long-sleeved shirt on overtop of her black t-shirt and buttoned it half way up.

Jack gave her an appraising look. "Well, that is quite the fashion statement."

Emily ignored the comment. "I don't suppose you have any boots stashed around here?"

"Actually," Jack grinned, "I do. In that big box right next to you." He indicated the box to her left. Emily found a suitable pair of boots from the box and put them on as well. Emily looked up after tying the boots and saw that Jack was still watching her. "You can look somewhere else now. The show is over."

Jack pretended to be upset for a moment then looked at Mike and Ted. "You guys need anything?"

Both Mike and Ted shook their heads "no".

Satisfied, Jack held his machine gun steady as they rumbled down the battle-scarred street.

CHAPTER 12

From the north, Clearfield had only one major road out on this side of the river, so they followed it for a few miles as it wound around the hill where it led to an overpass and the road split in several directions. They took the right fork and curved around to merge onto the overpass itself.

They continued along that road for several more miles, passing abandoned cars and destroyed stores. The road soon left the more populated areas and became very narrow as it looped along the left side of the river. The road carved into the hillside with a steep drop down to the rushing water below.

In the distance, Mike could see the tops of the power plant's smoke stacks getting closer. Shawville Station wasn't really that far away from Clearfield, but winding through all the hills made the distance much longer to travel.

They went around another sharp bend along the hill when the cliff face leveled off and Mike could see up into the forested hillside. He breathed a sigh of relief now that they had made it through the most treacherous part of the drive. Mike looked up into the woods and was enjoying watching the trees fly by when he caught a flash of movement up the hill. He peered intently into the woods trying to see more, but the brush was too thick.

He caught a glimpse of metal and then a flash of green skin.

Mike turned to the others and saw that Jack must have seen the same thing he did because he was staring hard up into the woods too.

Then, there was a break in the undergrowth and Mike could see what looked like a man in armor battling furiously against a horde of goblins. But just as Mike saw it, they vanished behind another small hill.

"Stop the truck!" Mike shouted as he pounded the side of the truck with his fist.

Everyone lurched forward as Darrell slammed on the brakes.

"What the..." Emily started to say, but Mike was already on his feet. "There is somebody up there fighting goblins," he said. "We need to help."

Emily looked shocked. "But what about the power plant?"

Ted stood as well and picked up his poleaxe. "You guys go on ahead and warn the plant." He caught Mike's eye. "We will catch up."

Before anyone could say more, Mike and Ted jumped out of the truck and ran across the road up into the woods.

Jack stood there holding Ol' Bertha and scanned the hillside. When he didn't see anything, he said, "Okay, Darrell, you heard them. Let's go."

Darrell nodded and the truck started forward again.

Mike was breathing hard when he held up his hand, signaling to stop. Ted came up next to him also sucking wind. The hill was a lot steeper than it looked from the road. Not to mention the added difficulty of climbing in armor, even pieces of armor, like they were wearing. That didn't include all the brush and undergrowth that kept pulling at them.

Mike paused to listen and was rewarded with the sound of battle. Deep roars and battle cries could be heard over the clash of steel and the screams of the dying. Mike thought the sound was close, likely just around this hill.

There must be more than one guy up there. No way was one person holding out that long and making that much noise... at least not against what sounded like an entire army of goblins. Their harsh shrieks and shouts nearly drowning out all other sounds.

Mike looked over at Ted and he nodded then held up his right hand. A spark appeared in his open palm and quickly spun into a small ball of liquid fire. It was only about the size of a golf ball, not nearly as big as Mike had seen him make before.

"Can't make a bigger one without my head feeling like it is going to explode," Ted explained apologetically.

"Better than nothing." Mike replied, and put his hand on Ted's shoulder. "Let's go show these critters who's the boss."

An evil grin spread across Ted's bearded face. Mike thought he looked quite imposing with his poleaxe and spinning fireball in his hands, his gore-encrusted armor and braided beard all making him look wildly possessed.

Mike checked his shotgun and loosened his sword in its scabbard. He hoped he looked as fearsome. With any luck, there wouldn't be that many goblins and they might scare some of them away. For all his bluster and reputation for charging recklessly into battle, Mike was actually a rather cautious man. That was why nobody would play him at chess anymore. He was always thinking several steps ahead and nearly always won. He saw all possibilities before he made a move. But when he did move, it was fast and brutal, making others think him reckless, when in fact it was a well-calculated move. Mike knew that sometimes the appearance of recklessness could be used as an advantage.

Mike sighed. He didn't have many shots and doubted he would have time to reload. He disliked charging into a fight that he had no idea what to expect, but there was no help for it. So, with another sigh, Mike started forward. They were as ready as they were going to be.

The sounds got louder as Mike and Ted made their way around the small hill. Men's voices could be heard shouting above the goblin's shrieking.

Mike and Ted rounded the hill and stopped. Below them, a virtual sea of goblins swarmed. Mike guessed that there must be over a hundred of the creatures.

So much for hoping there wouldn't be that many of them. At least the goblins hadn't noticed them yet, with their backs to Mike and Ted. They were focused on the line of men beyond them.

There looked to be only around twenty men down there battling against the swarm. The men were covered from head to toe in heavy plate armor that had strange symbols cut into them, and they all wielded either large war hammers or massive battle-axes that looked far too heavy for anyone to carry, let alone fight with.

As Mike watched, he realized that the men down there were short. The tallest were only a head taller than the surrounding goblins. But the goblins only came up to around Mike's waist, so he guessed all the men to be slightly above five feet tall. But where they lacked in height they made up for in width.

The men were incredibly broad. Even covered in the heavy plate armor like they were, Mike could tell they were impressively massive. They moved in their heavy plate as easily as if it was a second skin, and they swung their huge weapons with precision and ease that Mike couldn't quite believe. These men would challenge even the best Scadian company for discipline.

But even with their heavy armor and skill, Mike and Ted watched one of them fall, pierced through the eye by a goblin spear. The only reason they hadn't been overrun was that they were in a tight line stretched between a bottle-neck of two sheer cliffs. The goblins were funneled into the narrow area where they could only attack a few at a time.

Seeing the man fall to the goblin spear knocked Mike and Ted out of their trance. The swarm of goblins was between them and the other men. Their only option was to attack the goblin force from behind.

Mike grinned evilly. "What do you say to a little prostate exam?"

"I will bring the chili powder," Ted replied, with a wicked grin of his own.

Ted thrust out his hand and the small fireball shot forwards. Mike and Ted charged down the slope close behind. The fireball struck the back of the tightly packed goblins and erupted in a fiery explosion. A few goblins were incinerated and many others were torn apart by the force of the blast.

Mike and Ted charged into the rear of the stunned goblins. Mike was firing his shotgun in rapid succession, shredding the goblin ranks as Ted summoned up smaller fireballs and threw them at the closest groups of goblins as fast as he could.

Within moments, dozens of goblins lay dead or dying around Mike and Ted. Smoke obscured the battlefield as Ted's explosions burned and caught some of the undergrowth on fire. The surprise wore off all too soon and the goblins charged them. Taking his last shot, Mike dropped his empty shotgun, unslung his shield from his back, and drew his sword in one fluid motion.

A group of howling goblins rushed him, slashing with their swords and spears. Mike lunged forward with his sword pointing straight out and skewered two of the creatures at once. But when he tried to pull his blade free, it was stuck. Another goblin stabbed at him with a long spear and Mike blocked it with his shield. Kicking out, Mike pushed the dying goblins off his sword just in time to raise his blade and block a slash from yet another.

The goblin with the spear stabbed again and this time Mike spun around it and with a quick swipe at the wooden spear, cut off the iron spearhead. Mike continued his spin and blocked two more goblin slashes with his shield at the same time as he swung his sword in a horizontal arc, decapitating several goblins that had been charging him from his right side. Dancing away, Mike continued to block and stab wildly as he fought a desperate battle against his numerous foes.

As Mike whirled and slashed, Ted remained in one spot, blasting groups of goblins with fire as they came too close and carving into any others that made it through with his poleaxe. With his great height and the long reach of his weapon, no goblin could get close to Ted. He stood in the center of a burning ring of bodies, like some wrathful spirit.

A goblin with a spear lunged at Ted from behind, hoping to catch him unaware. But just before the spear entered his back, Ted twisted in a tight pirouette and swung his poleaxe like a golf club. The goblin lurched forward caught off balance, and Ted connected with the goblin's back mid-swing and launched it squealing into the smoke. Ted finished his pirouette and looked around, surprised to find that no goblins were attacking him, when out of the smoke two, huge shapes emerged.

They were a pair of creatures that resembled overgrown goblins. They had greyish-green, warty skin and long arms that nearly dragged on the ground, which was impressive since they both stood as tall as Ted. They had large eyes and long, pointed noses. Large drooping ears protruded from a mop of wiry hair and a horrible stench filled the air as the creatures approached. One held a massive wooden club in its large hands and the other held a pair of large, notched cleavers. They howled in unison and charged.

Ted summoned another fireball, but this one was the smallest yet. He doubted it would do much more than singe these creatures' skin. To make matters worse, Ted was getting a horrible headache and his nose had started to bleed. The magic was taking its toll and he didn't know how much longer he would last. Perhaps it was time to stop casting and fight the old-fashioned way.

The two monsters were just about on him when Ted threw his small fireball. It exploded in the face of the monster with the cleavers. The huge goblinoid howled in pain, then stopped and clawed wildly at its face, desperately trying to put the fire in its hair out. The other roared angrily and raised its huge club as it quickly closed the distance between it and Ted.

Ted dove to the side as the huge club smashed into the ground where he had been standing a moment before. Ted stabbed out with his poleaxe and caught the creature in the thigh. It roared in pain and swung its club around in a wild arc, knocking over small trees as Ted scrambled away. The other creature had put out the fire in its hair and was rushing in to help its companion. Ted was now caught between the two monsters.

Before the cleaver-wielding creature could close, Mike appeared out of the bushes and lunged at it. The creature moved remarkably quickly and dodged Mike's thrust, and brought its own cleavers down at him in the same movement. Mike pulled his shield up just in time, but the force of the blow splintered his shield and drove Mike to one knee.

Ted couldn't help because the club-wielding goblinoid was charging him again and it was taking all of Ted's concentration to keep from being crushed by its tree-like weapon. The creature swung the giant weapon remarkably fast for how relatively thin its long arms were.

But Ted needn't worry. From his knee, Mike stabbed upwards from under his shield and caught the hunched cleaver-monster in the stomach. The large goblinoid released its trapped cleaver, threw its head back and screeched in agony as Mike pushed to his feet and drove his blade further into the creature's bowels.

With a cleaver still stuck in his shield and his sword buried to the hilt in the goblinoid's gut, Mike punched out with his shield and crushed the creature's throat. The beast fell to its knees and slowly collapsed in a bloody pile at Mike's feet.

Not wasting any time, Mike ran over and joined Ted as he desperately battled the club-wielding goblinoid beast.

Between the two of them, the monster didn't stand a chance and was quickly cut down. Mike and Ted stood over the monster's corpse and looked around. The smoke from the burning brush had grown and obscured their vision. The clamor of battle could still be heard as monsters and men's voices shouted over the clash of steel, and shapes could be seen moving through the smoke.

Mike and Ted moved toward the sound of battle and soon found themselves face to face with an army of the large goblinoid beasts.

The big monstrosities were pressing the armored men's line hard and Mike feared that it would soon break. The armored men gave a marvelous accounting of themselves, cutting down monster after monster, but there were too many of the beasts as another armored man fell to the clubs and cleavers of the giant brutes.

The armored line retreated a step, but one man in the center broke away and tried to reach his fallen companion. He wore more ornate armor than the others, with what Mike thought looked like Norse runes carved into it. The man carried a large steel shield and thick bladed axe, both of which were covered with the strange runic shapes. He had a dark blue, fur-lined cloak that billowed out behind him as he dashed toward the prone form of his companion. Before he could get there, four brutes surrounded him, clubs and cleavers slashing.

Mike and Ted ran as fast as they could toward the battle, but they knew they wouldn't reach the cloaked man in time. As they ran, one of the brutes caught the man a glancing blow to the shoulder that spun him around. Another brute's cleavers chopped at his head, but his heavy helm protected him from the worst of the blow.

But then a creature even larger than the rest appeared behind the cloaked man and it carried an immense war hammer. The massive brute swung its hammer and before the cloaked man could react, it slammed into his back and sent him crashing to the ground several yards away.

The beasts howled in victory and raced to finish the kill. Mike and Ted were almost there, but Mike knew they wouldn't reach them in time as the largest beast raised its hammer over the cloaked man as he tried to rise.

Doing the only thing he could think of, Mike reversed his grip on his sword and hurled it like a javelin at the bloated goblinoid. Mike ripped the cleaver out of his shield and continued his charge. His aim was true, and the sword flew through the air and struck the monster square in the chest.

The goblinoid stared stupidly down at the sword hilt sticking out of its chest for a moment before it fell backward, dead. The other three brutes looked up from their prey to see where this new threat came from just as Mike and Ted crashed into them.

The cloaked man regained his feet and joined in, swinging his axe with more force and skill than Mike could have thought possible for a man who had just been sent flying by a huge war hammer.

Caught by surprise, two of the creatures died quickly to cleaver and poleaxe. The fourth lasted a little longer, but the three men quickly surrounded it and cut it down.

Before they could say anything, a deafening cheer went up from the line of men as the goblins attacking them suddenly broke and ran.

The armored men did not pursue the beasts; instead, they picked their way through the bodies and made their way to Mike, Ted, and their cloaked companion. Seeing that the battle was over, at least for now, Mike dropped the cleaver and pulled his sword out of the bloated goblinoid's chest.

It was only then that Mike realized they had no idea who these men were. Just because they fought the goblins didn't necessarily mean they were friends. But since the cloaked man didn't attack them as soon as the monsters ran away, Mike guessed they were not enemies. At least, not yet…

Ted came to stand next to Mike as the armored man in the cloak turned to face them and his armored companions gathered behind him.

Mike had been right about their height. The tallest of them came to his chest, but they were incredibly broad. Mike was a large man, well-muscled and tall, but these men made Mike look almost scrawny.

Adding to their large size was the intricate, heavy plate armor that completely encased each of them. It was of a style that Mike had never seen before and their weapons were of a peculiar design as well. The very metal the weapons and armor were made of seemed strange. It was a very dark, brushed metal with an unusual bluish tint to it. Adding to the strangeness was the runes that were engraved into both weapon and armor.

Mike was a bit of a history buff and knew some Viking runes, and these seemed similar to some he had seen, but were far more complex. The runes were mostly sharp and angular with a few spirals and curves worked in. Intrigued, Mike turned his attention to their apparent leader in the dark blue cloak.

He wasn't the tallest of the men, but he may have been the bulkiest. Mike guessed that under all that armor his arms were larger than Mike's thighs, maybe even both thighs! And his armor was very ornate. Blue and gold runes covered much of the armor in a dizzying array of patterns.

The helm was rounded at the top, but the bottom was hidden by a thick and high armored collar piece that guarded the man's neck. And unless Mike missed his guess, acted as a neck brace. The heavy neck guard gave the cloaked man the appearance of not having a neck at all.

He went from the top of his head straight into shoulder plates and massive, multi-segmented shoulder plates they were. The image of a castle tower was emblazoned on the left shoulder and what appeared to be three interlocking triangles were on the right.

His chest plate seemed to be one solid piece emblazoned with a strangely familiar symbol. The symbol was difficult to make out due to the large, black beard that jutted out from under the heavy helm, but it appeared to be eight spiked tridents radiating out from a central point as if protecting the circle in their center.

A tense moment followed as the two sides faced each other before Mike stuck his sword, point down, into the ground in front of him and extended his hand to the cloaked stranger.

"Michael Strazney at your service."

The tension grew as the cloaked man didn't move for several breaths. Then, ever so slowly, he hung his axe on his belt and carefully removed his helm, revealing piercing blue eyes set on a wide bearded face with thick, bushy eyebrows and a wide flat nose.

The bearded man put his helm in the crook of his arm and extended his other hand. But instead of taking Mike's hand, he took Mike's forearm in a tight embrace. Mike returned the gesture by grasping the man's forearm. It wasn't quite the handshake he expected, but it would do.

When the man spoke, it was in a deep rumbling voice with a strange accent to it. "Greetings Michael Strazney. I be Lord Aurvang Twinpeaks o' the Keepbuilder Clan dwarves."

CHAPTER 13

"Morons," Liz fumed. "Jumping out and charging off into who-knows-what. They are going to get themselves killed."

"Yup," Darrell replied without taking his eyes off the winding road and they lapsed into an uncomfortable silence, each lost in their own thoughts. Liz worried that she would never see Mike or Ted again. They could get killed out there and nobody would ever know. The thought of never seeing Mike again upset her more than she cared to admit.

Thinking of losing Mike made Liz wonder how her family was doing. Were her parents and brothers all safe up in New York? Had the same thing happened up there? Will she ever find out? There were just too many questions. Luckily, Liz lost her train of thought as Darrell rounded the last curve and Shawville Station appeared before them.

The power plant wasn't overly large, but it did have two very identifiable smoke stacks that towered over the surrounding buildings. The taller of the two stacks had vertical red and white stripes painted along its top half while the bottom half was the same tan colored stone as the smaller stack. Large plumes of white steam billowed out of the tallest stack and two smaller smoke stacks poked out from the main building far below the main stacks.

The main building rose several stories high and was surrounded by a variety of smaller buildings all connected by miles of crisscrossing pipes. Huge piles of coal were heaped around the buildings. Conveyer belts and other equipment wound between the pipes and buildings in a dizzying complexity. Some of the conveyer belts led down into the giant piles of coal and could be seen feeding streams of coal into the bowels of the plant.

The plant sat on the opposite side of the river, where the river took a sharp curve. There was only one old, steel bridge connecting the plant to this side and as Liz watched, they drove by the power plant and up to the lonely bridge.

The old bridge was covered in potholes and even some grating could be seen through the holes in the pavement, revealing the rushing water below. Darrell drove up to the intersection where the crusty bridge met their road and stopped.

"Well, that bridge has seen better days," Darrell noted happily.

"Just get us across," Liz muttered.

Darrell turned right and eased their way onto the old bridge. Liz swallowed nervously as she waited for the dilapidated old bridge to collapse and plunge them all into the river.

The truck bounced as it ran over the potholes and drove across the grating, and Liz held her breath. It seemed like an eternity, but within moments they were across the old bridge.

Liz let out a sigh of relief. "Well, that was fun."

"Yeah," Darrell agreed, "but now what?"

That was a good question. Liz had only been here once before and that was years ago when she was little and had been on a class field trip. The road they were on now continued straight, but Liz didn't know where it led. Shawville Station sat on their right with two roads leading towards it. One road looked to lead around the plant to somewhere behind it, while the other road led to a small gatehouse that broke up the razor-wire fence surrounding the entire plant complex.

Liz pointed to the gatehouse. "I guess we go there."

Darrell shrugged and drove up to the gatehouse and wound down his window. He stuck his head out and looked into the gatehouse. It was empty. Darrell leaned further out the window and looked all around, but he didn't see anybody anywhere.

"Looks like nobody's home," Darrell said.

Liz scanned the area as well. "Doesn't look like the goblins were here either."

"So, now what?" Darrell asked.

He was just starting to roll the window back up when a loud voice crackled to life.

"What are you doing here?" the voice asked.

Darrell and Liz nearly jumped out of their seats at the sudden sound. Darrell recovered quickly and looked back at the gatehouse and noticed the speaker sticking out of the gatehouse wall.

"We're here to warn ya." Darrell told the speaker.

There was a long pause.

"Warn us about what?" the voice asked.

Darrell looked at Liz and she motioned for him to continue. "The goblins," Darrell said.

"Goblins? Is that what those little green monsters are?" The voice crackled, followed by a short pause. "You guys are a tad late. We have been pushing back those things for nearly an hour now."

"Sorry 'bout that," Darrell replied. "But we got here as fast as we could. We came to warn ya that there's a big army of 'em headed yer way."

"How big of an army?" the voice asked.

"Hunnerds prolly," Darrell answered.

This was met with silence. Darrell looked at Liz again and she shrugged. They continued to wait, but no answer came. After several minutes, Darrell put the truck in reverse and was just about to leave when the voice came back. "If what you say is true, we could use all the help we can get," it crackled. "Come on in."

There was a loud clang and grinding sound as the gate slowly swung open.

"Follow the road and it will lead you to a small parking lot next to the main doors," the speaker voice said, then cut out.

Darrell put the truck back into drive and when the gate was open enough for them to get through, he followed the voice's instructions. The road narrowed and weaved through a forest of steel beams and thick metal supports that held up the tall conveyer belts that were way above them.

After they made it through the steel forest, they came to a small parking lot filled with the worker's vehicles. The parking lot was right next to the main building of the plant and a large set of steel double-doors was set in the wall next to the lot.

Darrell pulled up along the building, threw it in reverse, and backed the truck up to the large double-doors. He put the truck in park and everyone climbed out, weapons close at hand. Liz figured there were no goblins or anything nearby, but it didn't hurt to be prepared. Besides, the power plant gave her the creeps. Liz and Darrell met Jack and Emily in front of the doors.

"Now what?" Emily asked, as she looked around nervously.

Jack eyed the big double-doors. "I guess we go in."

But before they could move, the steel doors swung open and two men stepped out.

One was a large bear of a man with a great, round gut. He had short, black hair streaked with grey and a full grey beard.

The second man was slightly shorter and much skinnier. He appeared to be far younger. but even so he also had a little grey sprinkled in his hair.

The large bear-like man spoke first. "Welcome to Shawville Station. I'm Dave." He motioned to the smaller man. "And this is Jim. Now, who are you and what is this about an army of monsters?"

Liz stepped forward. "I'm Liz and these are my friends Jack, Emily, and Darrell. We just came from Clearfield. Half the town is burning and overrun by monsters."

Both men's eyes grew wide at the news. Apparently, they didn't know what was going on outside of the plant.

The shorter man, Jim, looked at Dave. "Larry and Steve will want to know what's happened. They have family in Clearfield."

Dave looked grim. "You're right and they aren't the only ones." Then he turned back to Liz. "What kind of monsters? And does it have something to do with all these blasted earthquakes?"

Liz shrugged. "I don't know for sure if it has anything to do with the earthquakes, but I would guess that it does. As for what kind of monsters... all kinds. We have seen what we think are goblins, orcs, kobolds, ratmen, and troglodytes." Liz took a deep breath as she saw Jim and Dave make faces that said they didn't believe her. So, she quickly added. "We are just giving them names, but there are at least five different kinds of monsters we have seen."

Dave ran his hand through his hair. "We were hoping that what we found were just some deformed animals or something."

"What did you find?" Liz asked.

Dave took a deep breath. "Slim was working down in the basement when he heard some crashing and screeching sounds. He was shooting clinkers out of the boiler at the time so he had his shotgun on him, and thinking that it was just some animal that got inside, he decided to investigate."

Dave took another deep breath and looked like he didn't believe what he was about to say. "But what he found were two small, green monsters trying to pry some pipes off the wall. When they saw him they tried to attack him. Luckily, Slim shot them both before they could reach him. Then he brought them up to the control room to show everyone."

Liz wanted to ask what a "clinker" was and why they would need a shotgun in a power plant, but she decided to leave it alone.

Dave looked down at Jim. "Most of us still didn't believe him, even after seeing the bodies. We thought it was just some elaborate prank. But then a few minutes ago, Jerry saw a few of the things running around outside the fence like they were looking for a way in. Then, you guys showed up armed to the teeth and saying an army of the weird buggers were headed this way."

"Well," Liz began, "I can tell you it's no prank. These things are real and they seem to be hell-bent on destroying whatever they find. We are calling these small green ones goblins so we can keep all the creatures organized. Now, how many people work here?"

Jim answered, "Twelve of us are here right now. After one of the bigger quakes a lot of the guys went home to make sure their families were alright."

Liz was shocked. "Twelve? That's it? But this place is huge."

Jim shrugged. "Yeah, that's it. We don't really need that many guys to keep it running. Only when something is getting repaired do we need more. We did try to call in a few more, but the phones aren't working right."

"Twelve will be fine." Jack said. "I brought four shotguns, eight rifles, and six pistols. So, we can arm everyone here and have a few to spare." He motioned to several crates in the back of his truck. "I also have all these boxes full of ammo. Hopefully, a thousand rounds will be enough for whatever is out there."

Dave and Jim looked impressed as they walked up to the truck. "I'm glad you came prepared," Dave said, as he looked over the supplies. "Let's get this stuff inside and handed out before this army of yours shows up."

Dave and Jim each took a large crate of ammunition, and everyone else grabbed whatever they could carry and followed them back inside the plant.

They walked down a dark narrow hallway and passed several doorways. Everything was made of dark metal and Liz couldn't tell if it was because everything was dirty or if the steel was actually that dark. The air had a metallic taste to it and some other odors that Liz couldn't quite place, grease maybe. Then Dave turned into one of the doorways and they entered a small room full of equipment, and went through it to enter another set of thick doors in the back of the room. They went down another narrow hallway and entered into a large room where one man sat surrounded by monitoring equipment. They were now in the heart of the plant.

"This is Control Room One," Dave said, as they made their way to the center of the room. "We will put the supplies here."

The control room was a large, circular area covered in blinking panels and control stations. Computer monitors filled the central hub of the room, while antique-looking boards and switches lined the outer walls. It gave Liz the impression of airplane controls on steroids. The array of flashing lights was enough to nearly make her sick. Large windows looked out onto the main floor where four gigantic turbine generators sat.

The unloading went quickly as Dave got a few other plant workers to help and then called everyone in the station to the control room. Soon, all the employees and Liz and her friends were standing in Control Room One around the pile of supplies that Jack had brought.

Once everyone was gathered, Jack told them what had happened to the town and how some people seemed to be gaining magical abilities. He told them how communications were going out and that the National Guard had made a safe zone downtown, but couldn't send any help so it seemed that they were on their own. These announcements were met with equal parts disbelief and dismay.

Jack told them how the power plant must be saved or there would be no electricity, since it was likely that the grid would eventually be knocked out. He then went on to describe the different types of creatures they had seen and what names they had been given.

"And now," Jack finished, "you all need to decide if you are going to stay here and fight or retreat and try to make it back to Clearfield."

The room filled with low muttering as the plant employees gathered together across the room and talked among themselves. Their discussion had gone on for several minutes when one of the men left the group and ran off. None of the employees seemed to care that the man had ran away.

They continued their discussion for a few more minutes before the man came back. He told everyone something that caused a lot of arguing and raised voices.

"I wonder what that's about," Jack whispered, as he and his friends stood off by themselves.

"I think we are about to find out," Liz said, as she saw the employee's group break apart and Dave walked up to them.

"We decided to stay," Dave said. "We couldn't live with ourselves if we just abandoned this place to some scrawny monsters. Besides, Clearfield and the surrounding areas will need power if they want to survive this chaos and it is up to us to give it to them."

"If the grid does go down, we will need to reverse the power output so that it flows back to Clearfield," Jim added. "Right now, all the power flows away from here. It will take time, but we can do it."

"Thank you," Liz said. And she meant it. She knew that without power everyone would be in even worse shape than they already were. Even though spring was here, there were still some bitterly cold nights and people would need their power to stay warm.

"Why did that one guy leave?" Emily asked.

"The power plants have an internal radio system so we can communicate with each other," Dave explained. "We sent him to radio the other nearby stations to see what their stats are." He took a deep breath and rubbed his eyes. "We didn't get a response from any of them."

"Wonderful. Looks like we really are on our own," Emily complained. "Now what?"

Jack checked his rifle and rested it on his shoulder. "Now, we prepare for the worst."

CHAPTER 14

The dwarves stood in a silent, imposing line behind Lord Aurvang Twinpeaks.

The fires were going out from Ted's fireballs and the smoke was slowly clearing out, revealing the carnage wrought by the short but furious battle.

Goblin bodies and those of the larger goblinoids littered the ground in all directions, but most were piled up around where the dwarves had made their stand. It was impressive that anyone had survived such odds considering how outnumbered they had been.

"I owe ye me life," Lord Aurvang's deep voice rumbled. "But I must ask. What manner o' being be ye?"

The question caught Mike off guard and it must have shown on his face as Lord Aurvang quickly added. "I mean no disrespect, but ye obviously no be a dwarf."

Mike laughed at that. "No, I'm not." Mike then realized how confused and scared these dwarves must be, stranded alone in a strange land and then saved by unknown beings. They held their composure remarkably well considering. Mike could only hope that he would take such an event so calmly. Although, truth be told, such an event was happening to him and he was looking that evidence in the face right now.

"We are humans," Mike said simply.

Lord Aurvang's eyes grew wide and a soft rumble of dwarf voices picked up at that announcement. "Odin's Breath!" Lord Aurvang said in disbelief. "Humans be a myth. Figures told in ancient lore."

Mike laughed. "We say the same of dwarves."

Lord Aurvang snorted at that.

Mike took it as close to a laugh as he was going to get.

Lord Aurvang looked around at the surrounding woods and frowned. "I owe a Blood Debt ter a human… how wonderful," he growled. "So, where be this place?"

"You are in America," Mike replied. "On Earth."

"America?" The dwarf looked thoughtful. "Never heard o' it, but Earth does be soundin' familiar…" Lord Aurvang's eyes narrowed dangerously. "How did we get here?" he scowled at Ted. "Did ye cast some sort o' dark magic on us, Wizard?"

Ted shook his head and held up his hand. "No dark magic," he shrugged. "Honestly, we are not sure how you got here either. Where are you from anyway?"

Lord Aurvang looked suspiciously at Mike and Ted as if expecting some trick. After a few moments, he must have decided that it wouldn't hurt so he answered. "Our world be called Svartalfheim."

Mike and Ted shared a look and Mike shrugged. "Got me," he said, but Ted looked thoughtful. "Svartalfheim. Hmm… that sounds familiar, but I can't place where."

One of the dwarves stepped forward and whispered something into Lord Aurvang's ear before stepping back in line.

Lord Aurvang looked at Mike and Ted. "Me Loremaster tells me Midguard been called Earth. This be true?"

Mike and Ted looked at each other a moment confused. Then Ted snapped his fingers and grinned. "Of course! Midguard. Svartalfheim. Yes! How could I have been so dumb? In Norse mythology Earth was called Midguard."

Lord Aurvang's scowl softened at that and he seemed to be almost talking to himself. "So, it be true then. Ye really are humans and we be on Midguard."

He shook himself and looked to Mike and Ted. "It be said that we dwarves lost contact with Midguard over two thousand years ago when the Great Portal Stones stopped workin'. The runelords o' the day could no figure out why and eventually the knowledge o' how they functioned was lost ter time. Since then, Midguard and the other realms have faded into myth. I never thought they actually existed... until now." Lord Aurvang squared his broad shoulders. "And now it seems we be trapped here."

Mike wanted to ask what he meant by Portal Stones and runelords, but he thought better of it and made a mental note to ask about it later.

Ted scratched his beard. "I don't know if you are trapped here, but I do know that it's not safe to be standing here all exposed like this." He looked around the woods uneasily. "Mike and I were heading to the nearby power plant when we saw you fighting. Come back with us and you can tell us how you came to be here, and maybe we can figure out a way to get you home."

Lord Aurvang thought a moment then nodded. "Very well." He made a hand motion and the dwarves formed up in a double line. Some of the dwarves picked up their fallen comrades and carried them on their broad shoulders as if they weighed nothing. Then he turned back to Mike and Ted. "But what be a power plant?"

Mike tried not to laugh. Of course, the dwarves wouldn't know what a power plant was. He realized that there would be many other words that seemed basic to him that would need explanations for the dwarves.

Mike and Ted turned toward the plant and began walking with Lord Aurvang at their side with the other dwarves following behind. "A power plant," Ted began, "is a building or complex where energy is created."

"A building?" Lord Aurvang looked shocked. "Not a magical tree? I heard tales o' magical trees in Midguard."

"Not a tree," Ted said. "I don't know of any magical trees in this world. We have a few legends, but none we can prove exists."

"I see." Lord Aurvang still looked confused. "How much magical energy does this 'power plant' produce?"

"Oh, it isn't magical energy," Ted explained. "It is electrical energy."

"Electrical?" Lord Aurvang rumbled.

Mike jumped in. "Like lightning."

"Lightning?" Lord Aurvang looked stunned and nearly fell. "Ye can produce lightning?"

"Not exactly," Ted said, in what Mike liked to call his "lecturing voice." "The plant produces electricity. Lightning is made of electricity."

Lord Aurvang shook his head in disbelief. "What kind o' sorcery allows ye to create the very stuff o' lightning?"

"It's not sorcery," Ted said. "It's science."

Lord Aurvang snorted and made a face that said he didn't believe a word of it.

Ted sighed, "I will show you when we get there." He looked down at the short, armored figure walking next to him. "So, how did you get here anyways?"

The dwarf lord looked like he wasn't going to answer, but then he shrugged. "Very well," Lord Aurvang rumbled. "Me retinue and I been traveling back from Hjalmstallr where we met with Thane Sven Thunderstone ter negotiate a new trade agreement fer King Hakon Keepbuilder. We be halfway back ter Borg Kastali when the ground began ter tremble. We did no think anything o' it until the air began ter… shimmer."

Lord Aurvang took a moment as he struggled to find the words he wanted. "It be difficult ter explain. The very air became … thick, like walking through tar and be cloudy like a fog. Then everything shook harder and the air shimmered more violently. It felt like we be being pulled in every direction at once and a great weight was smothering us. Then, as quickly as it began it be gone and we be standing in these here woods."

Lord Aurvang pointed to the striped smokestack. "We saw that tower and decided it be our best chance ter figure out what happened. But we be no alone."

Lord Aurvang growled deep in his throat. "There be gobs everywhere. Luckily, they seemed as confused as we and it gave us time ter find a defensible position. We be neck deep in gobs when the pair o' ye showed up. Ye confused them right good, too." Lord Aurvang chuckled, but it died on his lips as he remembered. "But then the hobs appeared. I never seen so many hobs together in one place before, and I guess the gobs hadn't either because they panicked and scattered in every direction. The hobs ignored the gobs and came fer us."

Lord Aurvang stared straight ahead. "I saw Vali go down ter their blades and I tried ter reach him, but there be just too many between us." He looked up at Mike. "Then ye arrived and killed their chief. The rest ye already know."

Silence fell as Lord Aurvang finished his story.

Ted broke that silence. "What are these gobs and hobs?"

Lord Aurvang's bushy eyebrows rose at that question. "Goblins and hobgoblins o' course. Don't ye humans know anything?" he snorted.

Ted held his ground. "I suspected as much. We humans know quite a lot actually. But we have never actually seen goblins or hobgoblins before today."

"Odin's Beard!" Lord Aurvang didn't try to hide his surprise. "Is that true?"

"It is," Ted replied. "We have legends of goblins and dwarves and all sorts of other creatures, but none of them are here. They have been nothing but stories until today. Humans rule this world."

"So, who do ye fight then?" Lord Aurvang asked.

Mike shrugged. "Each other mostly."

Lord Aurvang looked appalled.

Just then, the party rounded the last small hill and the power plant came fully into view. They had come out slightly north of the plant, but that suited Mike just fine since the only bridge was almost directly in front of them. Mike was glad to see that everything appeared normal there. The buildings didn't appear damaged and there were trucks in the parking lot. He breathed a sigh of relief when he saw Jack's truck pulled up to the main doors. There were even a few people walking around the higher levels of the main building.

They were making their way around the hill when strange hiss-like barking erupted from the woods behind them.

"Kobolds." Lord Aurvang growled as he hefted his axe and turned to face the sound.

Mike put a hand on his massive shoulder. "Let's get to the station. We don't need to waste time fighting."

Further up the hill between the trees Mike could see movement. Soon, the movement turned into a pack of small, scaled, dog-faced creatures. They barked louder when they saw the men and dwarves below them. Their greenish, scaly skin and dog-like faces glinted in the sunlight as they charged down the hill swinging their weapons in mad delight.

There were not that many, and seeing this the dwarves ignored Mike and all turned to face the rushing pack.

"We will make quick work o' these stinkin' kobolds," Lord Aurvang rumbled as he joined the other dwarves in an armored line facing the charging creatures.

The kobolds were halfway to them when more barking came from the right, then again to the left. Movement followed as more kobolds swarmed out of the surrounding trees. Mike guessed there must have been a hundred of them pouring down the hills.

"Umm..." Ted said, as he watched the kobold numbers quickly increase. "Maybe we should run."

Lord Aurvang snorted. "A dwarf does not flee!" The first kobolds were nearly on them as more sprang out of the trees. "But a strategic retreat be acceptable."

"Good," Mike said, as he backed away. "Let's go!"

Dwarves and men both turned and ran. Mike and Ted quickly outpaced the dwarves and their shorter legs as everyone sprinted down the hill with the kobolds close behind. Mike reached the bottom of the hill first and glanced backwards. The dwarves were several paces in front of the charging kobolds, but more of the creatures continued to pour out of the woods. Mike wasn't sure if the dwarves would make it. "Hey Ted," Mike shouted as they ran. "How about a little distraction?"

Ted glanced back and must have come to the same conclusion.

Still running, Ted looked back and pointed at the closest kobolds and concentrated. His nose began to bleed, but a moment later a line of fire shot out from his outstretched hand and the first line of kobolds screamed as they were engulfed in flames. The fire worked and gave the dwarves a few more precious steps on the approaching kobold horde.

CHAPTER 15

Liz had a great view from one of the upper balconies of the power plant as she searched for any signs of Mike and Ted or approaching goblins. So far, she had seen no sign of either. She was starting to get worried; Mike and Ted were taking an awful long time. Maybe something had happened to them. Who knows what could have been lurking up in those woods.

As she looked around, she heard a strange barking sound that grew louder until it sounded like a huge pack of dogs were going crazy. Liz tried to find the source of the barking, but she couldn't see anything. Then, a sudden burst of flames across the river caught her attention.

As Liz watched, Mike and Ted burst out of the woods and sprinted across the road followed closely by a small group of short, armored men.

A flood of small, scaly creatures pursued them. "Kobolds," Liz breathed.

Seeing the guys in trouble, Liz turned back into the plant and shouted. "Jack! Darrell! Get the truck! Kobolds are chasing Mike and Ted across the bridge!"

Jack and Darrell were still on the ground floor making plans with Jim on how to best defend the plant. At Liz's announcement, Jack and Darrell took off out of the door without a word. "Jim!" Liz shouted. "Get the gate open for them!"

The order was unnecessary as Jim was already speaking into his shoulder radio to tell Dave to open the gate.

Seeing that things were moving along, Liz turned back to the balcony and saw that Mike and Ted had crossed the old bridge and the other men were almost across with the kobolds close behind. Liz pulled up her rifle and found the leading creatures in her scope.

She took a deep breath and squeezed the trigger.

There was a puff of pink mist as three kobolds disappeared from Liz's scope view. She quickly worked the bolt and reloaded the rifle. Liz heard Jack's truck start up as she found a new target in her scope. Liz squeezed the trigger again and more kobolds died. She reloaded and was lining up for a third shot when the ground began to shake.

She reached out and had to hold onto the railing to stabilize herself as the quake worsened. Pipes rattled and shook inside the plant and Liz could hear men shouting to each other inside. She hoped the quake wouldn't damage anything or hurt any of the workers.

A few seconds later, the shaking subsided and Liz watched as Darrell drove the truck toward the gate with Jack standing in the back holding his large machine gun.

Mike and Ted were running hard and were almost to the gate when it slowly began to open. As it opened, Darrell roared through the opening and Jack fired Ol' Bertha into the oncoming kobold horde. Bullets tore into the mass of creatures and cleared some space between the kobolds and the armored men.

A few of the kobolds decided to try and scale the fence, but Liz quickly shot them off.

The kobolds were sitting ducks for the machine gun, running straight down the road toward Jack with no cover. Realizing this, the creatures abruptly stopped their charge, turned and fled.

The last of the armored men had just crossed through the gate when Jack stopped firing. The kobolds were in full flight now and were nearing the old bridge.

Liz watched as Jack said something to Darrell as they continued to sit there and watch the creatures' retreat. She guessed that Jack didn't want to waste any ammo, but he would wait to make sure the kobolds really did leave.

The last kobolds were dashing across the bridge when a strange horn sounded. At least Liz thought it was a horn. It sounded more like some animal wailing in agony than a horn.

The awful note was still lingering in the air when the forest all around the retreating kobolds began to quiver.

Suddenly, small green creatures burst out of the woods all around the running kobolds. Too late, the kobolds realized their danger as goblins quickly swarmed and surrounded them.

Liz watched in shock as the goblins continued to flow out of the woods and their numbers quickly dwarfed that of the kobolds.

The battle was short and violent as the goblins completely surrounded the surprised kobolds and tore them to pieces.

More of the small, green creatures continued to pour out of the woods as the goblins finished off the last of the kobolds.

Liz couldn't quite believe what she was seeing.

The goblins filled the ground from the bridge all the way up into the woods. There must have been a thousand of the ugly little creatures. She could only guess at how many were still up in the hills, hidden by the trees.

At first, Liz was afraid they were going to charge across the bridge right then, but after a moment she realized they were not going to. They just growled and milled around, staring longingly across the river at the plant.

"What are you waiting for?" Liz muttered to herself.

Jack and Darrell must have been thinking the same thing because they were still parked in front of the open gate watching the ocean of goblins on the other side of the old bridge.

Several minutes passed and the tension grew as the goblin voices grew ever louder and more excited. Liz could see the goblins straining to keep themselves from charging across the bridge.

The sound of heavy footsteps behind her made Liz turn around.

Coming up the steel grating steps were Mike, Ted, and one of the armored men. Mike was covered with several small cuts and had one of the station's radios strapped to his shoulder. Ted looked pale and his nose was bleeding, but otherwise he looked fine. Seeing them was like having a huge weight lifted off her shoulders.

Liz didn't know whether to laugh or cry, or to yell at Mike and Ted for taking off like that. She wanted to run over and embrace them, but held herself in check as she took in the third companion climbing the stairs.

The first thing Liz noticed about the armored man was that he was very short. She didn't consider herself that tall, being around five eight herself, but she was several inches taller than he was.

The man wore a thick cape and was covered head to toe in the most intricate and heavy-looking suit of armor that Liz had ever seen. He was impossibly wide and in his huge armored fist he held a wicked looking axe that was just as detailed as his armor.

She laughed to herself; she could just imagine how Mike was drooling over the thought of getting his hands on armor like that.

Liz waited as Mike, Ted, and the armored man reached the top of the stairs and stopped in front of her.

Liz's eyes narrowed. "You're late."

Mike laughed. "Glad to see you too." He motioned to the armored man. "I brought a friend."

The armored man hung his axe on his belt and took off his helm. He had a large mane of black hair and beard that nearly covered his whole face. Large bushy eyebrows and a wide flat nose took up most of his face. He appeared very fierce, but Liz thought she caught a mischievous twinkle in his eye.

"Lord Aurvang," Mike said, "this is Liz McAllister. A very good friend of mine."

Lord Aurvang stepped forward and gave a very formal bow, so low that his beard touched the floor. He straightened up and when he spoke it sounded like boulders grinding together. "A more beautiful creature I have never seen. It be truly a pleasure," he rumbled. "may Freyja watch over ye."

Liz blushed. She didn't know what to say to that. It was possibly the strangest and nicest thing anyone had ever said to her.

Mike cleared his throat. "Liz, this is Lord Aurvang Twinpeaks of Clan Keepbuilder. He is a dwarf."

****

Mike enjoyed watching Liz's reaction to that announcement. Her eyes bulged a little and her mouth opened slightly. She recovered quickly though and gave a bow of her own. "The pleasure is all mine, Lord Aurvang."

She looked about to say more, but the goblins' voices rose into a loud chant and Liz, Mike, Ted, and Lord Aurvang rushed to the balcony to see what was happening.

Across the river, the goblins were being worked into a frenzy. They stomped their feet and clashed weapons together as their chant rose and fell in a chilling cadence. The chant grew louder and louder until it rang throughout the valley.

"Odin's Breath," Lord Aurvang cursed. "There must be a shaman down there. Only they can rile up a force like that."

Liz brought her gun up. "What do these shamans look like?" she asked, as she peered through the scope.

Lord Aurvang chuckled and it sounded like stones grinding together. "Do ye think ye can kill the shaman from here?"

"Yes," Liz replied matter-of-factly, as she continued searching the sea of goblins.

Her confidence cut Lord Aurvang's laughter short. "I seen the power o'yer magical thunder weapons, but it must be over two hunnerd yards ter the army. There be no way ye could kill the shaman from here."

Liz never took her eyes away from the scope. "Just tell me what it looks like and we will see who is right."

Lord Aurvang shook his head in disbelief, but said, "Very well. The shaman will most likely be wearin' some kind o'robe er large feathered costume. But the real telling item is their staff. Every goblin shaman carries some kind of staff topped with a skull as a kind of totem."

"A goblin in a robe with a skull staff…" Liz muttered. "I should have known."

Mike couldn't help but laugh. That description was straight out of one of his fantasy books that Liz would make fun of him for reading.

Liz scanned the seething mass of goblins for several minutes until the chanting grew so loud that the ground began to quiver.

"Oh crap," Liz groaned. "There are three of them. It looks like they are performing some kind of ritual. They are dancing in a circle and waving their staves around." There was a pause as Liz watched. "There is a misty green glow forming between them."

"They be summoning evil spirits," Lord Aurvang growled. "Ye must break the circle before they finish the summoning."

****

Magnified in her scope, the goblin shamans could be seen clearly as they danced around in a small circle and waved their crude, skull-topped wooden staves wildly above their heads.

Two of the creatures wore large, feathered capes with wild-looking headdresses covered in the same strangely colored feathers. Both of their staves were topped with a small animal skull with other small totems and feathers dangling from it.

The third shaman wore a dark cloak that hid nearly all his features except for its long, pointed nose. It carried a dark staff that looked like it had been burned and was topped with a large ram's skull that also appeared charred. A bright green glow shone from the skull's eyes as the cloaked shaman whirled the staff above its head.

Liz watched, transfixed, as they spun about and slammed their staves into the center of the circle. They repeated this over and over, each time the skulls struck the ground the misty green glow in the center of the circle grew brighter.

The mist grew thicker and brighter as the goblin army chanted and the shamans danced.

Liz knew she had to act soon or their spell would be completed. Assuming the dark cloaked shaman to be the leader, Liz tried to focus on it, but her eyes kept being drawn back to the shapes forming in the mist. The glow was mesmerizing as the shapes of what appeared to be animals formed and dissipated in a rolling cloud inside the pulsing green mist.

The shamans spun faster and struck the ground with more force every second. The goblins around them also joined in the crazy dance, adding their bodies to the swirling rhythm. The green mist continued to thicken and expand as more goblins jumped into the ritual. It was like a goblin hurricane was forming with the bright green mist forming in the storm's eye.

By sheer force of will, Liz tore her gaze away from the light and tried to target the cloaked shaman. But with all the other goblins around joining in the dance and swinging their weapons she couldn't get a clear shot. As she searched for an opening the shaman began to spin even faster. They soon became a blur of motion around the quickly expanding green cloud.

Liz couldn't tell where one shaman ended and another began, but she knew she was running out of time. Saying a quick prayer, she pulled the trigger.

A green explosion ripped through the center of the goblin hurricane. Bodies rocketed through the air as the cloud detonated. Green fire erupted in writhing arcs from the ruined spell, consuming any goblin unfortunate enough to be in its way.

There was a sudden silence as the goblin chanting came to an abrupt halt. The silence lasted for several heartbeats as the goblin army stood in shock at the fiery display.

"Incredible," the dwarf lord breathed in awe. "I did not think such deadly range was possible…"

Mike chuckled darkly, "Well, that got their attention."

Liz thought that was a massive understatement.

A ripple passed through the goblin ranks as they shook off their shock and replaced it with anger. Their howls of rage echoed through the hills and the horde began to surge toward the old bridge.

Mike spoke into his shoulder-mounted radio. "Okay. Here they come. Everyone to their positions."

Thunder filled the valley as Jack unleashed Ol' Bertha into the charging goblin horde. The gun tore into the goblins crossing the bridge, but the green beasts didn't try to retreat. For every one Jack killed, three more took its place.

Within moments, dozens of goblins lay dead or dying, but the tide of creatures didn't slow. They screamed and ran on, fearless and full of rage.

Unable to stop the goblin advance, Darrell began to slowly back the truck up as Jack continued to mow them down.

Creatures disintegrated under the heavy barrage, but soon they were across the bridge and spilling out and spreading across the ground. Darrell backed the truck up through the still-open gate as Jack kept a constant rain of fire on the charging horde.

Once Darrell and Jack were through the gate, it began to slowly slide closed. Jack kept firing until the last possible moment when the gate clanged shut.

Darrell quickly backed them up until he reached the large coal piles outside the plant.

Mike spoke into the radio again. "Remember; kill any creature that looks like some kind of a leader first. Goblins are cowards at heart and without any bosses to push them the rest will give up."

Liz couldn't believe that killing a few leaders would make such a horde give up. Especially since they were in such a frenzy from her killing the shamans.

Liz watched in horror as the goblin wave rolled up to the fence and she knew there was no way they could stop such a force.

The goblins reached the perimeter fence and began to climb. The chain fence wasn't very large, but it was topped with barbed wire. In their haste the goblins that reached the top first got tangled in the barbed wire, but the ones behind simply climbed right over their struggling comrades.

"Fire at will," Mike shouted into the radio. A scratchy reply of "Which one's Will?" came back just before everything was drowned out by the thunderous sound of gunfire as the men of Shawville Station began the desperate defense of their power plant.

CHAPTER 16

Hundreds of goblins swarmed over the fence and sections of it collapsed by sheer weight of numbers. When the fence came down, Ol' Bertha roared back to life as Jack resumed firing on the green tide.

Goblins flew backwards as the defenders rained death down on them and others were shredded as Jack brought his powerful weapon to bear.

Even with all the carnage, the goblin charge didn't slow. There were so many goblins that only half of them had managed to cross the bridge, but half was more than enough to collapse the fence and overwhelm the facility.

Liz realized that even with the box of ammo at her feet, she didn't have enough bullets to really make a difference. She knew their only chance was like Mike had said; eliminate those goblins that were urging the others on.

She scanned the mob for any goblin that looked like it was leading the others and when she found one it died. However, all of her kills seemed to go unnoticed as the sea of goblins pressed forward.

Darrell was backing up again as the swarm raced forward. There were just too many of them.

"We are going to be overrun," Liz shouted over the screaming of the goblins and the roar of the guns.

"Not yet, we're not," Mike shouted back. "Watch."

He pointed to the outer buildings nearest the goblin tide. As they watched, towering jets of water shot forth and blasted into the swarm. The high-pressure water blew the goblins off their feet and sent them reeling backwards.

"Water cannons," Mike grinned. "They have them in case of a fire and the lines feed directly into the river, so there will be no shortage of water."

"Interesting," Lord Aurvang rumbled, as they watched the water cannons go to work pushing the army back.

The cannoneers worked in tandem, alternating sprays to keep the monsters away. But as impressive as the display was, after several minutes it became apparent that it wasn't going to be enough. There were simply too many goblins for the cannons to keep them all at bay. When one group was pushed back, more went around it, and as more goblins spilled across the bridge, it got harder to push them back. At first, only a few got through and they were easy prey for the defenders. But as time wore on, more and more goblins made it past the water cannons.

Goblins streamed in from all sides as they crossed the bridge and began to encircle the facility. Jack unloaded a steady stream of fire into the largest groups of goblins, but they kept coming like an unending wave. Darrell was forced to back up as goblins pressed in around them.

Liz kept picking off the biggest goblins she could find, but there were just so many it was hard to keep your eye on any one in particular for longer than a few seconds. Luckily for her, a few seconds was all she needed.

An impressively large goblin fell to Liz's rifle when she noticed a small avalanche coming down one of the huge coal piles. Looking up, she saw the cause of the slide.

A small goblin was climbing up the pile with a dirty banner clutched in one clawed hand. The banner was dark brown with a pale-yellow symbol crudely drawn on it. Liz wasn't sure what the symbol was supposed to be; it looked to her like a fanged jack-o-lantern face smiling evilly.

The climbing goblin reached the top of the pile and raised the banner over its head.

"Oh, no you don't," Liz muttered, as she brought her rifle up.

The banner-carrying goblin tumbled backwards with the top of its head missing.

"Grinners," Lord Aurvang scowled. "That be explain' it."

"Grinners?" Mike asked.

"Aye," Lord Aurvang replied. "The Grinnin' Gobs. They be a bunch o'fanatics. Zealots ter their vile spirit religion."

As Lord Aurvang spoke, the first ranks of goblins made it beyond the outer water cannons and reached the edge of the facility itself. Many charged ahead, heedless of any danger, while others began to climb the multitude of pipes and beams surrounding the buildings. Two of the men using the water cannons had to abandon their posts as the goblins climbed up from below them. Some of the other cannoneers stopped spraying the army and switched to knocking the climbing goblins down.

With less cannons pushing back the horde, the goblins surged ahead. As more goblins poured in, down on the ground Darrell was forced to back out of Liz's view, but she could still hear Jack's machine gun roaring.

The goblin army filled her vision. They were like a carpet of ants swarming over everything. She kept firing into the mob, but she knew deep down that it wouldn't make any difference.

There were just too many of them.

****

The large steel doors were locked and Mike knew that without any siege equipment it was unlikely that the goblins would break through.

That didn't slow down the goblins, however. They began climbing any surface they could dig their claws into. The green beasts were surprisingly agile climbers and quickly scampered up the exposed pipes.

A goblin head popped up over the railing further down the balcony to Liz's left. Mike saw it and charged forward. The goblin hopped onto the railing and then another joined it. Mike was still a few steps away when he fired his shotgun and blew them both back off the railing.

Mike reached the spot where the goblins had been just as another goblin head appeared over the railing. Mike slammed the butt of his shotgun down onto the creature's face. It squealed in pain and fell, knocking the goblins following it off the pipe as well. Seeing that he bought himself some time, Mike looked around to see how everyone else was faring.

Liz still stood in front of the doorway, firing at the goblins with grim efficiency.

The wind picked up and pressed her clothing against her, outlining her perfect curves and sending her dark hair streaming out behind her. Mike noticed that when she fired, she jiggled in all the right places.

"Bwahaha!"

Mike snapped out of his reverie and looked beyond Liz to Lord Aurvang further down the balcony who was roaring lustily. Goblins were climbing up in several places and the Dwarf Lord was waiting for them. He stood at the corner of the balcony, bloody rune axe in hand, laughing as he decapitated each goblin as they appeared over the railings. Mike thought it was like watching some gruesome version of whack-a-mole.

A flash of movement over Lord Aurvang's shoulder caught Mike's attention.

It was Emily, running along the balcony of an adjacent building with several goblins chasing her. As she ran, Emily drew an arrow, turned, and fired without breaking stride. Mike wasn't sure if it was a trick of the light, but he thought there was a strange glow coming off the arrow as it whizzed through the air. It struck the first goblin with such force that it blasted straight through it and lodged in the chest of the second.

Still running, Emily fired again, also skewering two goblins, and this time Mike was sure he saw a glow on the arrow. It was like watching a miniature comet as it left the bow and made a glowing trail through the air.

Emily grabbed ahold of a ladder and quickly pulled herself up. It was a retractable ladder and once at the top she pulled it up behind her.

The goblins howled and waved their weapons threateningly up at her but they were too late. Emily stuck her tongue out at them through the grating. She caught Mike watching her and blew him a kiss as the wind blew her long black curls around wildly. Then with a grin and a quick wink, she ran off around the side of the building and disappeared.

THE SHEARING

All over the buildings men and dwarves fought side-by-side as the goblins pressed in. When Mike and Ted had arrived with the dwarves, it had been decided that they would pair up the human workers with one of Lord Aurvang's dwarf guards. The plan seemed to be working rather well as the men used their guns to shoot the goblins and when the creatures got too close the heavily armored dwarves cut them down. The narrow balconies also played a major roll. They were just wide enough for one man, or dwarf, to stand on. That meant that the goblins could only attack one at a time.

But now only one water cannon was still operating. The others had been abandoned when the goblins swarmed their positions. The remaining cannon was guarded by two dwarf warriors and was using its high-powered spray to push goblins off the building in an attempt to stem the tide against the besieged defenders.

With the cannons no longer keeping the creatures back, the goblins had full control of the ground. They howled and pressed together, fighting each other in their haste to reach the defenders first. As they pressed in, they found more places to climb and the ugly little beasts were soon hanging all over the station.

There was a scratching sound from below so Mike leaned over the railing and saw that a gaggle of goblins were climbing up the pipe below him. He fired his shotgun and cleared the pipe of creatures. More took their place and other pipes were already covered in climbing goblins. Their filthy green skin made it look like a fungus was growing on the sides of the buildings.

Mike risked a glance behind him and saw that Liz still stood there, shooting goblins off the buildings and Lord Aurvang was on her other side looking like an armored mountain blocking the flow of a wild green river.

Mike turned back and emptied his shotgun into the climbing mass and cleared a few pipes for the moment. It wasn't enough, however, as more goblins reached the railing and began pulling themselves up. Mike raced around, knocking the goblins back as best he could, but he was quickly overwhelmed. Abandoning his empty shotgun, Mike drew his sword and shield and positioned himself between the green mass and Liz.

The goblins poured over the railing in a snarling wave and threw themselves at Mike with reckless abandon. He caught the first on his shield and used it as a ram to push the other back, as he pressed forward and stabbed into them.

He hacked and slashed at goblins, trying to push them back, but there were so many that even when he killed one they pressed right back in. Luckily, the beasts were armed with only their claws and small daggers, forsaking any larger weapons to climb the pipes.

The creatures came on wildly, stabbing and clawing at him from every angle. It was all Mike could do to keep from getting skewered. He blocked and parried with every ounce of skill he could muster, but even with that skill he still took many cuts to his arms and legs.

Mike stabbed down into one goblin and his sword passed through the wiry body and the grating underneath. More goblins pressed in and when Mike tried to pull his sword out, it wouldn't budge. It was stuck!

A goblin dagger slashed out at his exposed arm and Mike was forced to let go of the sword before he lost his hand.

Reaching behind him, Mike drew a long dagger from behind his back. It wasn't much, but it was better than nothing. The goblins kept stabbing at him and now that he lost the advantage of reach, he was slowly being forced backwards.

"I can't hold!" Mike shouted over the sound of screaming goblins and gunshots. He didn't know if Liz could hear him, but he couldn't afford to turn around and check.

Mike took a long cut to his forearm and nearly dropped the dagger. He jumped back, out of the goblins' reach for the moment when Lord Aurvang suddenly yelled, "Blódskuld! Catch."

Mike turned his head just in time to see a large steel mace come sailing towards his head. With more luck than any real skill, Mike reached out and snatched the mace out of the air and brought it down on a goblin's head.

It was surprisingly light for such a large weapon and it appeared to be made entirely out of some kind of silvery metal. Dwarven runes covered its flanged head and ran down the shaft.

The mace felt strangely good in his hand. Mike waded into the goblins and with each swing he felt stronger. He crushed heads and arms with ease as creatures fell before him. He pressed his advantage and drove the goblins back.

Mike had regained most of the balcony when a group of goblins suddenly dropped down from behind him, cutting him off from Liz and Lord Aurvang. He put his back against the wall and tried to fight off the goblins that were now coming at him from both sides. Surrounded, Mike blocked and parried furiously, but some strikes gouged his breastplate and more sliced into his arms and legs.

Dodging a swing from an impressively ugly goblin, Mike slipped on the slick blood-coated grating and fell. The goblins lunged forward, but before they could strike, a column of water blasted into the creatures and swept most of the goblins off the balcony. Mike quickly regained his footing and dispatched the remaining waterlogged goblins.

Free for the moment, Mike looked back and saw that the cannoneer had cleared all the goblins from this level and Lord Aurvang was also without enemies. The area around the dwarf lord's feet looked like a slaughterhouse and blood covered him from head to toe. He looked angry.

"Durned human taking away me kills!" Lord Aurvang shouted, and waved his axe menacingly through the air at the worker manning the water cannon.

The cannoneer paled at the sight of the angry dwarf lord and quickly turned away to spray another section of wall.

Mike looked out at the seething army of goblins. "Don't worry, there are plenty left."

That was a bit of an understatement. All the creatures they had killed so far hadn't even made a dent in the goblin host. Looking around, Mike saw that most of the defenders were being pushed back, nearly into the station itself.

The goblins couldn't be allowed to enter the plant. If that happened the creatures could spread out and run amok. The men and dwarves wouldn't be able to contain them and they would be swarmed.

They couldn't hold any longer. Mike put his hand on the radio at his shoulder to tell everyone to fall back to their secondary positions when a booming horn blast filled the air.

It was a deep rumble that Mike felt in his bones. He heard Lord Aurvang groan.

"What is it?" Liz asked. "More goblins?"

"No." The dwarf lord looked dismayed. "It be far worse," Lord Aurvang grated. "It be the Hill Clans."

CHAPTER 17

"Hill Clans?" Liz asked, confused. "Are they dwarves?"

"Aye," the dwarf lord grumbled.

"Then what's the problem?" Liz asked. "Aren't more dwarves like you a good thing?"

"Like me!" Lord Aurvang looked appalled. "I be no hill dwarf!" He proudly held his head high and puffed up his chest. "I be a true Son o' the Mountain."

Another deep horn blast rumbled through the hills. Before the last note faded, another type of roar filled the air as stocky figures burst out of the surrounding woods screaming war cries and brandishing axes.

It was hard to make out too many details from this distance, but to Mike it looked like the newcomers wore bright chainmail with some plate armor scattered about. They carried axes and spears, and wore large horned helms that revealed their bearded faces. Mike thought they looked like an army of short, angry Vikings.

The hill dwarves poured out of the woods behind the goblin army and drove into their exposed flank. A ripple passed through the goblin host as they realized they were under attack and turned to face this new threat.

The dwarves carved into them, spears and axes flashing.

"Ugh," Lord Aurvang moaned. "Rescued by Hillies." He shook his head sadly. "I will never hear the end o'it." Suddenly, goblins boiled up over the railings in a wave and hurled themselves at Mike, Liz, and Lord Aurvang, and the three were nearly overwhelmed by the sudden rush of creatures.

Liz fell backwards into the open doorway as Mike and Lord Aurvang were forced together by the goblin press. Liz quickly jumped back to her feet and drew her pistol.

Mike and Lord Aurvang were nearly pushed back-to-back on either side of the doorway with Liz stuck behind them. Mike bashed goblins left and right, but as soon as one fell another appeared. Lord Aurvang wrought terrible damage with his rune axe, but the goblins still came on, undeterred.

"Fer the Allfather!" Lord Aurvang roared and kicked out with a massive armored boot, sending the tightly packed goblins hurtling backwards. Before they could recover, the dwarf lord lunged forward and hacked madly at the stunned creatures.

Liz was momentarily shocked by the ferocity of his attacks, but she quickly recovered. Seeing that Lord Aurvang had matters well in hand, she turned to help Mike. He was still holding his own, but the goblins were trying to get around his broad form. Liz rapidly fired her pistol over his shoulder until she ran out of bullets. Her shots tore through the goblins, killing several with each shot and clearing some space between them and Mike.

Her quick thinking gave Mike the critical moment he needed to press into the goblins and begin to drive them back. He was a blur of motion as he pounded the goblins and sent them flying. Liz couldn't believe how hard Mike seemed to be hitting them. It was almost like there was some extra force hurling the goblins.

With both man and dwarf battling the goblins to either side of her, Liz had a clear space to move. She reloaded the pistol and began to alternate firing at the goblins attacking Mike and Lord Aurvang.

They did this for several minutes; Mike and Lord Aurvang battling furiously as Liz shot over their shoulders.

There seemed to be no end to the tide of goblins. Lord Aurvang showed no signs of fatigue and continued to slice into the goblins with unmatched savagery. He pressed up to the point where the goblins were climbing over the balcony and began decapitating them as they climbed, like he had been doing at the beginning of the battle.

Mike, on the other hand, wasn't fairing quite so well. His progress had stopped and he was desperately working to not lose any ground. Each goblin he hit was still being knocked away, but Liz could tell he was getting tired. His parries came slower and each attack was just a little closer to reaching its mark. His wooden shield was nearly destroyed, with pieces of it splintering off with each impact from a goblin weapon. Liz stopped assisting the dwarf lord and concentrated on supporting Mike.

Her pistol blazed and together the two of them pushed the goblins back. Even combined it was tough going. Liz could hear Mike's heavy breathing as he fought like mad against the never-ending goblin swarm.

Then, suddenly, Mike kicked out, knocking the last goblin off the railing. As it fell, it knocked the others that were still climbing off as well.

Mike turned and was about to say something to her when a look of panic crossed his face. "Liz run!" he shouted.

Confused, Liz looked around. Too late, she saw the bolt of crackling emerald energy streaking up towards her.

"NO!" Mike cried, as he jumped forward and brought his battered shield between Liz and the emerald bolt.

There was a deafening explosion as the bolt struck Mike's shield.

Instead of being incinerated, a nimbus of light blue energy materialized around them. The wooden shield blew apart under the force, but the emerald bolt sizzled over the blue shield. Then it dissipated into nothingness, leaving smoking metal and smoldering bits of charred wood strewn around Mike and Liz.

Before the last bits of wood had hit the ground, Liz was back leaning over the railing with her rifle, looking for the creature that had fired the bolt at them.

"Crap," She snarled.

"What is it?" Mike asked, as he joined her along the railing.

"Either that shaman with the dark robe is still alive or there was more than one, because I just saw one in the crowd. But before I could get a shot, he disappeared," Liz growled in frustration.

"Disappeared how?" Mike asked confused.

"Like a puff of smoke." Liz made a motion with her hand. "Poof."

"Interesting," Mike mumbled. "I'm sure he will reappear and when he does, we will kill him."

A moment later Lord Aurvang came stomping up to them. "That be a neat trick, Blódskuld," he rumbled. "That blast scared off all the cowardly gobs. Looks like we get a bit o' a breather."

"I think we are going to get more than that," Liz said, and pointed. "Look."

All across the facility the goblins had stopped climbing and were turning to face the dwarf force that had pushed halfway to the station. With the reinforcements gone, the men and dwarf defenders began to push the remaining goblins off the buildings.

Mike breathed a sigh of relief when he saw Emily and Ted emerge from around one of the buildings. Both were battered and bloody, but otherwise intact. In the distance, he could still hear Jack's machine gun firing, so he knew they were still alive.

Within minutes, the balconies were cleared and the men began firing down on the throng again. With the fire from above, the goblins couldn't organize any kind of defense, allowing the dwarf army to carve a bloody path through them.

Liz took up her rifle and joined the workers in picking off the goblin leaders as they tried to turn their forces around to face the dwarf army.

Before long, the goblin swarm started to break apart and scatter. They had held together longer than Mike expected, seeing how they were being decimated by the organized dwarf army and the human defenders.

With the immediate threat gone, Lord Aurvang rounded on Mike and growled, "So why didn't ye say ye be a wizard?"

"Because I'm not," Mike answered, as he shook the charred remains of his shield off his arm. "I can't use magic like Ted can. But I have been able to make shields like that one, and a sword to fight a demon."

"Demons!" Lord Aurvang nearly choked. "Odin's Breath lad! Ye killed a demon? How?"

"Well," Mike ran a hand over his shaved head, "I had help from a priest to kill one," he sighed. "And I can't control it. Things just happen sometimes."

"Hmm." Lord Aurvang looked thoughtful. "Protective shields and weapons ter fight demons…ye sound like a guardian ter me… yes, that must be it." He nodded as if satisfied with himself. "I didn't know humans could be guardians, but that indeed be the case, then ye need trained ter control yer powers. I think I can help with that."

Mike looked hopeful. "You are a guardian, too?"

"Gods no," Lord Aurvang laughed. "I be a Rune Knight o' Ogmar. A guardian be a Chosen o' Thor. It be their duty ter protect others from demons and the like. One o' me personal guard be a guardian. If he survived this battle, I will have him teach ye."

"Thank you," Mike said, and he meant it.

The thought of being able to control his abilities was exciting. Mike couldn't wait. As nice as being able to summon up a magical shield was, it didn't do much good when you didn't know how to summon it in the first place.

"Bah," Lord Aurvang made a dismissive gesture. "Think nothing o' it. I still owe ye a great debt. One that will not be so easily repaid."

Mike remembered that he still had Lord Aurvang's mace. "Ah, I almost forgot." He held out the rune-covered mace to the dwarf lord.

Lord Aurvang looked at the mace in Mike's outstretched hand, but made no move to take it. He eyed the weapon as if it he didn't trust it. "It be yours now. Keep it."

"I can't take this," Mike started to argue, but the dwarf Lord cut him off.

"Did ye notice anything strange when ye wielded it?" Lord Aurvang asked.

Mike thought a moment, not sure whether to tell him about the experience or not. The dwarf lord must know something if he asked the question, so Mike answered truthfully. "Actually, yes. It felt… good. Like it was meant to be there and the longer I used it the better it felt." Mike shrugged. "I know it sounds crazy, but I also seemed to hit them harder than I should have."

Lord Aurvang nodded like that was exactly what he had expected. "That wasn't yer imagination human. It has chosen ye."

"Chosen me?" Mike asked, incredulous. "But it's a mace."

Lord Aurvang chuckled again. "What ye have in yer hand be no ordinary mace. It be an ancient blessed impact mace forged by runelords ages ago ter help defeat the orcs and their demon allies." Lord Aurvang eyed the weapon in Mike's grip. "In the hands o' the hero Fugal the Sunderer it be a mighty weapon. Legend says that he could crush a giant's skull with a flick o' his wrist.

"Its name be Rikr Foerah, known as the Great Hurler, and it has chosen ye."

The dwarf lord looked at the mace in Mike's hands with longing for a moment then let out a deep sigh like a bellows. "I have carried it fer many years and it was never more than a simple mace fer me. Keep it and wield it with honor."

For the first time Mike took a good look at the mace. It was a beautiful weapon, made entirely of a silvery blue metal that was remarkably light. Six large flanges flared out to make the head. Golden dwarf runes were inscribed into the shaft and on the flanges themselves, and a small spike topped the head.

"How do I control it?" Mike asked, as he turned it over in his hands.

Lord Aurvang chuckled and shrugged his heavy shoulders. "As far as I be knowin', ye don't. The longer ye wield it, the stronger the bond will be. The stronger the bond, the more impact the mace will be."

Mike looked at the mace with a new respect. "Is every dwarf weapon like this?"

"Loki's Balls no," the dwarf lord replied. "It would take even a master runesmith decades, or centuries even, ter create such a weapon."

"Now, nearly every dwarf weapon does have at least a Lesser Rune o' Sharpening ter keep the blade from becoming dull. Those an apprentice runesmith can be makin' fairly quickly. But an axe such as this," Lord Aurvang held up his gore-covered axe, "is a master crafted weapon that only a rune knight like me self may wield." He held the massive axe up easily with one huge hand, but Mike knew that it must way a ton. It was another subtle reminder of just how strong the dwarf lord actually was.

The axe was indeed a marvelous weapon. It was made of a dark metal and had such an intricate pattern of silver and gold runes carved into its broad head that Mike couldn't tell where one ended and another began.

"I hate to interrupt," Liz said with a grin, "but I thought you boys might like to know that we won."

Mike and Lord Aurvang moved to either side of Liz and looked out over the railing. Sure enough, the remaining goblins were fleeing in every direction trying to get away from the pursuing dwarves.

The defenders let out a ragged cheer as the last goblins abandoned the field.

Lord Aurvang snorted. "Like there be any doubt."

Mike laughed and picked his way through the goblin corpses and retrieved his sword that was still stuck in the grating.

Liz rolled her eyes at the dwarf's confidence. "Shall we go down and thank our rescuers?"

That took the wind out of the dwarf lord's sails. He visibly deflated and grumbled something under his breath before slinging his axe over his back.

"Let's be getting' this or' with," the dwarf lord grumbled.

CHAPTER 18

When Mike, Liz, and Lord Aurvang reached Control Room One, it was a flurry of activity. Men and dwarves hustled about applying bandages and makeshift splints to the injured, and there were plenty of those.

To Mike it looked like nearly every warrior in the room had some kind of injury. He was glad to see that it looked like everyone had survived the battle, although there were a few missing.

Most of the injuries were cuts from goblin blades, but there were a few broken bones being set. The defenders had survived remarkably unscathed considering the odds against them. Although Mike had to admit the timely arrival of the dwarf army was the only reason they were all still alive.

Now that all the excitement was over and the adrenaline was wearing off, Mike became aware of all the wounds he had taken. His limbs burned like fire from the countless cuts crisscrossing his arms and legs, and his whole body ached from all the fighting. Suddenly, it was as if a great weight landed on his shoulders and it was all Mike could do to remain standing.

"Are you alright?" Liz asked, with concern in her voice.

"Fine," Mike mumbled. "Just need a breather is all." He took a few deep breaths and his head cleared somewhat.

Seeing Mike, Liz, and Lord Aurvang walk in, Dave got up from his chair and walked over to them. He had one arm in a sling and a large bandage wrapped around his middle, but he seemed in good spirits. "I'm glad to see you made it," he said with a tired smile.

"Thanks," Liz replied. "How is everyone else?"

"Pretty well considering," Dave said. "Cuts and bruises mostly. Terry got stabbed a good one and will need some stitches, I broke my arm, and Jim messed up his knee." He looked around at everyone getting patched up. "About time all those stupid safety training videos came in handy." Then he looked at Lord Aurvang. "I must say your dwarves did most of the up-close fighting. If it weren't for them we wouldn't have made it through so well. Thank you."

"Bah," Lord Aurvang rumbled dismissively. "We dwarves love a good scrap."

Mike smiled and shook his head. Only the dwarf could call facing hundreds of goblins with a few dozen humans and dwarves "a good scrap."

As Mike looked around the room, he spotted Ted sitting on the floor, leaning in the corner, so he made his way over to him. When he got close, Mike saw that Ted looked awful. He was pale and blood ran freely from his nose and right ear. He was also covered in so much blood that Mike couldn't tell if any of it was his own. Ted raised an arm in a pitiful wave when he saw Mike walk up.

"You look like Hell," Mike said.

"So, I still look better than you," Ted gave a sickly smile, then coughed up some blood that trickled into his already matted beard.

"What happened to you?" Mike asked.

"I was on hole watch," Ted coughed. "Bloody thing kept spitting out goblins."

"Oh, my God," Liz cried, when she saw Ted's condition. "We need to get you some help."

Ted coughed. "Why don't you just heal me up like you did to Mike?" The last words ended in a shuddering gasp.

Liz stood there dumbstruck for a moment. She had forgotten all about healing Mike.

"I don't know how I did it," Liz confessed.

"You have to try," Mike urged.

Without another word, Liz knelt down next to Ted and took his hand in hers and closed her eyes. She whispered a silent prayer and concentrated.

Nothing happened.

Then, slowly at first, a faint yellow glow appeared under her hands and soaked into Ted's. A heartbeat later his nose and ear stopped bleeding, and a few moments later his color returned and he took a deep breath. "Ahhh," Ted sighed contentedly. "Much better. Thank you my dear."

The glow faded as Liz let go of his hand and stood up. "You're welcome," she muttered distractedly.

Ted pushed himself to his feet as if nothing had happened. "So, what now?"

"Now," Mike replied, "we go see who saved us."

"Oh, no you don't," Liz growled as she turned to face Mike. "Come here." She reached up and grabbed his face between her hands.

At first, Mike thought she was going to kiss him right there, but instead she just closed her eyes. He could hear her muttering something and a moment later, comforting warmth filled him and all his aches abruptly faded away.

"There," Liz said, as she released Mike and stepped away. "Now you can go."

"Thanks," Mike said, then his eyes narrowed. "Wait. You aren't coming?"

"No," Liz replied. "I am going to stay here and see if I can help everyone else." Before anyone could challenge her, Liz moved off to the nearest injured worker.

"Can't say that I would argue," Ted muttered to Mike.

Mike nodded his agreement. "Well," he said, and put his hand on Ted's shoulder, "let's go see who rescued us before Jack and Darrell get back and try to shoot them, too."

Lord Aurvang grumbled deep in his throat, but didn't say anything as the three of them headed out of the control room. Mike glanced back as the door closed behind them. "Where is Emily?"

"Oh, she went back up with a few of the guys to keep watch in case the goblins come back," Ted answered.

As they made their way down the narrow halls, Mike saw several forms standing against one of the walls. When they got closer, he discovered that they were the bodies of the three dwarves that had died in the hills. And they were standing up!

"Um. What are they doing standing against the wall?" Mike asked, confused, as they approached the corpses.

Lord Aurvang didn't reply, just bowed his head reverently as they passed the bodies. Once they were several paces away, he took a deep breath and spoke. "When a dwarf dies, his body slowly turns ter stone. All o' the Fallen be positioned standing up ter await Ragnarok, when they be brought back ter life ter fight beside the gods."

"Fascinating." Ted scratched his beard. "But aren't you afraid something will happen to them? Say they fall over and break, or some creatures destroy them?"

Lord Aurvang chuckled. "No. We be no worried about such happenings. You see, we do no turn into any ordinary stone. We become Svartalsteinn, although many refer ter it simply as Dwarf Stone, and it be harder than steel. Nothing been able ter damage even the most ancient o' the Fallen. No that we leave them just lying about, mind ye. Nearly all be returned ter a Hold er some other fortress, if it be possible."

Further conversation ended as they reached the locked outer doors.

Once they unlocked the big steel double doors and opened them, they found Jack's truck idling in front of the opening with Jack standing in the bed and his machine gun pointed at the assembled dwarf army arrayed before them.

The army was more wild-looking than Mike had first guessed, but his Viking comparison proved to be rather accurate.

Every dwarf that Mike could see held either an axe or a spear with a round shield. Each of them was short with large beards of varying colors and wore large, chainmail shirts. Some even had pieces of plate armor strapped to them along with protruding spikes and blades. Their angular, open-faced helms all sported horns, horsetails, wings or some other kind of decoration giving the squat army a fearsome appearance.

The dwarves were waving their weapons threateningly at Jack and shouting at him while he just stood there not budging an inch. They must have seen Ol'

Bertha in action because none of the dwarves dared approach him.

"Oy! Hillies!" Lord Aurvang roared, as he stormed out from behind the truck to face the dwarf army. "Ye threaten me allies, ye threaten me!"

The assembled dwarves froze in surprise at the sight of the angry dwarf lord appearing before them and a soft murmur passed through the army. Silence fell as Lord Aurvang glared around at the assembled dwarves.

One of the dwarves stepped out from the throng. "Lord Aurvang," he said, with surprise evident in his deep voice. "What be ye doin' here?"

The speaker was taller than the dwarf lord, and his beard was flame red and braided in a complex pattern of knots. Blue runic tattoos covered his shaved head and ran down his massive, exposed right arm. The other arm was encased in a dark steel plate up to his shoulder while he wore a chainmail shirt underneath. A circular wooden shield was strapped to his armored arm and a large rune axe was clutched in his right. The axe wasn't as ornate as Lord Aurvang's, but it was still an impressive weapon.

Mike assumed this was their leader.

Lord Aurvang rounded on the dwarf that had spoken. "Ah, Jarl Deathkettle. I could be askin' the same o' yer self."

There was a tense minute as the two dwarves eyed each other. It became apparent that neither one wanted to answer the other's question first.

As the silence stretched, Mike was afraid they would come to blows. After what seemed like an eternity, the wild dwarf that Lord Aurvang had called Jarl Deathkettle sighed. "Very well, Lord. Me boys and I be headed off ter join with Thane Hardhelm at Draunupir ter push back several gob tribes that be movin' into the southern border when some foul magic brought us ter the woods north o' here. We heard the chantin' o' the gobs and we assumed they cast the spell that brought us here. So, we went looking fer 'em."

Jarl Deathkettle shrugged his massive shoulders. "Then, we heard the explosions and sounds o' battle, so we got here as fast as we could. We couldn't tell who was fightin' the gobs, but we figured they needed help. Any enemy o' those little buggers be a friend o' ours, as far as I be concerned. But then we get ter the door and this creature," he motions to Jack, "won't let us in."

For the first time, the jarl noticed Mike and Ted standing behind Lord

Aurvang. "What be these creatures that ye have allied yerself with?" he growled at the dwarf lord.

"These," Lord Aurvang shouted dramatically, so that all the assembled dwarves could hear, "be humans."

A chorus of shouts and cries of disbelief erupted from the assembled dwarves at Lord Aurvang's announcement.

Jarl Deathkettle laughed. "Do ye expect me ter believe that? Everyone knows that humans be nothin' more than a myth."

"Are ye calling me a liar, Deathkettle?" Lord Aurvang growled, with a dangerous glint in his eye.

"N-no Lord," the jarl stammered. "O' course not. It is just hard ter believe is all. If what ye say be true then where we be?"

"Midguard," Lord Aurvang replied grimly. "The humans here call it Earth."

"Midguard!" Jarl Deathkettle breathed in disbelief. The wild-looking dwarf suddenly became excited as a realization came to him. "That means the Bifrost be here."

He became more excited as he talked and Lord Aurvang groaned at the jarl's growing enthusiasm. "We could finally find Asguard!" Then the jarl looked directly at Ted. "Human! Where be the Bifrost?"

Ted found the dwarf's tone offensive and snapped, "I don't answer to *human*, dwarf. And why should I tell you where anything is?"

"Bah!" Jarl Deathkettle's face started to turn purple with rage. "Because we just saved yer miserable lives, *Human*," he added with a snarl.

"Try asking nicely, *dwarf*. And maybe I will tell you," Ted growled back.

"I will no 'ask nicely,'" the furious jarl exploded. "Ye will tell me now or I will rip it from ye," he said, as he took a step forward and raised his axe threateningly.

"Make my day, dwarf," Ted laughed, as he casually leaned against his poleaxe.

Ted raised his other hand and a ball of liquid fire burst to life above his open palm. A gasp of astonishment passed through the dwarf army and the term "wizard" and "sorcerer" were whispered.

The jarl held his ground, but he suddenly looked less willing to fight.

"Stop it both of ye," Lord Aurvang roared, and stepped between them. He pointed at the shaken jarl, "Ye will lower yer weapon. If ye threaten me allies again, I will take it as a personal insult." Jarl Deathkettle's face paled and he quickly lowered his axe.

"And yerself!" Lord Aurvang rounded on Ted. "Put that durned thing out!"

Ted gave an unconcerned shrug and the fireball disappeared in a puff of smoke.

Satisfied, the dwarf lord turned from Ted and stormed up to the jarl and began talking to him in a gruff language that Mike couldn't understand.

Mike reached over and spun Ted to face him. "What the Hell was that about?" Mike asked, in a loud whisper.

Ted shrugged again and scratched his beard. "Well, from what I have read the dwarves are usually notoriously stubborn and proud." An inner fire sprang up in Ted's eyes. "If we let them boss us around we will never be taken seriously. I had to show that puffed up meat-head that we humans are not some cattle to be pushed around."

Mike had read just as many stories involving dwarves as Ted had, maybe more, and he knew that Ted's display could have backfired terribly. "Yes, and you could have gotten us killed. Or did you not notice the army in front of us?"

"It was a calculated risk," Ted replied airily.

"Calculated my foot," Mike grumbled. "You just wanted to show off. Next time, warn me before you go trying to pick a fight with an army. You know how I hate surprises."

Ted flashed him an exaggerated wink and Mike groaned as Lord Aurvang and Jarl Deathkettle approached.

"Michael Strazney, Ted Koldun," Lord Aurvang began, as he and the jarl stood before them. "Let me formally introduce Jarl Baldor Deathkettle o' Clan Hardhelm."

"A pleasure to meet you Jarl Deathkettle," Mike said, and held out his hand.

The jarl scowled at Ted for a moment then took Mike's offered forearm. "Greetings, Michael Strazney." The jarl ignored Ted while he spoke. "I wish ter apologize fer any possible insult I may be given ye." His broad shoulders sagged and he bowed his wide head. "I be brought dishonor ter me clan with me ignorance o' humans."

With his head still bowed, the jarl went down on one knee in front of Mike and offered up his axe. "Therefore, I pledge me service ter yerselves until such a time as ye determine me knowledge o' humans be sufficient and me honor be restored."

Mike was shocked and confused. But without any better ideas, he reached out and took the offered axe.

It was surprisingly heavy. Mike struggled to hold it up with one arm and he hoped the strain didn't show on his face. He quickly lowered the axe and thinking quickly he said, "Very well. I accept your pledge." Jarl Deathkettle looked up and Mike was surprised to see relief on his bearded face. "But I admit we humans don't know very much about dwarves either. So, you will teach us about dwarves as we teach you about humans." Mike held the axe out to the jarl. "Do we have a deal, Jarl Deathkettle?"

The jarl grinned. "We do at that." The dwarf stood and took the offered axe. "And ye may call me Baldor."

"Alright Baldor," Mike said. "You can call me Mike and this is Ted." He motioned to his towering companion who continued to lean easily against his poleaxe.

"So, now what?" Ted suddenly asked.

"What do you mean, 'now what?'" Mike asked.

"Well, we came here to warn the plant about the goblins and defend them if they stayed," Ted replied. "And we accomplished that. So, now what?"

That was a good question. Mike didn't know what they were going to do now. He hadn't really considered what would happen if they actually saved the plant.

"Well…" Mike began, "I suppose we head back to Clearfield and see how the town is faring."

"But we can't leave Shawville Station undefended again," Ted noted. "A lot of goblins got away and might come back once we leave."

Mike saw that Ted had a good point, but didn't have an answer. Luckily, the dwarves did.

"I can be helpin' with that," Baldor rumbled. "We can return ter yer village with ye, but I will leave some o' me boys here to protect yer... *station,* until we have built better defenses."

He eyed the buildings around him critically. "And ye must explain what purpose these strange structures be havein'."

Mike tried not to look too eager. An army of dwarves would come in handy. "We would appreciate any help you can give us," he said as diplomatically as he could.

A sudden ripple passed though the dwarf army and many pointed up at something behind Mike and Ted.

"Bless me beard," Baldor whispered, as he stared over the humans' shoulders. "The sky be on fire."

CHAPTER 19

"On fire?" Mike muttered in disbelief, as he and Ted spun around and looked up.

Sure enough, there were great pillars of fire streaking through the sky. Bright columns of flame appeared and as they watched more sprang to life. Soon, the entire sky in Mike's vision was ablaze.

The air shook with a thunderous blast as one of the fireballs suddenly exploded in a brilliant burst of light.

"Meteors?" Mike asked, in awe.

Ted grunted distractedly. "Could be…"

"I didn't think there was supposed to be a meteor shower today," Mike said, not taking his eyes off the sky.

"There isn't," Ted answered, also not looking away from the fiery display.

"I hope none of them are big enough to reach the ground," Mike muttered to himself.

Terrified, everyone watched in horrified wonder for several minutes, mesmerized by the towering columns of fire that continued to burn across the sky.

Eventually, the hellish display lessened until only a few burning tails occasionally marred the sky.

"Well, that was fun," Ted said, as he looked back at the gathering.

"Ye humans got a strange concept o' fun," Baldor grumbled, still eyeing the heavens uneasily.

"Yes," Ted grinned, "we do." He leaned his poleaxe on his shoulder. "Now, I say we pack up and get back to town before there isn't a town to go back to."

Mike nodded his agreement. "Indeed. We've spent too much time here already."

"Not so fast," Lord Aurvang rumbled. "First, we must dispose o' these." He motioned to the mass of goblins corpses that were sprawled all around.

"Me clan will gather the scum up and burn 'em while the rest o' ye prepare," Baldor offered.

"Very well," Lord Aurvang said, and without another word he spun on his heel and stomped back around the truck and into the plant. Wasting no time, Baldor followed suit and went back to his milling army, bellowing orders as he went.

Mike and Ted were suddenly standing alone between the dwarf force and the plant complex. They shared a confused look, then shrugged helplessly and made their way up to Jack and Darrell, who were still guarding the doors.

"It is good to see you two clowns made it out alive," Mike greeted them.

Darrell snorted from inside the cab. "Like there was any doubt."

"Yeah," Jack said, "between Darrell's crazy driving and Ol' Bertha here," he patted the machine gun affectionately, "those little green buggers didn't stand a chance."

"I'm glad you fools were having fun while the rest of us were trying not to get killed," Ted growled at them.

"It weren't no walk in the park for us neither," Darrell shot back.

Ted groaned. "Was no"

"What?" Darrell asked.

"You said 'weren't no' it should be 'was no,'" Ted tried to explain.

"Oh, shut it, Ted," Darrell snapped.

Mike chuckled to himself. Listening to those two bicker was always a little entertaining, but before things could get out of hand he decided to jump in.

"Anyways," Mike said loudly, "how about Darrell and Jack stay here and guard the door while Ted and I go back inside and get Liz and Emily so we can head out?"

Jack nodded. "Works for me." Darrell also agreed, so Mike and Ted left the two of them to watch the door.

Once back inside the control room, Mike saw that things were very different than when he had left. Gone were the injured men and dwarves. Instead, just Dave sat at the control station watching the various monitors around him.

"Where is everybody?" Mike asked when he entered the room.

Dave looked up from his monitors and Mike could see the disbelief on his face. "She healed them all," he said in awe.

It seemed that Liz had managed to keep her healing power working. Mike was glad; some of the workers had looked pretty bad.

He was surprised that she had managed to help everyone, but instead of telling Dave that, he said. "Yeah, she is good like that," making it sound as though Liz healed people all the time. "So, where is everybody?" he asked again.

"Oh, that dwarf lord fellow came in here and chased everyone out yelling something about checking the defenses before they left. Is he going somewhere?" Dave asked anxiously.

"We are. Yes," Mike answered. "Now that this station is safe, we are headed back to Clearfield with the dwarves to clear the creatures out of town."

Dave looked less than pleased with that announcement. "But what if those monsters come back?"

"Don't worry," Mike reassured him. "Some of the dwarves are going to stay here in case the goblins come back. And when the town is secured we will come back, I promise."

"Thank you." Dave looked relieved and Mike could understand why. He wouldn't want to be left alone out here with goblins and who-knows-what-else prowling about in the shadows.

"No problem," Mike replied, as he and Ted sat down to wait.

For a moment, Dave looked like he wanted to say more, but instead he stayed silent and went back to watching his monitors. Mike was glad of the silence because a lot had happened in a short amount of time and he needed to process the day's events.

The day had started out so well, too. Granted, he hadn't been thrilled about Liz making him go to church with her, but discovering he had the power to fight demons was a definite plus.

He smiled to himself. Fighting the demon had been terrifying, but also exhilarating. Mike knew he shouldn't be so happy about encountering a demon, but he couldn't help it. It brought a lot of things into focus.

Mike had always been fascinated by the occult and stories of demons and how to defeat them. So, to come face-to-face with one and see it destroyed was a bit of a dream come true. Perhaps there was a reason for that.

Maybe his obsession with demonology wasn't an accident. Maybe deep down he had known he had the power to fight them, but it wasn't until one actually appeared that the ability manifested.

It may have been wishful thinking, but the more he thought about it the more sure he became.

Mike looked over to tell Ted about his revelation, but he saw that Ted was staring at the floor with his head in his hands, lost in thought. Mike decided not to interrupt and kept quiet. He wasn't the only one that strange things had happened to.

Mike thought about how Ted had suddenly gained his magic and Liz could somehow heal people. He then remembered the strange sparks coming off of Emily's arrows while they fought the goblins and he wondered if that was some power of hers. As far as he knew neither Jack nor Darrell had any supernatural abilities, but then again Darrell spent most of his time driving Jack around so Jack could shoot that ridiculous machine gun of his.

He grinned at that. Jack had always been dying to shoot that bloody thing ever since he "acquired" it from some Marine buddy of his. Mike had to admit that it was handy to have around. Especially since Jack had saved him with it when the ratmen had him and Liz surrounded outside his apartment.

Ratmen. Thinking of them made Mike remember all the awful creatures that had plagued them so far. First, it was the demon, and then the packs of ratmen, followed by goblins and kobolds. Then there were the lizardmen that Ted had fought, and also the creatures out by Emily's, and most recently there were the hobgoblins that had been attacking the dwarves.

Somehow through all of the chaos, they had survived. Mike believed it was mostly luck that had kept them alive this long. They could have easily been swarmed while they slept or some other time without warning. But now the time for luck was over.

They knew what was happening.

Monsters were invading and with the help of the dwarves they were going to push the creatures out and retake Clearfield.

He looked down at his battered form and shook his head sadly. He looked a wreck. Drying blood covered most of him; the majority of it belonged to creatures, but a lot was his own. Not to mention his poor breastplate that was covered in new dents and gouges.

He was mad at himself for letting it get so damaged. It looked like it couldn't take much more beating and he didn't have another one. Even if he did, there was no way he was going back to his place to try and get the rest of his armor.

Not only was his breastplate a mess, but his sword was also a notched ruin. Luckily, Lord Aurvang had supplied him with a marvelous mace. Well, Mike corrected, the mace had apparently "chosen" him, assuming he believed the dwarf lord's story.

Mike had heard legends of weapons that had feelings, but he didn't believe any of them. The mere thought of a sentient weapon was ludicrous. He looked at the mace suspiciously, then put his hand on it. When he did, a warm tingle ran up his arm.

Mike quickly pulled his hand away, and clenched and unclenched his fist to try and make the tingling go away.

The sensation was slowly fading when one of the control room doors opened. Mike looked up to see Jim enter the room followed closely by Liz and Emily.

Mike stood up as they approached.

Neither of them seemed the worse for wear. "Where is Lord Aurvang?" he asked.

Jim shrugged. "He stayed behind to oversee setting up more defenses."

Dave made a face. "You left him out there?" he grumbled, as he waved his hand, motioning out the window. "He will never find his way back."

"The dwarf said, 'We dwarves never get lost' and I wasn't about to argue with him," Jim replied.

"Wonderful." Dave rolled his eyes. "If he isn't back in a few minutes, I will radio for one of the guys to go find him."

Liz and Emily slid over to Mike. Liz watched Ted with concern in her eyes. "So, now what's the plan? Lord Aurvang said something about going back to Clearfield?"

"Yes," Mike answered. "Baldor agreed to bring his hill dwarves back with us and help clear the town of creatures."

"Who is Baldor?" Emily asked.

"His name is Baldor Deathkettle," Ted said, as he stood and joined the party. "And he is the jarl of the hill dwarf army that saved us."

"Jarl?" Emily looked confused.

Ted let out an exasperated sigh. "It's his title. A jarl is the Norse word for a chief or ruler." Ted looked thoughtful. "Or perhaps it is a dwarf word... hmm" He stroked his beard, lost in thought.

Before Ted could get onto one of his wild theories, Mike quickly said, "Now that that is settled, how about we go out and see if we can assist with the clean up?"

Mike saw Emily's questioning look and added, "The dwarves are gathering up all the dead goblins and are piling them up to burn them."

"I see," Emily said. "In that case, I think we should stay in here awhile longer."

Ted laughed. "I'm sure a little work won't hurt you."

"It's not the work." Emily wrinkled her nose. "It's the smell. Those ugly green things stink when they are alive, I don't want to think about how they smell dead."

Mike was forced to agree. The goblins did smell something awful. Somewhere between rotten garbage and dirty diapers would be a good way to describe them.

"As much as I hate to say it," Liz began.

"Then don't," Emily butted in with a grin.

Liz scowled but continued. "It would be rude to leave them to clean up. The least we could do is help gather the bodies. They did save us after all."

"Liz is right," Mike said. As much as he hated to admit it she did have a point. "We should go help."

"Ugh. Fine," Emily moaned. "We can go. But I am not touching any corpses."

****

Turns out the debate was irrelevant because by the time the friends made their way back through the plant and outside, the dwarves had worked remarkably quickly and had already gathered all the bodies into a huge pile and were preparing to light it on fire.

Liz was glad. Although she had argued to come help, she hadn't been overly thrilled with the idea of touching the dead goblins either. She heard Emily breathe a sigh of relief.

"Well, I guess that problem is solved," Emily chirped happily.

Liz chuckled, "I guess it is."

As they watched, the dwarves tossed the last of the goblins on the pile and started adding coal. Luckily, there was no shortage of coal with the massive piles all around to feed the immense boilers that powered the turbines.

A few minutes later, one of the dwarves lit the pile and soon the entire thing was engulfed in flames. The heap became a towering inferno with flames shooting dozens of feet into the air and a billowing black column of smoke climbed into the sky.

They stood at least fifty yards from the conflagration, but Liz could still feel the heat on her face. She was impressed at the power of the flames and she suspected it had a lot to do with the abundance of coal that the dwarves had most likely stashed throughout the mound.

The dwarves stood remarkably close to the bonfire and didn't seem uncomfortable in the least. Liz was impressed at how the heat didn't seem to bother them even though she was sure the temperature must have been sweltering.

The fire crackled and sparked, and soon the smell of roasting meat filled the air. But not the smell of a nice steak; this meat smelled rotten. Cooking rotten meat.

It was not a pleasant smell.

Liz covered her nose with her hands, but it didn't help. The stench was overpowering.

It was so bad she could almost taste it. Not only that, but the fumes were making her eyes burn. Next to her, Emily gagged and Ted wiped tears from his burning eyes.

"That is rather unpleasant," Mike coughed.

Liz thought that was a bit of an understatement, but as she looked around she noticed that again the dwarves didn't seem fazed in the least. Perhaps they didn't have a good sense of smell.

Liz looked over her shoulder at where Jack and Darrell were still parked by the door. To her amazement, Jack was still standing in the bed holding his machine gun, but now he was wearing a gas mask! She wondered where he had gotten that.

Liz shook her head. Leave it to Jack to have a gas mask lying around when he needed it.

But that wasn't the most shocking thing. Still in the cab was Darrell with the window rolled down, his head leaned back, and his eyes closed. His mouth hung open and Liz could just make out the sound of snoring. "Seriously?" she muttered to herself.

Emily heard her mutter and looked over as well. "Is he sleeping?" Emily asked, appalled.

"Yes," Liz replied. "Yes, he is."

"How can anyone sleep right now?" Emily said. "Especially with this stink everywhere."

Liz sighed. "If anyone could sleep at a time like this, it would be Darrell."

A low rumble suddenly filled the air. Liz looked around and quickly realized it was coming from the dwarves.

They were chanting.

It was a deep, mournful rumble that Liz could feel in her bones. It grew in strength and the melody became haunting. Liz was suddenly filled with an immense sadness that she couldn't explain.

The gloomy chant ground on as the dwarves moved about in an almost ritualistic pattern. The chant grew louder and the tone changed to something sounding almost hopeful.

As they watched, some of the dwarves bent down and picked up large lumps that had been laid out around the fire and set them over their shoulders. It took a moment for Liz to realize those lumps were bodies. Dwarf bodies.

Realization hit Liz like a hammer. They were the dwarves that had died in the battle.

The friends watched in silence as the dwarves rumbling chant grew ever louder and the bodies of the fallen were picked up. Once all the bodies were gathered, the dwarves formed a line and began to march toward the plant.

Liz couldn't understand the words, but she didn't need to. The chant grew louder and transformed into a sound that she would almost call joyful as the train of bodies approached the open doors.

Mike, Liz, Ted, and Emily reverently moved away from the door to make way as the fallen were carried past them and into the plant complex.

Liz was surprised that the string of bodies was so short. After such a large battle, Liz expected more casualties, especially looking at the huge number of dead goblins.

The living dwarves were chanting so loudly now that it began to echo throughout the hills. The beat became faster and the tone more joyful until Liz almost felt like dancing. The song continued as the last of the bodies were carried into the plant and were lost from sight.

The flames burned greedily and the pillar of black smoke spiraled higher and higher. The stench lessened as the bodies blackened and charred.

The song swelled and long minutes went by before the dwarves began marching back out without the bodies.

Once all the living dwarves had rejoined the chanting army, some of the dwarves brought out musical instruments and began to play.

A merry song sprang up, and from somewhere the dwarves produced large mugs and began filling them from several massive kegs that Liz had failed to notice before.

All of a sudden, there was a merry party around the corpse fire. Dwarves laughed and toasted each other as the musicians played and continued their rumbling song.

Liz was stunned by the sudden change in atmosphere. What had started out as a solemn funeral march had ended in a cheerful celebration.

One of the dwarves broke away from the party and approached them. He was an immensely thick dwarf with bright red hair and a beard that was a tangle of braids. He was taller than most of the dwarves Liz had seen and blue tattoos covered his head and ran down one arm. In those massive arms, he carried several large mugs full of some dark liquid. She wondered if this was the jarl that Mike had mentioned earlier.

When the dwarf got closer he said, "Greetings humans! We won a great victory today. Here," he said, handing each of them one of the foaming mugs. "drink and may the Gods watch or' us." He tilted his head back and poured the dark liquid into his mouth with much of the drink overflowing and running down his beard.

Her suspicions were confirmed when Mike greeted him. "Thank you, Baldor."

Mike and Ted then followed suit and drank. Emily looked down at her mug suspiciously and Liz did the same. It had a strange, earthy scent, almost like fresh tilled earth.

Liz didn't want to insult the dwarf, and it seemed to her that Mike and Ted liked whatever it was, so she decided to try it.

She poured a small amount into her mouth.

The sudden explosion of flavors shocked her.

It was like drinking liquid light. That was the only way she could describe it. The drink was sweet and creamy, and made her whole mouth tingle and a warm glow filled her. It was quite possibly the best thing she had ever had. It was like sunshine in a glass.

"What is this?" Liz breathed in awe.

Baldor wiped the foam off his beard with the back of his hand. "That, my dear, be Uberjuice. The best Hill Ale in all the Kingdom," he said proudly.

Liz had no doubt that this was considered the best; she couldn't imagine anything being more flavorful and wonderful. With a few big gulps, she drained the mug. The others must have agreed because they all quickly finished their mugs as well.

"So," Ted belched, "what is the occasion?"

Baldor scowled at him. "It be the Celebration o' the Fallen o' course." He said as if Ted were stupid for not knowing.

Ted scowled right back, but before he could reply Mike jumped in. "How long does this Celebration last?"

"Depends," Baldor shrugged. "Sometimes a few minutes, sometimes they last fer days."

"We don't have days," Mike replied. "Can you end the Celebration and have your dwarves ready to go soon? We only have a few hours of daylight left and I have no desire to be traveling in the dark."

Baldor nodded his agreement. "A good idea that. Hobs 'n gobs be bolder at night. Best not be exposed when the light fades. I will assemble the Clan." He collected the empty mugs, and with that he turned and disappeared into the swirling mass of celebrating dwarves.

Liz went over to the truck and woke Darrell up while Mike went back into the plant to tell Dave that they were leaving. Everyone gathered around the truck while they waited for Mike.

True to his word, Baldor and his dwarves were ready by the time Mike came back out.

Mike joined the others. "Alrighty. Are we ready?" Everyone nodded their agreement.

Baldor strode over and announced, "The Hardhelm Clan be ready ter march."

Liz watched as the sea of assembled dwarves milled around in a large mass waiting for the order to move. "How many dwarves do you have?" she asked.

"Near two thousand," Baldor replied proudly.

Just then the plant doors banged open and Lord Aurvang stormed out. "Lost! Dwarves don't get lost!" he shouted in rage. He spotted the truck and stormed over to Liz and the others followed closely by his guards. "Those... *men* sent someone ter come find me because they thought I be *lost!*" he fumed at them. "A dwarf does NOT get *lost*."

"I'm sorry Lord Aurvang," Liz replied quickly, and tried to defuse the angry dwarf. "You are the first dwarves we have ever met and we don't know these things."

The dwarf lord seemed to calm a bit at that. "Aye," he sighed. "I suppose yer are right at that. I forget meself."

"No problem," Mike replied easily. "We all have a lot to learn."

Lord Aurvang grunted, "Yes, well... be we ready?"

Baldor replied, "Yes, Lord. We be prepared ter depart."

"Good," Lord Aurvang nodded.

"Would you two like to ride with us?" Mike asked the dwarf leaders.

"No," Lord Aurvang replied. "The Keepbuilder Clan will act as the rear guard. But Deathkettle here will join ye."

Baldor looked ready to argue, but Lord Aurvang wasn't done. "Ye have an Oath to learn about the humans and to teach them about us. This be a good time for ye to begin yer lesson."

The jarl looked less than pleased but grumbled, "Yes, Lord."

"Awesomesauce," Mike said happily, as he rubbed his hands together eagerly. "Let's get going." He jumped up into the bed of the truck.

"I will ride up front," Emily said, as she ran around and got in the cab. Darrell looked pleased. Liz chuckled and climbed in after Mike, followed by Ted and Baldor. Lord Aurvang and his dwarves marched off to join the milling throng.

Once everyone was seated, Darrell pulled out and headed for the gate. As they drove by, the dwarves formed into a ragged column and began to follow the truck. The dwarves lined up shoulder-to-shoulder, four abreast and filled up the road.

Darrell was driving nice and slow so the dwarves could keep up. As he turned out of the gate and headed towards the old bridge, the dwarf army began to uncoil like a snake behind them.

Baldor was still grumbling to himself, obviously angry about being forced to ride in the truck. Liz didn't know what exactly he had done, but she felt bad for him anyways.

"Why do you take orders from him?" Liz asked the irritable dwarf.

Baldor snorted like that was the dumbest question he had ever heard. "He be a lord," the jarl said, like the answer was obvious. "And he be not just any lord, he be one o' the most powerful lords in the entire Empire."

Curiosity piqued, Liz asked. "And what makes him so powerful?"

The jarl let out a deep sigh. "All lords control a fortress-city. But Aurvang be the Lord of the Twinpeaks," Baldor said meaningfully, and looked around like everyone should know what that meant. When nobody said anything he sighed again, shook his head, and muttered. "But o' course ye humans don't know anything about that."

"The Twinpeaks," Baldor began, "lay under a huge mountain that be two identical snow-capped peaks, hence its name. But the Twinpeaks be no one city, but two that be connected by a massive underground highway. So, Lord Aurvang's recourses be nearly double that o' any other lord, making him nearly equal ter some kings in terms o' wealth."

Baldor paused to let his words sink in before he continued. "And not only be he a lord, but he also be a Rune Knight o' Ogmar. I be sure ye noticed his ornate armor and weapons. Those symbols be not just fer looks; they be powerful runes o' protection and strength, among others. Only another rune knight be knowin' what they all truly mean."

A grudging respect entered the jarl's voice. "Lord Aurvang's battle prowess be legendary, but more importantly he be a brilliant strategist. He has won more battles than any other living lord."

This information made Liz see the gruff dwarf lord in an entirely new light.

"But there be one thing I don't know," Baldor said, and looked over at Mike. "How ye got him ter owe ye a Life Debt."

So, Mike told how he and Ted had found the dwarves, and saved Lord Aurvang from the hobgoblins.

"Truly?" Baldor asked, in disbelief. "I never heard o' that many hobs working together before."

Mike nodded. "That is what Lord Aurvang had said as well."

"That be dire news," Baldor leaned back thoughtfully.

Ted suddenly spoke up. "I have a question and it has been bothering me for some time." He looked directly at the large tattooed dwarf and asked, "How is it that you speak English?"

Liz was surprised. That was an excellent question and she couldn't believe she hadn't thought of it before. *How could these dwarves from another world speak fluent English?*

"English?" Baldor rumbled confused. "I don't know what this *English* be, but we be speaking Common right now."

Ted leaned forward. "Here, we call this language English. How can you know it? If your ancestors met ours thousands of years ago they wouldn't have spoken English. It would most likely have been Old Norse or something similar." Ted was clearly intrigued. "It doesn't make sense that you can speak English."

"Well, I don't know what ter tell ye human," Baldor replied. "Every dwarf knows Common as well as Dwarvish."

"Fascinating," Ted muttered, as he leaned back and stroked his beard. Silence followed, as everyone was lost in his or her own thoughts.

After several minutes, Mike spoke up. "So, what is your world like?"

Baldor shrugged his massive shoulders. "It looks a lot like this one on the surface. But most o' our civilization be underground."

"And why is that?" Liz asked.

Baldor leaned forward. "Because the Gods carved us from the very bones o' the world, so deep within the stone be where we live. We only came ter the surface when the gobs and orcs tried ter dig their way ter our hidden halls."

"That sounds like quite the tale," Liz flashed the jarl a sweet smile. "Would you mind telling it to us?"

Baldor waved the question away. "It be a long tale and I would no be knowin' where ter begin."

"We have plenty of time," Liz pleaded. "And the best place to start is the beginning."

The jarl thought a moment then nodded. "Very well. But I be no loremaster and no have the gift fer the tellin' o' tales. Ter do the story justice I will start at the very beginning."

Baldor paused for a moment as he gathered his thoughts, then he began.

CHAPTER 20

"Our Lore states that the first dwarf created by the Gods be Motsognir," Baldor rumbled. "He be carved out o' living stone at the heart o' the world."

"Legend says he be eight feet tall with a great beard o' flame and that he could move through rock as easily as we walk through air."

"Motsognir burrowed ter the center o' the world and with the help o' the Gods, built the great city o' Holy Agartha that would later be the seat o' the Empire."

"After seeing how powerful Motsognir be, the Gods decided ter make all other dwarves less and that be when they carved the second dwarf named Durinn."

"Durinn would later be known as Durinn the Mighty after he unified the Clans under one banner and created the Holy Dwarven Empire."

Baldor looked at each of the humans expectantly, like he was waiting for one of them to say something about his story. When none of them did, he continued.

"Originally, there be ten Great Clans, each with their own king, who be unified by Durinn." The jarl puffed up his chest as he continued. "But Durinn had no Clan o' his own, so he used the lost secrets o' Carving ter craft his own wives. Thus, Durinn began his own Clan.

Ted spoke up. "How did he manage that?"

Baldor visibly deflated at that. "That," he grumbled, "be a mystery. We have no record o' how such Carving be performed."

Ted shrugged and motioned for the dwarf to continue.

"Now, three o' the Clans were destroyed in the Amalgamation War, but the remainin' seven bent the knee ter Durinn and named him Emperor."

"Now, the symbol o' the new Empire became the Eyegishiowlmer. Its eight spears radiating out from a central point, representing the original eight clans' unification and defense o' the new Empire. It be known in the common tongue as the Helm o' Awe. Ye should have seen it on Lord Aurvang's breastplate."

Every head nodded at that. How could anyone miss the giant circular symbol that nearly covered the dwarf lord's barrel-like chest?

"It also be the name fer the crown o' the Emperor. Legend says that Durinn himself designed it and any enemy that looks upon the Emperor's helm be paralyzed with fear."

"What does it look like?" Mike asked.

Baldor groaned and rubbed his eyes with a massive hand. "I don't be knowin' that either. No hill dwarf seen the Emperor in a thousand years."

"What?" Liz asked. "How has nobody seen your Emperor in a thousand years?"

"I didn't say 'nobody seen him,' I said no *hill dwarf* seen him in a thousand years," Baldor rumbled. "The Emperor does no usually leave Holy Agartha unless there be great need."

Liz still looked skeptical.

"Look," Baldor began, "have ye ever seen yer king?"

"We don't have a king," Liz replied smartly. "We have a President. And no, I have never actually seen him in person, but I know what he looks like."

"*President?*" Baldor mouthed the word as though it tasted bad. "What kind of leader be a *President?*"

Mike laughed. "Not a very good one."

Liz ignored Mike's remark. "A President is an elected leader. We all vote on who gets to be President every four years."

"Sounds silly ter me," Baldor said. "Who would want ter be the ruler fer only four years?"

"It's not about being the ruler," Mike said. "It's about getting rich and…"

Ted cleared his throat. "We can discuss the intricacies of the Presidency later. How about we let our friend here finish his tale?"

"Boo," Mike grumbled half-heartedly. "I was just getting ready to go on an anti-government rant."

"I know," Ted grinned back. "That is why I stopped you before you got a head of steam going."

"Good call," Liz muttered.

"Please continue," Ted said to the jarl.

"Now, where be it I was?" Baldor mused. "Ah, yes. So, except fer the occasional war with the giants, those days be ones o' prosperity fer the dwarves as the Gods walked among us and we grew inter a powerful nation. Many consider this the First Golden Age. With the help o' the Gods, the first rune lords created the Portal Stones that connected all of the capital cities. It be also in those times that the mythical runesmith, Dvalin Swordforger, taught the legendary smiths, the Sons of Ivaldi, his craft. He then went on ter create many marvelous things."

The dwarf's tone dropped menacingly. "But those glorious days be no ter last. Fer then came the orcs and muspell."

Baldor paused dramatically and Liz suspected that he was enjoying telling his saga.

"Muspell?" Ted asked. "Those are a type of demon, are they not?"

"Aye," The dwarf replied ominously. "The muspell be also known as Fire Giants. But most know them ter be demons."

Before today, Liz would have laughed at the idea of demons. But now the thought of them terrified her. She had seen one first hand and had no desire to ever encounter one again.

"There be a debate between our scholars or' which came first. Some say the giants summoned the muspell and they brought their orc slaves with 'em. While others believe the orcs had always been Above, but it wasn't until they discovered a way ter summon the muspell that they began tryin' ter conquer the Empire."

"Regardless, fer a thousand years we fought the orcs and their summoned allies, but it seemed as soon as we defeated one group another would appear. Eventually, the Empire was hard pressed by a massive alliance o' muspell, orcs, and their slaves, when the great Lord Hreidmar went before the Emperor and asked permission ter lead an army ter the surface ter face the enemy."

"Ye must understand," Baldor leaned forward, "up until this time, we dwarves had only defended our fortress-cities, never leaving the safety o' our underground empire. So ter actually go Above was unhearda."

"Surprisingly, Emperor Bjorn II agreed and Lord Hreidmar took four Clans ter the surface ter do battle. After nearly a hunnered years o' brutal fighting, Hreidmar and his Clans defeated the orc War Chief BloodFist at Trogar's Gap and crushed the vile alliance."

"Seeing how the Empire be vulnerable from above, Hreidmar petitioned the Emperor again and asked that some Clans be allowed ter live Above so they could protect the mountain halls from burrowin' enemies. But in this, Bjorn II refused."

"Hreidmar be wise and he knew livin' Above be the best way ter protect his people. So, he took the lords o' the three Clans that had battled beside him and again asked the Emperor ter let them leave. Again, he be refused."

"With glrious stubbornness, Lord Hreidmar did what he thought best and took his clans and left anyways. When Emperor Bjorn II heard this, he be enraged and sent an army ter bring Hreidmar and his wayward Clans back. But by the time Bjorn's army reached the surface, Hreidmar and his forces already locked themselves inside the fortresses they used during the last orc incursion."

"Seeing no other choice, the Emperor's forces besieged the rebel fortresses. But being unaccustomed ter fighting Above, the Emperor's army be quickly routed and fled back underground."

"Years passed and Emperor Bjorn II made several other attempts ter regain the lost clans. But he be never successful."

"Sometime later, a large army o' giants arose from the south and made war with one o' the Empire's cities. After many glorious battles, it be clear we could no hold out much longer. It was then Hreidmar and his people came ter the aid o' the besieged city and defeated the giants."

"However, the battle be no won without cost, fer in the final battle, the Giant King Drofn killed Emperor Bjorn II in a mighty duel before the vile Drofn himself be slain by Lord Hreidmar."

"In gratitude fer savin' the city, Bjorn's son, and new Emperor, Haldor the Sunbringer, decreed that any dwarf who wished ter live Above was allowed ter do so. Emperor Haldor then established the Kingdom Above and made Hreidmar its king."

"Four other Clans chose to join Hreidmar's four ter keep the foundation o' eight like when the Empire been founded by Durinn and tergether they be the Kingdom Above. From then on, King Hreidmar be known as The Chainbreaker fer breaking away from the Empire and his Clan also took on the name."

"King Hreidmar took his new Chainbreaker Clan and founded the great fortress-city o' Nidavellir and made it his capital. The other seven clan lords each founded fortress-cities o' their own, and each took the title o' thane. They pledged their allegiance ter King Hreidmar, who in turn pledged his allegiance ter the Emperor. This be considered the beginnin' o' the Second Golden Age."

"Fascinating," Ted said. "And this is where you are now? The Second Golden Age?"

"Ha," Baldor laughed. "No. The Second Golden Age lasted fer over a thousand years until a great host o' orcs once again attacked the Empire."

The dwarf rubbed his hands together eagerly, clearly enjoying himself. "Now, this be no any normal orc host. Usually a few tribes band tergether, but this time nearly every major tribe had gathered under one warlord ter make war on the Kingdom. We quickly lost several fortresses ter the combined might o' the unified orc tribes."

Anger entered the dwarf's voice as he continued. "When asked fer help, Emperor Dolgathar refused ter aid the Kingdom. He believed the orcs be a minor threat ter the Kingdom Above and o' no threat at all ter the Empire Below. But Dolgathar would soon discover the error o' his ways."

"Fer upon the sacking o' a Kingdom stronghold, the orcs discovered an underground highway leading ter the Imperial city o'Doffheim. The orcs descended on the city and utterly slaughtered its unsuspectin' inhabitants."

"Now, Emperor Dolgathar's sister lived in Doffheim and upon hearin' the news o' its destruction, Dolgathar flew inter a rage. He immediately called for a crusade against the orcs and their vile Warlord Grug the Rotten."

"Nearly all dwarves answered his call," Baldor said, with pride. "And with a massive crusade army at his back, Emperor Dolgathar met the orc hordes in an underground chamber complex known as Odin's Forrest."

"Odin's Forrest?" Mike asked.

The jarl sighed impatiently. "Yes. It be a massive series o' chambers filled with enormous stalactites and stalagmites that be so closely packed together that they resemble a forest o' stone."

"Now, we had the advantage o' fighting underground, but the horde be so immense that the outcome be still uncertain. It be no until Emperor Dolgathar himself met the Rotten Warlord and slew him in single combat that the orcs finally lost heart and be defeated."

"Seeing the ruin such a large force o' orcs could bring, and his thirst fer revenge not yet quenched, Dolgathar resolved ter continue his crusade. He then took his army and did something no other Emperor ever done before. He went Above."

In hushed tones, the dwarf eagerly leaned forward as he continued.

"Gatherin' near every dwarf he could along the way, Dolgathar soon amassed an enormous host the likes o' which never be seen before or since. With his crusade at his back, he made war with the orcs and began systematically destroying each o' their tribes one by one."

"But this was ter be no easy thing. Ye see, the orcs were spread across the whole o' the world and not only be there orcs ter fight, but there be also the threat o' goblin kind, giants, and all other manner o' beasts."

"The crusade lasted fer over three hunnerd years before the orcs were so hard-pressed that they be forced ter join together in common cause ter defeat Dolgathar and his crusade."

"But they be no alone, fer they had called fer aid as well. The evil orc warlocks used all o' their sorcerous powers and summoned legions of muspell ter join 'em."

"With defeat looming, the last o' the orcs amassed on the Fields of Gorthak just outside their final and greatest settlement. Their numbers, combined with the demons, be overwhelmin'. The now battle-hardened crusaders never seen an army o' such size before. It made their battered crusading army seem puny in comparison. The orcs and muspell swarmed or' the hills and fields like a living carpet as far as the eye could see."

"Undeterred, Emperor Dolgathar attacked. The battle lasted fer seven days and seven nights. Until at dawn o' the eighth day we did finally achieve victory. The cost be terribly high as we suffered catastrophic losses, including Emperor Dolgathar himself."

"But indeed, the orc menace be finally annihilated and so Dolgathar would ferever be known as The Orc Slayer."

"His two surviving sons decided that nothing like this should ever happen again. Then, the eldest son, Hannar Orcsbane, be Emperor and decreed that a new order be created with the sole purpose o' huntin' down and destroyin' every last orc and demon that escaped the slaughter. And so, the Imperial Order o' Wardens be created with Hannar's younger brother, Finn Demonslayer, named as the first High Warden."

"The wardens became primarily a demon huntin' order as the orcs be all but extinct. The wardens been very secretive and after a few thousand years they vanished like the orcs they been created ter destroy. They be since a thing o' legend, just like the orcs themselves. There still be some who believe the Order be out there still, workin' in secret ter protect us from the orcs and muspell," the jarl snorted. "A great pile o' nonsense the lot o' it."

"Regardless, that be over five thousand years ago. Since then, the Empire established their own fortresses Above ter protect their mountain halls, and the Kingdom be spread farther out inter the low lands. We be recovered from our losses so much that new Clans be formed and the Empire has grown ter dominate the entire Ironband Mountain Range."

"Eventually, we dwarves o' the Kingdom Above be known as the hill dwarves because many o' us live in the hills around the great mountain ranges. While those o' the Empire be more commonly known as the mountain dwarves, on account o' them all livin' deep inside their precious mountains."

Baldor relaxed as his story came to an end. He leaned back and grinned.

"And that, humans, be The History o' the Dwarves Accordin' ter Baldor."

"A good tale," Ted said. "But I have a few questions."

Baldor motioned to him to continue.

"So, first off, you said that Dolgathar…"

"Emperor Dolgathar, ter ye human," Baldor interrupted.

Ted held up his hands. "Sorry. Emperor Dolgathar then. Anyways, you said he fought the orcs for three hundred years. Are you telling us that dwarves live that long?" Ted said, with disbelief plain in his voice.

"Heh," The jarl chuckled. "O' course he didn't live three hunnerd years."

Ted nodded knowingly. "I thought not."

"He lived fer over five hunnerd."

Liz's mouth fell open. "What!?"

Baldor looked confused. "Ye humans no live that long?"

Mike laughed. "Ah, no. We don't. The oldest people are just over one hundred."

The jarl looked even more confused. "So, ye be saying that all o' ye aren't even a hunnerd yet?"

Mike shook his head no. "We are all in our twenties here."

The dwarf moaned and put his head in his hands. "I be talkin' ter children," he groaned.

Everyone laughed at the dwarf's dismay.

"And just how old are you?" Mike asked, still smiling.

There was a long pause as the jarl stared at his feet before answering. "I have seen over two hunnerd winters."

"Fascinating," Ted said, as he leaned forward. "Most stories agree that dwarves live longer, but I didn't think it would actually be true."

The jarl nodded. "True enough it seems. Most o' us live ter be around six hunnerd. Legend says that we used ter live well over a thousand."

"Hmm," Ted stroked his beard thoughtfully. "There are legends of ancient humans living for hundreds of years."

"Like Methuselah," Liz added.

Jack looked down at her. "Who?"

Liz sighed. "Methuselah," she repeated. "He is the oldest man ever recorded at over nine hundred years old."

Mike chuckled. "You don't really believe that, do you?"

"Actually, I do," Liz replied testily. "You can't tell me that after everything that's happened you don't believe that it's possible people used to live a lot longer."

Mike shrugged. "Fair enough."

Ted cleared his throat and everyone looked at him. "So, for my second question. What exactly do orcs look like?"

"Well…" Baldor scratched his beard. "No dwarf has seen an orc in over four thousand years. All we know be stories and carvings o' the beasts."

"From what I understand there be several types o' orcs. The smallest and most common were huge, muscular creatures, six feet tall and be various shades o' green."

"Like the goblins," Liz added.

"Aye," Baldor agreed. "But there be also the larger red-skinned orcs that be berserk warriors that be more bloodthirsty than even the other orcs be. It be said they had the greatest talent for the summoning o'muspell. It also be said that their red skin made them immune ter heat and they could control fire with a word, but they be no even the worst o' the orcs."

Baldor's voice dropped to a loud whisper. "The most powerful be the black orcs."

"Legend says they be the most massive o' orcs, tall and powerful, and the most cunnin'. It be said they could move through the shadows unseen and be the masters o' dark magic."

The dwarf raised his voice again. "Legend also says there be white and blue skinned orcs as well, but there be no confirmation o' such creatures er' existin'."

"All orcs did have a few things in common though. One be their blood-red eyes. Another be their tusks."

"Yes, yes," Ted interrupted, as he leaned forward with a hungry light in his eyes. "We all know what orcs look like. But what did they *wear*?" he asked eagerly.

"Hmm… that varies," the jarl replied. "Some tribes be said ter be rather simple and scavenged their armor, while others forged their own heavy plate. It wasn't anywhere near dwarf quality work mind ye, but by all accounts, it be hard ter break."

"So, they didn't wear animal skins and use stone weapons?" Ted pressed.

Baldor looked confused. "No that I ever hearda. Why do ye ask?"

"Earlier this morning, we encountered some massive green-skinned creatures with red eyes and large tusks."

The dwarf's eyes lit up at the news.

"But they wore ragged animal skins and had primitive stone weapons," Ted said.

"Interesting." Baldor stroked his large red beard. "Perhaps some orcs escaped the purge," the dwarf mused nearly to himself. "But most likely what ye saw weren't orcs at all. Some young trolls might look similar ter what they say orcs did. They be usually quite primitive."

Ted looked thoughtful. "Trolls, eh?" Then his face fell. "I thought for sure they were orcs."

Liz's sparkling laughter filled the air. "Oh, Ted," she laughed. "You can't be right all the time."

Ted scowled at her. "I sure can," he grumbled.

"Bwahaha," Baldor laughed. "Ye sound just like me old loremaster."

Ted just scowled at the chuckling jarl as well.

"Are ye sure ye aren't over a hunnerd?" Baldor asked.

Mike laughed from deep in his chest. "Yes, I am sure."

"But now it be my turn," Baldor said. "Ye have heard the history o' the dwarves, albeit a very short version. Now, I ask fer ye ter return the favor and tell me the human histories."

There was a short silence as everyone looked at each other.

"Ted?" Mike asked. "Would you be so kind?"

"Sure," Ted grumbled, "I'll tell it. But I'm not sure where to start."

The dwarf grinned wickedly. "The beginnin' usually be the best place."

CHAPTER 21

As they drove along the road headed back to Clearfield with the dwarf army marching along behind, Ted gave the jarl a brief overview of human history.

Liz sat back and tried to get as comfortable as she could in her corner of the truck as Ted began his story. This was going to take a while.

He began with cavemen and worked his way to the beginnings of civilization in Egypt and Ancient Mesopotamia before steering them into the Greek and Roman empires. Followed by the downfall of Rome and the start of the Dark Ages. Which, in turn, led to the Middle Ages, and how more advanced weapons and armor along with art led to the Renaissance.

Baldor listened intently and hung on to Ted's every word. Even Liz was paying close attention as she learned a few things she hadn't known before. Ted truly was a wealth of information.

He told the dwarf of the invention of gunpowder and steam engines that brought about the Industrial Revolution, and then the discovery of flight. Then how technology continued to advance until the First World War where planes and tanks were used in combat along with submarines. Which led into the Second World War and even more technological advances, like radar.

The jarl asked many questions and was very interested in how guns and explosives worked. He was surprised to learn that towns no longer used walls to defend themselves. Ted tried to explain that guns and missiles could destroy walls easily, but Baldor insisted that walls could be improved to stop even a bomb.

Liz would like to see what the dwarf thought of that idea after he sees an actual bomb go off. She chuckled to herself at the idea of the dwarf building a huge wall and having it blown to bits before his eyes. Silly dwarf.

Ted started talking about the political situations and ongoing tensions, but he saw that the jarl was not interested in such things, so he went back to technology and war.

The trip dragged on as they crawled through the miles and Ted kept talking. Over an hour slipped by until Ted's story finally came to an end. Just in time too, as they were getting close to town.

"And that is the History of Humanity According to Ted," Ted said proudly.

"Very nice, Ted," Jack said. "Now, shut up. I think I heard something out there."

Silence fell as everyone went on alert, trying to hear whatever Jack had heard. Several tense minutes passed before Jack relaxed. "False alarm."

They retraced their steps from earlier that day and crossed the overpass and got back onto the road leading to the center of town where the National Guard had their barricades set up. Liz hoped they were still there.

Tension grew the closer they got. What would they find? Was the town still standing? Was anyone still alive?

Eventually, they realized that most of the smoke was gone. Liz thought that was a good thing. If the smoke was gone that means places weren't on fire anymore.

Or, perhaps, there was nothing left to burn.

Liz banished those dark thoughts and tried to think positive. It was difficult for her after everything that had happened so far. She had seen innocent people murdered by creatures out of nightmares and still had no idea how or why any of it was happening. Perhaps it was the End of the World.

Liz laughed at herself. End of the World indeed! She had survived Y2K, the Mayan Apocalypse, two Raptures, and countless other supposed "End Times" and she was still here.

The truck came around the final bend down the hill into the center of town and they came upon their first barricade. Liz breathed a sigh of relief when she saw that the guardsmen were still there.

Jack waved to the soldiers as they approached and Liz noticed the young guardsmen's eyes grow wide when they saw the medieval army stomping along behind the truck.

When they pulled up to the barricade, Jack asked to speak with Lieutenant Bowman immediately. The guardsmen wisely didn't argue and they opened a section of barricade just wide enough for the truck to squeeze through. The young guardsmen stood in amazement as the dwarf army marched by.

It was a short trip through downtown to Grice Gun Shop where the National Guard command post was still located. It did look different, however.

There were a great many tents and rolls of camouflage netting hanging between the buildings. It looked like a small city had sprung up right in the middle of the street. Men and women in army uniforms ran about on various tasks while truckloads of supplies came and went. It was a flurry of activity that reminded Liz of a beehive.

The bustle slowed as Liz and her friends drove in followed by the mass of dwarves. People stopped what they were doing and stared at the strange sight.

Liz was afraid the dwarves would take exception to being stared at, but when she looked back she saw that the dwarves were completely ignoring the humans around them. They stomped in with a stoic menace about them.

She was glad of that.

The last thing she wanted was to have a fight erupt between the humans and dwarves. Neither side could afford that.

When they had gotten as close as they could, Darrell stopped the truck and everyone got out.

"What now?" Baldor rumbled, as he glared at the people staring at him.

"Now," Mike said, as he jumped down, "we go find the lieutenant and see what the situation is. Have your dwarves stay where they are until we know where we are going."

"Aye," the jarl agreed, and stomped over to the line of dwarves and passed the order along to the head of the column. He then came back to the group.

"Done."

Just then, a man came out of the camouflaged tent city and upon seeing Mike and the others he headed over to them. As he got closer, Liz saw that it was Sergeant Leah.

"I didn't think we would be seeing you again," the sergeant said, as he approached. "Who are *they*?" he asked, as he stared suspiciously at the dwarf army that stretched around the block and out of sight.

Jack laughed. "I didn't think we would be seeing you again either. And these," Jack motioned behind him, "are dwarves."

The sergeant's eyes bulged. "Dwarves?" He nearly choked on the word.

Mike let out an exasperated sigh. "Are you telling me after all the crazy shit that has happened you are still surprised?"

"Well..." Sergeant Leah stammered, then quickly recovered himself. "Are they friendlies?" he asked suspiciously.

Baldor stormed forward, huge muscles flexing. "Depends who's askin,'" he growled.

Mike stepped forward quickly. "Sergeant, this is Jarl Baldor Deathkettle, leader of these dwarves."

The jarl puffed up his massive chest. "Clan Hardhelm be ready fer battle, Lord," he said, with a slight nod of his large tattooed head.

Sergeant Leah returned the nod. "We appreciate any help you can give us. Now, please follow me. Lieutenant Bowman will want to see you immediately."

"Someone go fetch Lord Aurvang," Baldor rumbled. "He will need ter know what we face at once."

"I'll go," Emily said, and hurried off.

There was a tense silence as they waited for Emily to return. The minutes seemed to drag on until finally Emily returned with the armored bulk of Lord Aurvang close behind.

Everyone followed the sergeant as he made his way back through the shelters.

Those tents sprawled out farther than Liz had imagined. There were tents of all sizes and shapes. Some were obviously military in origin, while others looked like they were nothing more than an average camping tent. They packed the roads making it seem like they were traveling through a maze. After several blocks, they came upon a huge camouflaged tent with two guards posted outside. After speaking to the guards, Sergeant Leah quickly entered and the others followed.

Inside was filled with tables and boards covered in maps and charts. Pictures of different types of creatures were scattered around with multi-colored arrows and symbols scribbled on the maps. Liz guessed each color represented a different monster and where they had been spotted.

The sheer number of colors and markings on the maps were terrifying. Before Liz could get a close look at any of the details, she noticed the men huddled in the far end of the tent.

Lieutenant Bowman was hunched over a large map while several other soldiers were pointing at different spots and arguing.

Sergeant Leah cleared his throat and the men around the table each looked up. When Lieutenant Bowman saw the sergeant and the others, he quickly stood up and ordered the soldiers around him to leave.

When the soldiers were gone, Sergeant Leah brought everyone over to the lieutenant and they filled in around his map-covered table.

"Boy, I'm glad to see you guys again," the lieutenant began, with relief evident in his voice. "So, you warned the plant?"

"Yes, sir," Jack answered.

Emily snorted. "We did more than that."

Lieutenant Bowman's one eyebrow rose questioningly.

"The reports of an army out there were correct lieutenant," Mike said. "Turns out there were goblins and kobolds out there. Luckily, they fought each other first and gave us some time to get ready. In the end, the goblins won… there must have been thousands of them out there, sir."

"Thousands?" Lieutenant Bowman's surprise was plain. "How did you survive?"

"We were saved by an army of dwarves," Liz answered. She looked over at Baldor and the lieutenant followed her gaze.

Lieutenant Bowman didn't look surprised in the least to see a pair of dwarves standing before him. "So, the reports are true then," he said, as he studied the dwarves.

The lieutenant held out his hand to Lord Aurvang, correctly assuming who was in charge. "A pleasure to meet you. I am Lieutenant Bowman of the United States National Guard and currently commander of the Clearfield defenses on this side of the river."

The dwarf lord clasped the lieutenant's forearm. "Greetings lieutenant. I be Lord Aurvang Twinpeaks o' the Keepbuilder Clan. And this be Jarl Baldor Deathkettle o' the Hardhelm Clan," Baldor nodded to the lieutenant.

"How many dwarves do you have with you?" Bowman asked.

"Near two thousand," Baldor replied.

"Two thousand!" Bowman said. "I have heard reports of small groups of beings calling themselves dwarves, but I didn't quite believe it until now, and no group of them has been reported over fifty."

Bowman gave a deep sigh. "I have a great many questions for you jarl, but right now I have more pressing matters to attend to. You all have arrived just in time. We are preparing to push back across the river."

Lord Aurvang grunted. "What be on the other side?"

The lieutenant looked a little embarrassed. "We don't really know. Only a few of the scouts we sent over have come back and the ones that did all reported something different." Bowman rubbed his eyes wearily. "Some reported goblins, others saw kobolds, one even saw some large lizard-like creatures."

"Lizard-like?" Baldor scratched his beard thoughtfully. "Be they tall and slender with a leathery crest running down their backs?"

Shocked, Bowman nodded. "Actually, yes. How did you know?"

Baldor groaned at the news. "Because they come from the same place that I do," the jarl replied. "Those be troglodytes. And they be far more dangerous than any smelly gob or kobold."

"And why is that?" Bowman asked.

"Gobs and kobolds both be dangerous simply because o' their sheer numbers and savage nature. They reproduce like a plague and act like rabid dogs. Sometimes they are cunning, and a few can wield magic. But very few o' them have any real intelligence," Baldor explained. "Troglodytes on the other hand be, as a whole, far more intelligent. Luckily, there be also far less o' them than gobs or kobolds. However, what they don't be in numbers they make up fer in cunning and magic."

"Troglodytes, eh?" Ted muttered, as he stroked his beard absently. "They sound like the creatures that I fought around my house."

"Then ye be lucky ter be alive," Lord Aurvang rumbled to Ted before addressing the lieutenant. "How long do ye think it will take ter clear the rest o' yer village?"

Bowman shrugged. "To be completely honest, I have no idea. I can't say for sure what will be waiting for us over there."

The dwarf lord snorted. "Then I suggest ye retreat ter behind yer walls and await the dawn. Gobs n' kobolds prefer the night. With only little more than an hour o' daylight left it be suicide ter hunt them in the dark."

A look of defeat crossed the lieutenant's face. "I'm afraid we have no walls to retreat to."

"What?!" Baldor nearly choked. "No walls?!" He sputtered in shock. "I had heard that ye no longer used walls, but I didn't believe it. How do ye expect ter protect yerselves without walls?"

Without waiting for an answer, he rounded on Ted. "When ye said ye didn't need walls anymore I thought ye were joking! This is unacceptable. We can no mount a proper defense without walls!" Baldor fumed.

The dwarf lord shot the jarl an icy glare.

"Now," Lord Aurvang rounded on Lieutenant Bowman, "explain your plan."

Liz could tell the lieutenant didn't like being ordered around, but after a moment he bent back over his map and began.

"We are here." Bowman pointed to a spot on the map before him. "We have barricades on all the roads on this side of the river. But we are spread thin. Any decent sized assault will probably break through. So my staff and I have decided our best option is not to wait for them to attack us, but for us to move across the river and make it to the garrison at the Armory."

"I thought there wasn't any contact with the Armory?" Jack asked.

"There isn't," Bowman replied, "but while you were gone we were able to briefly establish radio contact with the Armory. At last communication, they had gathered other survivors and were just barely holding out against some of these… troglodytes. That was over two hours ago."

Bowman clenched his fists in frustration. "They could all be dead by now," he growled.

"Exactly," Lord Aurvang rumbled. "They all could be dead. And with only an hour or so o' daylight left it be suicide ter run out there and look for 'em."

"That's what I said," Baldor muttered, as Lord Aurvang continued. "The gobs will surround ye and tear yer forces apart. And if they don't, the kobolds or troglodytes will." The dwarf lord stared hard at the lieutenant. "We should stay here and wait till morning."

The lieutenant scowled, obviously not happy, but he suddenly relaxed and let out a long breath and he seemed to deflate before them. "Fine," he sighed, defeated. "We will wait until first light, then we march."

Lord Aurvang nodded as if he expected that the whole time. The two commanders then set about planning the town's night defenses. It was decided that many of the jarl's dwarves would be split up into groups to bolster each of the barricades. The remainder would patrol the streets and a few were tasked with scouting across the river. By the time all the plans were set, darkness had fallen.

The dwarf leaders went about organizing their forces while Mike, Liz and the others went back to the pub and grabbed some much-needed food.

They returned some time later with a few to-go boxes to find the last dwarves being sent out to their positions.

As the last dwarves marched off, Mike and the others approached Lord Aurvang and Jarl Baldor. Mike held out the to-go boxes to the dwarves.

"What be this?" Lord Aurvang asked, as he took the plastic box in his large hands and eyed it suspiciously.

Emily laughed. "It's food, silly."

Lord Aurvang scowled at her then sniffed the box.

"No, no, no," Liz sighed. "There is food *in* the box." She reached over and opened the lid for the dwarf lord. "See?"

Lord Aurvang snorted.

Baldor opened his box and took out the hamburger that was inside. He sniffed it experimentally then with a shrug of his massive shoulders he stuffed it into his mouth and took a huge bite. He chewed it for a moment then his eyes grew wide. "Odin's Beard!" he exclaimed, as bits of food flew out of his mouth. Not waiting to swallow he took another bite.

Lord Aurvang followed suit and tried his own burger. He had much the same reaction, and suddenly both hamburgers were gone and the dwarves were picking crumbs out of their beards.

"What *was* that?" Baldor breathed reverently.

"It's called a hamburger," Liz answered.

"Hamburger," Lord Aurvang tried the word and smiled. "I like hamburgers."

Baldor nodded his agreement and everyone laughed.

"I'm glad you like it," Mike said. "It is one of my favorites. Although you can't beat a good pizza."

"Pizza?" Baldor asked.

"Oh, you haven't lived until you have had a Scotto's pizza," Mike chuckled. "When this is all over, I'll get you one."

Baldor nodded. "If it be anything like this hamburger, then I look forward ter it."

"But now we must return ter yer commander," Lord Aurvang rumbled.

They made their way back through all the tents and were ushered into Lieutenant Bowman's command tent.

"Our forces are arrayed as planned," Lord Aurvang announced without preamble.

"Very good," Bowman answered, without looking up from his table.

Emily yawned. "I'm exhausted," she said, and stretched like a cat.

"Me too," Liz added, and everyone nodded their agreement.

Lieutenant Bowman looked up from his table. "I am sorry. I completely forgot," he said, as he pulled out another paper from the pile before him.

He studied the page for a moment then looked up. "I'm sorry, but all the buildings are in use. But Bob's down the street is in charge of giving out sleeping bags and tents for those that need them." He motioned to the door. "Go. Get some rest. You did well today and we have a busy day tomorrow."

"Works for me," Darrell said easily.

Liz could tell when they were dismissed, so she made her way out of the tent and everyone else followed except for the two dwarves, who remained with the lieutenant.

The friends made their way down the street to Bob's Army & Navy store and were given a sleeping bag and small tent each. Then they walked back and set up their tents a short distance from all the others that crowded the street.

"What we need is a fire," Darrell noted, as he sat down on the curb next to his finished tent.

"I think there have been enough fires for one day," Emily said, and then sat herself down next to Mike.

Liz couldn't argue with that, but she did agree with Darrell. Staying in a tent made her want at least a small fire.

"What *I* want to know," Ted said, "is why we can't stay in some of these buildings." He motioned up and down the street. "It is silly that we have to stay in a tent when there are perfectly good structures right here."

"It's because they are all in use," Mike answered.

"So, the good lieutenant says," Ted grumbled.

Mike chuckled. "Just look around."

Everyone did.

Liz wasn't sure what Mike was getting at. The street looked normal to her.

"See how there are lights on in every window?" Mike said. "All the people that made it here are packed into all the remaining buildings inside the National Guard's safe zone."

Jack yawned. "That's all well and good, but I'm too pooped to party."

"Agreed," Emily sighed. "How about we just get some sleep and worry about this tomorrow?"

Everyone finished setting up their tents and wearily crawled in.

Liz was glad. She couldn't remember ever being this tired before. Everything ached. She laid down and closed her eyes.

It had been a long, crazy day.

CHAPTER 22

Mike was abruptly awakened by the sounds of gunshots and screaming.

It was pitch black and he couldn't see anything inside his tent. He shot up and rummaged around for his armor, and quickly strapped on his battered breastplate and pulled on his sword belt. Grabbing his shotgun, Mike unzipped the tent and rushed out.

Bleary eyed, Mike stumbled out onto the street and searched for the source of the commotion. Armed civilians and soldiers rushed everywhere.

Mike bent over Liz's tent, but when he opened it he found it empty. Panic filled him. Where was she? Mike moved to Jack's tent and discovered he was also missing. A furious search turned up no one. Where was everybody?

Suddenly, Lord Aurvang came clanking around the corner with his massive rune covered battle-axe in hand and several of his guards following close behind.

"What's going on?" Mike shouted.

"What do ye think be goin' on?" Lord Aurvang growled. "We be under attack!"

The dwarf lord didn't slow down and charged past Mike, toward the nearby Nichols Street Bridge.

Mike growled under his breath. He knew they were under attack. He wasn't stupid after all. But since the dwarf lord wasn't going to give any more information, Mike decided to follow.

If there was one thing he knew about the dwarf was that he wanted to be in the center of the action, and that was right where Mike wanted to be, too. So, Mike hurried after the heavily armed dwarves.

With Mike's longer legs it didn't take him long to catch up. Once he did, Mike slowed down to keep pace.

They came out of the street and saw the bridge.

Black shapes darted about, obscured by darkness as they swarmed over the bridge. So far, the defenders had managed to keep the creatures away, but as Mike approached, several of the shapes ran under one of the few working streetlights on this side of the bridge, and he saw black fur and long hairless tails.

Ratmen!

They darted about trying to avoid the lights and scrambled towards the barricades as the guardsmen fired into them. Many of the large rodents were cut down, but a few managed to avoid the barrage and scramble over the makeshift wall. Those ratmen that survived the firestorm were quickly and efficiently slain by a line of dwarves.

It was hard to tell just how many of the creatures there were. Their dark fur and armor blended into the darkness across the river and with many of the lights not working there were numerous shadows from which to hide.

Mike began to sprint once he saw the battle and he quickly outpaced the dwarves with his long strides. He was almost there when a huge surge of ratmen leapt over the barricade and forced their way through the thin dwarf line.

One of the guardsmen fired into a group as it sprang at one of his comrades, but he didn't see the other beast that came flying at him. The ratman crashed into him and bore the guardsmen to the ground, clawing and biting.

Mike couldn't use his shotgun for fear of hitting the soldier, so as he ran, he reversed his grip and held the cold barrel. With a few quick steps, Mike reached the struggling pair and swung the gun around like a baseball bat. The blow cracked the creature squarely in the side of the head and the ratman flew off the soldier to lay quite motionless nearby.

THE SHEARING

The guardsman slowly climbed to his feet and Mike saw many scratches all over his face and neck, but none of them seemed very serious. Suddenly, two ratmen sprang over the barricade and dove at them.

The guardsman pulled up his rifle and blew both of the beasts out of the air to fall dead at their feet.

The bodies hadn't stopped twitching before more ratmen appeared over the barricade. Mike and the soldier fired into them as they came, but soon Mike was out of shells.

Dropping his shotgun, he pulled out his new mace with his right hand and his notched sword in his left. Then with a wild yell, he charged into the ratmen as the soldier behind him continued firing at those coming over the wall.

Mike spun wildly as he parried with his sword and struck with his mace. He looked like a tornado as he whirled around slicing and bashing anything that came too close.

But he could not keep up the momentum forever. As he started to slow, he had to stop attacking and focus on defending. Claws and daggers stabbed at him from every angle and soon he was being forced backwards.

More ratmen poured over the walls and the defenders were slowly pushed back. Mike wondered where they all came from. There were just too many.

The human and dwarf defenders were almost off the bridge when Lord Aurvang and his guard slammed into the line of ratmen.

Roaring battle cries, the mountain dwarves hewed happily into the furry beasts with wild abandon. The ratmens' claws and daggers couldn't find any openings in the heavy dwarf armor, and soon the surviving ratmen began to flee.

It was like watching a wave part around a large rock. The ratmen ran around Lord Aurvang and his guard to attack the men and hill dwarves on either side.

Mike still fought wildly with the ratmen, but the dwarves had slowed down their advance and he was able to strike back. One ratmen fell to his sword, with a blade through its neck, while another was blasted off its feet by the power of the ancient dwarf mace.

Frustrated, the mountain dwarves roared challenges that went unanswered. Wherever they moved to, the ratmen parted around them. Those ratmen that were too slow were brutally cut down.

A sharp command from Lord Aurvang broke the formation apart and the mountain dwarves spread out in a thin line across the bridge. Mike saw the ratmen pause as if trying to decide what to do. Their delay gave the defenders time to slay the last creatures nearby. The hill dwarves filled in the line between their mountain cousins and the human defenders quickly began reloading.

The ratmen packed together and filled the width of the bridge, and their numbers were lost to the darkness on the other side.

The two sides faced each other.

Not one to turn down a good fight, Mike joined the line of dwarves.

****

The smoking, brass casing hit the ground as Liz slammed the bolt home. With a deep breath, she pulled the trigger and another smoking casing rang against the pavement.

Liz stood on the road behind a line of cars facing the Market Street Bridge with several other people armed with high-powered rifles.

Scads of ratmen were climbing all over the large steel trusses of the bridge, trying to make it across to drop down onto the human and dwarf defenders on the other side.

The first attack had come as the ratmen had tried to rush across the bridge and overwhelm the few guards. Luckily, this bridge was well lit and they were spotted before they had made it half way across the bridge.

Liz had awoken when she heard the first shots from the guardsmen that opened fire on the sneaking beasts. Emily and Ted had joined her as she followed the sounds of fighting and they had arrived just as the first ratmen reached the barricades on this side of the river. The guards had almost been overrun, but dwarf reinforcements arrived and stopped the furry advance. Soon, people like Liz that had heard the commotion joined in the defense.

The combined forces quickly pushed the ratmen back across the bridge. They attempted to cross one more time before they realized the bridge was a shooting gallery. The heaps of hairy bodies that lay sprawled all over the bridge were evidence of their repeated failure.

After all the slaughter, Liz couldn't believe that there were still ratmen left to attack and they just kept coming.

She had been worried when the first creature had jumped into the river and tried to swim across. But her fears were soon put to rest as the high, fast moving water quickly swept them away.

The ratmen were persistent though. Once they realized that crossing the illuminated bridge wasn't going to work, they then decided to climb the steel beams that made the trusses for the bridge and cross that way. It was challenging to shoot them from between the beams, but so far the ratmen had only made it half way across.

Liz fired again and a small furry body fell into the rushing water.

Suddenly, there was squealing and movement across the bridge. Liz couldn't see much in the darkness, but something was happening.

She watched intently as large shapes began to move toward the bridge and into the light. At first she thought it was another type of monster come to join the ratmen. But as they got closer, she realized those large shapes were also ratmen - massive, armored ratmen.

These monstrosities stood a foot taller than their smaller counterparts and they were covered snout to tail in a thick, dark metal. Their weapons were also of a much higher quality than the usual rusty blade most ratmen carried.

The ratmen beasts roared and suddenly charged across the bridge. Everyone turned their attention to the monsters and began unloading into them.

Many of the brutes fell to the barrage, but not as many as Liz would have liked. Soon, they were half way across the bridge and coming fast. The defenders poured more fire into them and many more fell. But then it began to rain ratmen.

They had forgotten about the smaller ratmen in the beams!

The ratmen began dropping onto the guardsmen and clawing wildly at them. With their sudden appearance, the rate of fire quickly declined and the monstrous ratmen came nearly unchallenged.

With throaty battle cries, the dwarves launched themselves into the melee with wild abandon. Axes split furry skulls and claws tore at exposed throats as battle was joined.

The dwarves quickly cut down the ratmen that had jumped down, but then the huge armored ones crashed into the barricades and tore through them.

Pieces of wood and metal flew everywhere as the giant rats smashed their way to the defenders. The smaller ratmen continued to drop down from above as the large ratmen collided with the dwarves in close combat.

The human guardsmen were shouting orders and it quickly became apparent to Liz that they were falling back. How could they retreat and leave the dwarves all alone?! They would be torn apart!

Liz's fears eased when she saw that the soldiers were not retreating, just pulling back enough that they could continue to fire at the ratmen in the trusses.

The dwarves met the monstrous ratmen while the humans fired at the smaller ones above and together they halted the monsters' advance.

But not for long.

More and more ratmen joined the fray and the humans couldn't shoot them down fast enough. And the dwarves were hard pressed by their larger, better-armored enemies.

They were being slowly pushed off the bridge and no matter how many ratmen Liz killed, there were always more to take their place.

One guardsman was knocked down by a falling ratman and his rifle flew out of his hands. A young woman nearby saw him go down and yelled for him, but she was too far away. "NO!" she shouted, and reached out her hand.

Suddenly, a cone of force shot out from the woman and blasted into the ratman, sending it and several of its companions flying off the bridge.

The young woman rushed over to the guardsman and helped him up. The two quickly embraced, but then more ratmen fell down around them. The guardsman pulled out a pistol and quickly killed several of them before they could recover from their falls. The young woman unleashed another barrage of concussive force that sent ratmen bodies flying.

The constant assault from in front and above was taking its toll. The dwarves were being pushed back and the humans couldn't get organized enough to mount a significant volley.

All of a sudden, a hole broke open in the line and giant armored ratmen poured through. Liz fired rapidly to try and stem the tide, but there were just too many of them. The dwarves went into a full retreat as they tried to not get surrounded. Those humans not fighting off their own creatures fired into the giant ratmen to try and give the dwarves time to escape.

It was chaos as man and dwarf and ratman all battled each other in a violent swirl of death. The ratmen came on and pushed across the last barricade and were almost over the bridge.

Liz continued firing helplessly into the mass, but it was futile.

They had lost.

****

Mike's heart raced as the two sides eyed each other. Suddenly, the sea of ratmen surged forward. Grunts of surprise came from the dwarf line, as they must have expected the ratmen to retreat from their unified defense.

The dwarves roared battle cries and charged. The two sides crashed together. The sound was like many bodies being hit by cars, and the result was similar. The dwarves were the cars and they steamrolled over the ratmen.

It wasn't a battle so much as it was a rout. Axes and hammers rose and fell methodically as the dwarves pressed forward like some giant machine. The ratmen were cut down by the score as the dwarves pushed them back over the barricades and beyond. Within moments the fighting was over as the ratmen broke apart and fled into the night.

The dwarves stopped at the other end of the bridge and watched as the last ratmen faded away into the darkness.

"That'll teach those filthy ratmen ter challenge the Sons o' Durinn!" Lord Aurvang roared and raised his bloody rune axe high above his head.

A chorus of cheers erupted from the dwarf line in agreement.

The dwarves then made their way back across the bridge, throwing the corpses of ratmen over the sides and picking up the bodies of their fallen. Once back across, they began rebuilding the barricades. The humans took up positions across the bridge and kept watch as the dwarves worked. They were almost done when Lord Aurvang stopped and looked up. Several others followed suit. Lord Aurvang sniffed the air and one dwarf put his ear to the ground.

"They be comin' back," Lord Aurvang rumbled.

The other dwarf picked himself off the ground. "Indeed Lord. Sounds like three-hunnerd er so."

Lord Aurvang nodded and motioned for the dwarves to form up around him.

Mike wasn't overly worried about the reported numbers. The dwarves and humans could hold off that many ratmen on the bridge easily. He was curious how the dwarf had guessed the number of enemies just by listening to the ground.

Just then, Mike spotted a tall man coming through the crowd.

"Ted!" Mike waved to him. "Where the hell have you been?"

"Around," Ted replied vaguely.

Mike noticed fresh blood on his armor, but it didn't appear to be Ted's so he let it go. "You are just in time for another bridge battle," Mike grinned evilly.

"Ugh," Ted groaned. "I hate bridge battles."

"I know," Mike laughed. "But this one is for real. And now you have magic."

Ted's eyes sparkled mischievously. "That I do."

Mike and Ted made their way through the line of dwarves that spanned the bridge again. They found Lord Aurvang in the center. When he saw Ted, he gave him a slight nod. "Greetings, wizard."

Ted returned the nod and the two of them took places on either side of the dwarf lord. Several minutes went by with no sign of the ratmen. Mike looked over the dwarf's head and Ted shrugged.

A few more minutes passed by with no sign of the ratmen. Mike was about to leave when he heard the unmistakable clank of armor.

Soon, Mike could see movement in the darkness.

About time, he thought. All this waiting was driving him crazy. It would be good to finish off these little rats.

A sudden muttering erupted from the dwarves.

Mike didn't know what they were talking about, but a minute later he knew. What emerged out of the darkness were not "little rats." They were enormous rats, and not just enormous, but also covered in thick armor.

Lord Aurvang snorted. "I be wonderin' when these cowards would show themselves."

"What are they?" Mike asked.

"Those be Clan Rats," Lord Aurvang grumbled. "They be the backbone o' the ratmen swarms. The little ones be Pack Rats and be only a threat if they get ye surrounded. These on the other hand..." he motioned to the massive ratmen, "be far more dangerous."

Mike didn't need the dwarf lord to tell him these guys were more dangerous. Just looking at them told him that.

The men and dwarves watched as the giant ratmen made a slow advance across the bridge. Halfway they stopped.

A ripple passed through the center of the line as two strange-looking ratmen emerged. One was an albino and very tall with pure white fur and glittering red eyes. It wore a dark robe that Mike guessed was blood red, but it was hard to tell in the dim light. A long, braided rope was tied around its waist. It carried a huge sword that looked too long to wield, but it carried it with an ease that spoke volumes. This was no ordinary ratman.

The other was much shorter with grey fur and extremely large ears. This one also wore a robe, but it looked to be a solid black. In one furry paw, it held a long staff that was topped with a claw that clutched a large angular, crystal.

The pair of odd ratmen strode a few paces away from the others and stopped.

There was a long silence before one of Lord Aurvang's dwarves strode forward. He was taller than most and Mike guessed he might have even reached Mike's shoulders. His heavy armor was polished until in shined, and although it wasn't as ornate as Lord Aurvang's, there were still a great many runes carved into it. Instead of a helm this dwarf wore a simple hood over his head that disappeared into his armor. He had a large, braided black beard with silver clasps in it, and in his hands he carried the largest hammer Mike had ever seen. It was huge and silver with intricate runes covering its head and ran down the shaft.

The dwarf faced the pair of ratmen alone.

"What is going on?" Mike asked, confused.

"A challenge," Lord Aurvang replied. "The monk and sorcerer will face me guardian, Jerrik Ironforge."

So, this was the guardian. Mike eyed the lone dwarf with new curiosity, and he was looking forward to seeing what this guardian could do. But against two opponents it didn't seem like a fair fight.

"I will help him," Mike said, and began to step forward.

"No." Lord Aurvang grabbed Mike's arm and held him there. "Watch."

Against his better judgment, Mike decided to listen to the dwarf lord.

The dwarf guardian and the pair of ratmen came within a few paces of each other and stopped.

The short, grey ratman sorcerer seemed to laugh in a high-pitched chittering. "Flee or die, worms," it squealed in a reedy voice.

Mike was in shock. *It could speak*! The horrible rat-creatures could actually talk! Somehow this made them even more horrifying.

The Guardian Jerrik let out a deep booming laugh. "We be no afraid o' a few puny little mice."

The entire army of ratmen hissed in anger at the insult as the dwarves laughed. The ratmonk screeched in rage and abruptly sprang at Jerrik. It moved almost too fast for the eye to follow. The massive sword whistled through the air straight for the dwarf's exposed head.

Mike thought that was the end of the guardian, but at the last second Jerrik brought his massive hammer up and caught the blade mere inches from his face. He punched out with a massive armored fist and sent the ratmonk flying backward. Before he could recover, the sorcerer barked a spell and a bolt of dark energy shot out of his staff and streaked toward the dwarf.

Almost casually, Jerrik threw up a hand and the dark bolt collided into a bluish wall of energy and dissipated. The sorcerer barked another spell and several twisting ropes of red lightning flew toward the guardian.

He swung his hammer and connected with one of the lightning ropes. There was a brilliant flash and the rope disappeared. Jerrik spun away as the other two lashed out at him. One struck the ground and left a smoking gouge in the pavement.

Just then, the monk charged back in, huge blade whirling. Jerrik parried the monk's lightning quick attacks, but then one of the red ropes coiled itself around one of the dwarf's wrists.

With his arm held in place, the monk came on furiously. Jerrik was then forced to wield his immense war hammer with only one hand. He parried each of the attacks, then punched out with the top of the hammer and forced the monk backwards.

Another lightning rope streaked towards him, but Jerrik twisted away and with one motion swung his hammer at the rope holding his arm. There was another brilliant flash and that rope disappeared as well.

Before the flash had faded, the monk was thrusting at Jerrik's exposed back. The final lightning rope also whipped out toward him. At the last possible moment, the guardian dove away, and the monk and lightning rope collided. The rope wound itself around the monk and began to squeeze.

Jerrik then charged the sorcerer.

The sorcerer screeched and a massive wall of twisting flame-like energy appeared before it that Jerrik could not cross.

Mike thought that was the end of the monk, but he soon realized that the monk didn't seem to be hurt by the rope.

The monk twisted around in the grip of the rope. Then there was a crackling sound and the rope burst apart in a shower of sparks. With smoke rising from its red robe, the monk rushed forward.

The guardian abandoned the wall of flames and turned to meet the charging monk. Jerrik made a few motions with his free hand then charged the monk.

The giant great sword met the immense war hammer in a clash of metal.

But the sorcerer wasn't done.

With the guardian distracted once again, it conjured large, magical darts and flung them at the dwarf's exposed back.

Mike shouted a warning, but it was too late. Jerrik didn't turn around. The darts struck.

They hit a golden bubble inches away from the dwarf and evaporated. The sorcerer screamed in anger, and summoned several more spells and hurled them at the guardian. All had the same effect. They struck the golden wall just before reaching him.

While the sorcerer fired spell after spell at the dwarf, Jerrik and the monk traded blows faster than the eye could follow. They struck and parried in a deadly dance.

One of the monk's attacks scraped off Jerrik's armor in a shower of sparks.

Seeing the same force that was defeating its spells wasn't stopping the monk's blade, the sorcerer got an idea. It held its staff with both paws in the air and invoked an enchantment.

The crystal on the top of the staff began to writhe and twist in the claw. It elongated and billowed out until it formed a large red-ish blade.

Now armed, the sorcerer charged the dwarf's back.

Jerrik saw him coming and spun away so that both ratmen were in front of him. "Come and get me ye ugly little mice," he taunted.

As one, the ratmen screamed and charged, weapons whirling.

Jerrik laughed and jumped forward.

His war hammer was a blur as he parried both ratmen's attacks. Mike couldn't believe how fast he was. That hammer must weigh a ton, but Jerrik wielded it with ease.

The ratmonk reversed his next swing at the last second and the dwarf overcompensated and lost his balance. Seeing an opening, the monk stabbed forward. But Jerrik wasn't there. He took his momentum and rolled around the monk and came up behind him.

Before the monk could recover, Jerrik brought his massive war hammer down on the back of its head. There was a sickening crunch as the ratmonk collapsed.

The sorcerer stood there in shock as Jerrik extracted his hammer and turned to face him.

"Yer next, squeaky," Jerrik said, and tapped his hammer in the palm of his hand.

The sorcerer back peddled furiously, and began waving its arms around madly and barking things that Mike didn't understand.

A glow began to form before it that started to twist and grow.

Jerrik held up his hammer before him with both hands and whispered something into the hammer's head.

Then he pulled the hammer back and with a mighty heave threw the war hammer. It sped through the air and with a peal of thunder it struck the sorcerer.

The ratman flew backwards and fell dead with a smoking hole where its chest used to be.

There was a stunned silence as Jerrik walked over and pulled his war hammer from the chest of the sorcerer. He raised the weapon above his head and the entire dwarf force bellowed a roaring cheer.

The ratmen stood motionless as if not sure what to do. Then one of them stepped forward and charged Jerrik's exposed back. Others followed and soon the entire army of ratmen was charging across the bridge.

"Oh, no you don't," Ted muttered, and stepped forward. He held out his hand and a ball of revolving liquid fire appeared. The ball grew until it was larger than a softball. Then, Ted shot out his arm and the ball of fire streaked out and struck the center of the charging ratmen.

There was a massive explosion that knocked dozens of them back and set many of them on fire.

The explosion was just too much after the deaths of their champions and they lost the last of their courage. The ratmen stopped their charge and fled.

Ted dusted his hands off and nodded happily to himself. "That's better."

****

The ratmen were streaming over the abandoned barricades and Liz couldn't do anything about it. There were just too many of them. She stayed behind and kept firing until long after the rest of the defenders had fled.

Pockets of men and dwarves still fought to hold off the horde, but every moment more and more ratmen crossed the bridge.

Liz could just hear a soft rumbling in the distance behind her, but she didn't think anything of it at first. She was too busy trying to slow the tide. But then, the rumbling grew so loud that even she noticed it.

She glanced back to see a black truck barreling down the road. Darrell came roaring toward her with Emily and Jack in the back. The truck looked different somehow, but it took Liz a moment to figure out what it was. Then she got it; there was a snowplow attached to the front.

Where had they found a plow?

Liz shook her head in disbelief. Leave it to those two goons to acquire a snowplow when the town is under attack.

The truck careened down the street and Emily waved as they blew past Liz and roared ahead. Liz could just hear the sound of music blasting from the truck as it flew by.

The machine gun roared to life as Jack began firing at the groups of ratmen that had already crossed the bridge. Instead of slowing down, Darrell punched it and the truck shot forward straight into the ratmen army.

Bodies flew everywhere as the truck plowed its way through the center of the mass and kept going.

It was then that Liz realized it was getting lighter. She could see across the river now and the end of the ratmen. They weren't numberless after all. Really, there was just enough to fill the bridge and that was it.

Darrell's rampage had broken their charge and the ratmen were now trying to get out of the way of the truck. There was a line of bodies strewn about across the bridge after the truck's passing. Once across the bridge and through the ratmen forces, Darrell cut the wheel hard and then roared back toward the bridge.

Somehow Emily managed to keep her balance in the bouncing truck bed and fired arrow after arrow into the ratmen.

The ratmen were now confused. They didn't know whether to continue across the bridge to town or to go after Darrell.

Jack answered the question for them as he brought Ol' Bertha to bear. The machine gun tore through them even with their heavy armor.

Deciding to go after easier prey, the ratmen continued across the bridge and left the truck alone.

Liz saw the ratmen's charge was broken and the defenders needed to capitalize on it, but there was nobody around to push back.

"Forward!" Liz shouted, and waved her rifle in the air, trying to draw people's attention. "They are weak! Attack!" she yelled as loud as she could.

A group of dwarves nearby killed the last ratmen they were fighting, and ran over to Liz and began yelling with her. Other groups pulled together and soon there was a large force surrounding Liz.

They began a slow march forward with dwarves in the front and those humans still with guns behind. Together the rag-tag force pushed its way to the bridge. Liz fired until she was out of bullets then grabbed the axe from a fallen dwarf as they marched by. She knew she wouldn't be much use with an axe, but the defenders needed someone to rally around and it looked like she was it.

"Forward!" she shouted.

More humans and dwarves suddenly arrived from all directions, and soon they joined together and were pushing the ratmen back. With Jack unloading his machine gun on the ratmen from the other side and Darrell running over any that tried to escape, the ratmen were trapped.

They continued to push forward, pressing the ratmen together on the bridge and rather than face either side, the ratmen began jumping into the river. Liz thought some of the smaller, unarmored ones might make it, but the heavy armored ones wouldn't be so lucky. And even if they did make it across, there were people positioned the whole length of the river just in case anything tried to swim across.

Suddenly, the last of the surviving ratmen jumped off the bridge and just like that the battle was over as the first rays of sunlight peaked out over the hills and shown down on the battleground.

In the distance, Liz heard a few gunshots as those creatures that had made it across were being picked off.

CHAPTER 23

Although they had achieved victory, the cost had been high. Dozens had died during the night. But it could have been worse, Mike thought, much worse.

Mike wiped sweat from his brow as he finished dragging a ratman corpse onto the ever-growing pile. Jack dumped a furry corpse next to it. "This is my favorite part," he said, and kicked one of the small, mutilated bodies.

Mike grunted and heaved the corpse up a little higher. *Man, these things were heavy!* "I would rather do this than be one of them."

"I can't argue with that," Ted added from across the pile.

Mike, Ted, and Jack were working near the Market Street Bridge, close to where Liz had rallied the defenders a few hours earlier, while Emily and Liz had gone to help the wounded.

Under the direction of the dwarves, the three of them along with many others were piling all the ratmen corpses to be burned. The dwarves said the ratmen would quickly rot and spread disease if left alone.

Mike didn't relish the thought of dying of some horrible ratman disease after surviving battling the ratmen themselves.

It took over an hour, but eventually two large piles of corpses were finished. One large pile was next to either bridge that had been attacked in the night.

The bodies of the fallen dwarves and humans were separated and taken away.

When the town and bridges were again clear of any dead, the dwarves set fire to the corpse piles and tall columns of inky, black smoke spiraled into the clear morning sky.

The three of them watched as more corpses caught fire and the black smoke billowed ever thicker. Several minutes went by with the only sound being the crackling of the fire, and the hissing and popping of burning flesh.

Suddenly, someone shouted. "Movement! Across the river!"

Everyone spun around and readied their weapons.

"Where?" a guardsman shouted back.

"Coming down Coal Hill Road," came the reply. "I see movement between the trees, headed our way."

"To yer positions!" one of the dwarves boomed, and suddenly everyone was moving. Men and dwarves clamored about and gathered around the repaired barricades.

It all happened remarkably quickly. Mike was impressed.

Once everyone was in position, they waited.

A tense silence filled the air as the men and dwarves watched the tree line several blocks away on the far side of the river, waiting for whatever it was to emerge.

Mike saw movement between the trees.

It was hard to make out at this distance, but it was definitely moving faster than any creature he had yet seen.

The defenders gripped their weapons tighter as everyone saw the distant movement.

The blurring movement sped down the hill until it arrived at the base of the hill where the tree line ended and it appeared. But it wasn't any type of creature anyone expected.

It was an armored vehicle! And behind it was a line of army transport trucks.

They sped down the hill and turned at the intersection to drive directly toward the defenders. As they got closer, Mike counted over a dozen transport trucks before losing sight of them back to the trees.

The armored vehicle reached the bridge and slowed down as it crossed the battle-scarred terrain. Although the truck must belong to friends, the men and dwarves didn't budge from their positions. They had seen too much to trust anything.

The armored vehicle came to a stop right before the first barricade. The heavy door opened and a man in the uniform of the National Guard stepped out.

The guardsmen behind the barricades lowered their weapons and let out a cheer. Confused, Mike looked over to Jack for an answer.

"That is Captain DiSantos," Jack said.

Mike was surprised. The captain wasn't what he had been expecting.

Captain DiSantos was maybe slightly taller than average with a barrel chest and short, black hair with grey at the temples. His uniform was stained and wrinkled.

Looking him over, Mike wasn't sure what he had been expecting. Perhaps some tough looking drill sergeant type man that could chew nails.

This guy looked like somebody who Mike would drink with… and probably have had to drive home.

"*That's* the captain?" Mike asked incredulous.

"Don't let his appearance fool you," Jack answered. "He's one tough S.O.B."

Mike snorted.

For Jack to say that about somebody was quite rare. Perhaps there was more to this man than met the eye.

The captain walked up to the line of dwarf warriors that stood blocking his path. "Who is in charge here?" he asked softly.

"I am," came the gruff reply, and Baldor stepped out from the line.

"Ah," DiSantos said, as he looked down at the tattooed dwarf before him. "Would you mind letting us in?" he asked politely.

The jarl seemed surprised by the gentleness of the request. But before he could answer, a tremor shook the ground. It grew in strength until paint and rust began to rain down from the trusses above.

"Make way!" Baldor shouted, as he began pushing men and dwarves out of his way. Captain DiSantos ran back to his armored vehicle and quickly started forward. Within moments a path was made for the captain and his trucks.

As the transports drove by, Mike saw that each was packed with people. Raggedy men, women, and children huddled together in the cramped spaces. He was surprised to discover there were even a few dwarves seated among the humans.

As they hurried across the bridge, the earth began to shake even more violently. Mike was afraid they wouldn't make it across. This was the worst quake in some time. They were almost constant, but so minor that Mike almost forgot they were happening.

The convoy of military transport trucks was halfway across when the quake suddenly stopped.

Mike breathed a sigh of relief.

****

Liz slowly stood as the quake faded away. With the exertion of the day before followed by a long night with little sleep, she was exhausted.

She wearily ran a hand through her grimy, matted hair. Liz sighed as she looked down at herself. She was covered in sweat, dirt, and blood. Luckily, none of the blood was hers, but she couldn't say the same for the poor souls around her though.

Liz stood in a giant, green army tent that was a makeshift hospital. There were virtually no medical supplies left, only small bandages and a few thin blankets. Emily had gone out to search for more medical supplies from the surrounding buildings, although the hope of finding anything substantial was slim.

After the battle with the ratmen, they had come down here to help the wounded and when they arrived, Liz had discovered that she wasn't the only person with a healing ability.

Besides herself, Liz discovered five other people that could heal. But not all abilities were created equal it seemed. A local priest, Father Joe, a very old woman that Liz hadn't met yet and herself all seemed to be able to heal anything they came across. But there were others who could not.

One such person was a young woman named Mary. She could cure a sick person no matter the illness, or if a wound was infected she could clear it up. However, she couldn't actually heal the wound itself. Her powers seemed limited to infections.

Then there was a young nurse named Peggy and a middle-aged man named Mark that had the opposite skill. They could heal a wound, but couldn't stop an infection. It was discovered that if a wound was infected, it couldn't be healed until the infection was gone. So, the three of them worked as a team; Mary would go around first and cure any illnesses, then Peggy and Mark would take turns healing any physical wounds they may have.

Two dwarf clerics from Clan Hardhelm, that Liz was surprised to discover were female, supervised the care and healing of the patients. They were the first female dwarves that she had seen. Liz had expected them to be ugly like in many of Mike's games, but instead they were surprisingly pretty, although they looked nearly as tough as the male dwarves.

The two hill dwarf clerics were in turn being supervised by Lord Aurvang's personal cleric, the War Priest Vestri Skullsplitter.

He was short, even for a dwarf, and it was hard to tell under all his armor but Liz guessed he was just as well built as Mike, although for a dwarf that was almost scrawny. He wasn't nearly as impressive looking as most of the dwarves, but he wasn't as grumpy either.

Liz had spoken to him several times and instantly liked him. His frizzy, black beard and baldhead made him look almost comical. He was friendly and funny, and Liz discovered that he was an excellent healer that was eager to teach.

He explained to her that there were three types of healing. One came from the healers themselves. The healer could channel their own life force and use it to reinforce the life of another. But this was dangerous and could result in the death of the healer if they gave too much of themselves.

The second was by magic. This was very rare among the dwarves as they were naturally resistant to magic. They could capture magic and use it in their runes, but to actually use magic like Ted did was extremely rare.

The third was through prayer. Vestri explained that each dwarf cleric was a disciple of one of the gods. The two largest and most powerful groups were the Church of Odin, to which Vestri belonged, and the Church of Frigg.

By praying, one would call upon the gods' powers to heal others. But this took great faith and concentration on the part of the healer and it wasn't easy. Being a conduit for a god's power was taxing. Liz could attest to that. After each healing, she was more and more exhausted. Now she knew why.

Liz also learned that healers couldn't heal themselves.

She was glad for that piece of information.

Liz was relieved when Vestri didn't ask her who she prayed to. She didn't know how the war priest would react to her not praying to one of the dwarf's gods. But listening to the dwarf had shaken her faith a bit.

She had always believed in one God, but now other non-humans stood before her and worshiped other gods that answered their prayers. What did that mean for her? Was her faith wrong? Was there more than one God? If there was more than one that meant her God couldn't be the only one as she had been led to believe. How much of what she believed was wrong?

Or was there another explanation?

Just then, the earthquake had struck and Liz was forced to concentrate on staying upright.

"All right there, lass?" Vestri asked, concern evident in his voice.

"Fine." Liz lied as exhaustion threatened to overwhelm her.

"Odin's Arse yer fine." Vestri grumbled, as he stomped over to her. Reaching up nearly on his toes, the scrawny dwarf gently put one large hand on the side of Liz's face. Then her skin shivered with goose bumps as a cool sensation passed through her. It only lasted a moment, but as it faded she felt alert and refreshed.

Vestri dropped his hand from her face and smiled up at her. "Better?"

"Much," Liz sighed gratefully. "Thank you."

"Bah!" Vestri waved his hand dismissively and turned away. "It be what I do."

Liz followed the war priest as he made his way carefully through the injured. At each person, he would bend over, put his hand on them and whisper something, and then the wounds they had would heal.

Liz watched him do this several times before she asked, "Don't you get tired?"

Vestri chuckled as he bent over another patient. "O' course. But I be been doing this fer a long time. Ye could say I be a greater tolerance fer it."

He moved to another prone form and with his back still to Liz he said, "Actually, I am impressed that ye lasted as long as ye did. Ye did a great many healings fer only just discovering yer gift yesterday."

He moved on to the next patient. Vestri glanced back at Liz; there was a mischievous twinkle in his eyes. "If someone had told me yesterday that the most talented healer I would see in centuries was going ter be a human, I would have thought they be mad and tried ter heal 'em!" he chuckled to himself and turned back to his ministrations.

That last bit caught Liz's attention. "You can heal madness?"

"O' course," The war priest answered casually, without turning around.

Liz was stunned. *You could heal madness!*

She had been studying psychology in the hope of helping those with mental illnesses. But now she was told that it could be healed! This was a dream come true!

"Is it difficult to heal?" Liz asked excitedly.

"Aye. Only True Healers can cure madness. Or those with a special gift," Vestri said, as he stood and brushed his hands together like a job well done, which Liz then realized was indeed the case.

Looking around she saw that everyone in the tent had been taken care of. Most of them had left, while a few remained comfortably sleeping.

"And *you* can heal madness?" Liz pressed.

"Aye, lass. I be one o' the few," Vestri answered.

"Can you teach me?" Liz tried not to sound like she was begging.

Vestri though a moment and Liz was afraid he was going to say no, but then he answered. "Aye. I can try. But it be the most difficult and dangerous thing ter heal and there be no guarantee that ye will be able ter." His tone became serious. "It be takin' years ter master."

Liz wasn't afraid of a challenge. She welcomed it.

"Is there anything that can't be healed?" She asked.

"Aye," came the grim reply. "Death."

****

Mike, Ted, and Jack followed the convoy of survivors until they reached the command tent. Wanting to know what was going on, they made their way to the tent. Surprisingly, the guards didn't try to stop them. Apparently, they had been in and out so often that the guards assumed they were allowed in. Mike wasn't going to complain.

Inside they found Captain DiSantos, Lieutenant Bowman, and Sergeant Leah on one side of the table with Lord Aurvang and Baldor on the other.

They were arguing.

"We cannot stay here," Sergeant Leah growled.

"And where would you have us go?" Bowman growled back.

"DuBois," Leah replied instantly. "Or State College. Either of them would be better than sitting here and waiting for death."

"We don't know if either o' those places fared any better than here," Lord Aurvang said. "They could just as easily be overrun."

"Oh, so you want to stay here and die too?" Leah snapped.

"Dwarves do no retreat from the likes o' gobs," Lord Aurvang rumbled menacingly.

"We are not going to die here, Sergeant," Captain DiSantos said. "And neither are we leaving. This is our home and no amount of monsters are going to take it away from us." The captain stared directly at the sergeant. "We stay."

After a moment, Leah lowered his eyes. "Yes, sir."

"Good," DiSantos said. "Now, where do we stand?"

Lieutenant Bowman answered, "With your added troops, we now have around three hundred soldiers, fifty police officers, and somewhere around three or four thousand civilians with I'd say better than two thirds of them armed. Eight Humvees, a few dozen transport trucks, and the two Stryker armored vehicles you brought, sir."

"Get everyone armed with something," DiSantos said. "I don't care if it's a shovel. Nobody goes without some kind of weapon." The captain then turned to the dwarves.

Lord Aurvang spoke first. "There be fifteen mountain dwarves o' me personal guard under me command."

"And with me be near two thousand hill dwarves ready fer battle," Baldor stated proudly.

Captain DiSantos leaned heavily on the table. "So, we have a total of about fifty-five hundred troops. Along with four vehicle-mounted machine guns."

"Um, sir?" Sergeant Leah stepped forward. "Our machine guns are about out of ammunition, and the assault by the ratmen this morning used up most of our supplies. Unless you brought a lot back with you, the machine guns won't last long."

"Damn," the captain muttered. "The Stryker's are about out of ammunition as well. That is part of the reason we came here. We were hoping to resupply. But if you don't have any extra…Damn."

"Surely over five thousand warriors will be enough ter defeat whatever force o' greenskin rabble is headed our way," Baldor said.

"Rabble," DiSantos laughed, without any humor in it. "I would not call what is headed for us 'rabble'. My scouts report that thousands of creatures are headed this way, with more joining every second." He pointed to a spot just on the edge of the map. "They are here and moving right at us. I guess they will reach the other side of the river by nightfall. They will rest for the night and attack in the morning. If we…"

"No!" Lord Aurvang interrupted. "The gobs will no wait fer dawn. Like the ratmen, gobs prefer the night and will attack as soon as it be full dark."

"Damn," DiSantos groaned again. "That gives us less than twelve hours to prepare."

"That's not the worst of it," Sergeant Leah almost whispered.

"What are you talking about?" DiSantos asked.

"It isn't just goblins, sir." Leah swallowed nervously. "Our scouts also reported that there are larger monsters with them."

"What kind o' monsters?" Lord Aurvang rumbled.

"Huge monsters," Leah stammered. "Shaped like goblins, but appearing to be over six feet tall."

"Hobs," Baldor and Lord Aurvang said in unison.

"There were also some even larger creatures that had greenish-grey skin and large tusks."

Lord Aurvang and Baldor exchanged looks. "Trolls?" Baldor asked.

"That would be me guess," Lord Aurvang agreed.

The captain looked at the two dwarves. "What do we do about hobs and trolls?"

Baldor laughed. "We kill 'em o' course!"

Captain DiSantos' eyes narrowed. "And how do you propose we do that?"

It was Lord Aurvang's turn to laugh. He motioned to Mike, Ted, and Jack. "Gather 'round humans. I have a plan."

CHAPTER 24

Sun filtered through the trees as Emily sat alone on the grass, watching the river rush by, and her bow and arrows lay on the ground near at hand. She was seated in the small park between the Market Street and Nichols Street Bridges.

She had searched for supplies for over an hour, but like she had suspected, all medical supplies had already been gathered up. So, she had wandered around until she came across this small park. Needing some time to think, Emily took the opportunity to get some quality alone time.

A cool breeze ruffled her skirt and made her pull her camo shirt tighter around herself. Her hair streamed out behind her in a tumble of black ringlets and her green eyes sparkled.

"Hello, Darrell," Emily said with a smile.

There was a long moment of silence.

"How'd ya know I was there?" Darrell asked, as he appeared from behind a tree.

Emily laughed. "I could hear you breathing."

"Seriously?" Darrell plopped down beside her.

Emily grinned impishly at him, but said nothing.

Darrell fidgeted until he found a comfortable spot. "So whatcha doin'?"

"Thinking."

"Bout what?"

"Everything…" Emily said airily." And nothing."

"Sounds… fun."

"It is." Emily looked over at Darrell. "I'm surprised you still have legs."

"What?"

Emily chuckled. "Seems like every time I see you you're driving that stupid truck."

"It isn't a stupid truck," Darrell said. "It is a very nice truck." Then he looked confused. "What does that have to with my legs?"

"Ugh!" Emily threw her head back and groaned. "It was a joke Darrell. When you drive the truck we can't see your legs."

"Oh. Gotcha," Darrell muttered, but he still looked confused. Emily didn't press the matter.

Another breeze made her shiver. "Don't you ever want to get out and do something?"

"Nah. I'm good." Darrell shrugged. "I can't fight with a sword like Mike, and I ain't got no magic like Ted or that nifty healing power like Liz." He explained, "Only things I'm good at are shootin' guns and driving trucks." He looked sad and added, "An' I ain't got to do no shootin' yet either."

"So, you like carrying everyone around?"

Darrell brightened up. "Yeah, I guess so."

Emily laughed. "I guess that makes you our steed."

A lopsided grin appeared on Darrell's face. "Yeah, I guess it does." He puffed up his chest, raised his chin, and put his fists on his hips in a seated superhero pose. "Darrell the Steed. Barer of the Heroes of Clearfield. Part man. Part horse." He winked at the last and gently elbowed Emily. "And you know what part is a horse right?" he winked again.

Emily rolled her eyes. "In your dreams, Darrell."

Darrell laughed and relaxed into the grass. For the next several minutes they sat in an easy silence until Emily asked, "Have you seen the others recently?"

"Hmm… Mike, Ted, 'n Jack have been in the general's tent for over an hour. And I think Liz is still in the sick tent."

"It isn't a general's tent. There are no generals here."

Darrell shrugged easily. "Whatever."

After a moment, he looked at her and asked. "So, why did you sit in the one spot with the tall grass?"

"What are you talking about?" Emily asked, as she looked down.

She was surprised to see that what Darrell had said was true. The grass around her was over twice as tall as it was everywhere else. How did she not notice that before? Perhaps it was because the grass wasn't like that when she sat down. She had a suspicion of what was going on, but she wasn't about to tell Darrell.

"The longer grass feels nicer to sit on." That wasn't completely a lie.

Darrell eyed her suspiciously for a second, then he shrugged and went back to watching the water rush by.

After that, they lapsed into silence. It was peaceful for a while until Darrell started to fidget.

Emily gave an exasperated sigh. "Don't you have something to do?"

"Like what?"

"I dunno. Like clean a gun or put spikes on the truck or something."

Darrell's eyes lit up. "Spikes on the truck! That's a great idea!" He shot up from the ground. "I better hurry before the baddies get here!" And with that he took off, running back into town.

Emily watched him go and shook her head sadly. "If I had known it was going to be that easy…" she muttered to herself with a small smile.

Finally alone, she stretched out a hand over some short grass and waited.

Nothing happened.

Disappointed, she set her hand down.

Suddenly, the grass around her hand began to grow. They turned a darker, healthier green and doubled in size. Then several small buds sprouted up from between her fingers and blossomed into beautiful flowers. She put her other hand next to the first and that grass also burst to life under her touch.

****

Mike blinked in the sudden sunlight as he, Jack, and Ted finally came out of the command tent. It was a beautiful day and Mike hoped it wouldn't be their last.

As they had planned the defense of Clearfield, a dwarf scout arrived and gave an updated account of the enemy troops. What he had to report wasn't encouraging.

Based on the area that the monsters covered, the scout guessed that their numbers were over ten thousand. Which made their force at least twice the size of the defenders, and that number included the children and elderly that wouldn't be much help in the upcoming fight.

But Lord Aurvang proved to be a brilliant strategist just as Baldor had said. He quickly outlined a battle plan that would give them the best chances of victory. With the dwarves' knowledge of the monsters they faced and human technology, a plan had formed that everyone agreed on. Now, it was time to start implementing that plan.

Mike, Ted, and Jack split up and began searching every building and bringing everyone out to gather at the courthouse in the center of town. Soldiers joined in and then the people that they had recruited, and the announcement spread quickly.

The dwarves believed that guns alone wouldn't hold off the enemy and that everyone needed to know how to use an axe or some other weapon. Captain DiSantos agreed, and so they gathered everyone together and distributed weapons; guns from the National Guard Armory and Grice Gun Shop, as well as axes, spears, and shields from the dwarves.

Then they broke everyone into groups, and the dwarves and human soldiers began training them in the use of their weapons.

Only having one day to learn to fight wasn't ideal, but it was all they had.

It would have to be enough.

Luckily, this was central Pennsylvania where there were more deer than people. The vast majority of citizens that had survived so far had at least one gun and knew how to use it. And using an axe wasn't unheard of either, but chopping wood was quite different from trying to chop a goblin without getting yourself skewered.

Mike walked down the street headed for another building to search, when he saw the dwarf Jerrik Ironforge heading for him. So, Mike stopped and waited for him to catch up.

"Ye must come with me," the Guardian said without preamble, and then turned and stormed off.

"Sure, I'll go," Mike muttered to himself, before following the dwarf.

Jerrik led him to an abandoned street with buildings that had been far too damaged for anyone to take refuge in. He stopped in the middle of the abandoned street and waited as Mike caught up.

"Lord Aurvang tells me ye have Thor's Blessing," Jerrik snorted. "He wishes me ter train ye, but I don't believe a human can have such powers as they come from the mighty Thor himself. However, a request from Lord Aurvang is not one ye can ignore, so here we be." He motioned to the battered surroundings. "First, I must see that ye do indeed possess the Blessing," the guardian grinned wickedly. "The test will be simple; I will try to hit ye and ye must summon a shield ter block it."

Mike shook his head. "But I don't know how to do that. Things only happen by accident. I can't control it."

The dwarf's grin darkened. "Then ye are in fer a bad time."

Jerrik stood right in front of Mike and held up a large armored fist. "Ready?"

"I don't thi…" Mike began, but then Jerrik punched out and Mike flew backwards and landed hard on his back, the air knocked out of him.

"That wasn't fair," Mike wheezed, as he climbed to his feet.

"Battle isn't fair," the dwarf growled, and lunged forward, fists flying.

But this time, Mike was ready. The blow hadn't hurt as much as it appeared, and when Jerrik struck, he hit nothing but air.

The dwarf growled in frustration and pursued. But on each swing Mike danced away.

Luckily, Jerrik's reach was short and it was easy for Mike to use his longer legs and arms to propel himself away from the dwarf's attacks.

"Stand still ye great oaf!" Jerrik shouted, and charged Mike.

Mike dove away and laughed. "Now, why would I do that?" He back peddled quickly as the angry dwarf swung again. "I have no desire to let you beat me senseless."

Jerrik abruptly stopped his assault and stared at Mike. "Perhaps I been goin' about this wrong," he mused. Then he snapped his fingers. "I be havin' just the thing." He reached behind his back and brought forward his massive war hammer. "This should be enough motivation." He waved the war hammer dangerously. "Prepare yerself."

Before Mike could protest, Jerrik lunged, swinging the hammer so fast that Mike didn't have time to move. Mike threw up his arm just before the hammer struck.

There was a deafening boom as the hammer collided with a glittering blue shield.

Jerrik's mouth hung open in amazement. "It be true then," he breathed. "A human Blessed by Thor…"

"Told ya," Mike grumbled. He stepped away from the dwarf and the shield faded away.

"Now, how do I do that without almost dying first?" Mike asked.

Quickly recovering from his shock, Jerrik sat down and placed his war hammer on the ground in front of him. "Sit."

Mike wasn't sure what to think of the sudden change in attitude, but he figured it didn't hurt to listen so he sat facing the dwarf.

Jerrik closed his eyes. "In the First Age, the Great God Thor blessed certain individuals with the power ter protect themselves and others. These individuals came together and formed the Blessed Order o' Guardians. Since our inception, we guardians been instrumental in the protection and stability o' the Empire."

Mike shifted uncomfortably. "Does everyone with this ability join your Order?"

"No." Jerrik opened his eyes. "Not everyone with the gift joins the Order. Although most do," he added.

"Being a guardian is not merely an ability, but a state o' mind," the dwarf explained. "Ye must be one with yer powers and let 'em flow through ye in order ter unleash 'em." Jerrik made a fist. "Right now the power be inside ye, but ye are a fist, no lettin' anythin' escape. But ye must open yer hand and allow the power ter flow." Jerrik opened his hand and a soft blue glow appeared above his open palm. "The Blessings that come from the gods are the closest thing we dwarves have ter any true magic." Jerrik lowered his large hand, but the blue glow remained floating before him. "Try it."

Mike closed his eyes and took a deep breath. He held out his fist, palm up and concentrated.

Nothing happened.

"Feel the power inside ye," Jerrik instructed. "Release it."

Mike was no stranger to meditation. He used it often with his mixed martial arts training. But this was different. He withdrew into himself and searched for this hidden power. He didn't know what he was looking for, but hoped he would recognize it when he saw it.

Several moments passed and Mike didn't feel anything.

Then he saw it.

On the edge of his consciousness was a feeling that he couldn't describe. Concentrating on it, Mike imagined it as a bright light tucked away into a dark corner. He approached the sphere of light and picked it up. The orb pulsed with trapped energy and seemed to Mike to be begging for release. He wasn't sure how or why, but Mike took the orb in his mind and with a thought he tore it apart.

Light burst everywhere and filled Mike's entire being.

He was being swallowed by it, consumed in a blue fire.

His mind burned.

He wanted to scream, but he couldn't.

His soul was on fire! *NO!* Mike shouted to himself. *Control it!*

The inferno of fire and light threatened to sweep him away. Mike brought all his will to bear and slowly anchored his mind. Once locked in place, the power flowed and raged around him, but now he was the eye of the storm. It could not touch him.

Mike was in control as he let the power flow through him.

Jerrik watched intently as Mike's hand slowly opened. A sudden sparkling blue light appeared and revolved in the air above Mike's open hand.

THE SHEARING

****

"Another," Ted said, as he sat his empty glass down on the dark wood of the bar. Next to him, Jack drained his glass and set it by Ted's. "Me, too." Jack winked at the pretty girl working behind the bar.

Denny's Pub wasn't very busy right then. Mostly everyone in town was outside being quickly trained by the dwarves on how to not spear themselves. The only people in the pub were men and women that had the look of former soldiers.

With a shy smile at Jack, the serving girl refilled both glasses then moved off to help another patron farther down the bar.

"A great waste of time that is," Jack grumbled and took a long drink.

"A little training won't hurt anything," Ted replied.

"It would take weeks for them to be proficient enough with any of those weapons to be any threat," Jack continued. "Besides, if they work too hard they will just get tired and be even more useless come the fight."

"Normally, I would agree with you," Ted said. "But right now the people need confidence and something to take their minds off of what is coming. Learning how to swing an axe and thrust a spear is giving them both." Ted shrugged and took another swallow. "Who knows, maybe some of them will discover they have some ability."

Jack scowled at the mention of abilities, but Ted didn't notice and kept talking. "I was chatting with one old man who can shoot lighting from his walking stick. But when he tried without it, he couldn't even summon a spark. So I thought maybe it was the stick, but when I tried, I couldn't get it to do anything," Ted grumbled. "It's not fair. I can only summon fire."

Jack snorted and took another drink. "Oh, boo hoo. Poor me, I can only throw fire. That's not cool enough. I want lightning, too!" Jack mocked. "Where are my powers huh? Why can't I throw some fireballs or something? *That's* not fair," Jack grumbled into his cup.

"Maybe you just haven't found your ability yet," Ted offered.

Jack sighed. "Or maybe I don't have one." He drained his glass and motioned for a refill. "So, maybe you're doing it wrong."

"What?" Ted asked.

"The casting," Jack answered. "Maybe you are doing it wrong."

Ted's eyes narrowed dangerously. "And how did you come up with that?"

"Well..." Jack paused as he stared into his new drink. "Who's to say that creating lightning is the same as making fire?" he shrugged. "Or maybe you aren't thinking about it in the right way." Jack took a long drink then leaned toward Ted. "How *do* you make fire anyways?"

Ted swirled his beer around distractedly. "That is hard to explain..."

"Don't give me any of that crap," Jack growled. "You just don't want me to learn how to use magic so you won't have any competition."

"Competition?!" Ted laughed. "In your dreams! You couldn't compete with me!"

"Prove it then, o' mighty wizard," Jack mocked.

"Fine," Ted laughed and finished his drink. "I will tell you the secret." He set the empty glass down and leaned over conspiratorially. Jack leaned in excitedly. Keeping his voice low Ted whispered, "I think about it and then will it to happen."

Jack stared at him, confused. "What?" he asked in disbelief.

Ted sat back, shrugged and then grinned.

"That's it?" Jack nearly yelled. "You just think it and it happens?"

"Well..." Ted kept grinning evilly. "It is a bit more complicated than that. There is a tingly feeling and then... poof. Fire."

Jack smiled back and shook his head ruefully. "You're a sonofabitch, you know that?" He pushed himself away from the bar and made a fist. "Now, it's my turn."

"This outta be good," Ted laughed, and slid himself farther down the bar, away from Jack.

Jack stared hard at his fist for a while then suddenly opened his hand.

Nothing happened.

He tried again.

Still nothing.

He left his hand open and concentrated, staring at his open palm for several minutes, but there wasn't even a hint of a spark.

Disgusted, Jack sat back with a sigh. "So much for that."

"You have to really believe it," Ted said. "You can't just wish fire to appear. You must see the fire. Feel the heat on your hand and smell the smoke."

"Okay, okay," Jack muttered, and held out his hand again.

After several more minutes still nothing happened.

"Fine." Jack threw his arms up. "I give up."

Ted laughed again. "Maybe you weren't thinking about it right." Ted froze. "Wait…not thinking about it right… I've got it!" Ted snapped his fingers and a bright flash of electricity sparked between them.

Ted and Jack both jumped at the sudden crackle of light.

"How did you do that?" Jack asked.

"I was thinking about it all wrong," Ted said excitedly. "I was trying to make *lightning*. I should have been thinking about *electricity*."

Ted held out his open hand to illustrate his point. He spread his fingers. Suddenly, electricity arched between his fingers and danced across his hand.

Jack groaned. "Are you kidding me?"

****

The day wore on and the town continued its preparation for the approaching army. More barricades were constructed out of abandoned vehicles and building rubble, secondary positions were established, and debris was arranged to impede the advance of enemy troops, should they make it past the bridges.

The one good thing from all the destruction was the availability of lumber and other building materials, even if most of it was broken. It was all put to use. Doors and windows were boarded up and reinforced from both the inside and outside. Those deemed too young or too old to fight were protected as best they could, by being locked away in the topmost floors of the largest buildings in the center of town.

The dwarves handed out every spare weapon and piece of armor they had, and both the gun shop and the military surplus store gave out every gun and round of ammunition they had left.

The humans continued their rapid training under the careful supervision of the dwarves with brief periods of rest in between. Mike, Ted, and a handful of other members of the SCA in Clearfield also aided in the training of medieval weaponry and basic tactics.

Those individuals that had discovered they had some magical ability were pulled aside and organized separately. The preparations were going well and some of the soldiers even showed a few curious dwarves how to use shotguns.

Civilian tension grew as the hours passed by, but the mood of the dwarves only seemed to improve. This growing cheerfulness lessened the people's anxiety somewhat. When one of the guardsmen asked a dwarf why they were so happy, the dwarf replied that they were looking forward to a glorious death. This answer did little to improve morale.

The hour was getting late and the town was a flurry of activity as men and dwarves finished their final preparations. People armed with hunting rifles lined the roofs and windows of the buildings. Liz took her place on one such roof facing the Nichols Street Bridge.

Below Liz in the center of the bridge, the dwarves formed ranks four rows deep spanning the width of the bridge behind the first barricade. Behind them, three rows of National Guardsmen readied their weapons.

A similar formation was mirrored on the Market Street Bridge and further upstream at the Hyde Bridge.

Emily and other small groups of civilians and dwarves patrolled the streets and the hills behind the town in case of a surprise attack. No creatures had been spotted on the east side of the river, but it never hurt to be safe.

Jack had gone in search of Darrell and his truck, which seemed to have disappeared.

The sun was going down and had just touched the tips of the distant hills when a sudden horn blast filled the air.

The dwarves were sounding the alarm.

The monsters were here!

CHAPTER 25

Mike ran down the street as darkness fell. He made his way past the soldiers stationed at the various barricades along the Market Street Bridge and arrived at the first barricade in the center of the bridge where he found Ted waiting for him.

"What took you so long?" Ted asked, as Mike came up next to him.

Mike held up his left arm that was encased in armor and a large dwarven shield was strapped to it. "Had to pick up some new goodies from the smith."

"Very nice," Ted said, as he looked at the armor. "But where is the other one?

"Didn't have time to make it," Mike said, as he self-consciously looked down at his bare right arm. "Ah, well," he shrugged, "some is better than none."

"Are you two done?" Captain DiSantos growled. "Or do you want to compare shoes next?"

Mike and Ted managed to look embarrassed as they slunk past the captain and his guardsmen to join the ranks of dwarves at the front of the line.

The dwarves were positioned with several rows of spears in the front and those with axes and hammers behind. It was here they found Lord Aurvang and most of his bodyguard.

"Welcome, humans." Lord Aurvang greeted them cheerfully. "It be a good day fer a battle!"

"If you say so," Ted grunted in reply.

Mike looked around at the surrounding dwarves, but didn't see the guardian, Jerrik, anywhere. When Mike asked where he was, Lord Aurvang replied that he and the war priest were on the Nichols Street Bridge. Mike had been hoping to ask Jerrik a few more questions before the fighting started, but it looked like he would have to do without.

"So, now what?" Ted asked.

"We wait," Lord Aurvang answered.

And wait they did.

Hours passed as the defenders watched the monsters gather around the buildings on the far side of the river. As full darkness set in, there seemed to be no end to them; and still they waited.

The bridge had a few remaining lights, but beyond there was only darkness.

"What are they waiting for?" Mike asked impatiently.

As if on cue, there was a sudden shrill horn blast from across the river.

"You just had to say something, didn't you?" Ted grumbled.

Mike grinned wickedly as the first goblins charged onto the bridge out of the darkness.

"Down!" Captain DiSantos yelled from behind them.

As planned, Mike, Ted, and the dwarves all took a knee as the goblins ran toward them. The goblins ran even faster when they saw the dwarven line on its knees.

"Fire!" Captain Disantos shouted.

Gunfire erupted from the ranks of soldiers and carved into the rushing goblins. The tightly packed beasts were mowed down like wheat in a field. The creatures had no chance against such organized firepower.

It was a slaughter.

Within minutes the bridge was covered in goblin corpses.

Then, as quickly as it had started it was over. The last goblins fell and there was an eerie silence after all gunfire ceased.

"That was easy," Mike muttered. Then he noticed the sounds of gunfire in the distance. *The other bridges must still be under attack,* he thought. Hopefully, they beat back the goblins as easily as this bridge had.

"Yeah. Too easy," Ted agreed.

"That be a test," Lord Aurvang rumbled. "They be probin' our defenses." He shook his bearded head. "I did no expect this level o' cunning from the gobs," he admitted sourly.

Mike could hear the rustle and clank of the creatures milling about in the darkness, but they didn't attack.

"What are they waiting for?" Mike growled. He was eager to test his newfound powers and finish these monsters once and for all. The echoes of gunfire continued.

"Ter see if the other bridges fall," Lord Aurvang answered darkly.

****

Liz fired and another goblin disappeared from her scope in a puff of green mist. She looked up from her rifle for another target when she realized there were no more enemies.

She scanned riverbanks, half expecting the goblin forces to be spilling out of the river. She didn't really think it likely since those filthy ratmen hadn't been able to do it. But perhaps the goblins were better swimmers.

She watched for a long minute and when no goblins appeared she relaxed a bit. Maybe the monsters had given up already. She doubted it, but it was a nice thought.

Another horn blast split the air.

Wild shrieking erupted from the darkness across the river, and then with a sudden rush the goblins reemerged. But this time they were not alone.

Tall, slender, lizard-like creatures with spiny crests running down their backs and leather straps crisscrossing their bodies charged alongside the goblins.

Liz recognized them as the creatures that had attacked Ted at his house. Troglodytes, he called them. She didn't really care what they were called. Just so long as they died.

The guardsmen and civilians opened fire, and the charging monsters practically melted before them. *Yes.* Liz thought. *They died just as easily.*

Right before she leaned back into her scope, Liz saw one of the troglodytes in a dark robe wave his hand in a strange motion. Then it pointed a finger at the defenders and a sudden light blossomed from its fingertip. A ball of fire shot out straight toward the dwarf line.

Liz cried out in panic, but one of the dwarves calmly stepped forward and held out a hand like a crossing guard. She cringed as the fireball exploded. But to her amazement, the dwarf stood there unscathed with the guardian remains of a shimmering wall fading away before him.

So, this must be the guardian that Mike had spoken about. Liz hoped he had more shields ready because she doubted that was the only time he would need it.

The radio sitting next to her suddenly crackled to life. "Concentrate on the sorcerers!" the voice commanded. "Kill the casters!"

Liz quickly scanned the charging mass and found the sorcerer that had thrown the fireball. It was waving its scaly hand in the air again, but before it could finish the spell she pulled the trigger and the sorcerer's head disappeared and its lifeless body crumpled to the ground.

Suddenly, a bolt of greenish lightning shot out from the charging monsters and was blocked by the dwarf guardian.

Liz spotted a feathered goblin shaman. She pulled the trigger as three more spells flew from the screeching horde.

Below, the guardian blocked two of them, but the third erupted on the dwarves' shield wall.

More spells flew; burning fireballs, green lightning, and glowing darts of energy. Some were absorbed or blocked by the dwarf guardian, but more and more made it past him to strike the defenders behind.

Liz tried to find the casters, but it was difficult to spot them in the seething mass of creatures. A flash of red cloth suddenly appeared and she saw another sorcerer. It died with a hole in its scaly chest.

The dwarf line was taking a beating, but somehow it was still intact. Liz guessed the dwarves must have some kind of protection spells worked into their shields. There was no way a normal wooden shield could hold up to such a withering barrage, but they did.

Besides the guardian, Liz counted five other heavily armored dwarves of Lord Aurvang's clan spaced out along the dwarf line. She wondered if they had something to do with it.

More magical attacks streaked towards the dwarves and exploded along their shields, while the goblins and troglodytes continued their charge and were cut down by precision gunfire.

The radio continued to chatter away next to her as the different units gave orders and informed the others of what was happening. Liz ignored most of it, until she heard that the guardsmen would be running low on ammunition soon if the enemy wasn't slowing down.

Through her scope, Liz saw another sorcerer readying a spell.

She pulled her trigger.

****

Ted swore as a magical blast nearly knocked him off his feet. Quickly regaining his balance, Ted pointed at the offending sorcerer and a fireball of his own suddenly blossomed and shot toward the ugly troglodyte sorcerer.

The monsters had reached the defenders' line and were locked in a vicious melee with the sturdy dwarves as the humans behind them continued shooting into the creatures further back.

The sorcerer made a motion and the fireball hit an invisible wall. But Ted had expected it and before the fire dissipated he shot the sorcerer with his pistol.

It seemed that the enemy casters could only block one type of attack at a time and Ted quickly capitalized on it, using his spells and pistol to devastating effect.

Other people that had discovered they wielded some sort of power were also spread out along the line, adding their own abilities to the chaos.

Mike stood in the center of the bridge right behind the line of dwarf spears, blocking any magical attacks with summoned walls or force. But he couldn't protect the whole bridge and some spells made it past him to strike the defenders.

Lord Aurvang strode back and forth along the line bellowing orders over the noise of battle. He had initially been shocked that the goblins and troglodytes were fighting together, but he quickly recovered from his surprise and began redirecting the defense of the bridge to compensate for this unforeseen development.

Another explosion ripped into the dwarf line and the monsters surged ahead trying to break through. Ted threw up a wall of fire giving the dwarves enough time to recover before the monsters pressed in.

Spears stabbed as axes and hammers rose and fell. Explosions ripped through both sides as magic was cast about with wild abandon. Goblins screamed and dwarves roared as the battle raged.

A sudden surge by the monsters caused the dwarf line to bend dangerously inward. A moment later, an organized barrage from the human soldiers cut a swath through the monsters and with impressive organization the dwarves reformed their line. The green tide of monsters crashed back in, but their momentum had been lost.

Ted threw a crackling bolt of lightning into the swarm and was rewarded with the sound of screams as goblins and troglodytes were electrocuted.

"Hold the line boys!" Lord Aurvang bellowed to the dwarves, as he approached where Ted was fighting.

Just then, a strange warbling sound rang out from the darkness.

Lord Aurvang froze.

"It can no be," he breathed in disbelief.

Another warbling call rang out from the darkness across the bridge.

A crackling bolt of energy blasted a dwarf mere feet from Lord Aurvang, but he didn't even flinch. He was paralyzed as he stared into the blackness across the bridge.

"They can no stand each other," the dwarf lord muttered.

Ted was just about to ask what he was looking for when the goblins and troglodytes at the far end of the bridge suddenly scrambled away, and two giant shapes lumbered out of the night.

Tall and muscular with glossy, green skin, the lanky monsters towered over their companions. Large, yellow tusks jutted up from their lower jaws and large, pointed ears drooped from their relatively small heads. Their legs were short, but their arms were so long that their huge knuckles dragged along on the ground as they walked. They didn't wear anything but an animal skin loincloth and carried no weapons that Ted could see.

"Jungle trolls," Lord Aurvang groaned just barely loud enough for Ted to hear. "Impossible."

"Why is it impossible?" Ted shouted over the din of battle.

Lord Aurvang had a haunted look on his face when he turned to Ted. "Trolls be no fought alongside gobs and trogs in thousands o' years. No since…" the dwarf lord paled, "Odin's Beard."

The trolls strode onto the bridge and the soldiers opened fire. The trolls bellowed in rage as the bullets riddled their massive bodies, but they charged ahead, heedless of the gunfire or the creatures below them, crushing goblins and troglodytes alike under their massive feet.

The trolls' charge snapped Lord Aurvang out of his shock and he turned to Ted. "Wizard! Throw yer fire at 'em! They can regenerate from any wound but a burn. Only fire 'el kill 'em!"

Ted nodded and turned to face the charging behemoths. A spark appeared in his hand and a moment later he threw a large ball of liquid fire at the nearest troll just as it reached the barricade, and the first line of dwarves who were still locked in combat with the other creatures.

The fireball exploded on the troll's chest and it screamed in pain, but it didn't stop. Its chest still ablaze, the beast crashed through the barricade as if it were a pile of sticks, and then began swinging its massive arms about wildly, knocking dwarves away like they were children.

"Bring them down!" Captain DiSantos screamed from somewhere behind Ted.

The soldiers responded, and discarded their other targets and concentrated all their firepower on the troll. But the bullets seemed to have little effect, except to make them angrier.

With no gunfire raining down on them, the goblins and troglodytes pressed forward, seizing the advantage and straining the dwarf line.

The bullets had little to no effect, and as Ted watched, the bullets embedded in its skin were pushed out and the wounds began healing. The only place the bullets remained was the burned area on the troll's chest.

Ted holstered his pistol and picked up his poleaxe. He hoped the poleaxe would be a better weapon against such a monster, but he also hoped he wouldn't have to get close enough to use it.

The dwarves hacked and stabbed at the troll's legs with abandon. But no sooner did they strike, than the wounds began to heal.

"Use fire!" Lord Aurvang bellowed, as the second troll burst through the barricade and began to wreak havoc among the dwarves.

Ted concentrated and formed another fireball, but this one was larger than any he had ever made before and his head began to throb painfully. The orb revolved and grew in the air like a soccer ball of lava. Summoning every ounce of power he could, Ted made the spell as large as possible, and then when he thought he was going to burst, he released it.

The magma cannonball screamed through the air and sped toward the flailing troll. There was a deafening explosion as the molten ball erupted on the side of the troll's head and the bridge shook with the force of the blast.

There was a horrible shriek of pain as part of the troll's head exploded and the rest of its face began to melt. The troll fell to the ground, screaming, trying to hold its ruined face in its hands. One of the mountain dwarves stepped forward and using his thick war hammer, swiftly crushed the troll's skull, ending its misery.

But even with one of the huge beasts down, the goblins and troglodytes streamed through the gaps the trolls had made and the dwarves were hard pressed on every side.

"Fall back!" Lord Aurvang bellowed, as he hacked a goblin in two. "Second positions!"

The dwarves responded immediately and began an organized retreat as the soldiers provided cover fire.

The last troll barreled forward, furious at the loss of its companion, roaring in anger and throwing dwarves around like rag dolls. Ted tried to summon his magic, but he couldn't concentrate. The last spell had drained him. A few brave dwarves stayed behind to distract the troll while the others made their slow retreat.

Nearby, Mike fought several troglodytes at once, crushing one with his mace and parrying madly as the others stabbed at him. Ted wanted to help, but he couldn't get his body to respond. His mind was cloudy and slow.

Suddenly, a large hand grabbed ahold of his arm and roughly pulled him backwards. "Come on Wizard," Lord Aurvang growled. "Now be no the time ter stand about."

Ted spun to face the dwarf when a goblin lunged out of nowhere and stabbed at the dwarf lord's exposed back. Without thinking Ted thrust his poleaxe into the goblin's chest as Lord Aurvang continued to drag Ted away, heedless of the danger.

The defenders continued their organized retreat until they reached the second barricade where they reformed their lines as the human soldiers kept up a steady rate of fire on the monsters. Magic still exploded on both sides as the sorcerers and gifted humans continued to exchange spells to devastating effects.

The enraged troll casually crushed the last dwarf before it and then lumbered toward the newly formed line. The smaller monsters made way for the troll as it warbled its unsettling call.

Ted tried again to call the fire, but it still eluded him.

The troll reached the second barricade and easily crashed through it, tossing cars and rubble out of its way as if they were nothing. Dismayed, the dwarves attacked, trying to hamstring the beast, but having no success. The bullets from the soldiers were having little effect as well. A few small fireballs exploded on the huge beast's green skin from the gathered humans, but none of them had the same power as Ted's. The small blasts were only singeing the troll's thick skin.

Thinking fast, Ted remembered the old man that used his staff to channel his power. Perhaps Ted didn't need to summon fire directly; perhaps he could just catch something on fire. Concentrating, Ted focused on his poleaxe.

Slowly at first, the blade of the poleaxe began to glow cherry red and soon it looked as if someone had just taken it out of the forge. Sparks began to fly off of it and small flames flickered along the length of the blade.

Ted grinned evilly. *Yes*, he thought, *this will do nicely*.

One of Lord Aurvang's mountain dwarves charged the troll, wielding what looked like a heavy mining pick. The dwarf dodged a swipe from the troll and got behind the monster. Then with a mighty swing, he drove the pick behind the troll's knee.

The troll screamed in agony, and with a quick backhand sent the offending dwarf crashing into one of the bridge trusses, but the pick remained lodged behind its knee.

The dwarves surrounded the troll and desperately hacked at it from all sides.

Ted saw his chance and charged the wounded beast with his burning poleaxe held high. He lunged and with a mighty swing cleaved into the troll's exposed neck. Black blood fountained and hissed as it contacted the burning blade.

The troll thrashed wildly, but Ted quickly swung again and cleaved deeper into the thick neck. The troll clawed helplessly at his ruined neck. Ted drove the burning blade into the charred wound one more time and with a wet gurgle the troll collapsed.

"Reform the lines!" Lord Aurvang bellowed from beside Ted. "Push them back!"

With no trolls left to absorb the spells and gunfire, the goblins and troglodytes were quickly forced back as the unified defenders drove into them.

Suddenly, a chilling horn blast split the air.

It was unlike any sound Ted had ever heard. It chilled his blood and sent shivers down his spine. He looked questioningly at Lord Aurvang for an explanation and was shocked to see the dwarf Lord had gone pale as a ghost.

"Impossible..." Lord Aurvang whispered.

Ted noticed all the dwarves had the same reaction. They were frozen in stunned disbelief.

"What is it?" Ted asked nervously.

Lord Aurvang didn't answer.

The expression on many of the bearded faces was the closest thing to fear Ted had seen on a dwarf. Most dwarves seemed to relish the mere idea of battle and were eager to get into a fight. But now they were afraid, and anything that made a dwarf afraid should terrify humans.

Ted stared into the darkness across the river and saw movement. Large shapes formed out of the blackness and marched in organized lines into the faint light of the bridge.

Black and red armor glinted in the light, and a forest of spikes and horns arose from the dark heavy plate. Horned helmets with wide, segmented guards flowed into the armor.

At first Ted thought they were being attacked by an army of huge samurai that were wearing ugly, green, demonic masks, but then he realized the ugly, tusked visages were actually their faces!

Large, slightly curved swords were clenched in armored gauntlets and small banners waved from their backs as row after row of the huge warriors marched onto the bridge.

"Impossible…" Lord Aurvang breathed in disbelief. "They be extinct!"

"What are they?" Ted mumbled, but he was afraid he already knew the answer.

Lord Aurvang clenched his rune axe tighter and set his feet with grim determination.

"Orcs," the dwarf lord rumbled darkly.

Another chilling horn blast erupted from the darkness and the legion of orcs roared and charged, enormous katanas held high.

CHAPTER 26

The trees creaked in the wind as the sounds of battle echoed through the hills. In the wooded darkness in the hills above Clearfield, Emily crept through the trees, searching.

Below her, Clearfield was visible and the battles raging on two of the bridges were clear to see. Flashes from the soldiers' guns and streaks of destructive magic illuminated scenes of horror. Part of Emily was glad that she wasn't down there, but another part wished she were. It felt wrong to be so far away while her friends fought the monsters that threatened everyone.

A soft rustle and clank in the darkness ahead made Emily freeze. The sound continued and she crept forward. Through the trees she could see dozens of dark shapes trying to sneak through the brush.

So, it seemed that dwarf had been right and the monsters did send some of their warriors to launch a surprise attack from the rear.

Emily grinned wickedly to herself. The surprise would be on them. She had been sneaking through the woods since she could walk. These poor creatures didn't stand a chance.

She motioned with her hand behind her and after a moment a dozen dwarf scouts armed with heavy crossbows emerged from the gloom around her.

Emily was still surprised at how silent these dwarf scouts could move. As far as she had seen, most of their kind were loud and clumsy in the woods. But these were hunters, silent and deadly.

She pointed to the noisy monsters, and the dwarves nodded their understanding and silently faded back into the darkness.

Emily followed the creatures for several minutes until she thought the dwarves should have been in position. Then she quietly nocked an arrow and searched for the leader.

It didn't take her long to find the largest monster that was shoving the rest before it. Emily quickly crept forward to get as close as she could. The darkness could easily hide a branch and she didn't want anything messing up her shot.

Emily didn't make a sound as she moved over a carpet of leaves and sticks. When she got closer, she saw that the noisy creatures were goblins. The monsters were just a few yards away when she stopped, and in one smooth motion she drew her bow back and released the arrow.

The leader flinched, and Emily feared she had missed. But then the creature slowly toppled over, dead before it hit the ground.

Sudden twangs echoed through the woods and a dozen goblins fell, pierced by dwarf crossbow bolts. The beasts howled in confusion as they searched for their hidden attackers, and Emily shot seven more arrows before another volley of bolts skewered a dozen more goblins.

The remaining goblins scrambled about and Emily enjoyed watching their confusion as she picked them off, one by one.

Another barrage from the hidden dwarf scouts and then there was a sudden silence.

Nothing moved as Emily scanned the darkness for movement. Seeing none, she emerged from her hiding place and approached the killing ground.

Goblin bodies were scattered everywhere with arrows and crossbow bolts sticking out of their small green bodies. The dwarves emerged from the darkness and some set about recovering their bolts while others disappeared back into the woods.

Emily gathered as many of her arrows as she could find, and then she and the dwarves set off back into the trees, looking for any more creatures.

It didn't take long before she heard the telltale scrape and clank of armor again in the distance.

Emily grinned and nocked another arrow as she disappeared into the darkness with a dozen stocky shadows following silently behind her.

****

The black armored orcs howled as they smashed into the dwarf line with unbridled fury, their long blades a blur. But the stocky dwarves held them with stubborn determination. At first, the dwarves were shocked at seeing their ancient enemy back from the dead. But as he watched, Mike saw a change come over the dwarves.

As the orcs roared and charged onto the bridge, Lord Aurvang was still in shock, but that shock quickly evaporated and was replaced with an almost insane joy.

A huge smile split the dwarf lord's bearded face and he waved his massive rune axe above his head. "Come on! Ye filthy orc swine!" he bellowed. "Come meet me axe!"

He got his wish as a few orcs broke through the first line of dwarves and rushed the dwarf lord. Lord Aurvang jumped in and filled the gap, and in a whirl of motion he fought three black armored orcs, his massive axe meeting their long swords in a deadly dance. He decapitated one and split another nearly in two, laughing wildly the whole time.

But where the dwarf lord cut down his enemies, the other dwarves were not having such luck. The orc armor was proof against only the most accurate strike, and without the aid of a heavily enchanted weapon like Lord Aurvang's rune axe, the dwarves were being pushed back.

"Fall back!" Captain DiSantos shouted. "Final positions!"

Just then, several black bolts of writhing energy shot out from the orc lines and blasted into the defenders. Sergeant Leah was directing the retreat when the missiles exploded and ripped him apart.

The line shattered under the bombardment and the orcs poured in, deadly blades carving gleefully into their enemies.

The remaining defenders broke and fled.

****

The radio crackled to life with the order to retreat.

Liz cursed as she and the other sharpshooters on the rooftops took a few more shots as they desperately tried to create some space between the retreating men and dwarves, and the pursuing horde.

A few yards separated the last defenders from the front line of monsters when Liz stood up and ran across the roof, then scampered over a narrow plank to the adjacent rooftop. The other shooters did the same, falling back as the monsters poured uncontested into town.

****

Mike, Ted, and the remaining defenders pounded down the street in full flight with the orcs close behind. They rounded a corner and came across a tall barricade made of building rubble stacked on top of a line of ruined vehicles. An awaiting soldier quickly moved a towering tractor-trailer to give them room to dash through the opening, and as soon as the last dwarf was through, the soldier pulled the truck back to block the entrance. Fresh soldiers lined this new barricade as the weary defenders joined them.

The orcs and their allies appeared around the corner and roared battle cries when they saw this new barricade before them. They charged ahead and crashed into the walls, scrambling up the rubble and vehicles, trying to reach the humans that unmercifully fired down on them.

The concentrated fire devastated the ranks of monsters that sought to mount the wall. But too soon the guns slowly stopped firing as the defenders ran out of ammunition.

Now uncontested, the huge, armored orcs, scrawny goblins, and vicious troglodytes scaled the barricade, forcing the soldiers atop the wall to resort to using their short bayonets and combat knives to try and repel the heavily armed monsters.

The soldiers were no match for the orcs fury and were quickly pushed off the barricade. But the defenders had regrouped behind the wall while the soldiers on the barricade bought them precious time and were ready when the orcs flowed over the wall and dove into them.

The orc host was so large that it filled the entire intersection and began to overflow down the other streets.

"Now!" Captain DiSantos called into his radio.

****

"Now!" crackled across the truck radio.

Darrell revved the engine. "It's go time!" he shouted back to Jack, who was anxiously seated in the bed.

"About time," Jack grumbled, as he stood up and grabbed his machine gun.

"Yeee hawww," Darrell shouted, as he hit the gas.

The truck shot forward and barreled down the street. Tires squealed as they rounded the corner at break neck speed.

Charging down the street toward them was a sea of black armored orcs.

On the far end of the street on the opposite side of the horde, two IAV's each appeared at the end of a street, as did the Humvees equipped with heavy antipersonnel weapons.

The orcs were surrounded as armed vehicles raced forward.

Thunder echoed down the streets as the machine guns roared to life.

Blistering rounds of lead tore through the tightly packed orcs.

Windows opened along the length of the streets and rifles began firing down onto the confused monster horde. The large beasts died by the score, cut down by scathing gunfire that rained down from all sides.

But the orcs were not so easily confused as their goblin and troglodyte lackeys. They quickly recovered from their initial shock and began charging down dark alleys and tearing through windows to escape the death trap.

The organized battle lines quickly broke down as the orcs and other creatures scattered. Large groups of defenders were positioned around the town at key intersections with support from above, and as the monsters scattered, they collided with these defenders and the whole town quickly degraded into a chaotic, bloody battlefield.

Devastating spells flew from both sides and buildings everywhere caught on fire. The crash of weapons and gunfire rang through the streets, drowning out the screams of the dying.

****

Liz was perched in the corner of a rooftop and watched as a black truck with a snowplow fitted with crudely welded-on spikes barreled down the road. It was hard to see much in the darkness, and the flickering light of the many fires made shadows dance and look like something was there when there really wasn't.

Liz recognized Jack standing in the back, firing his machine gun into the packed monsters below.

She caught motion above the truck and saw a goblin looking out a shattered window. The creature suddenly leapt from the opening with a dagger raised over its head, right above Jack's back.

Liz snapped her gun up and fired.

The goblin flew backwards and crashed into the wall with a hole in its chest. Jack kept firing, oblivious to what had just happened.

An explosion caused Liz to turn around and she saw a dark robed troglodyte sorcerer throwing bursts of shimmering energy into the window of a nearby building. She quickly repositioned and fired.

The sorcerer died and a young girl briefly appeared in the ruined window before vanishing back inside the building.

Shouts of alarm erupted below her as a pack of orcs suddenly emerged from a dark alley and surprised a group of dwarves that had been following a pair of wounded troglodytes.

Liz recognized Baldor among the dwarves and she got a few quick shots off, killing several orcs before they knew what was happening. The dwarves quickly finished off the remaining beasts.

Liz had to reload and to her dismay discovered that she was on her last magazine. She had to make these last rounds count.

From around a distant street corner a group of civilians armed with dwarven weapons were being pushed backwards by a significantly larger force of goblins.

Liz knew she couldn't waste all her ammunition on the one group, but didn't know what else to do until she spotted the large hobgoblin directing the surrounding force of goblins.

The hobgoblin's head exploded and the goblins paused, looking confused. Thankfully, the humans seized the opportunity and charged into the goblins, pushing them back around the building and out of Liz's sight.

She wanted to follow and help the people below, but Liz knew she would be of more use up here on the roof, providing support from above. She trusted that with the hobgoblin leader dead, the humans would be able to defeat the unorganized goblins.

At the far end of the street another group of orcs appeared, chasing a few wounded guardsmen. One of the orcs was especially large and had a banner attached to his back. He looked like a leader.

Liz found him in her scope.

****

Mike and Ted fought back to back, in the center of a swirling melee of guardsmen, dwarves, orcs, goblins, and troglodytes.

Soldiers surrounded Captain DiSantos as they desperately fought a mob of goblins. Nearby, Lord Aurvang shouted a battle cry as he challenged a pair of massive orcs.

An orc appeared before Mike and he blocked its sword with his shield, the force of the blow making his arm go numb. Mike dove away and brought his mace down on the orc's knee with bone shattering force. The orc screamed and fell, clutching its ruined joint.

Before he could finish off the wounded orc, three goblins rushed Mike and he was forced to retreat as they slashed at him with their serrated blades. One of the mongrels suddenly burst into flames and Mike crushed the skull of another. The last died when Ted's burning poleaxe took off its head.

Mike was breathing hard when another orc came at him. He jumped back and Ted stabbed the orc in the gut.

Another orc ran at Ted's exposed back, but Mike was too far away to intercept. The orc slashed at Ted, but his blade bounced off an invisible wall inches away. The orc howled in rage, and a surprised Ted spun around and released a lightning bolt point blank into the orc's chest.

Nearby, a dark robed sorcerer unleashed a wave of destructive force that pulverized a group of guardsmen. Corporal Allen appeared out of the swirling battle and fired on the sorcerer. But the bullets disintegrated before reaching the robed orc and the beast retaliated with a dart of sickly yellow light that struck the corporal square in the chest.

The dart vanished inside the young corporal, but it didn't seem to have any effect. Apparently unharmed, the corporal fired another burst at the sorcerer. But then, he suddenly dropped his rifle and cried out in pain as something moved beneath his skin. He clawed desperately at his eyes and tried to scream, but when he opened his mouth a fountain of wriggling maggots poured out. His eyes abruptly ruptured and more worms tumbled out of the ruined sockets. Within moments, Corporal Allen was consumed from the inside out by hungry maggots.

The corporal's skeletal remains hit the ground just as dozens of orcs suddenly appeared from a side street, and Mike knew they would soon be overrun. But then there was a roar of an engine, and a black truck abruptly plowed into the orcs. The surprised beasts were skewered by the crude spikes on the bloody plow and completely mauled by the powerful vehicle as it careened through them.

The truck came to a screeching halt and Jack jumped down, unloading his AR-15 into the remaining orcs as he came. Once all the nearby beasts were either all dead or dying, Jack made his way through the raging battlefield to Mike and Ted, shooting anything that came too close.

Darrell peeled out and drove at the largest group of orcs. Dwarves dove out of the way as Darrell smashed into the helpless orcs and continued down the road until he roared out of sight.

"Where the hell is he going?" Mike shouted to Jack.

"He said something about 'bowlin' for orcs' or something," Jack answered with a shrug.

An orc lunged at Jack and it fell dead at his feet with several holes in its chest.

A sudden commotion arose from the orcs.

Mike searched for the source of excitement.

"Bwahahaha!" Lord Aurvang's laughter boomed over the sounds of battle. "There he be lads! The stinkin' warlord himself! Kill 'em and their army will shatter!"

The dwarf lord pointed with his rune axe at the far end of the street where Mike discovered the largest orc he had ever seen.

CHAPTER 27

Emily limped down the dark, empty street with all of the remaining scouts she had been able to find.

That last fight had been rough. There must have been over a hundred goblins sneaking along with a very grumpy shaman. They had waited until several other scouting parties had joined with theirs before attacking, but even then it had been touch-and-go for a while.

The goblins had pushed them out of the woods and into the outskirts of town before Emily had finally managed to put an arrow in the shaman's chest. Without the shaman's protection, the rest of the goblins were easy targets for the dwarven crossbows.

Emily stopped above the body of the shaman and retrieved her arrow from its corpse. She was down to her last three arrows, the rest lost back in the woods, and she needed every one she could find.

The light from several fires and the sounds of battle told Emily that the army of monsters had broken through the bridges and had reached the town, so she decided that there was no point in staying in the woods. She and the scouts would be better used in the streets where the actual fighting was.

Just before moving on, she noticed the scepter still clutched in the dead shaman's clawed hand. The scepter was tall, at least compared to the short goblin, and looked like a long, knotted tree branch. The top of the staff curled around the largest piece of labradorite Emily had ever seen. Bones and feathers hung from the staff and one large animal skull grinned evilly at her.

For some reason she couldn't explain, Emily picked up the scepter.

She was surprised when she felt a faint jolt go through her arm, followed by a strange sensation of vertigo that passed so fast Emily wasn't sure it had even happened. But now she noticed that the scepter felt warm in her hand and strangely… good. She couldn't quite explain it, but holding it felt right. Like it was supposed to be there.

Emily stood and continued her limping walk toward the sounds of battle. She made it several steps before she noticed that the dwarves weren't following.

She turned to look at the scouts and saw that they weren't looking at her, but at the scepter in her hand. She was about to ask what the problem was when she realized there was a soft greenish light on her.

Looking at the scepter, Emily saw an eerie greenish light emanating from the eyes of the skull.

"Well, that is interesting," she muttered under her breath.

Emily looked at the dwarves then. "Well, are you all going to just stand there or are we going to go help our friends?" Without waiting for an answer, Emily spun around and strode toward the flickering lights and sounds of death.

Emily grinned to herself when she heard the rattling of the scouts following her.

She didn't notice that her limp was gone.

****

The warlord stood head and shoulders above its bodyguard, its glossy, black lacquered armor plates and helmet trimmed in gold. A large banner with an odd symbol was strapped to its back. Large spikes protruded from its armor and in its huge fist was a long staff topped with a blade like a wide, curved sword at the end.

Liz could see the warlord approaching the intersection far down the street just as the radio call went out telling everyone to converge at the warlord's location. This was the dwarves' ultimate plan - find the warlord and kill him. Everything hinged on that.

According to the dwarves, the orcs had some kind of telepathic ability to make other creatures follow them. That was why the goblins, troglodytes, and trolls had joined together. Something the dwarves said would never happen under normal circumstances.

Lord Aurvang explained that the orc warlord was the focal point that all of the orcs telepathic connections were hinged.

He was the linchpin.

If he died, it would sever his hold on the other monsters and they would be free of the orc influence.

Liz looked around and saw chaos everywhere. Groups of orcs, goblins, and troglodytes swarmed everywhere. Groups of dwarves fought bravely against the hordes and desperate humans battled for their lives. Gunfire and spells flew through the air to wreak havoc on both sides. But dwarf bravery and human desperation wouldn't be enough. There were simply too many monsters. Scores of the beasts died, but more always took their place.

The defenders were fighting a losing battle, but salvation was within reach.

Liz found the warlord in her scope. He had his back to her as he entered the intersection.

Heart racing, Liz tried to calm herself.

She knew the curved orc helmets could deflect a bullet. She had seen it happen. And the heavy body plate could stop a bullet cold. With his back to her, there was no good opening since the helmet fanned down to cover everything to the shoulders.

Liz decided her best shot would be for the space under the arm. The warlord just had to raise his arm and she would have an opening.

The battle progressed, and the warlord and his bodyguard stood in the center of the intersection directing his forces around him. The humans and dwarves were pressing in from every side, but the monsters had superior numbers and with the direction of the warlord, were holding the defenders.

Only one group of humans and dwarves were making significant progress toward the warlord. Liz saw one goblin fly through the air to crash amid its comrades. She searched for the cause and found Mike wielding his impact mace and leading a group of dwarves spearheading into a mass of goblins. In the center of the dwarves was Ted, as he threw fire at the tightest clusters of monsters.

Next to them was Jack, leading a group of human soldiers that shot and stabbed their way forward.

To Liz it looked like they were having a competition to see who could reach the warlord first. Knowing all of them too well, she knew that was exactly what they were doing.

But they both might be beat by Lord Aurvang and a few of his bodyguard who were carving a bloody path straight for the orc warlord.

The warlord saw her friends getting closer and it roared a challenge and raised its spear-like weapon. That was what Liz was waiting for!

Taking careful aim, she sighted in on the warlords exposed armpit.

Liz squeezed the trigger.

The sharp click of an empty chamber sounded loud in her ears.

"Damn!" Liz swore, and threw down her useless rifle.

She looked around desperately for somebody else to get a rifle from, but she was alone on this rooftop and there was no one any closer to the warlord that she could get to.

Of all the times to run out of bullets it had to be now, she fumed.

With no other options, Liz grimly drew her pistol from her leg holster that only had one remaining magazine as well. She knew there was no way she could hit the warlord from so many blocks away with a pistol. She had to get closer.

She drew the slender sword she had taken from a ratman the night before. Although she had some fencing experience, Liz hoped she wouldn't need to use the small blade.

Armed with both pistol and sword, Liz made her way down from the rooftop to the mostly dark street below.

****

A sporadic crackle of gunfire dropped the last goblins, revealing dozens of massive orcs making up the warlord's bodyguard.

The orcs raised their weapons and roared a challenge.

The men and dwarves shouted defiantly back.

The two sides hurtled together with crushing force. The orcs carved into the men and dwarves with reckless abandon, eager for blood. Bullets ricocheted off orc armor as orc swords rebounded from sturdy dwarf shields.

The organized lines quickly vanished as combat was joined, and the swirl of battle carried the combatants around in a maelstrom of violence and death.

Mike caught an orc's large blade with his round shield and struck out with his mace. It caught the orc a glancing blow on the shoulder, but with the extra impact of the enchanted weapon, it knocked the monster off its feet.

Using the momentary advantage, Mike brought the mace down in a devastating chop and crushed the orc's skull with an explosion of bone and brains.

A roar behind him made Mike spin around just as another orc swung viciously at him. Mike blocked with his shield just in time, but he stumbled backward from the force of the blow. The orc swung again and Mike dove forward under the swing and smashed his mace into the orc's knee. The beast howled and clutched its shattered knee, and Mike finished it off just as Ted stumbled up next to him.

A pair of tall orcs lunged forward. Ted put up a hand and a jet of fire shot out, catching one of the orcs full in the face. The tusked beast dropped its sword screaming in pain and tried to put out the fire that was consuming its face. Ted drove his still burning poleaxe into the roasting orc's gut.

Mike deflected the other orc's swing and quickly punched out with his shield, crushing the orc's throat. It collapsed, trying in vain to breath.

Mike left it to its slow death.

Three more orcs came roaring at them and Mike kicked one away as another charged him from behind. He danced away, but within moments Ted was swept away by the chaos of battle.

Nearby, a group of dwarves had formed a tight circle and were surrounded by roaring orcs. Mike tried to make his way to them, but an explosion knocked him off his feet. When he got up, the dwarves were gone. Nothing but a smoking crater remained where the dwarves had been a moment before.

Suddenly, Jack was next to him covered in gore, and he smiled crazily at Mike. "Aren't you dead yet?" he shouted over the sounds of battle.

"You wish," Mike shouted back, with a wild grin of his own.

A large orc with mostly red armor suddenly rushed Jack. Jack pulled the trigger of his rifle, but nothing happened. Mike jumped between them just before Jack got skewered and just barely blocked the thrust with his shield. Jack reached over Mike and stabbed the orc in the eye with the combat knife attached to the end of his rifle.

"What did you do that for?" Jack grumbled. "I had him right where I wanted him."

"And where was that?" Mike shouted back. "With his blade in your gut?"

More orcs lunged at them and the conversation was cut short.

Mike parried wildly as he tried to keep the orc at bay. This one was far more skilled than the others. It was all he could do to keep its long blade away.

Jack was having the same trouble. Apparently, they had made it beyond the regular orc soldiers and had reached the elite warriors. The orc Mike faced had elaborate armor and there were strange symbols etched into its sword. The beast battling Jack had armor of a different style and its sword gave off a reddish glow as it blurred through the air.

The orc with the red, glowing blade drove Jack backwards with its furious attacks. Crying out, Jack took a long gash along his arm as he fell to one knee. Sensing victory, the orc brought its curved sword above its head and then down in a brutal chop.

Jack raised his rifle at the last moment and lunged backwards. The glowing sword carved right through the gun, splitting it in half and continuing to slice a long cut in Jack's bulletproof vest.

"That was my favorite rifle," Jack growled.

The orc swung again and Jack dove to the side at the last second. As he rolled, Jack drew his pistol. The orc heaved its glowing sword out of the pavement and lunged. Jack fired his pistol point blank at the orc. Bullets bounced off helmet and armor as the orc crashed into him. Jack unloaded his pistol as the huge warrior bore him to the ground.

THE SHEARING

Mike saw Jack go down, but he couldn't help as he whirled and danced away from the angry orc that was trying to cut him in half. A group of soldiers were brutally cut down by a pack of black armored orcs and a dwarf warrior was beheaded a few yards away. The defenders' momentum stalled and the orcs pushed forward.

Here he was pissing around with this orc as his friends died around him, Mike growled to himself. No matter how hard he tried, Mike couldn't find an opening in the orc's defenses, and seeing Jack and the others fall enraged him.

Furious and without really thinking about what he was doing, Mike summoned two walls of force on either side of the red armored orc and caught it in between them. Surprised, the orc thrashed about crazily but couldn't get away. Mike's anger boiled over, and by sheer force of will he brought the two walls together.

There was a sickening crunch and the orc was pulverized, armor and all.

Suddenly, the ground heaved beneath Mike's feet and he crashed to the ground. Before he could get up, a rain of magical bolts tore into him.

Another wave of bolts shot forward, but Mike summoned a shield and the missiles were absorbed before reaching him.

He stood slowly, smoke rising from his scorched body, searching for his assailant. It didn't take Mike long to find him.

A relatively small orc in an elaborate dark robe strode toward him. Clenched in its fist was a tall, black staff with a gem held by a long blade on the end. Mike couldn't tell if its skin was black or just such a dark green that it looked black, but either way he knew this must be the one who summoned the burning bolts. But even more surprising was the massive figure standing next to the sorcerer. The warlord.

Before Mike could move, a streaking silver shape blew past him.

It was Lord Aurvang.

The dwarf lord bellowed a war cry and launched himself at the orc warlord. The massive orc laughed as he blocked the dwarf lord's swing and struck back with his long-bladed weapon. Lord Aurvang sidestepped the thrust and drove at the orc's armored face.

Mike missed what happened next as the sorcerer sent another blistering array of spells lancing toward him. Mike blocked some of the barrage, but one exploded in front of him, knocking Mike flat on his back. The sorcerer unleashed a fireball as a shaken Mike tried to stand.

But then, Ted was there. He raised his hand and a wall of fire absorbed the sorcerer's attack.

"Go help the dwarf," Ted shouted to Mike without turning around. "This one's mine."

The sorcerer pointed his black staff at Ted and said something Mike didn't recognize. Then a glob of purplish energy shot forward.

Ted's eyes grew wide as the purple orb blazed toward him.

Mike thought he heard Ted muttering something that sounded like 'bubble' over and over again, but before Mike could figure out what it meant, the glob struck.

A blinding flash of purplish light consumed Ted in a crackling release of energy.

"NO!" Mike cried, and he lunged forward to help his doomed friend.

A hand on his shoulder held him back.

Spinning around Mike saw that it was Jack.

Mike stood stupidly there for a heartbeat, unable to believe his eyes.

"Miss me?" Jack smiled wolfishly.

Wild laughter behind Mike made him turn back.

The purple energy dissipated and standing there was Ted with a soft golden glow surrounding him, laughing wildly.

"It worked!" Ted giggled gleefully. Then he saw the surprised look on the orc sorcerer's face. "Oh, yeah. Now it's my turn," he said, and pointed his poleaxe at the sorcerer.

A bolt of fiery energy shot out of the head of the poleaxe straight for the robed orc.

The orc brought its own bladed staff up, and the fiery energy struck a purplish shield and exploded around the orc.

"Come on!" Jack shouted, and pulled on Mike's arm. "We have a warlord to kill."

Breaking his eyes away from the awesome sight of Ted and the sorcerer exchanging spells, Mike followed Jack away from the magical display.

They found Lord Aurvang in a furious duel with the massive warlord. Mike could see the orc had several gashes in his armor from the dwarf's powerful rune axe, and Lord Aurvang had a slight limp with blood flowing down one leg. But neither seemed to be slowing.

Suddenly, Lord Aurvang slipped in the blood around his feet and he fell heavily to one knee. The warlord howled and punched out at the stricken dwarf with such force that it sent him flying through the air to crash into the corner of a building. Part of the wall collapsed and buried the dwarf lord in a shower of bricks.

The warlord saw Mike and Jack coming and laughed as it turned to face them.

Jack reached the huge orc first and rained a series of blows that was almost too fast to see. Mike noticed that Jack was using the same black katana that the orc had cut his gun in half with and Mike was impressed. He didn't know that Jack knew how to use a sword that well. But even Jack's lightning-fast attacks weren't good enough. The warlord parried them all with his bladed staff and even managed to counter with a few slashes of his own before Mike joined in.

Together Mike and Jack desperately battled the mighty orc warlord to save Clearfield.

The orc seemed to be everywhere at once, no matter where Mike struck he was there, and when Jack slashed from the other side, he blocked that, too. Mike waded in harder, bent his will to getting more force out of his enchanted mace. On the next swing, the orc blocked the mace with his bladed staff and the hardened staff handle shattered.

The warlord howled in anger, but didn't relent. Instead, it picked up the broken pieces and held a piece of the weapon in each hand as it parried and stabbed at its two attackers.

Out of the corner of his eye Mike saw Ted still trading spells with the orc sorcerer, but Ted was looking tired and his spells were having less effect, while the sorcerer's spells kept their deadly energy. Mike knew they had to end this quickly because Ted wouldn't last much longer.

Pain blossomed along Mike's leg as the orc's blade sliced into the meat of his thigh. Mike cried out in agony and stumbled. The warlord stabbed at Mike's head, but Jack's blade was there and pushed the thrust away. Surprised, the warlord was off balance and Mike used that moment to bring his mace down on the orc's iron shod foot.

The armor crumpled like paper beneath the enchanted weapon and the orc screamed in pain as its foot was crushed.

The warlord reeled backwards trying to keep his weight off his mangled foot as Jack lunged in. The blade took on a reddish glow as Jack drove it into the orc warlord's side.

The warlord dropped the broken haft of its weapon and clutched at the blade stuck in its chest. The mighty orc raised the bladed end of the weapon and brought it down in a deadly arc at Jack. Just before the blade reached him, Mike's shield deflected the blow and the orc fell to a knee with the glowing blade still lodged in its chest.

The warlord growled and swung again, but there was no strength left in its arm. Mike knocked the blade away and with a mighty swing, brought his mace down on the orc warlord's head.

With a resounding crunch, the powerful mace cracked the warlord's helmet and skull beneath like an egg. The massive body slid free of the sword and crumpled to the ground.

Lord Aurvang's announcement about the warlords binding was proven at least partly true as howls of pain and confusion filled the air as the warlord's link was severed. However, the rest of the horde didn't die with the warlord.

A sudden roar and a burst of rubble announced Lord Aurvang's arrival as he heaved himself out of the pile of debris. "Where is that overgrown gob?" he thundered angrily.

Then he saw the body lying at Mike and Jack's feet, and his face turned purple with rage.

He charged into the nearest group of orcs with a berserker fury that was terrifying to behold.

Mike saw most of the orcs standing around dumbly as if they didn't know where they were. The humans and dwarves seized the opportunity and drove into the stunned horde with a vengeance, and cut them down unmercifully.

THE SHEARING

Only one orc wasn't stunned.

The sorcerer.

Ted was leaning heavily on his burning poleaxe with blood running down his nose and ears, surrounded by a golden shield so faint that Mike could hardly see it. He knew there was no way they could reach Ted in time.

The orc sorcerer sent a wave of concussive force at Ted and the golden shield burst in a shower of sparks.

The orc chuckled darkly as it prepared a final spell.

The dark robed sorcerer raised its staff and shouted something in a strange language while pointing the weapon at Ted.

Suddenly, a whining sound erupted from behind the sorcerer and a bolt of green energy burst around the orc. He howled in pain as the energy crackled around his robed form. Smoke arose from his burning body as the green energy burned through the cloth and charred the flesh beneath.

The whining sound grew louder and then deepened to a throaty growl as a fountain of blood abruptly erupted from the sorcerer's neck. A spinning blade appeared as it chewed through the screaming orc's shoulder and carved a bloody path across the orc's body, splitting him from shoulder to hip.

The first rays of daylight lit the street as the sorcerer's corpse landed with two wet thuds and revealed Liz, standing there covered in blood and holding a gore-encrusted chainsaw. Emily stood further down the street as a green glow slowly faded from her outstretched scepter.

The chainsaw abruptly cut off and Liz wiped some gore off of her face.

"Are we late for the party?"

CHAPTER 28

With the death of the warlord, the combined horde of goblins, troglodytes, and orcs began to fight amongst themselves. The warlord's psychic link had held the goblins and troglodytes in thrall. With his death, they had been freed and they immediately turned on their former allies. The organized horde disintegrated into a wild carnal house of death, relieving the pressure on the defenders and giving them time to regroup.

It took several hours, but eventually the humans and their dwarf allies managed to push the last of the warring gangs of monsters out of Clearfield.

Then began the long process of gathering the slain and disposing of the corpses.

The citizens realized that it would be a waste to discard the fine orc armor and weapons, so the dead orcs were stripped of their possessions and then the humans claimed them for themselves.

Many strange artifacts were discovered by the victors, including several enchanted swords, like the one Jack now carried. The dwarves refused to touch anything that was made by the orcs, so nearly all of the spoils were divided out to the surviving humans.

The dwarves decapitated the orcs and placed their heads on spikes near the entrances of the bridges and all around the town. They claimed it would deter any future attacks and the humans weren't about to argue. Anything that could prevent another attack would be most welcome.

They had achieved an unlikely victory, but the cost had been terribly high. Hundreds had died saving the town from the horde and there was very little ammunition left. What remained was dispersed to the sharpshooters positioned around the rooftops and the guardsmen on patrol.

They still had electricity thanks to the efforts of the workers of Shawville Station who rerouted the power toward Clearfield. But television, Internet, and phones were all still dead. No word reached them about the fate of the outside world.

They were alone.

****

That evening found Mike, Liz, Ted, Jack, Darrell, and Emily sitting around a table in Denny's Pub with Baldor and Lord Aurvang.

"But if it be made o' beef then why it be called a *ham* burger?" Baldor rumbled between bites.

"It's not named for the type of meat," Ted answered. "The name originated in the town of Hamburg in Germany to describe their meat-based products."

The jarl snorted. "Ye humans be a strange lot."

"I, too, have a question," Lord Aurvang said, and he turned to Mike. "I noticed durin' the skirmish around the warlord that ye crushed an orc between two o' yer Svalinn Fields." The dwarf lord stared hard at Mike. "I be known o' many guardians, but none ever been able ter move their Field once summoned, let alone crush an enemy between two ov' em."

Mike was taken aback by the sudden questioning. "I didn't even know the power had a name," Mike admitted honestly. "And I don't know how I did it. It just kinda happened."

"Perhaps we can use our powers differently than dwarves," Ted offered helpfully.

Baldor shook his head. "There be tales o' the ancient wardens bein' able ter do miraculous things with their Svalinn Fields. But since they vanished, no one knows fer true."

Lord Aurvang and Baldor looked at Mike suspiciously before they both burst into laughter.

"Bwahahaha!" Lord Aurvang boomed. "Could ye imagine a *human* warden?"

"That be the most ridiculous thing I ever heard!" the hill dwarf hooted merrily.

Suddenly, the door to the pub banged open and a young soldier burst in. The soldier spotted Lord Aurvang and hurried over to their table.

"Lord Aurvang, sir," the soldier gasped. "You need to come with me."

"What be the matter lad?" the dwarf lord rumbled between bites.

The soldier was breathing hard and he took a deep breath before continuing. "Our scouts have returned and brought news, sir. The captain requests your immediate presence."

"Well, that doesn't sound good," Jack mumbled with a mouthful.

"Very well, lad." Lord Aurvang stood up. "Take me ter 'em."

The others all stood as well. "We're coming, too," Liz said. It wasn't a question.

The soldier looked about to argue, but Lord Aurvang simply nodded and motioned for the man to lead on.

They made their way through town to a secluded clearing several miles into the woods where Captain DiSantos and Lieutenant Bowman were waiting for them.

"What be the matter Captain?" Lord Aurvang asked, as he stomped up to the two men, followed closely by the others.

"We don't know yet," DiSantos replied almost sheepishly. "We got word from this scout here," he motioned to a dwarf scout that stood nearby, "that they had discovered some creature and that you needed to see it immediately." The captain shrugged. "I thought it best to call for you rather than wait for them to return first."

"A sound decision, Captain," Lord Aurvang rumbled approvingly.

And then they waited. It was a pleasant day with the birds singing as the evening sun shined through the first new leaves of spring.

A rustle of trees announced the scouts before they pushed through the brush. The two stocky dwarves grunted and groaned as they dragged a massive shape between them.

Liz was impressed. She hadn't seen a dwarf struggle to move anything before, let alone two of them working together. Whatever it was must be exceedingly heavy.

The scouts dragged the massive form up to the gathered onlookers and deposited it before them.

Liz saw it was a massive body with four thick dwarven crossbow bolts sticking out of it. The monster was covered in course, dark fur and had gigantic hooves where its feet should have been. It wore a white armored kilt and a strange golden armor covered in odd designs that Liz thought looked like hieroglyphics.

Its clothing was strange, but it didn't prepare her for the massive head of a huge bull. Enormous black horns protruded from the wide skull and an elaborate striped head covering was draped over its massive shoulders.

"What in Odin's Beard be that?" Baldor breathed.

"That," Mike replied, "is a minotaur."

"Don't you have them in your world?" Ted asked the confused dwarves.

"No," Lord Aurvang rumbled darkly. "This creature no be o' Svartalfheim."

Liz looked at Mike nervously. "Then where did it come from?"

Ted stroked his beard thoughtfully. "There must be more than one world connected to ours."

Liz stared at the minotaur's corpse and wondered what dreadful consequences this new revelation would herald. They were already lost and adrift in a sea of monsters, cut off from the rest of the country and low on supplies. *How had all of this happened? Was anyone else still alive? Could they survive another assault?*

She didn't know the answers, but she was afraid they would soon find out.

EPILOGUE

The burning sun beat down on a sprawling, golden city.

Light glittered off beautiful temples and towering stepped pyramids that dominated the skyline. In the center of the ancient golden city was a grand palace complex that arose above the rest. A massive wall separated the metropolis from the lush jungle surrounding it, like a golden jewel in a sea of brilliant green.

Inside the great golden palace was a huge room with large maps covering every wall. In the center of the room was an elaborate table set with a miniature city and the surrounding countryside. Small, stylized marble cat and eagle statues marked locations in and around the city, while a clump of bull statues was grouped at the far edge of the board.

Three figures stood around the table as one of them repositioned some of the small statues. At first glance they appeared to be men, but upon closer inspection it became obvious they were not.

The largest figure towered over the other two. He was a dangerous looking beast, large and muscular, covered in golden fur with black and brown spots and a wide face with very feline features, much like a jaguar.

He wore nothing but a long, green loincloth trimmed and armored in gold.

Next to the large jaguar man was a slightly shorter female eagle-like creature with more delicate features and elegant dark brown feathers. Golden plumes protruded from around her head. A vicious looking beak extended from below large, angry eyes.

A fine, tight fitting dress revealing one shoulder covered most of the bird-like woman's lithe body. The material was a bright shade of purple with gold and black angular designs worked into the fabric. Several large, golden bracelets festooned her wrists.

The last individual was short but regal, and covered in fine, pale gold feathers. He had large, cunning eyes and a wide, golden beak dominated his face. Large feathers with the tips dyed green stood out from his head in a stunning crest and an angular crown of gold set with jewels rested upon his brow.

He wore long, red robes covered in golden geometric patterns. Golden chains adorned his neck and wrists while large, golden rings decorated his delicately feathered fingers.

The large cat-man moved the bull statues closer to the miniature city.

"How long before they are at our gates?" the short birdman asked in a sharp voice.

"Two days. Perhaps less," the eagle woman chirped.

"And can we stop them?" the birdman asked nervously.

"My warriors will stop them," the big jaguar growled proudly.

"Don't be foolish Xkeatean," the eagle woman snapped at the jaguar man. "This isn't some rabble of Majava." She held up one of the bull figures. "This is a legion of Isfet, led by the Son of Apep himself," the eagle woman screeched.

Xkeatean's eyes narrowed dangerously. "I know exactly who is coming for us, Sireek. For unlike you, I have actually faced them in battle," he growled.

Sireek's feathers ruffled in anger.

"Enough. Both of you," the golden-feathered man snapped.

"Apologies, Tlatoani," Xkeatean and Sireek said in unison. When both looked sufficiently chastised, he continued. "This great city has never fallen to an enemy and I do not plan on starting now. Do we have any allies nearby?"

Sireek shook her feathered head. "Jahangir and his Gurkan mercenaries are still a week away. We will need to hold until then."

Tlatoani looked at the board as if wishing something would appear that he had missed. But no such thing came and he exhaled heavily.

"What of the Primat?" Tlatoani asked. "Has the Great Ape sent word?"

Xkeatean laughed. "The Primat don't care about us or anyone else for that matter," he shook his head ruefully. "They will be in for a surprise if the Destroyer defeats us, because they will be next."

Sireek glared at Xkeatean. "I have already sent envoys to Mahoroba and Cibola, but I have not received a response from either."

"So, we are alone," Tlatoani sighed. As if to accentuate his point, a slight tremor shook the room, but only lasted a moment.

Tlatoani smiled sadly. "As if the Destroyer at our doorstep wasn't bad enough, these ever-growing earthquakes may be the end of us."

"Perhaps the wards will keep us safe," Sireek volunteered.

"They will not stand against the Destroyer's magic," Xkeatean replied. "He and his sorcerers will tear this city apart unless we go out and meet them on the battlefield."

Sireek scoffed. "You go out there and they will tear *you* apart."

Xkeatean growled deep in his throat and bared his teeth.

Just then, the door banged open and another large jaguar-man burst in.

He was obviously a soldier and wore an armored shirt made of interlocking gold plates and an armored skirt of a similar green to Xkeatean's.

He charged into the room and fell to his knees before Tlatoani. "Oh, Great Speaker! I come bearing glorious news!" the soldier announced excitedly.

"Well, what is it boy? Speak!" Tlatoani squawked.

"It is the Destroyer, oh, Great Speaker," the warrior trembled. "He and his Legion are gone!"

"What?!" Xkeatean bellowed.

"What do you mean 'gone'?" Tlatoani asked.

The warrior swallowed nervously. "Our scouts went out to spy on their positions, but when they arrived there was no trace of them. They are gone."

"Blessed Huitzilopochtli!" Tlatoani breathed.

"A trick," Xkeatean growled.

"Where did they go?" Sireek asked the warrior.

"We don't know Priestess," the warrior answered. "They vanished without a trace."

Sireek looked thoughtful at this.

"I told you it is a trick," Xkeatean rumbled. "They want us to think they are gone so that we lower our guard." The large jaguar pounded a furry fist on the table. "Double the guard and increase the patrols. We will not be caught unawares!"

"At once, Lord Xkeatean," the warrior replied, and quickly rushed back out of the room.

"Might I suggest another possibility?" Sireek asked.

"Of course, my dear," Tlatoani smiled reassuringly at her.

"As you know, there have been reports of people vanishing without a trace for a few days now," Sireek began. "And so far, there has been no explanation. But I believe I may have found the answer."

"Oh? And what is that?" Xkeatean snarled. "Did you just remember that you sacrificed them all?"

The Priestess ignored him.

"I was searching through the Archives for clues when I discovered a reference to the time when we kefali were conquerors," Sireek said. "And not just here. But in other worlds."

Xkeatean laughed. "Children's stories."

"No," Tlatoani said with such conviction that Xkeatean and Sireek froze. "There is something I must tell you." The Speaker seemed to age before their eyes and he spoke as if the weight of the world were upon him. "The stories are true, Xkeatean. There once was a time when we kefali could travel to other worlds. They wished to spread Order across the universe."

Tlatoani rubbed his eyes wearily. "This has been kept secret ever since crossing the Veil was lost to us millennia ago. Only the Speakers and other kefali rulers have been entrusted with this knowledge."

"I had suspected this might be the cause of the disappearances since they began, but now that you, Priestess, have come to the same conclusion, I am forced to agree."

"I suspect those that have disappeared were pulled to another world."

Xkeatean shook his head in disbelief. "Assuming what you say is true, does this mean we are under attack? How do we defend against such a thing?"

"I don't know," Tlatoani replied. "I will consult the Magi and Lector Priests. Perhaps they have some arcane knowledge that will aid us."

"Regardless, we must pull all of our forces back inside the walls in case this really is some kind of trap," Xkeatean pressed.

"And if it is not?" Sireek asked. "If they truly did cross this… Veil?"

"Then the Destroyer is in another world," the Tlatoani said grimly.

"And may the Gods have mercy on it."

THE END…

About the author

N. J. Colesar enjoys ancient history, mythology, playing games, and painting miniatures. Raised in Clearfield, Pennsylvania, he currently resides in Pittsburgh with his wife and children.

Origins of Myth

DARKENERGY

STEEL CITY SERIES: BOOK 2

N.J. COLESAR

DARKENERGY

STEEL CITY SERIES

THE SHEARING
ORIGINS OF MYTH
BIRTH OF LEGENDS

AUTHORS WANTED

Entanglement Interactive is looking for new and experienced authors to help us expand the ever-growing DarkEnergy universe!

No experience? No problem!
We love to hear from first time authors.

INTERESTED?
Visit: **www.entanglement-interactive.com/submissions**
OR
Email: **submissions@entanglement-interactive.com**

Made in the USA
Las Vegas, NV
16 October 2022